The Labyrint
By
Christopher Cartwright

Copyright 2019 by Christopher Cartwright
This book is protected under the copyright laws of the United
States of America. Any reproduction or other unauthorized
use of the material or artwork herein is prohibited. This book
is a work of fiction. Names, characters, places, brands, media
and incidents either are the product of the author's
imagination or are used fictitiously. All rights reserved.

Acknowledgements:
*I wouldn't be able to write any of these books without the help of a
multitude of people who have assisted along the way. Specifically, I
would like to thank Bic for all the help she provided behind the
scenes, and without whom, this book wouldn't have come to fruition
in its present form.*
*I would like to thank my editor, David Gilmore and my team of proof
readers – without them, you would be receiving a far inferior version
of the book you read today – JC Barb, Rohen Kapur, Mike Riley, Kris
Densley, Mykel Densley, Liia Miller, Leslie Miller, Peter Gifford,
Ross Jarratt, Joannie Jenkins, Sheelagh Rogers, Jacquie Gilfillan, and
Colleen Mundis.*
Thank you!
Christopher Cartwright.

Prologue

Rhyolite, Nevada – Fifteen Years Ago

Ethan Jones held his breath and listened in the dark.

It was a quarter past seven in the morning and he knew exactly what he was going to do. What he didn't know, was why he felt compelled to do it. Call it childhood bravado, peer pressure, or just plain stupidity… it didn't matter. The fact was, if he was caught, his old man would try to kill him. If he was lucky, it would be the leather strap. Hard to kill a boy like that in a fit of rage. He would draw plenty of blood, but even so, would struggle to kill him. No, the greatest risk was that his father would lash out and simply beat him to death with his fists. Either way, one thing was certain – he didn't intend to get caught.

The silence was finally interrupted and he was rewarded with the sound of the screen door closing on the timber frame, followed by his father's heavy boots treading on the well-worn porch steps. The eight-year-old subconsciously held his breath, waiting for the shriek of the pickup truck's ancient hinge and the subsequent rifle-shot report as the heavy door slammed shut.

He listened to the sweet music of the V8 motor rumble to life, signaling his reprieve, exhaling long and slow with relief. Stones crackled under the tires as the truck turned and pulled away from the house. He pictured the truck moving up the track toward the road and waited until he heard the motor race as his father planted his foot on the accelerator, driving up the main track toward the highway.

After the sound came and went, he left the relative safety of his room and tip-toed to the kitchen. From there, he peeked through the cloudy old window, looking for the tail of dust heading south toward Beatty. A microscopic smile creased his lips. He was finally *alone*. At his age, a single night could seem like a lifetime; especially when his father was drinking – which was always.

Suddenly aware of his empty stomach, he headed for the almost-antique refrigerator. The old timber boards creaked under his feet, despite his attempts to step around the noisy spots in the floor he'd memorized over the years. He pulled the heavy snap handle on the Kelvinator and gazed at the space where food should be. Plenty of liquids clinking in there, but nothing to satisfy his hunger. The only non-alcoholic item was a giant glass bottle of orange juice, which he took from the door. On tip-toes, he awkwardly poured some into a small glass, making sure to leave plenty behind. He took down a packet of Saltines from the larder and removed a few from the box.

As he ate, he focused his gaze on the light coming up from between the floorboards beneath the table, trying to see the stones and sand under the kitchen. He could feel the heat rising up from there already, warm against the bottom of his bare feet. He knew today, like most days, would be hot as hell. He also knew his father wouldn't be back until midnight at least, because today was Saturday – his favorite day of the week. Optimism flooded through him and his thoughts turned back to where they'd left off, gaining traction as the fog of deep sleep slowly lifted.

Ah yes, the pistol!

He made himself finish eating before heading to his father's bedroom. He crossed the room and stopped to listen hard, just to be sure. He double-checked the distant view again. Nothing. Just the constant buzz of a million flies, going about their business, and the glare of the Death Valley sun – already shimmering off the stony surrounds.

He crossed the forbidden threshold of his father's room. The point of no return.

Get caught from here on in and his dad would make him pay with blood.

The smell of five thousand alcoholic snores still hung thickly in the musky, stifling air. The moth-eaten translucent drapes hung limply from the curtain rail, the same dirty white as the other fabric in the room. Odorous singlets and socks here and there, beer cans on the furnishings, mashed cigarette ends in the overflowing ashtray on the nightstand.

He grinned.

It was the nightstand that held the prize.

Ethan knelt down beside the bed and pulled open its wooden drawer. It sat on the side of the bed where his mother used to sleep, years ago – when she was still alive. Her side had been the closest to the door. Some part of him ached to be able to creep to her in the night, as he once had, and be received into her perfumed embrace.

In the open drawer, to Ethan's relief, the bundle was sitting exactly where his father had left it. He was sure it had not been disturbed. He could smell the faint scent of machine oil over the camphor sweetness of the timber, and memorized again exactly how the package was positioned in the drawer, with part of the oil emblem visible on the t-shirt rag in which it was wrapped.

Again, he paused a beat and listened.

All clear.

It had been long enough now, he decided, that his father would be too far from home to make it worth returning for some forgotten item. He took up the bundle and laid it upside down on the yellowed sheets of his father's bed. He unwrapped the parcel and stared at it. A treasure. An item of real power. A Colt Lawman .357 Magnum revolver. A *police* gun. He ran his finger over the writing inscribed on the burnished black barrel.

He read out loud, *"LAWMAN MARK III."*

He traced his pointer finger down the barrel, over the chamber and felt the indented inscription of the pony standing passant on the front of the timber stock. He grabbed up the weapon and weighed the steel and wooden pistol. It was heavy in his small hand. He loved the feeling of the gun in his grip. He thumbed back the chamber lock and tilted the weapon, feeling every bit an expert as the cylinder tumbled open.

He knew the gun was empty but checked it again – inspecting the barrel and chamber, then flicked the chamber closed. With reverence, he gently cocked the two-stage hammer and eased the revolver through its firing cycle. He squeezed the trigger but controlled the grip-top of the hammer to stop it from flying forward and damaging the precious firing pin in a dry fire.

At eight years of age, Ethan had read every gun review he could find on Google at the school library computer, and he knew this weapon well. He knew his father's example was old and worn, but as reliable as any gun ever made. He left the packet of .357 rounds in the drawer – to be certain that his father didn't notice any were missing – and bundled up the t-shirt rag again – making sure to replace it in the exact position he'd found it. Perhaps it would pass a cursory inspection if his father was drunk enough. He shoved the revolver in the back waist of his jeans, pulled his shirt down over it, and headed for the blinding light of the day outside.

The hot blanket of the Nevada day enveloped him as he stepped out and onto the porch. He brushed away the instant fly strike and eased the door closed silently, always the opposite to the way his father did things. He headed out back to the barn where a box of long forgotten .38 Specials lay in a tub and picked it up, stuffing it in to his back pocket. In the distance he heard his best friend, one of the few neighbors they had, named Joshua Rowe, admonishing his little sister, Mia, about walking too slow.

Ethan grinned.

He knew they would be at his house soon, just like *every* Saturday.

He popped out into the sun from the dark barn, squinted and shielded his eyes, gauging the distance of his friends. No time to load the weapon now, he decided. He could surprise them later. He whistled at the two children walking single file up the drive, and they changed course toward the barn. Ethan started walking north, away from the homestead, and they picked up their pace to catch up to him.

"Where are we going?" Josh called. He was the same age as Ethan, but smaller in stature, and had always looked up to him.

"Montgomery Shoshone!" Ethane called over his shoulder, not giving any quarter.

"Wait up!" Josh pleaded. "The mine? Why?"

Ethan stopped walking and turned to face the two smaller children, now about fifteen yards away and scurrying to catch up.

"Let's go shoot some rats!" he said, pulling the gun from his waistband and holding it aloft like a starter's pistol.

"We're not allowed down there," said Mia, before sticking her thumb back in her mouth to quell the rising anguish she felt having spoken aloud to the bigger, meaner boys.

"Don't be a stupid baby!" Ethan snapped back. He turned and looked directly at the boy, excluding the little girl with his body language. "C'mon Josh, let's leave your sister here if she's gonna be such a *baby*."

"Where'd you get the gun?" Josh asked, his eyes wide and transfixed by the weapon.

"What, this?" Ethan replied, pointing the pistol straight at the boy who instantly cowered away. Ethan hovered, enjoying the power differential for a few moments "Don't worry, it's not loaded." With a smirk of condescension, he added, "Not yet, anyway."

"You got shells for it?" Josh asked, trying to regain his composure.

"Yep. 38 Specials. Whole box of 'em." Ethan said. He pulled the weighty shells from his baggy jeans' pocket and handed them to the smaller boy, who was now completely under his power. He watched in delight as Joshua chastised his little sister, attempting to hurry her along as he set a pace for the forbidden mine shaft.

Joshua and Mia followed along with Ethan, through a chain-link fence marked 'No Entry!' and on into the complex of huts adjoining the abandoned mineshaft. They approached a gateway leading into the shaft itself and Ethan pushed on the protective wire gate, forcing a small opening. "Hurry up, ya babies!" he yelled back at Josh and his little sister. He noticed the girl was some distance behind, her attention diverted to one of the nearby derelict huts adjoining the mineshaft entrance.

"Felix!" she called out, "Hey Felix!"

Ethan watched a small black and white cat trot over to the girl. It arrived at her worn out old cowboy boots, mewled, and swirled around her legs until she bent over and patted its head. It was a scrawny looking thing; he felt instantly overtaken with contempt for the creature, revolted by the girl's attention as she cooed, kneeling down, trying to cuddle it.

The cat was wily and slipped from her grasp, preserving its freedom as she clumsily grabbed at it in kindly pursuit. The little girl giggled and chatted to the cat, stroking his back and playing along. The whole display annoyed Ethan to no end. He stepped away from the mineshaft entry and moved toward the approaching boy.

"Hand me those bullets," he commanded Josh, his hand outstretched.

Josh could see what was on Ethan's mind but acquiesced, despite his dread, and passed over the box of shells. "Ethan, please don't."

"Who's your friend?" Ethan called to the little girl, ensconced in her play with the little cat.

Without looking up, she called back, "This here's Felix. Best mouser in all the land!"

The cat had returned to his position a short distance from the girl, leaning in to get the most pleasure from brushing up against a wood and stone hut. It leapt, chasing a grasshopper, playfully stalking its prey.

"I hate cats," Ethan said quietly. He fixed his attention on loading the cartridges ruefully into each chamber, allowing a wicked smile to creep across his face.

Josh said, "Ethan, please don't. She'll tell for sure."

"Looks like a feral to me!" Ethan called out. "I'd suggest you hop out of the way, Mia."

Without hesitation he raised the pistol, braced his arm, aimed, and squeezed off a round. A spout of dust kicked up right next to the cat who froze, hunkered down and flattened its ears back for a moment, then with a flick of the tail, continued on with its mission. Ethan raised the pistol again, and this time aimed directly at the cat.

Mia, who had been frozen in terror, lurched into his field of fire, trying to save the cat. "Felix! No!" she screamed. This snapped the cat into action, and it bounded off along the siding.

Ethan tracked the cat as it jumped and sprang along the building. He brought another round from the pistol, just in front of the cat, who in turn bucked wildly, suddenly aware of the danger as the shot rang out and kicked up the dirt in front of it.

He was laughing now, enjoying the thrill of his newfound power.

The cat paused again, its head cocked, trying to determine where the shots had come from. Mia was screaming at the cat to run.

Josh steeled his resolve and said, "Hey, that's enough, Ethan… it isn't funny anymore!"

The cat suddenly got the idea and started running away.

Ethan leveled the barrel of the Lawman III, his eyes squinting as he narrowed in on the target.

Mia ran for the cat, bravely and stupidly placing herself between the shooter and his target. Josh, realizing what was about to happen, grabbed up his little sister, restraining her from running after the still-moving cat. He lifted her up from behind and she kicked out, arms squashed against her waist in his grip.

Ethan was vaguely aware that she was screaming.

He returned his eye to the gun's sight; slowing himself down by holding his breath, then exhaling with deliberate control. The cat was drawing near the edge of the building and Ethan pushed the muzzle to aim a half a foot in front of its head and gently squeezed. The gun felt completely weightless in his grip as the thrill of the moment consumed him. The round exploded from the gun, sending a small mound of dirt up into the air. The cat screeched and ran off, disappearing into the disused mine shaft.

"Felix!" the girl screamed, following after the stray cat.

Ethan started laughing at the sight…

Josh turned to him, angry now. "What the hell is wrong with you? You could have killed it!"

"So what if I did?" Ethan replied. "It's just a stupid feral cat. There's a million of 'em around this town."

Josh looked at his little sister, then back at him, defiant, red-faced in the heat, chest heaving with ragged breaths, nearly silent.

Ethan realized he needed to make this easier on Josh if he didn't want the littler boy to tell on him. "I actually didn't mean to get the damned thing, okay? I was just messing around. I'm sorry."

Behind them, Mia looked pleadingly at her brother and said, "I wanna go home."

Josh wavered, his eyes darting between his sister and best friend, unsure of what to do. His face twisted in a hardened grimace, certain that either option was going to make him unpopular with someone. He frowned and said to Ethan, "We'd better go home. I can keep her from talking, but not if we make her stay here any longer."

Ethan nodded. A slight twinge of fear overcoming his bravado. If she talked, he was a dead man. He nodded. Looked at the little girl and said, "Come on, Mia, we'll take you home."

Mia remained silent, but her eyes locked with his in blazing vehemence.

Ethan shrugged. "I don't know what the big deal is. It was just a feral cat!"

Josh went to pick his sister up to carry her, in a rare display of brotherly affection.

A tail of dust billowed upward in the distance.

Josh's eyes narrowed. He yelled, "Hide! Someone's coming!"

Ethan stared at the motorcyclist riding hard.

In a level voice, set to avoid revealing the fear that was rising, he said, "It appears we have a visitor."

*

Mia's lips turned upward in a malicious grin.

She almost hoped they would all get caught. That would serve her brother and Ethan right. She imagined it being Ethan's drunken father. The man would go ballistic. He would probably beat the lot of them halfway to death. It would be worth it, just to watch Ethan suffer. She glanced at her brother who stood shoulder to shoulder with Ethan, staring at this new threat. She hated Ethan, and she hated her brother for always siding with him. Their neighbor had always tormented her, and the cat was just another example in a long line of insults from the boy.

Ethan turned his attention to her. "What the hell are you smiling about?"

She placed her hands akimbo, her face plastered with a rueful smile. "I told you, we're not supposed to be here! You're gonna get into *big* trouble!"

"Shut up!" both boys yelled at her in perfect unison.

She desperately wanted to run home, to be home, away from this frightful situation and out from under the tyranny of her brother and his friend. She knew it was hopeless, though. They weren't allowed to be behind the wire fence and which was now a football field away, plus a stranger was coming in fast, *and* there was nowhere to go.

"I'm going to hide in those bushes!" she called to her brother as she ran to a nearby stand of saltbush and dried out looking trees, ducking down as low as she could go and peering out. The boys tumbled in after her and all three of them looked out toward the road, listening to the incoming engines.

Mia recognized the howl of a small motorcycle engine being thrashed out in front of a much bigger car motor, and the three kids jostled for space in the saltbush cover as the two vehicles came into view up the dirt road.

The motorcycle was a trail bike, being ridden hard by a man without a helmet and out in front of a black Chevrolet Suburban; the kind she'd seen on all the cop shows. The SUV was closing in on the motorcycle and as he rounded the trail head, he hit a deep gravel rivulet and lost the motorcycle out from under him.

The rider tumbled a few times, making her think that he might be dead… before he sprang up and started running, glancing now and again over his shoulder, but headed directly for the stand of bush in which they were hiding.

Mia could see the man's face strained with the effort of running, his clothing filthy with dirt and his arms bloodied from the fall to the gravel. The huge car now easily caught up with him and he slowed to a stop, defeated. He leaned down, stiff-armed and elbows planted on his knees, breathing hard. He was looking directly at the copse of vegetation where they were hiding, his face a painful grimace.

The man glanced directly into the bushes at her.

Mia's heart slammed in her chest and she felt as though she might vomit. The man's piercing blue eyes seemed to drill through the bushes as though they weren't there at all. The little girl stifled a shriek, and instantly received a pointed elbow to the ribs from her brother. The black SUV stood idling behind the man, dust still swirling behind it. The front doors opened, and two pairs of office shoes crunched onto the gravel.

"Hands behind your head, interlace your fingers and get on your knees!" commanded the officer exiting the passenger side, his pistol trained on the man from between the open door and SUV cab.

The man slowly stiffened to his full height, and arranged his hands as directed. He stared directly in to the bushes, as though deep in thought. His expression was neutral, relaxed, as though he wasn't alarmed – just calmly waiting for things to play out. Mia noticed his breathing had become entirely controlled, and he stood completely at ease.

Mia slowly looked to her left and saw the two boys kneeling beside her, peering through the gaps in the thick scrub, transfixed by the drama unfolding before them. They breathed quickly with mouths open, silently, unmoving.

"I said get on your knees!" the passenger-side agent yelled, slowly moving to flank the man, keeping his distance and pistol aimed.

The man turned to look at the agent to his left but didn't move to obey the command to kneel. A show of defiance. The second agent walked up behind the man, holstered his weapon and took a plastic zip-tie from his coat pocket. He roughly applied the tie to one arm and then moved the man's hands down behind his back and bound his wrists together. The agent reefed on the new yoke and kicked at the man's knees from behind, forcing him into a kneeling position.

"Like I said, on your knees, soldier." He redrew his weapon and aimed it at the back of the man's head, execution style.

"I'm sorry it has to end like this for you. I know what you've been through."

Mia's heart pounded in her chest; she wondered if the other boys could hear it as the blood coursed in her ears.

The man raised his voice, speaking loudly. "You're not going to kill me here."

"Oh yeah? Why's that?" replied the executioner, sneering.

The man spoke with confidence, "Because whoever's hiding in that bush over there is going to witness it. They've got your Secret Service license plate and have seen your faces. Even if no one believes them, there will be an investigation – and we all know the president can't afford that right now."

Both agents seemed to waver for a moment, and then directed their attention to the scrub. The man at the side kept his handgun pointed at the prisoner but turned his head and looked directly where Mia was hunkered down in the long grass.

The Secret Service agent looked directly at her.

She spotted the recognition behind his sunglasses.

This time there was nothing she could do. A loud scream issued from deep inside her chest before she could do anything to stop it.

"Quick!" the agent yelled. "Go silence her!"

*

Ethan saw the man to the side of the prisoner take off running and bring his firearm up to bear upon the scrub. The fear and dread that had rooted him silently to his hiding spot was replaced by a rush of adrenaline that stood him up. He noticed the man's jacket was apart and his tie was flapped over his right shoulder as he closed the distance between them. Ethan watched the agent's shoulder as he turned the gun toward him and caught a glimpse of a flash before the snap of the round passed by him, causing his ears to ring.

Ethan raised his own pistol without hesitation, leveled the barrel at his attacker, and squeezed the trigger, emptying the barrel of its remaining five rounds. Each of the bullets found their target, center mass, tearing through the agent's white shirt. Each point of impact blossomed red, morphing quickly from bullet holes to blotches.

The agent, still running, went down and crashed face-first into the dirt.

As his mark dropped, Ethan saw the prisoner push up and back hard, from his kneeling position, and smash his head backward with force, causing a violent collision with the other man's chin. The would-be killer, off balance, issued a round from his own pistol which went high and wide as he fell backward, but still managed to graze the prisoner's shoulder as he'd turned to stand up completely.

The prisoner, recoiled by the round's impact, reacted quickly and launched himself forward, unleashing another blow from his head to the man's face, with this one delivered squarely by his forehead to the bridge of the other man's nose. The middle of the man's face instantly erupted in a gush of blood.

The armed man went down hard, landing flat on his back.

Without hesitation the prisoner was on him, planting a desert boot firmly against the man's throat. The downed man squirmed and gagged for a time, arching his back and kicking out in a futile attempt to resist. When he was finally still, the prisoner stepped back, his chest heaving from effort. With his forehead streaked by the other man's blood, he shook his head slowly – as though remorseful of what had happened.

Ethan was disturbed from the scene in front of him by the sound of movement. He turned, tracking his empty weapon toward the commotion behind him. Mia was still screaming in a high-pitched wail and Ethan caught a quick glimpse of Josh as he picked her up and ran. Apparently running for their lives, he watched as they headed in the direction of their homestead, nearly a mile away.

He looked back and saw the stranger was walking toward him. "You may as well come out now kid!"

Ethan was suddenly glued to the spot where he stood.

The visitor grew closer, Ethan got a better look at him. He was tanned, well-built but lean, and wore cargo fatigue pants over the top of desert boots. He had about a week's growth of beard and scruffy, brown, short wavy hair. His t-shirt was torn and filthy, and a bandanna hung loosely around his neck – the man looked like a Special Forces operative, about three months into an operation.

The visitor stared at him with sharp, piercing blue eyes. With a smile at the corners of those eyes he turned and presented his bound wrists to the boy.

Wriggling his fingers, he asked kindly, "Little help?"

Ethan shoved the pistol into the waistband of his jean shorts and took his folding buck knife from his pocket. He approached the man and confidently sliced the zip-tie binding his wrists.

"Thanks," said the visitor, rubbing his wrists.

"Your shoulder's bleeding," Ethan said, matter-of-factly.

"Just a scratch luckily," the man answered with a wince as he touched the deep graze, gently oozing blood at one end. He took his bandanna from around his neck and wiped his face, then expertly wrapped the wound on his upper arm.

"We should call the police," Ethan said, his attention straying to the two bodies lying in the red dirt.

"I think that would be an exceptionally bad idea," the man answered, not unkindly. "You and I just killed a pair of federal agents. What do you think will happen if we call the police?"

Ethan thought about that for a second. He had grown up on the crappy side of every place he'd ever lived. He knew exactly how it would go – it would end badly. "Well, what should we do?"

"I think you should go to the trunk of that SUV and bring out the two shovels inside over here, so we can bury these men."

"How do you know there are shovels in the truck?"

The man made a wry grin. "Because they were supposed to be used to bury me."

*

Together, the two dug into the hard, red earth.

Ethan watched the man work with the shovel. He was strong and persistent. He showed the boy how to use the tool properly and for some hours they toiled, barely exchanging a word. The shadows were long on the land when the man helped him climb out of the hole, six feet deep at least.

"You want to go get us some water?" the man asked. "Take your time if you need to."

The boy quickly made for the house, his limbs aching from effort. He was filled with relief that he wasn't going to have to help move the bodies. He had been dreading confronting the corpses all day.

WHO WAS THIS MAN?

WHAT HAD HE DONE TO THE SECRET AGENTS FOR THEM TO WANT HIM DEAD? SHOULD I BE AFRAID OF HIM?

He filled a canteen from the house and drank the warm tap water deeply. He hadn't noticed how parched he was until that moment. He refilled it, intending to take it to the man, but leaned against a tree – sitting for a moment.

When he opened his eyes, he knew he had slept. Fear bolted through him and he jumped up. It was nearing dark, and the sky was ablaze with pink and orange, the last of the daylight.

He found the man sitting on the ground. Nearby the dirt was slightly darker – the only sign of their handiwork. Ethan knew that by mid-morning tomorrow, there would be no sign of the hole in the soft red dirt.

He sat down next to the man and handed him the canteen. The man still glistened with sweat and smelled of work.

"I thought you'd left me," the visitor said, taking the canteen gratefully. He opened it and drank back most of the contents in one long draft. He offered the boy the last bit, Ethan shook his head and the man finished it off to the last drop. "Thanks," he said, and tossed the boy the tin canteen.

Ethan just stared at him in silence.

The visitor asked, "Did you hear what they said to me?"

Ethan, mesmerized by the fact that he'd killed and buried a man today, couldn't find the strength to lie. Instead, he nodded. "A little."

"So now you know the lengths they would go to keep their secret."

"Yes, sir."

"And I don't need to tell you the lengths they would go to keep YOU quiet."

Ethan had already witnessed the lengths that they would go in order to keep someone silent. "No, sir."

"Good."

The man groaned with effort and stood.

He withdrew a metal container the size of a cigarette box from his cargo pocket. He showed it to the boy. It was small, but robust. It seemed weighty in the man's palm and had an insignia on the top, something ancient. The boy stared at the picture for a moment, it depicted an intricate maze – and at the center, a single three-dimensional stone in the shape of a key. The boy hoped that he was being shown something that wasn't going to spell his own imminent murder.

The man walked a short distance to where two large boulders stood beside the stand of low trees and scrub where the children had hidden, hours before. Ethan knew them well. He had climbed both and searched the distance many times, being that they were the tallest things around the area.

The two stones stood side by side, like two opposing tips of matching icebergs.

At their base, the man dug into the dirt again. He weighed the tin in his hand for a moment, and then, as if decided on something, threw the box in the hole and quickly covered it up. Ethan relaxed. He figured the man probably wasn't going to kill him, after all.

He looked the boy straight in the eye and knelt down. Ethan held his gaze but said nothing. The visitor asked, "Do you think you could find this place again if you needed to?"

"Sure."

"Are you certain?"

"I said I could, didn't I?" Ethan answered, his normal cocky attitude starting to return.

The man's face was set hard, but his deep blue eyes showed intelligence and kindness. He leaned toward the boy and spoke slowly, seriously. "All right, now you'd better listen."

Ethan nodded, dumbly saying, "Sure."

The visitor continued. "Someday, hopefully a long time from now, I'm going to die. God willing, it will be at home in my own bed. If that day happens to come along sooner than I hope, it's going to be on the news – in fact, it's going to be big news. If that happens, I want you to come back here and dig up that case. Inside it is a computer hard drive. You know how to use a computer, right?"

"Of course."

"Right. So, make two copies. One of them, send to the Washington Post and the other, to the New York Times. You keep the original. Got it?"

Ethan's curiosity overcame all his anxiety. He felt like an accessory now, a co-conspirator – no longer the fearful boy. "What's on the hard drive?"

"Secrets."

"About what?"

"Something that needs to remain secret for the time being, but one day, must come out." The soldier looked hard at the boy. "Whatever happens, you must swear to me you won't ever open that case until I'm dead. If you do, both of us might as well be dead already. You understand?"

"Yes, sir."

"If you ever hear of my death… dig it up and mail it that very day. You got it?"

"I got it."

"No matter what."

"No matter what," the boy echoed.

The visitor stared at him, his expressive blue eyes searching, as though they could read him. They leveled, and the man seemed to accept Ethan's promise. He clasped him on the shoulder. "Good man."

The visitor rose to his feet and walked to the black Chevrolet. He reached in and started the motor, then looked over the cab from his position standing at the driver's open door.

As he climbed in, Ethan jumped up and ran to the vehicle. "Wait!"

"What is it, son?"

"How will I know if you've died?"

"You'll hear about it. My father's worth a lot of money. He has a lot of friends in Congress. He'll make a big thing about it all… so you'll hear about it… and when he does, you'll come back here and dig this up and do as I've asked."

Ethan nodded. "Sure… but I don't even know your name."

The visitor grinned. "My name's Sam Reilly."

Chapter One

Ik Kil Cenote, Yucatán – Present Day

Birds called in the dense jungle canopy, their clear back and forth echoing against the high stone walls that surrounded the jungle pool, sunk almost one hundred feet below the surface of the earth. High, high above, just a sliver between the treetops, gleamed a blinding piece of Mexican sky. Once, centuries ago, the Mayans had looked up from just this place, at the same piece of sky.

Trailing vines reached from the opening at ground level all the way down to the clear water. Huge black catfish swam lazily below the surface like guardian denizens, their whiskered faces occasionally breaking the still water in their endless quest for something edible. Waterfalls tumbled from the high stone walls, breaking from some hidden wellspring deep inside the rock to cascade, splashing, into the pool.

It looked like a perfect postcard, a tranquil jungle pool, hidden and pristine.

But it wasn't. This place held secrets.

Below the surface of the water, a vast maze of tunnels snaked off from the pool and deep into the earth, like arteries spreading away from a heart. The water coursing through them was the lifeblood of the land, here. But none of that was visible. Not here.

A carved stairway descended from ground level, clinging to the smooth edges of the cenote, but the stairs themselves were empty at the moment. The steep stairs had once been used by the ancient Mayans centuries ago, as citizens made their pilgrimage to the pool for both recreation – and deadly ritual.

The cenote of Ik Kil was considered sacred by the Mayans, who used the site for human sacrifice to Chaac, their rain god. Jewelry, gold, and bones had been excavated from its deep water by archaeologists and specialists. Who the bones had belonged to was a more complicated story. The pool rarely gave up her secrets without a fight. It was a mystical place, full of history and violence.

The man sitting on the swimming platform was here today for neither ritual nor recreation and yet perhaps there were, in fact, elements of both. His blue eyes trailed the still surface of the pool, unbroken by any movement other than the occasional catfish on the prowl and the splash of the cascading waterfalls. The man wiped the sweat off his brow as he waited. The oppressive jungle heat seeped into his pores and the scent of earth and water clogged his throat. It felt thick enough to drink.

Then, there. Was that a ripple? The man watched harder. As he did, a dark shape swarmed upward, cutting through the clear water's depths. It appeared to be bigger than the catfish, but not by much.

A man broke the surface with a gasp, shaking water out of his hair and wiping it from his eyes. He wore no more dive equipment than a mask and snorkel, having descended to the depths to meet them on their own terms. When his vision cleared enough to make out the man on the platform, he frowned, blowing spray. He swam over and clung to the side. When he pushed himself up into the sun, startlingly warm on his chilled skin, his muscles bunched and gleamed.

"Well?" he asked, hauling himself out onto the platform, trying not to drip on the waiting man or his equipment. "Any news?"

Sam Reilly grinned and assessed his soaking, breathless friend.

Then he dug in his pack and handed Tom Bower a towel. "He's here."

Chapter Two

The sun blazed on the scrubby road as Sam and Tom arrived topside.

Tom was still toweling his hair with his shirt and raised his eyes at the sight that greeted them. "Doesn't exactly travel light, does he?"

A small convoy of three black Jeep Sahara Wranglers stood at the ready alongside the scorching Mexican road. The last Jeep in the convoy was towing a small hyperbaric chamber, a not-so-gentle reminder of the risks when SCUBA diving uncharted, and labyrinthian, underwater cave systems. Sam squinted into the bright sun in appreciation – the gleaming black caravan made an imposing, sexy front of machinery. The impressive vehicles looked built to withstand – and return – cartel gunfire and Sam wondered exactly what their host's connection was.

The Jeeps were dusty from their trek through the unforgiving landscape, a stark contrast to the man who waited outside, hands tucked in his pockets with his simple cotton shirt hitched up outside them. He chatted amiably with people Sam could barely see – the flat, rugged faces of local laborers, built for hard lives and long stories and as much a part of the land that surrounded them as the rugged stones and spiky yucca sprouting from the thick jungle carpet.

Sam reflected that Tom might have a point, but it didn't matter. He'd rather be over-prepared than under, and even if it was a show to impress them, at least it looked like they were dealing with a man who knew what he was doing.

Sam shrugged and hitched his bag higher on his shoulder. "He's the one in charge. Not everyone's got lungs like you."

He started forward with a wave and the man's face broke into a wide smile; his bright white teeth sharp and startling against the canvas of his deeply tan skin.

"Mr. Reilly!" the man called out, his hand outstretched, and starting forward through the jungle.

Sam took it with familiarity, and said, "Armando! It is good to see you, my friend."

The man was roughly the same height as him, their eyes meeting level. Though they had exchanged many emails and several phone calls in the past few months, this was the first time they'd met in person and Sam was struck by the man's commanding presence. He was well built and with a no-nonsense awareness that made Sam think he'd spent some time in the Mexican army; most likely before going off to college and diving into the ancient history of the land he'd been raised in. He'd dedicated his life to unearthing its secrets.

He and Sam shook hands firmly, warmly. The man transferred his steely grip and his bright smile to Tom. "Armando Ayala," he said, looking Tom square in the eyes.

Tom returned the gaze, a brief smile on his lips. The man was a renowned historian and archeologist that specialized in Mayan artifacts. Sam had spoken highly about him on multiple occasions. "Tom Bower. Pleasure to finally meet you."

Sam started to hitch his bag higher, but a local was already collecting it from him. He relinquished it with a shrug of thanks. To Tom, he said, "Armando has spent the last ten years sifting his way through thousands upon thousands of the four hundred and fifty-year-old Mayan testimonies recorded during the Spanish Inquisition."

Tom's brows rose. "Sounds like… enlightening reading. Not light, though."

Armando laughed, an easy sound. "No, not light reading. How much do you know about the history of the conquest of South America, Mr. Bower?"

Tom slanted a glance at Sam and raised a sardonic brow. "I know they came in search of gold, as much as land. The quest for El Dorado took them deep into the Amazon, but the mythical city was never found."

Sam scratched his neck and held in his laugh. He still had a small pouch of golden pearls he'd taken from *the* Tomb of El Dorado, back in his house in Oregon.

"Actually, they were after much more than gold and arable land..." Armando explained. "The conquistadors wanted power. They wanted economic supremacy. And there were a bunch of heathen natives taking up space, getting in the way. In the 1700s, the Spanish hold on the continent was shaky and needed to be solidified. Since money proved a questionable means of motivation, they turned to something much more reliable – violence in the name of religion. The conquistadors' priests put South American 'heretics' on trial and forced them to divulge the locations of their temples of worship, where they celebrated their pagan beliefs." Armando's lips tightened. "And once those heretics had 'confessed' under pain of death, most of them were killed anyway and their holy places destroyed."

Tom shook his head in solemn regret. "The Spanish weren't the first to use religion to forcibly achieve their goals, but it certainly looks like they perfected it."

"These people were my ancestors." Suddenly the Mexican grinned. "But they were a clever bunch, and rumors of a mythical place lived on. Of the gateways to the gods, Elysium, Xibalba." He glanced between Sam and Tom. "You've heard of these gateways?"

Sam spread his hands. "Just what you've sent me. I confess, I was totally ignorant before that."

Armando's smile slanted. "What about you, Mr. Bower?"

"You might want to refresh my memory. Sam filled me in a little bit about the project, in terms of the technical diving required, but nothing about the history."

Armando gestured to the Jeeps which waited like panting panthers in the sun. "Shall we retire to somewhere more comfortable? There is water in the car, and some refreshments." He'd noticed Tom's damp hair, Sam's sweat. "And, they are air-conditioned."

Sam allowed a smile to crease his lips. "Sounds good."

They settled inside the roomy Jeeps.

Armando said something in gunfire Spanish and the driver handed him two bottles of sparkling water from a cooler between the front seats. Armando passed them out to Sam and Tom, who accepted with thanks. The bottles were followed by wet wipes, and the scent of disinfectant mingled with the scents of sun and dust. After wiping his hands, Sam finished half his bottle of water before wiping his mouth.

Sam said, "I'm sorry, I'm not used to this heat."

"She's a brutal Mother, Mexico," Armando said with a smile.

"Tell us more about this Xibalba." Tom turned to the historian, getting down to business. "I did a quick free dive into the cenote, but I wasn't really sure what I was looking for. Beyond an entrance, I didn't see much."

"Some people think it's in Guatemala. Others think cave systems in nearby Belize are the entrance to Xibalba. But they're wrong. It's here. Here in the Yucatan." He smiled. "In some Mayan legends, the Milky Way is viewed as the road to Xibalba. It was a holy place for the ancient Mayans, a place of sacrifice, death, and rebirth. Riches unimaginable. Incredibly valuable from a historical standpoint as well as in terms of treasure, such as gold, silver, and breathtaking jewels." He straightened his cuffs. "I've dedicated my life to finding it, once and for all."

Tom raised his brows. "Have you had any luck?"

Armando laughed. "Yes, actually. Persistence pays off in treasure hunting, as I'm sure you know. There were originally three specific locations that I believed might lead us to Xibalba – and a fortune in gold."

Sam leaned forward, water forgotten. "Where were they?"

Armando's eyes gleamed. "In the North Yucatan Peninsula. We've ruled out two of them already."

Sam's breath quickened and he settled back, pulling at his collar in the heat. "Leaving just the one, correct location? Is that it?"

Armando spread his hands with a soldier's talent for self-deprecation. "That's what I'm hoping."

But Tom was frowning. "If you know where it's located, and you know how to get to it, why bring us in at all? Not…" he added, rubbing his nose, "that I'm complaining. I'm just… confused."

Armando grinned, rueful. "Because it's a lot harder to reach than we, meaning us, are capable of reaching," he admitted, glancing at the driver through the partition of the Jeep. The man said something in Spanish and Armando laughed.

Tom's brows rose. "Oh yeah? How come?"

Armando smiled. "Because it would take a world expert in cave diving to reach." He glanced between them and the Jeep rumbled to life without their being asked. "You want to know what Xibalba is, gentlemen. It's much simpler to just show you."

Chapter Three

The Jeep jerked and rumbled over the deserted roads.

The flat landscape stretched for miles, blending into the horizon in a wall of heat shimmer and haze. Sam peered out the window, glad of the air blowing past them. With the windows open and the air-conditioning on full blast, the temperature inside was almost tolerable. He loosened his collar in the wind.

Armando noticed his gaze and smiled. "Ah, yes... the Yucatan. Flat and barren. We'd be crazy to look for anything hidden, here. But that is what Xibalba wants you to think. Just as certain butterflies camouflage themselves to look base and unappealing, this land also hides her secrets."

Tom wiped sweat off his brow. "I'm sure she does."

Armando gestured out the window to the shrubby pale dirt. "Below the earth spreads a hidden life-web that has determined the direction of human settlement on this land for thousands of years."

Tom swigged from his bottle of water and wiped his mouth. He gestured with it, toward the landscape framed by the Jeep's window opening. "You mean the water table?"

Armando winced at hearing it described so crudely. "I suppose you could say that. I'm referring, of course, to the vast network of underground rivers and cenotes." He turned to Sam with a gracious gesture. "We've spoken about them, Mr. Reilly."

Sam wracked his brain, feeling like an idiot. "You're talking about the maze of linked cenotes?"

Armando laughed. "Not 'see-notes'. It is pronounced 'say-NO-tay'. From the Mayan word 'd'zonot', which means 'water hole'. These days, it can refer to any subterranean chamber that contains permanent water, underground lakes, pools... while some of them are singular, many are caves filled with pools and linked by underwater passageways or sometimes sinkholes, where a cave ceiling has collapsed. A bridge between the surface and all that lies below." Tom's brows rose, and Sam knew he was recalling his recent free dive site. He ran his hand through his still-damp hair, as if feeling it anew. Armando saw it and nodded. "The Mayans considered cenotes to be sacred spaces – entrances to their underworld. More specifically, to Xibalba, home of the gods, abode of one's spirit after death."

"But where did they come from?" Tom asked, gesturing toward the arid landscape. "This place doesn't exactly look... moist."

"It doesn't now. But time changes all things. Millions of years ago, the Yucatan peninsula was actually a sprawling coral reef." Sam stared in disbelief at the dust thrown up by the Jeep's passage over the rough road. "During the last ice age, the water levels dropped, exposing the reef. The coral died and the jungle invaded." Armando gestured dismissively to some unknown location. "You can still see coral fossils inland – far inland. They're quite common." He shrugged, and then continued despite their skeptical faces. "Centuries of carbon-matter build up created the forest floor you stand on today, but beneath, massive cave systems were formed as the coral dissolved. They're spectacular, and if you have the time, you should visit them. Well." His face changed. "What's *left* of them, anyway."

Sam blinked. "What's left of them? Why? Are they in danger?" He knew that Mexico was wracked by fault lines much like California, and it wasn't impossible to imagine how such a fraught topography could wreak havoc on a delicate system of caves.

But Armando shook his head. "No, not in the way you think. And in some cases, what's 'left' of them is actually a good thing."

"How so?"

"You see, many of the caverns have already collapsed. When the ice age ended, the caves flooded as sea levels rose. The water levels you see now leveled off around a thousand or so years ago. Give or take a few hundred. Scientists have carbon dated artifacts found in some of the caves in this area back almost ten thousand years."

Tom let out a low whistle. "Wow."

Sam leaned forward, his elbows on his knees, his instincts and interest, piqued. Things were starting to make sense. "And you think that Xibalba is in one of these cenotes?"

Armando spread his hands. "It is the most likely scenario." His smile quirked. "Cenotes have been having something of a moment recently, in the scientific community, which is what made me think of it. In the past decade, archaeologists have found everything in their depths- from ancient, fossilized remains of camels, to giant jaguars."

Tom sputtered a laugh. "Camels?! Are you serious?"

"Among other things… mammoths, sloths, horses… The flora and fauna were very different here, ten thousand years ago." Armando continued. If he found Tom's interruption elementary or objectionable, he had the grace to hide his distaste. "Human skeletons have also been discovered, with some being the oldest found in the Americas to date. All of these treasures, once thought lost, were found in underwater cave dives."

Tom shot a glance at Sam, looking suddenly uneasy. Sam recognized a person girding his sensibilities to the often-messy facts of history. "They found people in there?" He shook his head. "You go off to the water hole and you fall in, hit your head, and… Man. Rough day."

Armando laughed. "More than you know. Apart from human remains, they have found many artifacts not native to the area, which suggests they were brought in from the outside because they had value. Wooden artifacts, for example, that would not have otherwise been preserved. Weapons, idols, tools, jewelry, jade, textiles…" He waved his hand. "But that's not the most interesting part. The fascinating thing is, many of these objects appear to have been intentionally damaged before being thrown into the underworld – as if the sacrificer was killing the object before it was sacrificed." He paused to gauge their expressions. "Even the humans."

Sam's brow furrowed in thought, but he wasn't surprised. They were Mayans, after all. "Human sacrifice?"

"Yes. It's undisputedly true that certain cenotes contain large numbers of human remains: male, female, even young children and infants."

Tom stared. "Children? Infants?" His lips twisted in disgust. "That's barbaric."

Armando held up his hands, neither defending nor condemning his ancient ancestors. "Most people imagine the Mayans flinging beautiful women into the pit of hell, but research shows it was more commonly young men – young men who were either purchased or captured while their parents were working in the fields; warriors captured in battle; or even high-born, young nobles captured during conflicts with neighboring clans. They were usually killed prior to being thrown into the cenote." His lips quirked. "But not always."

Tom folded his arms. "I still think it's barbaric."

Armando's eyes widened in surprise. "You were a warrior, from what Sam tells me, and your country fully supports the death penalty. This is the same thing."

"But they're criminals! These people were executed for the gods!"

Sam jumped in. "And Christians have done terrible things, too – the Crusades, the inquisitions…" He shook his head. "Better not to get into a one-upmanship of ancient cruelty. Better to just be glad we weren't born back then."

Tom squirmed. "Just weird to think I was diving in someone's grave and had no idea."

Armando shook his head. "History is brutal, but it is not all doom and death." He smiled at Tom. "Don't worry, Mr. Bower. The Mayans didn't fling people to their deaths in all the cenotes. Only in certain ones. Others, purely recreational or domestic."

Tom laughed but didn't sound convinced. "That's a relief."

Sam leaned back against the leather seat as he processed this. "So, you think the Mayans only believed that certain cenotes led to the underworld? And you've found a few of them? Or at least the most promising ones?" He trailed off as Armando continued to watch him put the pieces together. "Maybe I'm off on something. I assume Xibalba was one of those sacred, sacrificial ones?"

Armando just smiled as the Jeep veered left and they headed south, out of the glare of the sun, and Sam felt the temperature cool immediately. Tom, on the right side, wiped his face again and shifted away from the window. Armando's smile grew, slightly.

"What do you know about the Chicxulub crater, gentlemen?"

Sam folded his arms. "That it was one of the most important geological discoveries of the twentieth century. It changed the course of history."

Armando glanced at Tom, a practiced lecturer giving everyone in the class a chance to prove their mettle. Tom shrugged. "What he said."

Sam glanced at him in surprise. "You don't know about the Chicxulub crater?"

Tom rolled his eyes. "I wouldn't even know how to spell it."

Armando laughed. "Don't worry, Mr. Bower. Most people don't, despite the fact that it has found a fairly prominent place in science."

"By all means. Enlighten me."

"Geologists discovered that a distinct difference in fossil assemblage noticed first in the nineteenth century actually occurred instantaneously- a record of the extinction of most of the species on Earth. Most notably the-"

But Tom was already nodding, seeing where this was going. "The dinosaurs. Right. I got it."

Sam shook his head, frowning. "That's great and established. But what does it have to do with Xibalba?"

Armando glanced out the window. "That's a little more complicated. Most scientists think this mass extinction was caused by the impact of a seven-mile-wide bolide."

"A seven mile what?" Sam asked.

"A bolide is an extremely bright meteor, and which, when it comes to earth, creates an exceptionally large impact. The word comes from Greek, meaning "missile"."

"Ah." Tom nodded. "So, we're talking about a comet the size of a small city."

Armando smiled. "You do know your history. So you also know the story: the bolide hit Earth in the northern Yucatan; its impact blasted massive amounts of debris into the atmosphere. This debris cloud blocked the sun, and without the sun, plants couldn't photosynthesize, other living things could not survive, et cetera, et cetera." Armando spread his hands, an academic enjoying a predictable lecture's surprise twist. "They also believe it created a two-mile-high tsunami and generated enough heat to set forests on fire."

Sam and Tom gaped, and Armando chuckled. "But, as impressive as those facts are, they do not concern us. What concerns us is that the Chicxulub crater is the result of this bolide – this comet's impact."

Sam shook his head, unable to stop from thinking about the current state of the planet. Humans constantly underestimate the raw power of nature and how much they do not understand. "God bless global warming."

Tom glanced at Sam, as if concurring. "So it's this impact that made the caves? The network of cenotes?"

Armando shook his head. "No, but there is a link. When the comet collided with Earth, it created a fault, a fracture line, around the impact crater. It is this fracture which interrupted- and continues to interrupt- the flow of the groundwater, diverting it up and around the fault line so that the water must find its way back down. It does so by dissolving the porous limestone strata and that is what has created the system of cenotes that is of interest to us."

That made sense to Sam. He imagined the water trickling back through and added it to his growing repository of subterranean geographical knowledge. "That makes sense."

"What is of even more interest to us is that there is a second boundary fault intercepting the groundwater. Most of the geologists I have spoken to dismiss the theory, but I have spent the past ten years testing it and it is irrefutable. Whereas the first created caves and cenotes reach the surface, the activity of this fault, instead, PREVENTS the water from rising, and pushes it deeper, widening the openings and drilling them much farther underground – into hell."

Sam looked at Armando. "You think the ancient Mayans built Xibalba along the fault line at the end of this tunnel system?"

"No." Armando leveled his gaze at Sam. His voice, in the hot, dusty Jeep was low and reverent as they rumbled over the dry ground. "I think this tunnel system is Xibalba."

Chapter Four

The Pyramid of the Magician

The caravan of Jeeps sped down the road while inside, Sam tried to process everything he had just heard. It was a lot to take in. When Armando had contacted him last month, he'd known the man was smart. What he hadn't realized was that he might be crazy. Sam scratched his ear. Yes, there were undoubtedly caves running through the water table in Mexico, and yes, there were undoubtedly interesting artifacts to be found in those caves. But the gateway to hell… the mythical land of Xibalba?

He always thought better when staring into space, so his gaze migrated toward the window quite naturally. The slightly tinted windows of the Jeep shaded the bright sky beyond.

There, a magnificent and unexpected sight caught his eye and for a moment he didn't quite know what he was seeing, in the way that truly awesome edifices tend to do when one comes upon them without warning.

"Whoa!"

It was not the most eloquent of reactions, but it was honest. Armando glanced at him in surprise. "What is it?"

"Exactly." Sam pointed out the window. "What *is* that?"

Beyond, set like a jewel in a ring of jungle, rose a magnificent four-layer, stepped pyramid, visible high above the treetops. The ancient, worn steps betrayed its age, moss-covered and pocked with time. From this distance it looked like it had magically appeared out of the jungle, as if it'd been here since the beginning of time.

Armando followed his pointing finger, saw where he was looking and smiled. "Ah," he said. "That, Mr. Reilly, is the Temple of the Magician."

Tom leaned far across the back of the seat to see where Sam was looking. "My god," he said, sounding awestruck. He leaned closer and Armando gestured to the driver, who slowed. "It's huge."

Sam grinned as the view of the huge structure slowed and stalled in the middle of the tinted window. As the tint on the window lessened under the shade of the sun, the structure came clear. "Not exactly subtle, is it?"

"It's actually even bigger than that."

"Bigger?!" Both Sam and Tom swung to stare at Armando, who smirked a bit. "You must be joking."

Armando shook his head, amused by their reactions. "The Pyramid of the Magician is actually just a piece of the ruin complex of Uxmal. You can't see the rest of it from the road because of the trees, but there is more. Uxmal was one of the largest ancient cities in the Yucatan."

"Largest meaning, how many?"

"Well, not large compared to today's standards. But a city population of twenty-five thousand, especially in AD 600-1000, was a lot of people."

"What does it mean? Uxmal."

Tom was unclear whether or not Sam was merely trying to make a good impression on their guide or really didn't know the meaning. Armando replied, "Uxmal means 'thrice-built' in the Mayan language. It probably refers to the number of layers in El Adivino."

"I thought that meant fortune teller," Tom said.

Sam looked at Tom in surprise. "How do you know that?"

Tom looked sheepish, shooting a glance at their companion, not wanting to set himself in a bad light. "No reason."

Sam grinned. "Come on, Tom. How do you know the Spanish word for fortune teller?"

Tom glared at him and folded his arms. "I had a bad encounter in Tijuana one summer, all right? Best not to get into it. Let's just say that *that* word is about all I remember."

If Armando found Tom's explanation infantile, he kept it to himself. "The name comes from a Mayan legend. According to one version, a magician god named Itzamna constructed the whole pyramid in one night, using only the strength of his magic. Another tale holds that it was not a god, but a boy 'not born of a woman'." Armando shifted his glance between them. "Perhaps you've heard the tale?"

Both Sam and Tom shook their heads. Armando gestured to the driver to pull over, allowing them to idle on the side of the road to soak in the majestic view of the temple as the tale unfolded. They were both spellbound by Armando's delivery; the man was a born storyteller.

"Long ago, an old crone lived here, in a hut. It was just jungle then, with a small village. She was a witch, mourning because she had no children. She wanted one, so badly. Finally, not knowing what else to do, she took one of her hen's eggs, wrapped it in a blanket, and nestled it in the corner of her hut. She tended it daily until finally, a small creature hatched out of the precious shell. It was like nothing she'd ever seen, but it was a baby nonetheless, and she was overjoyed.

"The woman called the creature her son and took good care of it. Within a year it was walking and talking like a man. She was very proud of him and told her son to challenge the King to a trial of strength. Her son didn't want to go, but he loved his mother and so he brought his challenge to the king. When the guards presented him to the king, the king ordered the half-sized man to lift a stone that weighed a hundred pounds."

Sam grinned. "Probably as much as the half-sized man weighed?"

"That's what he thought. He returned home to his mother, crying, whereupon the witch told him to tell the King that he would lift the stone, but only if the king would lift it first. He must have proof that it is not an enchanted stone. So the dwarf returned and told the King what his mother had said. The king was amused and, being quite a strong man, proceeded to lift the stone easily. The dwarf then did the same. The king was nervous… and tested him with other feats of strength. Each time the king performed first and the dwarf matched it.

"The king, furious that he was being beaten, told the dwarf that he must build a house higher than any in the city or he would be put to death. The dwarf begged his mother for help – he was a little irked at her, as she was the one who had gotten him into this situation, but she told him to simply go to bed, to trust her, and to not lose hope. The dwarf did so and upon waking the next morning, found this pyramid," he gestured to the window, "the Pyramid of the Dwarf, completely finished and taller than anything else in the city. AKA, the Pyramid of the Magician, and Casa el Adivino."

Sam asked, "What happened when the king saw it?"

"Well. When the king saw the building, he summoned the dwarf, intent on putting an end to this upstart once and for all. The dwarf must now collect two whole bundles of Cogoil wood – very strong, very heavy – for the king to break over his head. If the dwarf survived this torment, he could have his turn to break the wood over the king's head."

Tom said, "Good for him. King sounds like a real…"

Sam nudged him and Tom shut up.

"Certain he was not going to survive, so certain, in fact, that he was going to be flattened like a pancake- the dwarf ran to his mother, who again told him not to worry and gave him a magic tortilla to put on his head for protection."

He spread his hands and continued his tale with the practiced cadence of a man for whom storytelling had been bred into since birth. "The trial was held in front of the entire city, most of whom were enchanted by this plucky dwarf and eager to see the results of the confrontation."

Sam smiled. He had an interest in stories with heroes who beat the odds. "What happened?"

"Of course, the King broke one whole bundle over the dwarf's head, with great flair, but it failed to injure the smaller man."

"Of course it didn't."

"The King knew he was in trouble. He longed to bow out, but he could not lose face in front of his subjects. So what else could he do? He told the dwarf he could have his turn."

Sam stared at the Temple of the Magician outside the window. Even though the story was just a legend, it was easy enough to believe these events had in fact taken place inside it. He could almost hear the roar of the crowd.

Sam leaned forward, amused. "Well? Don't keep us in suspense!"

Armando laughed. "The dwarf beckoned the king to kneel so he could reach, which was humiliating enough. The first crack of the stick across his head made the king see stars; the second split his skull. The people cheered, and the dwarf was hailed as the new king."

Sam laughed, satisfied with the tale. He suppressed a smile, his eyes meeting Armando with genuine curiosity. "Was he a good one?"

Armando shrugged. "Legend says he was the best."

For a moment they sat in silence, and Sam wondered exactly why Armando had told them the story, amusing as it was. There had to be more than a history lesson in there. Was it possible that they, Sam and Tom, were going to be going up against an equally, seemingly-impossible foe for which they would have to rely on wits- not cleverness? It certainly seemed possible. The Mayans were portrayed as being brutal warriors, but people always forgot just how advanced- and intelligent- their civilization actually was.

Armando redirected their gaze to the imposing structure. "All of the reports I've found in my research indicate that Xibalba is meant to be beneath a great temple – with the temple sending people to heaven, while the cave system beneath, sent them to the underworld of hell."

Sam stared at the massive temple, imagining what might lurk in the depths beneath. The spell of the story still filled his thoughts, and the growl of the idling car created a thrumming background that made legends seem entirely possible. "The entrance to Xibalba is in there?" he asked. "Underneath the Temple of the Magician?"

Armando glanced at the driver and the car sputtered as the driver hit the gas and began to move again. The historian settled back into his seat and straightened his pants as outside, the temple receded from view. "No, Mr. Reilly," he chided gently. "What would make you think that? The entrance to Xibalba is on a nearby farm."

Chapter Five

The farm was lush and green, full of bougainvillea and oleander rioting in colorful splotches among yucca and jacaranda trees. The caravan of Jeeps swung into a long drive, passing pools and fountains. Whoever lives here is loaded, Sam thought.

Armando read his thoughts. "This was the house of a local magistrate," he said. "Rather a brutish man, and not too smart. He'd had no idea he was sitting on something so valuable."

Sam laughed. "And I'm sure you don't plan on telling him. He must have asked some questions, though. Why does he think you're here?"

Armando shrugged. "I never told him. What I did was get a friend of mine on the board of the Yucatan Department of Urban Development to unearth an inconsequential item of arcane historical importance attached to this site." He grinned. "I don't even know what it was, and I probably couldn't remember it even if I did. It took some persuasion, but he eventually sold the land for a song." Armando shrugged his shoulders nonchalantly, "Everyone walked away happy. His large ego was sated by some vague promise of something or other. I promise you both, he slept like a baby that night; no doubt, visions of the family name dancing beneath bright, glitzy lights rotating in grand fashion, blasting the face of an inscribed memorial stone out front, forever memorializing his sacrifice in preserving our country's historic past."

Sam's brows rose as they traveled over the lush paradise and a massive house emerged from the greenery. In the distance, he saw mango groves march over hills, like soldiers in the sun. "You own all this?"

Armando shrugged modestly. "Well. Now I do. It will take years of excavation, you see. I didn't want to deal with bureaucracy at every turn." He glanced at their faces and raised his own brows. "You must agree it was the simplest solution for all involved, no?"

Tom shot Sam an unreadable look. "Right."

As the locals unloaded the gear necessary for the dive and prepared to carry it through the jungle, Sam sat on the patio with Tom and Armando. Even from several yards away Sam could hear the workers shouting at each other in an unintelligible Spanish dialect while they unloaded the diving gear from the Jeeps. Piles of equipment had been plopped on the dusty ground and now rested hazily under their own unhurried, settling dust cloud. Sam couldn't help but feel a pinch of gratitude at the shade offered by the patio's broad portico overhead as he observed the laborers toil; muscles ripped and dripping with sweat, ferrying load after load of equipment from point A to point B, all beneath the Yucatan's relentless blaze. *And*, Sam thought, *in second-hand tank shirts, no less.* He couldn't help but shake his head in admiration.

While Tom and Armando discussed the transportation of the heavy equipment and who would carry the heaviest equipment, Sam held his glass of horchata and stared into the foreboding tree line of the jungle, thinking about the trip ahead. The memories of the last jungle he had been in superimposed themselves over this scene and he swore he could feel the wind rushing through his hair as he parachuted from that ancient plane, the bullets whizzing by inches from his face...

"Did you hear that? Sam?"

Sam snapped out of his trance. He knew that voice. He turned to Tom. "What?"

Tom sighed with the patience one would expect from a parent explaining the same thing over and over to a curious child. "Armando was explaining that we will have to make the dive one at a time." His gaze revealed nothing and for a moment Sam wasn't sure he'd heard correctly. "Without partners."

Sam cringed at such a thought. Diving alone? That would be absolute suicide. In any normal SCUBA dive, it was critical to have a diving partner. Without one, you could go down and get stuck in seaweed or have an equipment malfunction, and with no help you'd stay down there forever, a skeleton amongst the foliage. Not only had Sam heard horror stories of cocky and careless divers drowning as their tanks detached or they got stuck in a tight squeeze, he also had stories from his own personal experience. He and Tom had gone on countless SCUBA dives, both together and with other partners. There had been more than enough instances in which neither of them would have come out alive if they had gone in alone, and even considering going in alone chilled Sam to the bone.

Their gaze met without the need for words.

Tom turned to Armando. His tone echoed that of the academic's tone earlier in the Jeep- a man who knew his corner and knew it well. A tone spared from being labeled condescension by politeness, and politeness alone. Sam knew the anger was spurred by fear.

"Armando, you have to understand, dives are actually very dangerous alone. According to the United States Marines, almost twenty percent of divers-"

"Please." Armando held up his hands. "I know the stats and I know that it is not without risks. But I have sent men down in these caves, or caves like them, three times before. And trust me – diving in these caves, having a partner with you…" He looked at them straight, as if he wished it were different. "This only endangers both parties. I speak from experience."

For a moment, no one spoke as they considered their options.

Finally, Sam shrugged. "I'll go, Tom."

Tom shook his head stubbornly. "Fat chance. If there's an emergency, you get stuck or worse. Just no way…"

"I've got less chance of getting stuck than you."

Armando broke in, hands raised to deter an argument. "It is a question of space, gentlemen. You must understand that some of these crevices are extremely narrow, and the likelihood that you would be able to help one another in such an event… say, for example, you, Mr. Reilly," nodding toward Sam to illustrate his point, "make it through a narrow crevice successfully. You beckon Mr. Bower, here, who is much broader than you, forward. Because of your prowess, you think you can manage. He gets stuck. Not through any fault of his skill, simply because of his size. And then…" He spread his hands, helpless. "He can't get out and now, Mr. Reilly, *you* are stuck in the chamber beyond." He looked at them levelly. "You must consider which benefits outweigh the risks."

Tom set his chin. "At least you'd have company when you go."

For a moment, they sat in silence. Sam had been around enough dying men to know that the company of a friend sometimes made all the difference in the world.

Armando tilted his head and Sam wondered again if he'd had military training. "Yes," he allowed, finally. "That is true. You would have company."

Sam turned to him, running a hand through his hair. "There are no other options?"

"No," replied Armando. "As I said, there are portions of the tunnel that are very narrow – ten inches, even a foot in diameter, and we'll all be endangering ourselves if we clog the system up with bodies."

Sam considered this carefully, yet he knew that Armando was right. They would have to make the dives individually.

"All right, we'll go separately," conceded Sam.

Armando smiled, triumph fierce behind his eyes. Tom snorted, but Sam saw the gears turning behind his eyes, too. Finally, Tom got to his feet. "I'd like to see you dive with SCUBA gear while getting harpoons shot at you by the Italian mafia, Mr. Ayala," he said. "Or get out of Dragon Cave by yourself." He jerked his thumb at the men loading up the trucks. "You need me, I'll be helping out while I can."

Sam laughed. Low morale was dangerous morale. "I guess you'll be taking all the SCUBA tanks out of the truck yourself!" he called after.

Tom turned, glowering. "You bet your ass I will!"

"Really? How much would you say my ass is worth?"

"Guess we'll know when you haul it up out of hell." Tom scratched his forehead, fighting a grin, and Sam knew he was seduced by the thrill of the chase. "Guess it should be worth at least a couple of bucks."

Armando laughed, and Sam got the sense he knew exactly what Sam was doing. His estimation of the man rose when he said with a wink, "Oh, a couple of bucks? I wouldn't bet on that. Sounds like a lot."

By now the conversation had taken a joking turn and the locals had gathered around, watching the exchange with amusement. Though they spoke minimal English, it was clear they understood the dynamic.

Tom scoffed. "How about you carry these tanks through the jungle, Mr. Reilly? I'm sure your enthusiasm will make them feel like little pillows."

Sam's laugh was interrupted by a shout from the overseer, who gestured at the loaded Jeeps.

"Everything off. Time to go." The broken words would have sounded terse and unfriendly from anyone else, but the man's beaming face and friendly tone proved that it was merely the language barrier – he was proud to show off his English skills to these foreigners. He glanced inquiringly at Armando and said something in Spanish. Then he rubbed his fingers together in the universal sign for money.

Tom and Armando looked at each other and burst out laughing.

Sam brushed his hands. Mission accomplished. All the equipment had been unloaded during their bickering. Sam couldn't help but crack a smile, despite his anxiety at the perilous trek awaiting them. He'd faced perilous treks before- they both had, and a good team made up for quite a bit.

Trekking through a jungle with diving equipment was a lot easier said than done. Tom and Armando had formed a temporary alliance and forced Sam to lug all three tanks. However, as the humidity levels went through the roof and the mud got thicker the deeper they traveled into the jungle, the carts the two had opted to use to pull instead of carry the tanks dug deep into the ground, grinding them to a halt.

Sam had never been much of a tree-hugger. He was more interested in beating the jungle and getting to the treasures it hid, but it was impossible not to be intrigued by the new types of plants and insects that he saw everywhere. He looked to his left and there were exquisite flowers in shades of violet to green, with endless variations of numbers of petals. He looked right. A tree towered above him, branches reaching to the sky and shielding their skin from the harsh rays of the sun.

Occasionally, Armando would hold his arm out, stop the group, and stab a surprisingly wicked-looking knife into a seemingly random tree. He would then stick a wooden spigot into it, like a cork into a wine keg. After a few moments, water would begin dripping out like a leaky faucet. How Armando found the right kinds of trees, Sam had no idea. Tom and Sam had both learned trail craft in the Marines, and it had served them well on a number of occasions during deployment and after. But this was a whole other level – these were not skills acquired and filed away because someday they might be useful. This was the locals' everyday life; and their motions reflected this bone-deep familiarity. Of course they knew the ins and outs of the jungle.

As he trudged forward, Sam suddenly realized that he no longer had to fight the vines to stumble through. Was the jungle clearing up? Sam looked up hopefully. "Hey." He reached out and tugged the shirt of the nearest man who hoisted a SCUBA tank on his head like some kind of science fiction crown. "How much longer?" At the look of incomprehension, he mangled a sentence he wasn't even quite sure was Spanish.

To Sam's dismay, the local laughed in a bright show of teeth that reminded Sam of those flowers. He waved his hand into the distance, again and again, his meaning quite clear: 'We're not even halfway there' gesture. The hand dipped, then, demonstrating a motion like a plane coasting in for landing. The man grinned and slapped Sam's arm in encouragement. *Don't worry,* Sam interpreted, *the next part's all downhill.*

A regular hiker would have sighed with relief at the notion of an easy downhill climb. Sam knew better. Downhill treks, especially on a dense jungle floor full of vines, leaves, and other tripping hazards, were the most dangerous part of any jungle hike. His worry was tripled by the fact that each hiker was carrying just about his own body weight in gear. The three empty air tanks hanging from the ropes he'd slung over his shoulder had already started to take its toll, and the prospect of gravity increasing on them weighed his heart, too. His muscles burned with every step, the unyielding plastic fibers digging into his sweaty t-shirt. There was no way he could keep going, at this rate. From what he could hear, it wasn't much better for his friends either. They were panting like dogs in the humidity. Sam plopped himself down on a rotting log off to the side and practically threw the tanks off his back and into the mud, relieved to have them off.

Sam said, "Guys, I call time. Let's take a break."

Tom, having similar thoughts, set his equipment down next to Sam's. As the duo watched the rest of the group stumble down what seemed to be a near vertical hill while bantering effortlessly back and forth with the ease of people who do this all the time, Sam suddenly noticed something.

"Hey, who is that new guy?" He pointed.

Tom stared blankly, trying to home in on whatever Sam's finger was pointing at. "Where?"

"Over there. There. The guy carrying less stuff than anyone else." Sam tried not to sound annoyed but, if the man had room to spare, he'd be happy to share.

Tom scanned the group, searching as the team stopped to take a break in a distant patch of shade. Sam watched as the man in question took a lengthy drink from his water bottle.

"Oh, he's the doctor. An anesthesiologist. Apparently Armando isn't taking any chances with the team's safety on this expedition."

"We have a doctor?" Sam's brows rose. "I don't know if that makes me feel better or worse." He squinted. *There is nothing about this man that indicates his profession*, he thought. As he watched, jealous, he put his water bottle away and took out a sandwich, devouring it in a matter of bites. Sam's stomach growled.

He rubbed his hands on his pants to cover it up and pushed to his feet. His body groaned in protest. "Hey, let's go. We don't want to get left behind."

As Sam and Tom resumed their downhill climb, Sam quickly realized that although the locals were slow, they were faster than he or Tom could ever hope to be. By the time he reached some level ground, he was panting. Armando, waiting for him at the base, seemed barely out of breath.

"We're here," he announced. Without looking back, Armando plowed through a wall of bushes and disappeared.

Sam and Tom glanced at each other, shrugged, then followed.

Sam tripped over a few thick roots that were sprouting one on top of the other and lost his balance when the gear on his back shifted, causing him to tumble hands-first into the bushes Armando had slipped through. It was not the graceful entrance he'd have preferred, but the foliage easily gave way; almost as if it wanted Sam to see what was on the other side.

The first thing that caught his eye was the brilliant radiance of the pool before him. Sam had witnessed such amazing shades of blue and green only once in his lifetime. At the Tomb of El Dorado. This time however, it was nature's work and not centuries-worth of gold piled up. The colors almost appeared layered; the middle depths cast in deep shades of navy and the edges a marvelous turquoise. The pool was surrounded by reeds, like a crust and forming a barrier several feet wide. This natural barricade would have to be traversed with care prior to entering the water. Doable but, even still, something itched at the back of Sam's mind. Something felt *off*.

"Are you sure this is the right place?" Sam asked tentatively. "Sure, it's beautiful and all, but it looks like the cover of a travel brochure for South America more than anything else. What's so special about it?"

Armando opened the map gripped in his right hand and made a show of squinting. He turned the map this way and that, then checked it against the pool. "Yep. This is the right place."

Tom's forehead furrowed in puzzlement. "This is supposed to be the entrance to the Highway to Hell. I expected something more dramatic than this. Something... sulfurous, at least."

A local spoke up, speaking as his focus shifted between Sam, Tom, and the cenote. Sam raised his brows. "Translate?"

Armando wiped his face with a handkerchief and pocketed the large square of fabric. "He says that it might look normal, but it is very special."

"Disguise." The local drew his thumb across his forehead, serious. "Xibalba."

Sam considered the pool in a new light. Well, that made more sense, at least. "He's saying they left it unmarked for a reason?"

The local seemed to understand. "Not special. Seems. Conquistadors not…" He shrugged, unable to find sufficient English but Sam got the picture.

"I guess that's as good a solution as any."

Armando grinned. "So good it has remained hidden for centuries."

"But you're sure this is the right place?"

Armando's voice hardened. "That's what we're hoping you'll help us determine."

Tom was eyeing the pool with an engineer's trained eye. "Where's the opening then?"

Armando shook his head after a subtle nod toward the locals. "They refuse to go under, and they refuse to dive. The entrance is down there, but where, exactly…"

Sam was beginning to see why they'd been called in after all, as the local who'd spoken earlier lowered his chin and spoke fearfully, "Cannot risk. Cannot find. Curse."

"A curse, eh?" Sam looked at Tom who, despite his words on the patio, seemed to eye the crystal water the same way some men look at boats and cars. "I guess we're gonna be the guinea pigs." He laughed. "You want to go first?"

Tom jumped at being caught longing and then grinned sheepishly. Dropping all pretense, he shared what Sam had already read on his face. "You bet I do!"

Chapter Six

Tom looked down at the inviting crystalline waters below, the slight breeze disturbing the surface of the pool and sending out ripples that went on endlessly in the calmness. If he closed his eyes, he could imagine himself relaxing all alone at the community pool on a scorching August afternoon, enjoying the water as the pool emptied during the hourly break.

The journey to Xibalba would be long and arduous. From what Armando had told them, it would take every bit of his maximum dive time of three and a half hours to reach and return. To improve the odds, he would dive using a closed-circuit rebreather system.

He opened a large duffel bag and laid out his Dräger Closed-Circuit Oxygen Rebreather on a canvas mat. The rebreather was originally designed for military use, police diving, and search and rescue, but to Tom, their rectangular, rigid aluminum backpack gave them the awkward appearance of an astronaut's personal life-support system. Mounted on either side of this backpack were two gas cylinders. One was filled with oxygen and the other, a diluent called Trimix.

He and Sam methodically and efficiently worked their way through their dive equipment, slowly going through the laborious process of preparing each part for the dive.

Tom opened the aluminum backpack. Inside was an axial-type scrubber unit filled with the granular absorbent used to remove CO_2 from the closed-circuit during the dive. He removed the half-used cartridge and replaced it with a brand-new unit, filled with five pounds of soda lime and then reinserted it, locking the lid with a heavy-duty thread.

He then began to test the unit for leaks. Two leak tests were conducted. These were generally known as the positive and negative pressure tests and are designed to check that the breathing loop is airtight for internal pressure lower and higher than the outside. The positive pressure test ensures that the unit will not lose gas while in use, and the negative pressure test ensures that water will not leak into the breathing loop where it can degrade the scrubber medium or the oxygen sensors.

Next Tom tested his full-face mask for leaks.

He took a deep breath and started pre-breathing the unit. It was a process of breathing normally for about three minutes before entering the water to ensure the scrubber material gets a chance to warm up to operating temperature, works correctly, and that the partial pressure of oxygen within the closed-circuit rebreather is controlled within the predefined parameters.

Tom inhaled effortlessly.

The gas he breathed was humid and warm, rather than the dry, cold air divers are used to with compressed air and a SCUBA cylinder and regulator set up.

He checked his gauge for two things.

One, that CO_2 levels weren't rising, meaning the new soda lime scrubber was doing its job correctly and two, that the partial pressure of oxygen within the closed-circuit remained within the initial set point of 1.3 bar.

Tom ran his eyes across the top reading, where a nondispersive infrared sensor showed that the CO_2 levels weren't elevating. Below that, his glance stopped to examine the reading from the oxygen analyzer. It showed the partial pressure of oxygen as 1.3 bar.

Three minutes later, he said to Sam, "I'm all good to go."

Sam double checked his equipment, giving him the all good signal.

Armando's voice rose up and spilled over the loud crowd. "Good luck, Tom. I wish I could come with you."

Tom raised one eyebrow and gestured to the pool. "Thanks Armando. You're welcome to come with me, if you like."

"I wish I could, but there's no way I would survive a dive like this," the Mexican historian confessed as he parted the reeds and approached Tom. His face turned serious. "You've got all the equipment? Everything ready?"

Tom double checked his dive equipment. "All good." He waddled over to the edge of the cenote and splashed the surface with his flippers.

Sam swept a magnanimous bow. "Then we're ready when you are."

Positioning the full facemask on himself, Tom dipped into the waters below, head first. The water was warmer than he expected. Tom didn't like it. Instead of perking him up and keeping him on his toes, the water enveloped his body like the towels his grandmother used to put in the dryer to warm for him after he got out of the pool. The feeling was visceral and relaxed him. He shook himself free of the memories. Warmer meant more comfortable, and in a high-stakes dive like this, the last thing he could afford to be was comfortable.

Tom glanced back at the colorful blurs of Sam and Armando above the surface still rippled by his entrance. As the ripples calmed, he turned his focus downward, intent on getting this done as soon as possible.

The water was as clear as air beneath the surface, too, a friendly blue expanse vastly different than the ice-cold blackness of the Tomb of El Dorado. Tom stared straight ahead and squinted through his mask. Even with the transparency, he couldn't see an end to the cenote, which was too bad – because that was where he had to go.

Tom groped at his hip, removing a spool of dive-line. He wrapped it around the entirety of a relatively large limestone boulder. He gave the line a firm tug to confirm the knot would hold. It was his lifeline to the surface world – the one for those still living.

He shivered despite the warmth and kicked himself forward.

Even before the cave system started, he could see the cenote expanding in all directions, almost inviting him to explore its secrets.

Tom looked at his compass. The passageway before him headed on a bearing of 308 northwest. According to the mystical and antiquated map that Armando possessed, it seemed to match the historic references leading to Xibalba. He swam toward the darkest corner of the cenote. The warm water, while only mildly annoying before, was really starting to get to him. Tom was trained for diving in the ocean, where he had gotten used to the biting cold. The warm jungle water made him almost feel dirty.

As he traveled through the cenote, his sense of unease escalated. There was something off about the entire place. Was it the mystical powers of Xibalba? Tom distinctly remembered the bubbling feeling deep in his belly that he'd felt as Sam and he got near the Tomb of El Dorado, long hidden from tomb raiders. That had been months ago, and he could recall the visceral feeling even now, as if it had happened mere seconds earlier.

Somehow, it felt the same.

Tom forced himself to smile. He hoped this adventure would involve fewer guns and people with bad teeth. Far ahead, in the cave, he caught sight of something. A way in perhaps? He picked up the pace.

He'd only been swimming maybe another minute before he knew what had happened – the outline of a gaping hole in the wall. He saw it quite clearly, quite suddenly, and in its entirety. While all the water around it was blue, it seemed to shift to an insidious black at the opening. The sensation of something supernatural was stronger than ever. Like a curtain of death closing in on him.

Tom swam through.

Entering the deep black of the void, he quickly switched his flashlight on.

Illuminated by the beam, he could see that the cavern beyond the opening's threshold was larger than he'd imagined. While falling far short of the near abandoned-mansion feel of the Yellow Dragon Cave they'd navigated to reach the Tomb of El Dorado, Tom certainly felt small. He had to swing his head back and forth to illuminate each side. From what he could tell in the glare of the lamp, both sides of the cave appeared to be a kind of marble, almost blackened beyond recognition by impurities. He swam closer and ran his hand over the right side. *Rough, not artificially smooth.* This place wasn't some man-made death trap, at least. Then, he noticed the wall was getting closer to him. Was he not swimming straight? Tom looked ahead.

No. They were closing in on him.

He could feel his breathing getting shallower and more labored with every flipper stroke and he fought to keep it steady, to pull in through the respirator. He summoned the image of Darth Vader and tried to feel like the super villain, capable of destroying planets. It was a trick he'd used ever since he'd learned to dive, and it always made him feel better in tricky situations. He'd never told Sam.

It didn't work as well as he'd hoped. This was bad.

After twenty years of diving, I should be able to control myself at this point, he thought, angling himself slightly to avoid an outcropping of marble. If his air tank was penetrated, he was too far in to swim back out on one lungful of air. It wouldn't kill him instantly, but it would kill him nonetheless.

Armando had told the group that they were diving individually to make sure they had enough space to turn around should they need to backtrack to the point of entry, but Tom wasn't sure if that possibility had *ever* been an option. It certainly wasn't now.

With no choice, he continued down the long, narrow, and almost perfectly straight passageway, then stopped.

Up ahead, was a deadly choke point.

Chapter Seven

Tom stared at the choke point.

Almost a perfect circle, it had a diameter of two feet, making it wide enough for an adult to slide through, but impossible for a SCUBA diver with equipment to breach. Tom shined his flashlight inside. Like most choke points, the narrowest constriction opened to a much larger space inside.

He focused the beam of his flashlight through the opening, scanning the chamber beyond. The space itself looked like it could accommodate a large bus, making it easy for him to turn around once inside. That was, if he could get there in the first place.

It was the classic catch twenty-two.

Although he might have been able to squeeze through by himself, there was no way he could manage with all the gear he was carrying and without his SCUBA equipment, he would drown. He shifted his position, considering any possibility of turning around in the narrow passageway.

Impossible.

That left making his way through the choke point as his only option – and that meant holding his breath while he did it.

Chapter Eight

Tom took a couple of deep breaths.

He mentally ran through each individual step of the process. First he'd undo the Velcro straps that held his buoyancy control wing and his closed-circuit rebreather system. Next, he would need to drop to the seabed, allowing enough room above him to maneuver his equipment out in front. If he made it that far, he could then easily pass his gear through the narrow constriction. If he was lucky, he could follow right behind – that was, if his loop hoses reached.

He squeezed his dive wing's air release.

A small burst of air bubbles escaped, sending him ever-so-slightly negatively buoyant. Unlike a traditional open-circuit SCUBA system, where you can control your short-term buoyancy by breathing in or out, breathing never altered one's buoyancy on a closed-circuit loop. In a closed-circuit setup, gas never left the system. If the air expanded in the diver's lungs, it would deflate the wing balloon, never altering the diver's overall buoyancy.

Tom gave an equally small burst of air into the closed-circuit and his buoyancy turned neutral, his descent easing to a stop just ten inches off the rocky seabed.

He took another breath, collected his thoughts, then began the process of removing his dive equipment.

The Velcro came off easily, but the next phase of the process was harder. Slipping free of his CCR system felt more like a Brazilian jiu-jitsu wrestling match, but inside a constricted cave, underwater and with an opponent who knew how to instantly choke you if you made one wrong move. To make matters worse, the passage was barely wide enough to slide it free.

Tom breathed out as far as he could, gaining precious inches between the limestone walls, his deflated lungs, and the CCR dive system. He gently pulled the tank and aluminum backpack over his shoulders, until they couldn't move any farther. He pushed hard, trying to free it, but it had become lodged.

For a second, nothing moved.

Panic rose in his throat and his heart pounded. If he didn't wriggle free, there wouldn't be enough room to take another breath.

He maneuvered his arms forward, but in his current position the angle was all wrong. It meant that all the effort had to be generated from the smaller muscles of his triceps, and it wasn't enough. He tried only twice. Any more than that would be a precious waste of oxygen and strength; on something that would never work.

Instead, he turned his efforts to the larger, stronger muscles of his legs.

With his feet finding purchase on a small vertical ledge, he pushed hard. A small, muffled crunching sound filled the chamber as he pushed off. The dive equipment slid free and now floated in the void, middle of the passageway.

He closed his eyes and took a couple of deep breaths, trying to consciously slow his heartrate.

Tom swallowed. He'd just dodged a deadly bullet.

Careful not to disconnect the loop pipes that connected him to the CCR system, he slowly eased it through the opening. He gave the tank a gentle nudge, and it slowly cruised through, and then stopped – just shy of the large chamber on the other side.

It was the loop pipes that had prevented it from making it through.

He cursed silently to himself.

That left only one option. He needed to disconnect from the CCR system – and that meant removing his dive mask.

He took a couple more deep breaths, closed his eyes and removed the dive mask – blindly passing the entire CCR system through the choke point, until he could no longer reach it.

Now his turn.

Tom angled his head downward and grabbed the edges of the entrance. With a precision mastered over years of military training, he kept his arms tight against his body and flicked his feet to move forward. He came out unscathed on the other side.

Flawless, he praised himself, *victorious*.

And then, in the void of darkness, he realized he couldn't reach his dive mask.

Chapter Nine

Tom was an expert cave diver.

But in the darkness, blind panic began to flood over him, trying to drown out any rational thoughts. Without a facemask, his vision was nothing more than an obtuse blur. Unable to breathe, he frantically searched the chamber for his dive mask. His outstretched fingers ran through the gravelly seabed in front of him. He spread his arms wide, like one would to make a snow angel.

He forced himself to open his eyes. The saltwater stung. Without a dive mask, his entire field of vision was no better with his flashlight on or off.

He mentally pictured the outline of the chamber, reconstructing it from memory. It was roughly the size of a bus, maybe a little wider in parts, and potentially much longer. The fact was, if he could see at all, he could probably swim around the entire chamber within twenty seconds but, lacking vision it was a completely different story.

Tom visualized the dive equipment being pushed through the choke point.

It was neutrally buoyant making it easy to move through the water, gliding like silk. He thought about Newton's First Law.

An object will remain at rest or in uniform motion in a straight line unless acted upon by an external force.

He had needed to give it a decent push to slide it through the opening, but with the resistance of water, nothing moves very fast or far.

So where did it go?

Tom began a systematic grid search, focusing on those seven or so feet closest to the choke point. When he reached the wall at the end of the chamber he turned around and kicked off the wall like a competitive swimmer. He did this four times, crisscrossing the chamber, in slow, determined movements.

But his dive mask nor equipment materialized.

Panic raged in his hypoxia-driven madness, but he didn't allow it to take over. He had time, not a lot, but some. He was a strong swimmer and an extremely competitive free diver, capable of holding his breath for upward of five minutes.

It was a puzzle, but it had a simple answer.

Even Newton would agree the damned thing couldn't have gone far.

Tom turned and following the edge of the flooded cavern, felt his way back to the choke point. He carefully turned around and stopped. Despite his urge to quickly kick off in search of the dive equipment, like some hidden prize, Tom forced himself to remain perfectly still.

And that's when he realized he was floating across a gentle current and into an unknown passageway.

Chapter Ten

It was the one and only clue Tom needed.

Elation surged as he imagined the only possible explanation. The dive gear had been pushed through the choke point only to become picked up by an underground current and dragged elsewhere.

He swam hard in the direction of the current.

His heart raced and his lungs burned. Maybe twenty feet along the passageway his fingers reached the dive mask. His fingers grasped the mask as if his life depended on it – which it did – and placed it on his face. He depressed the purge button and a large bubble of gas cleared the flooded mask and rebreather circuit of debris and water.

He took a couple of deep breaths and calmed himself.

The beam of his flashlight shot across the narrow confines of the subterranean river system. The water moved horizontally, despite the passageway being level. If he had to guess, it was related to a distant tidal pattern, rather than a natural, fresh water source.

Tom scrolled through his dive gauges on his heads-up-display. The purging process had expelled way too much of his gas supply. There was enough to get back, but not a lot more than that. He should have turned back immediately but after the effort to get through the choke point, Tom needed to see whether his efforts had been worth it. If not, he could at least rule out this particular passageway for Sam.

He took a new spool of dive line and tied it to a protruding section of the rocky passageway. The tunnel was narrow, but not so narrow that it would be difficult to turn around in – not yet, anyway.

Letting the spool unwind, he swam north, along the new tunnel.

His deliberations about how best to get himself through the tiny opening within the cave wall had wasted time. Tom flicked the flashlight beam ahead of him, half expecting to face yet another opening he'd be forced to squeeze through. To his surprise, the tunnel widened, revealing what seemed to be a corridor. He remembered what Armando had said.

Had he reached the flooded passages of Xibalba?

Well, heck, he thought. *That was easy.*

He tried to remember what Armando had told him about Xibalba. *Would it be better if he actually knew anything about Xibalba,* Tom reflected, *instead of just offering conjecture? Gateway to hell, human sacrifice… hadn't he also said something about a maze?*

What he did remember was that 'Xibalba' roughly translated to *Place of Fear. Well,* he thought, looking around the dark passageways, a chill crawling up his spine…

That sounded about right.

Xibalba was the underworld in Mayan mythology, Armando had said. Ruled by the Mayan death gods and their helpers. According to the Popol Vuh – a creation narrative written by the K'iche' people before the Spanish conquest- the ten gods were often referred to as demons and lorded over the different realms of human suffering: sickness, starvation, fear, destitution, pain, and ultimately, death. He remembered the gods had worked in pairs because Tom had thought of Sam and made a joke about it. Down here in the dark it wasn't as funny. They'd had names like Flying Scab and Gathered Blood, Pus Demon and Skull Staff. They and their minions fulfilled their duties, dragging souls down into the underworld.

Tom's eyes narrowed. Too easy, indeed.

Slowly swimming through the passageway, he realized that it must have been a hallway at some time. The steps that rose under him seemed to be designed almost in an effort to deter entry; each step just a little taller than comfortable for anyone but a very tall man.

Before Tom knew it, he had reached the end of the passageway, revealing that the cave branched off.

Abruptly, a memory of Armando's distant voice popped in his head.

"It's a maze," he had said, pointing to the dead middle of his map. Damn. "But as far as we have been able to ascertain, it all goes to the same place. It sounds strange, I know, but that's the way it is. Just choose a path and commit to it."

This didn't change the fact that Tom felt incredibly uneasy with the whole dive. He glanced at his dive gauge. He was running dangerously close to the point of no return. He made the conscious decision to go just five minutes farther, and then turn around – no matter what he found.

His heart raced. He swallowed down the fear. He couldn't afford to get nervous. He looked around and decided to just take the wider passage. Maybe he wouldn't feel like he was getting suffocated this time.

And, this time, nothing seemed out of the ordinary. It looked exactly like the one that he had entered through. *Or, maybe it was the same one?* Tom swore he had seen that same rock on the ground a few minutes earlier. No. His eyes were playing tricks on him.

He was distracted from his growing concern when he saw another tunnel branch up ahead. He took the right side, again. A couple minutes later, Tom was starting to get nervous. He had been trained never to panic, but he would have to head back soon if he wanted to survive. The oxygen gauge was now an ugly mix of green and orange, marked thirty percent. Fifteen minutes left. Every single passageway he went through looked the same. The uneasy idea that it was a circle pestered him, but he'd yet to cross his unspooled dive line. Surely he was traveling deeper into the earth, but he felt like he was going nowhere.

All right, screw this. Tom twisted his body to turn around and leave. He'd have to get out quick or he'd wind up as just another body; the classic fool who'd decided to explore one passageway too many.

When he turned around, he came face to face with something that didn't belong...

A single SCUBA diver flashlight floated – its beam still bright against the gravelly seabed.

Chapter Eleven

Beneath his dive mask, Tom's lips curved upward in the slightest of grins.

A flashlight didn't belong anywhere near his location. Not this deep underground. There wasn't enough of a current to have carried it in from the outside, and the fact that it still shined brightly meant that it hadn't been left on for very long. A few hours, at most.

He switched off his own flashlight, just to be sure it wasn't a reflection. But the ghost flashlight continued to glow luminously. No, he hadn't imagined it, unless the cave's supernatural vibe was more real than imagined? Tom's eyes, having adjusted in the dimness, identified a slight curvature in the passageway's meandering. It didn't seem possible, yet–yes, a soft but unmistakable glow had revealed itself–and it was coming from up ahead; and *around a corner*.

Before he could think about it too much, Tom wasted no time paddling to reach it.

Then his gaze dropped. Lower, lower…

A flashlight inconspicuously rested on the pebbles on the ground of the passageway. And it was turned on, its light angled eerily towards the way he had come from. How the hell? Irritation masked his fear, and he kicked forward impatiently, scooping the object up. Upon inspection, Tom noticed that it was a standard underwater flashlight. These things only had enough power to keep working for a few hours, at best.

Tom felt the hair on the back of his neck stand up. Someone was here. Very recently. Carefully looking around the dark room, he realized that the flashlight wasn't the only equipment left behind. Divers' strings, spare tanks, a flipper… someone, maybe more than one, had made a big mistake and it most likely ended in a loss of life.

But where were the bodies?

Tom flashed the beam of his light across the walls of the passageway. The visibility wasn't the greatest, the surrounding water was noticeably dirtier; the silt here had been recently disturbed.

The passage ended here. Had the passage continued, Tom still couldn't fathom how anyone could have traveled far without a flashlight or fins. None of it made sense.

His oxygen indicator beeped, then beeped again three seconds later. And it would continue to do so, indicating that the tank capacity was under ten percent, until he ran out of air. Unless he wanted to repeat this poor fool's big mistake, Tom had no choice but to go up to the surface.

He tucked his spool of fishing line behind a rock so it would stay in place for Sam. Then, swimming urgently yet calmly, Tom turned around and followed his fishing line back toward the entrance. Exiting proved to be significantly less difficult than the trek in. Knowing exactly where to go, Tom expertly tugged along, careful not to break it. Knowing Sam as he did, he'd no doubt he'd be on the mysterious flashlight caper like flies on shit and with the SCUBA line he'd laid down — the diver's breadcrumb — Sam should arrive at ground zero in half the time it'd taken Tom.

He was cutting it close. Gripping his flashlight and kicking hard, Tom's only thought was *you'd better be worth it, lamp,* at the same time his air tank sputtered out.

Tom's throat burned and his vision vacillated between bright and dark as he kicked his way toward the surface, his focus locked on the light above. He didn't let go of the flashlight as his vision darkened further, struggled against the instinct to breathe. Alarms sounded in his heads-up-display, warning him that the carbon dioxide levels were rising dangerously high and the partial pressure of oxygen was falling.

He kept going, kicking harder.

There. Light up ahead, a distant glow.

Tom swam toward it but the closer he got, the light seemed to disappear. Even the light of his own flashlight dimmed until it was all but gone, and he was left once more in complete darkness.

Chapter Twelve

Sam watched the stilled water above the cave.

It had calmed a long time ago and become a surface of glass. Flies and mosquitoes buzzed all around Sam's body like tiny planets in orbit, searching for any opportunity to swoop down and collect some sweat and blood. Sam slapped the air uselessly in annoyance. Curiously, no matter how many swarmed their group, they never seemed to collect on the pool. He distinctly remembered playing in the lakes near his house in the summer as a kid and splashing away any mosquitoes that landed near them. It was always so satisfying to see them speed off in surprise. He remembered how he and James Longley used to crouch at the edge of the lake, paper cups at the ready. After finding the clusters of tall eggs, they would scoop them up and let them hatch into larvae before letting them go. Then nature's process would start all over again.

Sam missed those days, when everything was simple. He turned to one of the locals who seemed unfazed by the insects.

"Why aren't there any mosquitoes on the water? I thought they loved to lay their eggs on the surface."

The local let out a short yet hearty laugh. Apparently, his English comprehension was better than his execution. "Si, si. Normally. This one no. Mama knows it is sacred. Fish?" He shrugged, exaggerating his eyebrows to make sure Sam got his point. "Where?"

Sam hadn't thought of that. "There aren't any fish, are there?"

There wasn't any *Tom*, either. He stared at the pool and the endless expanse far ahead of them, and then back at his clock. Four minutes ago, Tom should have popped his head out and given them some critical information. Sam's mind shied away from worst-case scenarios, but forced himself to consider them. Was he stuck down there, or was he just taking a little longer? Maybe Tom had found something and was exploring before he came back. But then again, Tom was just like Sam: Military training dictated we always arrived early, not late.

"Hey! Armando!" he called over, where the man was smoking a cigarillo with the locals, apparently conversing about some sort of logistics issue. "I'm going in. Something's happened."

Armando started. "No, you can't. You're only going to get you both killed. How many times do I have to tell you it's too tight for more than one person?"

"I don't care. He's my brother. I can't just leave him down there."

Armando seemed to understand this but Sam didn't care. He'd already made up his mind.

Having already put his dry suit on a long time ago, Sam started to prep his oxygen tank for the dive. He was always at the ready, primed for action no matter the occasion. And if they died together, at least Sam went down trying to save his best friend. Loyalty trumps all.

Just then, one of the locals shouted. He was speaking fast, pointing down at the water. Sam's eyes followed.

Was that something moving? Sam looked more closely. There was a black shape coming from the opening Tom had disappeared through almost forty minutes prior. Sam paused his prep, sighing with relief.

Then he frowned. It was evident, with the clear water, that despite the distorted depth perception and flurry of bubbles that Tom wasn't moving.

Without hesitation, Sam kicked his shoes off and jumped into the water. Years of dive training had perfected his underwater breaststroke kick. The powerful pectorals he'd spent years cultivating, whether at the city pool or vacations on the cape, the work now paid dividends, allowing him to cut through the water like a blade toward Tom's motionless body. It was a visceral urgency that eclipsed all else and thankfully, a rare experience. The last time was when they'd swum for their lives— under water and in battle mode— through the pitch black depths of Yellow Dragon's Cave.

He didn't notice the warmth of the water nor its clarity as he struggled to reach his friend. All he noticed was that it felt like he was moving through air, but in slow motion. He felt like he was dreaming by the time he finally got to Tom, grabbed him in a lifeguard's hold and desperately kicked his way toward the surface.

The panic had taken a toll on his breathing, all right. He had been in the water for less than half a minute and already his lungs felt as if they were about to burst. Still, Sam held tight even as Tom's muscled bulk rebelled, sliding ever so slightly downward with every kick of his legs. *Come on, why the hell isn't anyone helping me?* Hauling two-hundred-and-fifty-pounds of dead weight through water, opposing gravity, was no easy task–not even considering the full complement of diving gear along for the ride.

When he finally surfaced arms were waiting to haul them up, however, and Sam collapsed down with Tom on the pool's sandy edge. As the locals stripped Tom's equipment off of his heaving body in a flurry of Spanish, Sam noticed a jarred look on Tom's face. He was awake. Never in their adventures had Sam ever seen Tom look so surprised. Sam took off the straps of the air tank, helped him sit up and encouraged him to breathe, recover. *He's probably still in shock*, Sam thought as he read the air levels remaining in the tank. Zero percent. He was at *zero percent*. Divers were trained to always be at the surface before their tank reached *fifteen* percent. The fact that Tom's tank was below that meant he'd either made a colossal mistake along the way or had found something very, very interesting.

When his breathing had gone from slow, steady gasps, to a regular in and out rhythm, Tom swiped his hair out of his eyes and weakly held up a flashlight Sam hadn't taken note of in his flurry to get them to the surface. It was inconspicuously small but looked rugged. And it was still on.

Sam reached over and tried to shut it off for him.

Tom pulled it away with a grunt.

"What?" Sam frowned. "You want to keep it on?"

Tom shook his head. "It's not mine. I found it down there, turned on, just like this." Sam's face must have portrayed his shock because Tom continued on. "That's not all. I looked around, and there was a lot of equipment scattered around. Somebody was down there in the last twenty-four hours and by the looks of it, they're still down there somewhere." He blew the drops of water that had collected on his lips from his sopping hair away with an air of frustration. "Or they died and I can't find their bodies. I really don't know what to make of it."

What? Armando had said no one else knew the location of Xibalba. Was it possible that wasn't the truth? Even more unexplainable was, even if someone did know the location and had set out to dive the site, why they would leave all their gear behind? Even if they'd had to surface quickly, they surely would have kept their flashlights with them to navigate the dark tunnels. Sam shook his head. A million questions and only one way of answering them. He grabbed a towel and started to mop his body so he could suit up. "Rest here. I'll check it out."

Tom sighed. "I knew you would say that." He relinquished the flashlight. "I left you the line, so you'll know which way to go. But be careful. The walls... they're different from anything I've ever seen."

Looking at Tom's face Sam knew he wasn't just saying empty words. He genuinely looked as if he'd just completed a monumental task he'd never want to attempt again.

"All right. I'll take care of it. Help me suit up. I'll need the rebreather."

Armando stood by their side, listening in and translating everything to the locals, as they looked on, expectantly. They, who'd lived here for centuries and hadn't dared go inside stood resolute, proof as to why, before them.

They broke the conversation and started scrambling to get the equipment ready. The two gas cylinders mounted on the pack contained Oxygen and Trimix. For a depth dive such as this, oxygen became less and less efficient as pressure increased. To fix this, mixing other gases such as Trimix allowed the divers to use the oxygen more efficiently, even under incredible pressures.

Sam placed his mask over his face. Tom turned around and harnessed the rebreather kit on Sam's back and connected it to his mask. After checking that all systems were in good working order, Sam waddled to the edge of the pool and prepared to dive in.

He stopped when he felt a gentle pressure on his shoulder. He turned to find Tom peering at him and cracked his neck, eager to get on with it.

"The string should lead you directly into that room. You're also going to have to take off your tank and push it through the choke point." For no reason at all, his patient tone reminded Sam of the time his dad had taught him to ride a bike.

Turning around to fall into the water, Sam took a last look at his companions' faces.

"Good luck," said Tom.

Giving a last all-good symbol with his index finger and thumb, Sam fell back and beneath the crystal waters.

Chapter Thirteen

Sam swam through the clear water to the string that led to the opening. Though he understood the reasoning for the strength and slimness of the line, he wished it was a little easier to see. He had learned a long time ago that he should never touch or tug on a path string. Sam remembered feeling that paralyzing tightness of the walls closing in on him the first time, a dozen feet underwater, and the panic had overwhelmed him. He had grabbed on to the trailing string for security. Wasn't a good idea then and surely wasn't a good idea now, diving solo.

As he swam through the huge maw which somehow had darker water than everywhere surrounding it, Sam looked up and his jaw dropped.

The passageway swooped far above his head and expanded far more than he expected on both sides of him. He couldn't contain the sigh of relief that escaped his mouth and went into his regulator, creating a Darth Vader-esque sound effect, which somehow was both echoed and swallowed by the massive chamber.

He had never told anyone he had claustrophobia. At least, no one other than Tom. Though Tom had always had suspicions – they'd grown up together, after all, and had been in plenty of tight situations over their years of adventures- but those suspicions had never been confirmed until they'd trekked through the narrow passageways in South America and he couldn't squeeze through them without hyperventilating and stopping every thirty seconds.

It was a moment of utter shame, but Sam was thankful that Tom had never made fun of him for it. Claustrophobia was his one and only fear and he hated how insecure it made him feel. Eventually he had come up with some techniques to master it; he didn't want to be a burden to his group, and he would never forgive himself if he'd allowed himself to back out of a challenge. But that still didn't change the fact that the walls still felt as if they were squeezing in on him.

Years of swimming in the open ocean had made Sam a master at consistent and smooth forward movement in the water, and now his muscle memory enabled him to not even think about it. Inspecting his surroundings while swimming allowed him to keep moving without paying attention to what he was swimming through.

He felt the first tendrils of fear creeping in and pushed the sensations to the back of his mind, fiercely. He didn't have time for doubt, not even a hint of panic. He could not afford to freeze, not now. It was possible there was a person in there depending on him, even if Sam did not know who that person was.

If he was honest with himself, though, Sam didn't believe that a person was alive in these caves. Of course, he knew Tom had seen some evidence, and there undoubtedly had been someone down here- probably still was. But Sam knew the way dives worked. He had a sinking suspicion- not quite yet a certainty- that he was on a body retrieval mission, not a search-and-rescue.

Sam drew up short, confronted by a wall. When he looked up, he realized that he had come to what so far was the tightest part of the cave. The fishing guide line led into an opening that was barely two feet wide, maybe even narrower. Sam suddenly felt nauseous. The dark, deafening silence of the underwater passage was already pressing down on him like invisible hands, and now he was expected to crawl through an opening meant for something the size of an ant? And, without getting any of his equipment stuck or broken in the process?

You must be joking.

Jesus, how did Tom even manage? Sam briefly considered turning around. Maybe he could come back down here with Tom

Idiot, no. He couldn't bear to explain to them as to why he couldn't follow a simple path, already laid down by a trusted diver. And Tom had just come out of this hellhole unconscious and sputtering. Putting his best friend through that again would be torture.

Sam took a deep breath, calmed himself and faced the hole. Methodically, he took inventory of everything on him. Before going in, he had taken the largest air tank. He knew that Tom had struggled to make it back to the surface with the smaller size and Sam might be down here even longer than Tom. To follow up and possibly find more information, he'd need the extra oomph if he was going to be carrying a passenger.

Sam thought, *I've got my regulator, and tank, nothing else.* He hadn't needed to bring string or navigation equipment: Tom had already blazed the trail with his fishing line. He did have the compass in his dive pocket but that didn't take up any space at all, and there was no point in getting rid of it, especially if he might need it later.

Maybe if I make myself thinner and longer… Taking a deep, shivering breath, Sam took his gas tank off and held it on top of his head. It made him feel like he was hiking back through the jungle with Armando and his team, but it also made him an entire foot thinner and 3 feet taller.

Positioning himself right against the opening, he sucked in his stomach as far as it would go and then started kicking in very small motions; as much as the narrow passageway would allow. The cavern walls dug into his fins as his feet hit the rocks continually, kicking up sediment in the otherwise clear water. His heart felt like it would pound out of his chest and all Sam wanted was to be elsewhere, doing anything else, than be in this godforsaken tunnel trying to fit through this godforsaken crack to save someone who was probably already beyond saving.

Damn you, Sam Reilly, he thought. *Damn you and your heroics*. He squeezed his eyes shut until he could feel himself on the verge of tears.

He kicked some more.

And more, without pause.

Sam found his legs had been hijacked by his body's autonomous fight-or-flight response system, autopilot had been engaged and cessation of motion unlikely until he could pull his brain back from the cliff's edge of claustrophobia. Not wanting to risk getting stuck by stopping prematurely Sam kicked for what seemed like an eternity, until he sensed the surrounding walls begin to open up.

Taking a deep breath, pausing mindfully, pulling forth the technique he'd employed in the past to bring his body back in line with his psyche. Within seconds his adrenaline levels had receded and Sam took a look around, finding himself healthily buoyant and in the calm depths about midway across a large cavernous room — and according to Tom's guide line, exactly where he was supposed to be.

Sam opened his eyes fully under his regulating mask, still slightly foggy from sweat and his quick breaths, noticing that the tight hole had opened into a hallway and which showed signs of being underwater for eons. To his side rested a deteriorated stairway with marine fauna glazing each step in a thin green layer.

Continuing to recover, this discovery provided a welcome distraction. Sam squinted closer and finned forward. The steps seemed a little too high for anyone's comfort. He doggy-paddled the rest of the way to the stairway, unslung his air tank, and set it aside as he sat on one of the steps. When he was sure that all his equipment was secured and the string remained in plain sight, he leaned over to the tank and checked his oxygen gauge.

Eighty-three percent. Damn.

In. Out. In. Out. The tank's meter vibrated with every inhale and exhale, but he could tell his heart rate had slowed significantly.

Welcoming the short respite, he planned out the return trip. Great that he had made it through, but now, even worse, he would have to return through the same passageway. The familiar flash of panic blinded him momentarily, but Sam fought it down into his stomach and stowed it away. He would cross that bridge when he came to it.

Breathing easier, he wanted to turn his mind to something else. Pointing the flashlight ahead of him, he could see what appeared similar to Mayan inscriptions on the wall.

Focus, Sam heard his sensible side say. You're here on a mission.

Still, he detached his helmet light and swung it around in a wide arc, taking in all his surroundings. Mayan inscriptions spanned all the walls and the engravings seemed reflective under the shine of the light. They were capped with some sort of metal and knowing the Mayans, it was probably a form of silver.

His one world history class in college had served him well, but these inscriptions were different. And the way the stones were placed around the entire room inexplicably triggered a primal uneasiness in Sam. The whole system felt hostile.

"Feeling like I've overstayed my welcome," Sam muttered to himself into his regulator, just to hear a human voice, despite the waste of air.

He swam forward, following Tom's string. In front of him two tunnels branched off into different paths, just as Tom had described the maze. Sam felt himself center. Okay, getting lost in an underwater maze might be scary, but Sam could deal with scary a lot better than tight.

Continuing onward, Sam followed the string with both hands, ignoring the internal voice of his instructor. He gripped tight as worries and thoughts buzzed like bees in his head. He couldn't hear anything but the rush of his own blood, and the occasional bubble release of the rebreather. The passageways were even more intricately designed the deeper that Sam traveled into the maze. *The ancient Mayans must have had a lot of time on their hands*, he thought to himself.

The string began to feel looser and looser as he followed it through every single turn and passageway. When it ran into the wall, he looked up. He'd found where Tom had wedged it tight between the wall and a rock, so he must be near the...

Shining the flashlight around, he saw the fins and diving equipment Tom had mentioned. He was in the right place. Cold leaked into his neck, having nothing to do with the chillier temperatures deep under the earth.

Now it was time to look for a body. The water was as still as a corpse and Sam knew that whoever's body was down here couldn't have gotten far. If anything, the body should have floated up and away by now, as the bacteria inside would cook and release gases, essentially making the corpse one nasty hot air balloon.

Starting with the right, Sam swept the ceiling with his dive light, checking every nook and cranny for anything that could indicate a passage into another room or anywhere that the mystery diver could have found passage.

Now sweeping back and forth, Sam's light caught on a patch of a darker dark. Of course. He swung back, to reveal that there was a small opening above the entrance of the cave, certainly larger than the hellish tunnel he'd been forced to navigate earlier, but small enough to pass unnoticed without careful review. Tom must have missed it when he turned around to get out before his oxygen depleted; thankfully Sam had the advantage of the rebreather and bigger air tank.

Sam swam up and cautiously felt around the opening, then shined his flashlight into it to aid his search. The sides were smooth, unlike the unrefined entrances he'd already come through. Maybe this cave was the one that held the secrets they had entered the pool in search of to begin with.

He peered closer, pulling himself up like a schoolboy at the side of the pool. Through the hole, Sam could see refraction in the water, meaning there was air up there. Bingo, he thought, as he swam through it.

It was easily big enough for a grown man to fit through, yet it was curved around the opening so that it was near impossible to see unless you were specifically looking for it. Even then, any novice would have mistaken it for a small curvature in the rock.

Popping up at the surface, Sam was surprised to find a hallway that was designed like the underwater ones that he had just come through except that… well, it wasn't underwater.

As Sam surfaced, he was instantly relieved of the tight feeling from the damp suit. His skin relaxed and the water slid off his face in droplets.

Working through his surprise, he hauled himself up and out onto the ground. Things were starting to make sense, maybe. He took his fins off and carefully placed them on the ground right next to him near the water. His hand hesitated over his mask, but Sam ultimately decided against it, choosing instead to breathe through the rebreather. He had heard too many horror stories of divers getting excited about a dry cave underwater, taking their mask off, and dying of hypoxia as carbon dioxide filled the space with invisible poison, with nowhere else to go.

Time to explore the cave.

He shined his flashlight around. He jerked back in surprise. There, where there should be nothing, was a young woman collapsed on the ground.

Chapter Fourteen

Sam quickly moved toward the woman as fast as he could in the diving suit, heavy with water. The suit thrashed around on the cold rock floor, making loud slurping noises that resonated through the caves. The woman before him remained motionless. For a second Sam thought of Tom's limp body when he was pulled out of the water in the nick of time.

There was no question that this was the owner of the equipment down at the room that he had just come from— there could only be so many explorers lost in a secret cave.

That wasn't his main concern, though. His main concern was why she had collapsed. There were several possibilities and Sam's military mind flashed on all of them: an injury, lack of oxygen, drowning…

He knelt next to her. She didn't move. She was still breathing, but her pulse was weak. There were no other visible signs of injury, but he knew that a head wound might not show.

Then, as he listened to the rebreather, a small thought intruded: What about hypoxia?

The cavern was tiny and it wouldn't take much time for carbon dioxide to replace the oxygen in the air in such a small space, especially if there'd been no clean air moving in or out. His father had yelled at him for constructing blanket forts for just this reason and, if Sam hadn't kept the rebreather in, it was very likely he could have suffered the same fate.

Now, kneeling beside the woman, Sam realized he was sweating, beads of salty liquid mixing in with the musty cave water drying off his skin.

She was lying face down. Sam crouched beside her and took hold of her forehead from the top and torso. Quickly, carefully, he turned her on her back, mindful of the possibility of a neck injury. Normally, he would have checked for water in the lungs, but she was too far from the water-side to have collapsed of drowning. And there was no easy way to do it. Besides, she was breathing on her own, albeit shallowly. No need for mouth to mouth. If it was hypoxia, that would only make it worse.

He checked her pulse again. Very weak, but she was alive. The fact that there was a pulse meant that she was just out of oxygen. At least he hoped that was it. He knew he could give her his oxygen tank and hope that she woke up in the cave, but there was no telling if she was ever going to wake up. And the longer he waited inside, the more anxious those on the outside would get. And the higher the chance that someone would come after him and do something stupid to try and bring Sam back.

Sam paused to briefly consider any other solutions, but there weren't any. He would have to get her back outside. And he had to act now, before her condition worsened or any more people got injured.

"Okay, if you're going to go, then let's go," he muttered to himself. Sam got his footing under himself on the slick rock, then leaned forward and carefully picked her up from her back, marine-style, and dragged her back to the water side. Even wet, she was lighter than he thought, and easy to carry. He wondered how old she was. Her unconscious state and her wet hair made her look anywhere from thirteen to twenty-six.

Sam perched on the edge of the water and quickly got into his fins. Time for the mask. With the hand of a practiced diver, Sam quickly split his oxygen-Trimix mixture into both tanks. This would automatically deactivate the rebreather. The countdown started now. Sam briefly shuddered at the thought of limited time, yet they had no choice. He'd worked under the gun before, and besides- they still had fifteen minutes. They would make it in fifteen minutes. They had to.

Sam took his tank pack off and attached it to her, cinching the straps so it wouldn't slip off. He would just have to worry about carrying his. And quite possibly carrying her.

Hearing the hiss as both tanks activated, Sam glanced at the tanks' oxygen levels. Both at around thirty-five percent. Should be good enough for the trip back. Thankfully, since she was not conscious, this would actually help lower their oxygen usage: Her shallow breathing meant that she would probably run out of the air more slowly. Sam reattached the two tanks and began filling his up to forty-five percent.

If she threw up, she would suffocate in her own vomit. He shuddered. That wasn't a pretty way to go. He would just have to push both of them back up to the surface before she died.

A thought popped into his head, so surprising and sudden that he slipped the fill and struggled to start it again.

What if she wakes up halfway through and panics?

It was possible with the increased oxygen flow, and her brain reactivated to more normal levels, he thought, as the tank resumed its fill. As long as he didn't waste any time getting lost or getting scared and he kept his wits about him in the tight passageway and got her through with no problems, they would have enough air.

And if the worst happened… well, Sam would just have to leave her there, as she had left her equipment behind on the cavern floor. It wouldn't be the first time he'd been forced to abandon dead weight.

It didn't mean he had to like it.

Best not think about that now.

Carefully, he eased her body down into the water, sticking his legs out straight under her to make sure she didn't sink all the way down. She floated like a log as he disconnected the rebreather from his tank and made the final adjustments to their air systems.

Then, collecting his wits and sending up a prayer to whatever ancient gods were listening Sam slid in off the ledge next to her.

She wobbled with his entry and started to sink. He steadied her and tried to figure out how he was going to manage. As he thought, he adjusted this nameless, unconscious woman so that she faced head-first to the entrance. He kept her right next to him, lifeguard-style, so he could help her if it was needed. He hoped again she would not wake up in transit.

He checked everything again, once more for luck. Her tank was working, her mask gently fogged. Her lashes lay on her cheeks as if in sleep. Behind the glass, damp with the residue of her toxic breath, she looked quite young.

Sam jumped in and all the way under.

If he'd thought coming into the cavern and navigating the system was nerve wracking, doing it in reverse with a passenger on limited air was doubly so. The currents caused by his own passing constantly disrupted her, and so she knocked against him in a syncopated motion that made his own transit more difficult than it had been on the way in. He wished he dared drag her along with some force, but he was terrified of disrupting the connection between mask and tank and killing her by accident. As shallow as her breaths were, it was a good bet he wouldn't even know anything was wrong until it was too late. Unconscious as she was, too late was too late.

He eventually worked out a pattern that allowed him some regularity, and he'd been in enough tough spots to know that rhythm could be the difference between success and failure. He repeated the steps, and repeated them again until he hit his stride, and then he held his breath with intent focus so he didn't lose it. He was making good time through the narrow passageways. First, he would follow the string a few feet ahead to make sure it was the right direction, then come back and push the woman ahead of him along the path. He couldn't afford to break the string, so he had to plot his movements carefully, but nor could he allow her to sink and detach from her regulator. So he had to paddle as fast as he could right beside her to keep her afloat. It was terribly awkward, but he sank into a survival mentality himself, and his awareness narrowed to his fake breathing, her fake breathing, the feel of the cool-warm water on his skin, and the darkness.

One stroke at a time, he crept toward the entrance.

When he reached the narrow passage that had detained him in the beginning, he pushed down the rising panic and found it easier than expected. Her life, quite simply, depended on his lack of fear. As it had before in rare moments of grace, that fear evaporated with stunning speed, resulting in a clear, certain focus.

Now. The question became: Who was going to go first?

After a quick deliberation, the best plan, he decided, would probably be to get himself through first and pull her through, second. With the tanks depleting by the breath, speed mattered, and this option seemed like it would get them to the other side the fastest. Right or wrong, Sam knew he had to stay focused and alert and with a backup plan at the ready.

He maneuvered behind her and carefully slid the tank off over her head, making sure it was still attached by the straps. Then, holding it awkwardly in one hand, he removed his own.

Carefully, as if he were working with explosives, Sam sidled as close as he could to the opening, dragging her with him and nudged his tank through. Then, in quick succession, he went through himself, before he had time to think about it. He went in head-first, kicking hard and reeling around to still keep hold of her hand, her tank. Quickly he looped his arm through his tank's strap to free up his hands, then, blessing her thinness and general pliability, guided her through. He scraped her shoulder in the process, but it was better than hitting her head. The connections between tank and regulator and mask remained solid.

In the relative safety on the other side of the wall, Sam didn't even stop to revel in his triumph over the claustrophobic space. He simply reattached the tanks, quick, precise, and certain, and then resumed his guide-pull-glide maneuver back along the string, back toward the exit, back toward freedom.

At long, long last, a glimmer of light peeked in the distance. Sam felt like he was seeing a sliver of heaven's glory through dark thunderclouds. As the light illuminated the tunnel exit more and more clearly, he called on the reserve of energy he knew he didn't have, needing to rely on the sometimes robotic, but always impressive, capacity of the human body to overcome physical obstacles if the mind is strong enough. He kicked harder, gaining a rhythm and losing himself in it as he stroked strongly for the surface, trailing the unconscious woman closely behind. As he went, he played the same game he'd developed to get himself through swim team practice decades ago, a game he had played countless times since. Five more strokes. Five more strokes. Five more strokes.

It worked as it had always worked.

The light got brighter, grew and blossomed, and he had the odd sense that he was witnessing a surreal kind of dawn, despite the fact that by now it was late afternoon. Maybe almost evening. In the growing glow, he could see the brown reeds all around the lake, waving beyond the surface like a damn Dali painting.

Sam surfaced, gasping. The regulator hissed in the real world like some science fiction man-machine. One armed, he groped for the ledge, treading water as he did so. Through the foggy mask, he saw a flurry of motion but oddly, heard no sound as the locals, some of whom had been lounging by the edge smoking cigarillos and some who'd been playing cards, waited for Sam to return. Now they looked over from their repose, taking in the scene. They cheered Sam's arrival in a jocular fashion, but when they saw the woman's head pop out next to him, they upended their logs or rocks in their shock. Sam fought to spit out the regulator, passing off the woman's arm to some other arm already reaching down to give him a hand.

"Help her, unconscious, hypoxic, I think," he panted, as the rubber and metal left his mouth and swung on its clip by his shoulder with a small thump.

The locals all shuffled uneasily at the water's edge, apparently unwilling to approach the mystical pool. Now Sam could see that it was only Tom willing to get on his knees and haul the woman out. It was Tom who laid her gently on her side, disconnecting the regulator from the borrowed tank so she could breathe fresh, clean air. Fiery impatience surged through Sam and his vision blurred. These men were willing to haul equipment to bring up treasure, but they wouldn't help a dying woman? What did they think she was?

Possessed?

His irritation was diverted by Armando pushing through the ranks of the babbling locals. Armando silenced them with a curt command in Spanish, panting. When he saw the woman on the ground before them, his eyes widened in surprise.

"Fetch the doctor!" he shouted, and several men called back in a chain of alert. Sam, breathing hard from his swim, saw commotion at the back of the group already moving forward. In the face of approaching help, Armando laughed, uneasily. "Sam, you do get results! You found an entire woman in there! You should've brought me along."

"Save it, Armando. That's not funny." Sam pulled off his mask in anger and cast it aside, glaring at their erstwhile boss. There was little that got his ire up like a man mocking a woman, particularly a defenseless one, no matter what his station. He didn't care if the man was paying him.

Armando had the grace to look ashamed. He snapped his fingers at the locals, forcing them forward and glancing back to check the doctor's process. "Get her some help. She's been down there for hours." He turned back to Sam, who was still in the water, half in, half out. "Right. Let me help you," he said, as Sam, struggling against the exhaustion of hauling the woman's dead weight and his own, plus their equipment through the narrow tunnels on no air, flailed against the side of the pool, suddenly too weak to pull himself up. He tried without success to grip Tom's arm, who was trying to haul him out.

Armando leaned over and grabbed Sam under his armpits and hauled him out onto the bank, suit and tank and all.

Sam slithered out and sprawled on the ground, feeling the earth under him with unutterable relief, unable even to react as he watched the doctor and the locals carry the woman he'd just rescued, who remained unconscious, further up the embankment where she was at less risk of falling back in the water.

When he realized Tom and Armando were helping to pull off his equipment, he did his best to aid them. Finally, he pushed himself up to his knees, then his feet. When the ground stayed steady, he kicked off the rest of his gear and jogged to where Tom and the local doctor were crouched over the woman's body. He had to see that she'd made it. If she hadn't, not only would some seriously important information go up in smoke, but all of Sam's efforts would have been for naught.

Hell, the small, prideful part of his brain interjected, unable to shut up. He had managed to haul himself through that damnable tiny cavern twice to get her out. Didn't that count for something?!

Tom's voice broke his thoughts. "Sam! I think she's waking up!"

Sam spun.

Tom was right. The doctor had turned the woman on her side, and she was now coughing violently, the action wracking her thin shoulders. She was short of stature, he saw now that she was free from the distortion of the dark water and of his own desperation, and slim – like a gymnast or an acrobat. No wonder she hadn't had that much trouble navigating those damn tunnels. Her wet hair was still plastered to her skull, but it was drying quickly in the hot sun, even though the sun itself was sinking. A distant part of him noted that it would be evening soon, and the wilds of the jungle night would emerge.

The doctor, locals, and Armando went back and forth in Spanish and Sam only realized the doctor was speaking to him – in English – when the man repeated the question.

"You found her unconscious? No sign of blood in the water?"

"I- yes," he said, startled, struggling to remember. "She was unconscious when I found her. And she wasn't under the water. She was above it – there was a tunnel at the top –" He cast around, looking for Tom. "There was a tunnel, just at the top, that's why you missed it- and when I went through, it opened up into something above the waterline. I found her like this- she was still wearing her mask- I think it was-"

Suddenly, the woman opened her eyes. Her coughs stopped and she stopped shaking. Her whole body went rigid and her eyes locked right on Sam's. He froze.

Her eyes were bright, cold. Distant. Though she looked straight at him, Sam got the sense she was seeing something far away. Something that might not even exist.

Her lips opened and she said something, so faint it was barely audible. Sam leaned closer. Despite the utter silence of the rescue team, he still couldn't hear her.

"What?" he said gently, softly. "What did you say?"

The woman's gaze circled, taking in the circle of men who surrounded her. Sam wasn't sure whether she saw them or not. He knelt in front of her as the doctor crouched behind, cradling her head from behind. "Miss," he said, low and urgent, leaning closer. Behind him, he could feel Tom creeping closer, too. "What's your name? Is that what you're saying? Your name?"

Her gaze wandered, and then it locked on him, straight in his eyes. Her lips formed the word again. Then, faint and almost incomprehensible, a sound slipped out.

Sam jerked back. Had she just said what he thought she said? "What?" he said, totally blank.

Her gaze held the intensity of madness as she whispered the word again. "Xibalba."

It was the only word she spoke, before her eyelids flickered and she drifted into an unconscious coma. Her face went blank and she sagged against the doctor's grip, unmoving.

The doctor said, "Quick! We need to get her into the hyperbaric chamber."

Chapter Fifteen

Sam's eyes locked on the young woman's face.

She was young, much too young to die. Her pale skin already had some color. She had shoulder length brown hair tied back. She had the slim and wiry figure of an athlete. At a glance he doubted she was any older than twenty, if that. She looked like she was close to death, but she was breathing on her own at least.

He frowned.

What the hell were you doing in there?

Recreational SCUBA diving had become a popular pastime. Plenty of young people SCUBA dive, some even enjoyed the dangerous specialty of wreck dives or cave dives. But she wasn't just cave diving. Where she had reached, she might as well have been on the moon. There were less than a handful of expert cave divers who had a chance in hell of getting that far, and that included Tom and he both. It was world class, right there.

Yet, some sort of *kid* had done it.

Was it stupidity, bravado, or something entirely different?

Well, he reflected, there was always the gold. But looking at her now, she seemed an unlikely ruthless treasure hunter. The girl was lanky and thin, which might have been ideal for getting in the nooks and crannies of the underwater caves if she had the stamina. Or maybe it was just her manner, desperate to find a legendary treasure and take the riches.

Sam recalled what Armando had said earlier about bringing him and Tom in on the project.

We tried to go on our own, but none of us were capable of reaching Xibalba – already, we've lost three world-class cave divers.

Sam turned his gaze to Armando. "Do you have something to tell me?"

Armando shrugged; his face blank. "About what?"

His eyes narrowed. "About why I found a woman – barely more than a kid – deep inside the cave system?"

"I don't know what you're talking about. I've never laid eyes on her until today."

Sam met his eye. Armando wore a mulish expression of obstinacy. If he knew something, he certainly wasn't going to tell him about it. "This woman wasn't working for you?"

"No, of course not." Armando made a mock frown for dramatic effect. "What sort of person do you think I'd have to be to bring in a mere child to do my deadly work?"

"You didn't seem to have a problem asking Tom and I to do it for you."

Armando grinned. "Come now, we both know I'm not twisting either of your' arms to give you the chance to be the first in more than four centuries to lay eyes on Xibalba. We both know you and Tom would have done anything to get on my team."

Sam nodded. Armando was either lying or he wasn't. Either way, he wasn't about to find out – and one thing the man was definitely telling the truth about was that he and Tom would have done anything short of kill, to be the first to reach Xibalba. "Okay. So how does a girl like her come to know about the entrance to Xibalba?"

Armando made a half-grin. "The Mayan legend is common knowledge in the region."

Sam didn't buy that explanation for a second. "Sure, but how did she know that this particular cenote led to it?"

"Beats me," Armando admitted, turning to head back down to the main campsite, clearly finished with the direction of Sam's discussion.

Tom completed the routine maintenance on his rebreather system, setting it up so that it would be ready for his next dive. He stepped up next to the hyperbaric chamber, his eyes running across the chamber's sole occupant.

Turning to Sam, he asked, "What the hell was she doing in that cave?"

"I have no idea," Sam replied, shaking his head. "But she knew about Xibalba."

Tom said, "And if she knows about it, I think there's more to this than Armando has led us to believe."

Sam nodded. "I agree. That's why you and are going to have to make another dive – this time together."

Chapter Sixteen

Armando knew that Xibalba wore many faces and survived many myths.

Despite the plethora of stories which portrayed Xibalba as one big death hall, the truth was that Xibalba was actually a number of individual structures. The most important site among all of them was the House of the Lords, placed at the entrance – the only way in. Each successive structure served as a test so only the worthy, or the quick of feet, would make it through.

If, by some miracle, you were worthy and quick of feet and passed all the way through the maze, the final test was the Xibalban ballcourt. Here, the ancient Mesoamerican Game of Death would commence. The players could only use their elbows, knees, shoulders, and feet to place the hard rubber ball into hoops placed around the grass-padded field. While the game traditionally had religious significance, Mayan myth told of the story of Hun Hunahpu and Vucub Hunahpu, two plucky brothers who angered the gods so much that they were sentenced to play against each other, their own blood, on the battle court of Xibalba. Hun Hunahpu, the loser, was promptly decapitated.

Legend had it, however, that if someone made it through, they would be greeted by the most sophisticated underground city imaginable. Gardens somehow grew without sunlight, vines snaked over carved rock walls, over the different temples and houses where people lived and thrived. In the middle of this paradise stood the Temple of the Lords, towering over all the homes and hostels, nearly scraping the top of the massive cavern that concealed the city.

Xibalba's defenses were many and mighty. But no matter how secretive or how well defended it was, trespassers always found ways to get in. Roads leading up to secret entrances above ground were riddled with booby traps and tests that only someone who truly knew the place and lived there would be able to avoid or pass. There were rivers that were said to have run across the entrances; first a river of scorpions, a tide of shiny black scales. Next, a river of the boiling blood of sacrificial victims. Finally, a river of pus.

Beyond these rivers was a crossroads where travelers had to choose from among four routes that spoke in an attempt to confuse and beguile. Their voices whispered like the wind, whispering secrets, whispering lies and tempting words. Voices of loved ones long past called unseen, cries of help pierced the air from invisible travelers requiring aide. Illusion or real? No one could say. Each traveler had to decide for themselves.

If one passed through the crossroads successfully and walked along the right route, upon surpassing these obstacles, one would come upon the Xibalba council place, a grand hall where it was expected visitors would greet the seated Lords.

Lining the pathway that snaked its way to the top of the temple, a series of chambers lay nestled amongst the jungle wilds along the sides. Mannequins that looked real as life were seated between the Lords on ornate thrones just like the ones the Lords sat in, to confuse and humiliate people who greeted them. The confused visitors would be invited by "servants" of the mannequins to sit upon a bench in front of the throne, only to be cooked alive as chains that clenched around their feet locked them to the bench which rested upon glowing red coals.

Only a few ever got this far, even in the history of all the myths. Only a few could walk to the end of the road where they could face the Lords of Xibalba. Proud, haughty, and blessed with long life, the Lords of Xibalba would then entertain themselves by humiliating the triumphant travelers in this fashion before sending them into one of Xibalba's deadly houses of pain for more tests and lordly entertainment.

Six houses of torture and tests awaited anyone that made it this far. The first was the Dark House, pitch-black as a nightmare and deadly silent. In the impossible darkness, the longer one stayed in it, the harder it was for them to find the exit. Their hearts would pound, their ears would ring, their breath would quicken. They would pant. The darkness and silence would render them insane.

The second house was the House of Cold. The bone-chilling frost would be enough to freeze the muscles of a human being in three minutes. Third was the Jaguar House, a jungle within a room filled with magnificent felines denied meat and water and thirsty for human flesh. The fourth was the Bat House. While many would underestimate the bats at first, the vampire bats would swarm anyone that entered, sucking the blood dry of any living creature that dared to enter. The penultimate was the Razor House, where knives stuck out of the walls, flying from one side to the other without warning, without rhyme, without reason. Their flights were completely random, and their blades were always kept sharp.

And lastly, the final chamber, was the Popol Vuh, the Hot House filled with fires and heat, stoked with wood and coals until the air was thick with shimmering torridity, so thick one's breath seared one's throat and their lungs shriveled in their chests.

If, by luck, skill, or the whims of the gods, anyone who got through all of the tests set before them, they would find themselves placed in front of the Lords who would glance between themselves and then, begrudgingly but respectfully, acknowledge their power and grant them entry.

That was what Armando knew of Xibalba.

If he only knew how *little* he knew...

Chapter Seventeen

Sam suited up faster than last time, eager to get on with it and find answers.

They both jumped into the water with splashes that echoed off the walls of stone. They sank below the crystalline water with no change in visibility between liquid and air except a slight magnification. Sam fought against the slimy feeling the hot water induced in him, wasting no time giving Tom the thumbs-up, and they were on their way.

Now that they knew where to go, Sam and Tom silently propelled themselves into the yawning opening. The string was exactly where Sam had left it, floating slightly to the right of them. They took a firm yet delicate grasp of the line and followed it all the way down to its end. Sam bit back his fear and pushed through the crevice.

When they reached dry ground, gasping, Tom took off his regulator first and turned to Sam as they struggled to clamber up and on to the dry steps.

Sam asked, "Where is it?"

"I don't know," Tom replied, glancing around. "Listen, there's no other way to go but this. It had to be here. Right?"

"Right, right," Sam sputtered, pushing his mask to the top of his head. "Want to take point?"

Tom peered into the darkness and flicked the flashlight on his head to max brightness. He turned and peered into the pitch-black passageway. "Might as well. The walls seem smooth," he said, stroking them. "This is definitely artificial. Manmade."

Sam rolled his suit down to his waist and felt the wall for himself. Manmade. "Let's go," he said.

They walked through the darkness and Sam kept checking his watch because it felt like they'd been walking for forever. But the glowing green numbers showed it had only been five minutes. They walked some more, yet nothing revealed itself. He began to wonder if they were going the wrong way. The combined bright beams of their flashlights did nothing to penetrate the oppressive darkness. By now, their suits were completely dry and Sam was left shivering from the sudden cold. He cocked his neck back and forth to crack his joints, fighting the fear brought on by the close quarters of the surrounding walls. The tunnel was getting narrower.

As his spine snapped and bent, something caught his eye.

He shined his flashlight to get a better look. The walls were now covered from top to bottom with Mayan symbols. He squinted, stopping Tom with his hand. "Check these engravings out. Any clue what they mean?"

Tom kept moving ahead, unperturbed. "Sorry, forgot to brush up on my ancient Mayan before we came. Catch me later."

"No, no." Sam peered forward. "These are different. It looks like they all say the same thing." He touched them. There was something familiar about them. He stalled, remembering a souvenir from his travels. Someone had given him his name scratched on a piece of stone in ancient Mayan using the symbol designating respect. "I think it's a... name." He wracked his brains and saw again the glowing computer screen where Armando had emailed him information about the legendary city he hoped to find. "I think it says... Xibalba."

Tom snorted. "City of the dead. Great."

They kept going, traveling in silence and awe, occasionally running their fingers over the walls to really confirm that they were, in fact, going into Xibalba. Sam hadn't expected it to be so easy. He reminded himself to keep alert, thinking *where are all those tests and trials?* He'd just opened his mouth and said, "We should have run into something by now —"

He was cut off by a horrendous crashing sound which echoed in the corridor, deafening him.

"Tom!"

Tom said, "It's all right. I'm fine but check this out."

Sam swung his beam around to see his friend standing in front of him holding a long, chalky white bone. Probably a femur. "There are skeletons everywhere."

Sam moved the light.

It was true. The ground was littered with bones.

The skeletons neatly sat, facing each other, smiling with their dead skulls and dead teeth as if they were expecting visitors. Some of them still had clothes on. One wore the curved armor of a Spanish conquistador. Sam crouched down and brushed the dust off. Beneath, it was still brilliantly shiny. Gold. Seated next to him, a skeleton wore a black tunic that had probably been brown at some point, and a beautiful spotted fur across its shoulders. Clearly, there had been a struggle as the Spaniards had tried to force their way in, and the residents of Xibalba fought valiantly against the guns. Even more unnerving were the bodies in the familiar wetsuits and SCUBA equipment that Tom and Sam now wore.

Spears and knives protruded from the suits, revealing how they had died.

Sam's mind raced to the obvious and his gut clenched into knots. Booby traps. He'd watched Indiana Jones like everyone else, just as he'd heard the legends – iron spears, crushing walls, and giant axes.

He wiped his hands on his pants, hurrying forward. "This is gruesome."

He'd reached the end of the hall, watching his step and trying to keep within Tom's footprints, thanking the gods for the centuries that had robbed Xibalba of its deadly intent.

A whir was the only warning he had before a knife flew through the air and bounced off the hard cave wall opposite, right between them. So close, it nicked his face.

He touched the blood with a mix of relief and terror. "That was close."

Tom said, "Too close."

They hurried on, extra careful.

It wasn't long before they entered a large cavern, much like the underwater caverns at the caves, but completely dry. In the middle, a huge door made of stone sat expectantly. It peaked at least four heads taller than Sam.

Sam looked at Tom who was scanning the setting with a practiced military engineer's eye. "What do you think?"

Tom shrugged. "Nothing obvious, but…"

He eased forward before Sam could stop him and walked right up to the door and inspected it closely.

Sam fought to keep his heart in his chest, half expecting the floor to sink and the walls to slide forward to crush them both.

Tom turned around with a grin. "Looks like someone's beat us to it." He reached forward and pushed it open with some effort. "Not even locked."

The door led to another opening. It was as empty as the first chamber except now a pedestal lay broken on its side, the intricate granite shattered and crushed. Either it was deliberate or someone had been rushed to take whatever was there, off it. Or they had been… deterred. By something.

Sam and Tom rushed forward, both fighting a growing feeling of foreboding. In the back of his mind, Sam reminded himself that they still had to return. They always had to return. If they made it to the inner sanctum, whatever secrets Xibalba had to share, she still had to let them leave...

Another door. This time, while it was the same height, it was round and made of a black stone. The darkness seemed to suck in all the flashlight's luminescence. Tom knocked on it. "Obsidian."

Sam's eyes narrowed. His heart picked up its tempo. "You're kidding me."

"Afraid not."

"To my knowledge, the Mayans never worked with obsidian and if they had, it's highly unlikely they would have developed the masonry and lapidary skills required to achieve the level of craftsmanship necessary to construct this door's delicate features out of obsidian. You know what this means, don't you?"

Obsidian, in general, fragmented or shattered when people tried to work with it. Even using modern lapidary technique, it was a difficult stone to work with and almost impossible to shape. There was only one group of people they'd ever heard of who'd appeared to have harnessed a near-mythical affinity with the stone.

Tom's eyes narrowed. "The Master Builders were involved in the development of Xibalba?"

Sam expelled a prolonged breath of air. "It would appear so."

"Any idea where this door is going to lead us?"

"If what Armando tells us about Xibalba is correct, it should lead to the underworld of the dead." Sam grinned. "Or it leads to a Master Builder temple? And what better way for the Master Builders to ensure their temple remained hidden throughout the ages than to wrap it in a shroud of myth and legend and relating it to a city guarding the underworld?"

Tom nodded. "I guess there's only one way to find out."

Sam suppressed a small grin. "After you."

Tom shrugged and tried to turn the ornate golden handle on the door's edge, to the right. He shook his head, glancing back the way they'd come. "This one's locked."

"Any ideas on how to open it?"

"We could take a ton of C4 and shatter the entire thing, but chances are we'll get stabbed by obsidian shards or the entire cave system will fall down upon us. Probably both." Tom shook his head. "We could…"

But Sam had stopped hearing him. Instead, his eyes focused on the pattern etched into the doorknob. It was the same pattern that sprawled across the door in a series of spirals forming a maze, or the intricate pathways of a secret map.

It was a pattern he'd seen once before, long ago, and had hoped never to see again. He thought he'd left this hell behind him. But here in the darkness in the gateway to the underworld, hell had reared its ugly head once more to look Sam Reilly in the face.

His face darkened, but he remained silent.

Tom noticed the change in his demeanor. "You okay, Sam?"

Sam expelled a breath of air. "Yeah, I'm fine. Sorry, I was just contemplating how to get through the door."

Tom nodded, unsure whether or not to take Sam's response at face value. He continued, "If we want to open the door to the labyrinth, we'll need to find the key."

Sam felt his heart form a lump in his throat. "What did you say?"

"We'll need to find a key."

"No. Before that…"

Tom bit his lower lip, the muscles around his jaw tightening. "What? I think I was saying we'd need a ton of C4 to dent this door."

Sam shook his head. "You mentioned a labyrinth."

Tom turned the palms of his hands toward the vaulted ceiling. "Yeah, so?"

"What makes you say that on the other side of this door is a labyrinth? What made you think of that term, specifically?"

Tom shrugged. "Honestly, I didn't give it much thought. Armando mentioned that Xibalba was protected by a maze-like labyrinth of hidden passages and flooded tunnels like the ones we had to dive through to get this far. Why do you ask?"

Sam turned his gaze away from Tom, his eyes fixed on the obsidian door. "It's nothing. You mentioned the labyrinth key and it startled a hidden demon from my past."

Tom arched an eyebrow. "What's the labyrinth key?"

"Something from my past and a secret hell that I've promised to keep buried for the remainder of my days." Sam turned to Tom, meeting his eyes. "I'm sorry. It doesn't have anything to do with Xibalba or this obsidian door. Nothing more than the coincidence of a name. Let's get back to the surface and find out where we can locate that crystal-shaped key."

Chapter Eighteen

Xi- balba… Xibalb-a… Xibalba…

The water crushed against her temples until Mia felt like her brain would squeeze out of every hole on her face. The edges of her vision darkened as she kept pumping and pumping, forward, forward. A race of sheer will against her body.

And then she remembered nothing.

Had she made it out of the water? If not, she should be dead by now, her body lying at the bottom of the cave floor, rotting like everyone else who had come before her. Maybe she *was* dead already. It honestly wouldn't be a bad way to go – painless, with the added benefit the cartel wouldn't be able to find her.

From the distance of her mind, Mia shuddered. The goddamned Black Muerte Cartel. The root of all her problems yet also, so much joy. It had seemed glorious in the beginning; endless highs, the feeling of power. She'd felt invincible and fearless, like no one could touch her.

Not even her own brother.

She didn't remember when the drugs had changed her from warrior to victim. She just knew the crystals had burned her nose and her lungs and her veins and little Mia was gone for good. She'd do anything to get more. It took more and more to get that feeling.

And *more* meant she needed money.

Money meant sauntering up to violent-looking men in cutoffs and tank shirts, relying on her high school Spanish to get an 'in'. Money meant impressing them with her street smarts, her quickness, and size. Mia had a great memory. The crack didn't affect that. And soon, just like that, she was doing retrievals and odd jobs for the second-largest cartel in Mexico.

Soon, the stealing had taken the place of the drugs. Most of the time, anyway. It gave her everything she'd always wanted. Control.

Whatever the boys wanted, to satiate their desires, Mia would steal it for them. She knew all the tricks for stealing anything. And they loved her for it. About a month ago she'd strolled into some noble's mansion in London dressed as an art critic, picked up an expensive statue, stashed it in her duffel bag and walked off. She'd laughed when she read the news the morning after. She was still laughing and the stories were still running, in London, at least. She'd stolen it over a month ago. Didn't London have other things to write about?

Boring. Mia hated being bored.

But this mission had been unusual. That was what had drawn her to it; so was the conversation she recalled with her boss.

"Mia? Ready to go out again?" Ramone had asked. They were still basking in the glory of their recent masterly-planned heist and Mia was snacking on crackers and caviar with Cheez Whiz from the can.

"Already? Don't you want to wait until all the fiasco dies down? You know what happened to Juan and his gang when they tried busting five museums in a week."

Her boss waved his fleshy hand. "Yeah, yeah, but this is special. We might even get more of a cut this time."

Mia missed her mouth. She wiped some cheese off her lip, flicking away the crumbs. "Always down for more money. What is it?"

"See, down where the Mayans used to live, they had an underground temple. Called it Xibulbous or Xibaldo or whatever. Highway to Hell." He grinned. "Sexy, no? The route to the temple was dangerous, but now it's all abandoned, so anyone can get in." The grin widened. "And you like a little danger, don't you?"

Mia rolled her eyes. "And?"

He shrugged. "Big Boss said it wasn't treasure but something else he wants. And he wants you to go get it for him." *He should get dental work done while he was here*, Mia thought. It was cheap in Mexico. "What do you say?"

Something else he wants. Drugs? Mia popped the rest of the cracker in to her mouth and swallowed. She wiped her hands on her shorts. "I say when do we leave?"

He wagged his fat bejeweled finger. "Ah. Not 'we'. You. I'll set up all the flights and give you a guide who will go along with you. I'm staying right here."

Fat ass couldn't fit on a plane, eh? All she said out loud was, "Huh. Weird." She gave him a flirty smile, just to stay in practice. "At least tell me what I'm looking for."

He leaned in. "A key," he whispered.

She gave an incredulous smile. "A key? To what?"

The man laughed. It was big and boisterous. "To the labyrinth, of course."

Chapter Nineteen

Yes, Mia thought she was dead. The first thing she felt when she woke up was the water sloshing in her throat and mouth. Instinctively Mia spat it out, turning her head to the side. She looked back up to see a pair of eyes staring back at her. A surprised look ran across the man's face but not before Mia saw what else was on his mind. She had seen that look countless times: When a man was attracted by her prettiness but confused by her rough edges, scars, and bruises, they just put on a dumb face, as if she was an equation they just couldn't solve. It had happened enough times that the information simply slid under her skin like someone else's sweat.

The man blinked and pushed his wavy hair out of his eyes, composing himself.

Mia coughed and spat, turning her face away. "Get out of my face."

"Good morning to you, too," the man muttered sarcastically. His sun-dried locks glistened like the water she laid next to. "Tom, she's awake."

"Great. Can I get out of this diving suit first?" This voice was gruffer, deeper.

"What the hell do you want from me? I don't even know who you are!" Even as she said it, Mia knew it wasn't true. Those ice-blue eyes stuck in her mind and she swore she'd seen those before. In Rhyolite, Nevada, the first time she had fought tooth and nail for her life…

Well. There was always a first time. It certainly hadn't been the last.

He didn't seem to recognize her though. His eyes simply remained empty. Not cold, but not kind either. He didn't trust easily. Mia recognized the signs. "You were nearly dead when we came across you in that cave. We brought you out and you lapsed into a coma. You spent nearly twelve hours in a hyperbaric chamber."

Mia struggled to sit up and discovered she was trapped inside some sort of steel contraption. "Where am I?"

"Uxmal, Yucatán – Mexico."

She grimaced. "I'm still outside the cave?"

"Afraid so," Sam replied. "We were going to move you but were afraid the trip might kill you. What's more, we had to make a second dive because we were worried that you weren't the only person trapped down there. Were you?"

She blinked. "What?"

He smiled kindly. "Were you diving on your own or did you have a partner?"

"I was on my own," she lied.

"That's a relief," he said. "I sure didn't revel in the idea of a third trip down that road to Hell."

Something about what he had said brought her memory out of its fogginess. "How did you even find me?"

"We were here diving the cenote. Somewhere deep inside – farther than anyone with good sense should ever attempt – and came across you in a dry chamber. I don't know how long you had been there, but you weren't conscious when I found you." His eyes narrowed. "What were you looking for in Xibalba?"

Mia put on a look of surprise and innocence. "Ze ball ba? What's that? I didn't know it had a name. I'm just here diving the cenote, just like you."

The one called Tom snorted. "Yeah, right. We heard you sleep talking all about it while we tried to keep you alive."

Mia felt her cheeks flush a deep shade of red despite the chill she felt from almost drowning. The man continued. "You look too young to even be here exploring sacred, ancient caves. Who set you up?"

Rule number five of the Black Muertes: Never snitch. "No one. I'm here of my own accord."

Sam and Tom glanced at each other and shrugged. Yes. Reilly had aged, no doubt about it, but now she was sure it was the same person. How she'd choose to confront him, she didn't know.

Looking around she realized for the first time where she was. "Where's my stuff?"

The same deep voice from earlier- Tom- replied. Now she could get a good look at him. Plain and huge. She filed this away as he appeared contrite. "We couldn't save any of your equipment." He spread his hands. "There wasn't space. And there wasn't time. Our priority was to get you out."

Mia dismissed this, pushing down her panic. Her dive bag! It contained everything she'd come here for!

Sam leaned over and grabbed something out of her view. He tossed it to Tom. "Everything except your dive bag, anyway. It was on you, so it made the trip, inadvertently." The tall and imposing figure handed her the wet bag. It looked tiny in his huge hands.

He hesitated, like he didn't want to give it back and she just sat there, anticipating.

Finally, he released his hold on it. She snatched it to her and felt the outside, hoping against hope it still contained its precious cargo as the key's distinct outline presented itself. She breathed an internal sigh of relief.

"You got anything important in there? Find anything in the tunnels?"

"You didn't snoop? I'm touched." She sighed. "Listen, I'm sorry. I don't mean to snap at you. I'm grateful – so grateful for what you did. I've just had a rough day."

The men softened, just as she knew they would. "What were you doing in there anyway?"

Mia shrugged. "Diving. I didn't see too much, though. I only got as far as where I stopped." They glanced at each other again. "Might be a minute before I think of going back in though."

The big one's eyes clearly said he didn't trust her. Mia wasn't worried. Lying well was what she did for a living.

The men glanced between themselves, and then Sam Reilly seemed to come to a decision. "Listen, how did you get out here?"

She shrugged. "Hitched."

He shook his head. "We'll have our charter plane drop you off at the nearest airport." Tom and the man shared a look. It was evident they'd known each other for a long time. "Look, we won't ask questions, we just want you on your way so we can work on our own project."

Mia ran her fingers over the object in her bag. So they *were* looking for the same thing after all. Maybe that was why her Boss had wanted her to get in and out so quickly. How he knew about them, she had no idea. The Cartel worked in dark and mysterious ways; even she didn't dare to find out.

She swung her bag to her shoulder and looked at the evening light. "You want me gone?"

"It's nothing personal, no offense."

"No offense taken. I thought I was about to get arrested. My ride isn't scheduled to return for another week, so I'll have to work out someway to get out of here."

"Where would you like to head to?"

"I'm meeting up with some friends in Mexico City."

Sam nodded. "There's a local airstrip nearby. If I can arrange for a ticket on a flight to Mexico City, would you take it?"

She arched an incredulous eyebrow. "Are you serious?"

Sam shrugged. "It's the least we can do."

She smiled. "Then hell yes I'd like a flight out of here."

Chapter Twenty

Sam watched her go.

There was a small airstrip carved out of the jungle twenty odd miles away and he had promised the young woman that one of his guides could arrange tickets for her on a local carrier.

Armando greeted him a few seconds later. His brow furrowed with concern. "Well? What did she tell you?"

Sam said, "She was here for a cave diving vacation, exploring the ancient cenotes and had never heard of Xibalba. What's more, she says she didn't get any farther into the dry chamber or reach the obsidian door."

Armando's eyes narrowed. "Do you believe?"

Sam grinned. "Not even slightly."

"And yet still you let her walk free from here?"

"She's an American tourist who came to the Yucatan and now wants to return home. What do you suggest I should have done, imprisoned her against her will?"

Armando shrugged. Then, in a tone that sat uncomfortably on the fence between a threat and a joke, he said, "If it helped us find the secrets of Xibalba."

Sam met his eye, trying to read the man, but failed to discern any truth. "Armando, I know that you have spent your lifetime searching for answers hidden within the vault known as Xibalba, but you know by now that some things have a price too great to pay."

"Yes," Armando agreed. "It's all right, I wasn't serious. But I do want to know how you intend to extract whatever secrets Mia appears to have been intentionally keeping from us."

Sam said, "I've arranged for someone I trust to follow her. Once Mia reaches Mexico City, my contact will report back to me with details; where she goes, who she speaks to. If she did reach the inner sanctum of Xibalba at the request of someone else, we'll hear about it."

"What about the obsidian door?"

Sam's lips parted in an open smile. "What about it?"

"How do you plan to get through it?"

"I'm not sure we can at this stage."

"You're kidding me." Armando kept his voice calm but his eyes betrayed disappointment, darkened with anger. "All the modern wonders of science and you can't break a two-thousand-year-old door?"

Sam's eyes, previously drifting across the cool waters of the cenote, turned and met Armando's eye. "We could do that if you like, with C4. The obsidian would shatter into a million pieces, but there's every chance that in the process we'll bring down the entire chamber."

Armando's eyes flashed daggers. "So do it! Then excavate the mess and let's take a look at what's been hidden all this time."

Sam licked his lower lip, laughed. "I don't know where you think all this is meant to take place, but we're talking about a confined cave, located deep beneath a mountain and flooded with water. It's nearly a day's preparation just to reach the damned dry chamber!"

"You think it would end up taking years to remove the rubble?"

"Armando, if that chamber collapses, I doubt anyone will ever set eyes on Xibalba again."

"So then, what are we supposed to do?"

"We'll need to find the key."

"I don't suppose you know what it looks like or even where to find it?"

Sam handed him a sketch of the crystal-shaped key they were looking for. "It looks like this."

Armando ran his eyes across the strange sketches. "I've never seen anything like this. We might as well give up now."

"Not quite."

"Why?" Armando arched an eyebrow. "What do you know?"

"I sent a copy of this image to a friend of mine. She's a computer hacker by trade, but she's capable of finding the proverbial needle in a haystack when no one has a clue in which country the haystack was even made."

Armando's eyes narrowed. "She's that good?"

"No. She's better," Sam said with certainty.

Armando grinned. "What did she find?"

"Apparently the crystal key was found by early archeologists, inside the burial chamber of the Pyramid of the Magician."

Armando's voice was quick, almost frantic, when he spoke. "Where is it now?"

Sam grinned. "Located in the Mayan World Museum of Mérida."

Chapter Twenty-One

Mexico City

The plane ride was identical to the one Mia had taken to get to Mexico in the first place. It was bumpy and noisy, like a bus full of elementary schoolers going on a field trip to the aquarium. Under them, hundreds of acres of thick foliage blocked her view of the ground. Even now, the unusual sight mesmerized her. In the arid lands of Rhyolite there were few plants and no trees. To her side sat a local, dressed in athletic wear but still sporting tribal tattoos. He played some kind of game on his phone and didn't look at the greenery once.

Before she knew it they were on the ground. The pilot didn't even turn around in his seat but the native took a break long enough from his game to give a sidelong glance at her and her bag, jerking his head to the left. It was the universal sign for *get out.*

Mia grabbed her bag and got.

And just like that, she was out safe and sound, with what she'd wanted. The guide would have to find his own way out. But she knew he wouldn't. She knew what he'd find.

She left the airport and headed three blocks south toward a payphone. She passed a woman walking her dog, a well-kept golden retriever with a big grin and flowing with the simple happiness of being able to go out for a walk.

It was nearly eleven a.m. by the time she found herself dropping a peso into the phone's slot and dialing a number from memory. She waited for the dial tone to change, indicating someone on the other end of the line had picked up the phone. A slight pause on the line was the only indication the caller had answered, the silence, what she'd expected.

"I have it," she proclaimed.

A second later she put the phone down on its cradle and exited the booth.

Outside the payphone and standing on the opposite side of the road was a woman, her face hard, eyes blue above an impish grin, framed by a short outcropping of brown hair and staring at her. The woman was patting a dog. A good-looking golden retriever. Still looking happy but no longer walking jauntily along the walkway.

It gave Mia more than a little pause.

There was a chance the woman had merely been walking her dog in the same direction as her. No reason to suspect taking a dog three blocks for a walk should be cause for concern, but in the back of Mia's head, alarm bells were going off.

The very same alarm bells which had managed to keep her alive, this long.

Was she being followed?

And more importantly still, who wanted to know her agenda?

Mia's heart raced. It might be nothing but then again, it might be everything. She didn't have long to lose her tail. There was a pub at the end of the street that she knew well, with a bathroom out the back which exited to an alleyway. She'd never used it for such purposes but knew if she needed to escape it'd be her best bet.

She moved quickly, taking purposeful, determined strides across the road and toward the pub. As she closed the pub door behind her she spotted the dogwalker quickly change direction, turning to follow her and confirming Mia's suspicions that the woman was indeed tailing her.

Momentarily out of the woman's line of sight, Mia dropped any pretense of coming to visit the pub for a drink and instead began to race toward the bathroom.

She reached the door just as her pursuer began talking to the bartender. It was obvious she was asking where Mia had headed because the publican soon gestured toward the bathroom. Mia locked eyes with her pursuer for a moment then closed the bathroom door, securing the lock behind her.

From there Mia moved quickly. She climbed on top of the toilet and up through the narrow opening of the window with all the grace and skill that would have made a contortionist proud.

She dropped down onto the alleyway several feet below, landing with a lithe feline-like grace. Mia drew herself up to her full height and sprinted to the mouth of the alley.

A blue Ford Lincoln pulled out in front of her and its rear passenger door swung open. She climbed in and immediately slammed the door behind her.

A man, seated across from her, asked, "May I see it?"

She dug into her pack, unzipping the secret compartment that ran along a hardened section of the back of the bag and pulled out an intricate stone key made of obsidian, etched with a series of swirls, like one giant labyrinth. "Here, it's all yours."

The man smiled. "Well done! This will make him very happy, Mia."

The Ford Lincoln sped away.

She glanced out the bullet-resistant windows. There, on the corner of the road, she spotted a golden retriever. It kept staring at her. She smiled at the lone dog; it wasn't the dog's fault its owner might have wanted to be the death of her.

For a moment, she could have sworn the dog had cocked its head at her, as if in recognition.

Chapter Twenty-Two

Mayan World Museum of Mérida

It took nearly two days of negotiation to convince the curator of the Mayan World Museum of Mérida to relinquish the ancient Mayan key into Sam Reilly's custody for a period of two weeks. Sam had explained that he wanted to run a geological analysis of the strange crystal offsite, at the Mexican Institute of Geology and determine if the crystal had originated from a local mine site they were exploring. In the end it was Armando Ayala's reputation as a famed historian that got them across the finish line, the curator eventually agreeing to sign off on the loan and a not-so-small donation to the museum.

Sam signed the various legal forms making him responsible for the crystal key and placed a U.S., two-million-dollar bond as security.

At one of the museum's many archival desks, Sam switched on the overhead light and, using a jeweler's loupe, examined the strange crystal key.

It was made of pink, smoky quartz crystal.

The stone was quite beautiful to look at. Upon closer inspection, a series of small veins of gold formed unnaturally straight lines throughout the mysterious haze of smokiness. They were set in an array of up-down strokes, similar to a rudimentary electronic key which used a series of on-off switches to differentiate its radio frequency against that of other keys. If he had to guess, the gold had somehow been artificially inserted into the quartz. There was no way it was a natural, geological development. Still, it seemed impossible to believe the ancient Mayans possessed such lapidary skills nearly two thousand years ago.

But. There was nothing to suggest the Master Builders hadn't.

Armando glanced at Sam. "What do you think?"

Sam grinned. "I think whoever made this key? They possessed technology thousands of years more advanced than the ancient Mayans."

"But you think it is, in fact, the key to the obsidian door?"

Sam nodded. "I'm almost certain of it."

"Then what are we waiting for?"

"Nothing. Let's go. Tom will have brought in the rest of the diving supplies by now and we should be able to make the journey through the underwater labyrinth, hopefully access the obsidian door, and into the heart of Xibalba."

"Excellent work!" exclaimed Armando, beaming with pleasure. "They told me you were the best, Mr. Reilly, and I think I am now starting to believe them! Thank you!"

"You're welcome."

Sam was about to secure the key in its case when the curator wished them good luck with their project and mentioned they were already very lucky because the key had only just been returned after its display at a private historical function.

Sam looked up at the curator through raised eyebrows. "Excuse me, did you just say this stone key was only *just returned this morning*?"

"That's right," the curator confirmed.

"Who borrowed it?"

"I'm afraid I'm not allowed to release that information but I can tell you that the gentleman who arranged to borrow the key was a wealthy businessman."

Sam and Armando frowned. "Did he have it three days ago?"

The curator thought for a second. "Yes. He borrowed it four days ago, to be precise, and returned it today. Why?"

Sam thought about Mia, the girl who he'd rescued from the depths of Xibalba. It was the final confirmation he needed that the young woman was more than a mere tourist, diving the cenote. But the question remained, did she achieve her goal and enter through the obsidian door?

If so, what was she looking for?

And what had she found?

Sam turned to the curator. "Thank you very much for your help, sir. We'll take good care of the crystal key and return it within the timeframe agreed upon."

"I'm sure you will," the curator replied, shaking his hand.

Sam carefully secured the crystal key into its purpose-built, protective metallic casing and he and Armando stepped out of the building. The museum was built on two hectares and had three levels, representing the three worlds of the Maya: Sky, Earth, and Underworld. The main building was built in the shape of a ceiba tree, the sacred tree of life to the Maya.

His cell phone rang. He picked it up and spoke to Genevieve briefly before ending the call.

Armando's eyes narrowed. "Is everything okay?"

Sam nodded. "Yeah, but we might have a problem."

"What?"

"That was my friend who followed Mia when she left the airport in Mexico City. She tracked Mia to a nearby payphone where she made a call and was picked up about ten minutes later by someone in a blue Ford Lincoln."

Armando frowned. "So, we lost our lead?"

"No." The lines across Sam's face deepened. "The license plates were run against the Mexican Drivers and Motor Vehicle register and matched up with one owned by the Black Muerte Cartel."

Armando's eyes narrowed. "She was working for the cartel?"

Sam nodded. "It would appear so."

"The question is, why would the Black Muerte Cartel have any interest in Xibalba?"

"Why indeed?"

"Whatever it is, they won't leave it alone now that we've arrived," Armando warned.

Sam grinned. "Then we'll just have to be quick."

Chapter Twenty-Three

Entrance to Xibalba, Yucatán

Sam met Tom at the entrance to the cenote the next day. Tom had re-provisioned their diving equipment with more than a dozen oxygen tanks and set up a series of safety deposits throughout the cave system to make it easier to reach the obsidian door.

They donned their wetsuits and closed-circuit rebreathers and prepared for their dive. Armando's men stood guard over the cenote with AK-47s.

If the Black Muerte Cartel were interested in the contents of Xibalba's inner sanctum, Sam didn't want to take any chances.

Sam parted the reeds and entered the shallow cenote, descending into its warm depths, disappearing into the dark subterranean passageways. They moved quickly, with the silent efficiency and teamwork acquired through years of working together. They quickly passed through the chokepoint which had nearly killed Tom the first time he'd tried to maneuver through it and soon reached the dry chamber.

Once there they exchanged their oxygen cylinders with a pair that Tom had stationed the day before to allow them to exit the chamber quickly if need be.

Removing their dive equipment and wetsuits, they opened their dry bag and swapped into dry clothes and hiking boots. They retraced their journey across the deadly boobytraps that had killed so many before them until they reached the obsidian door.

Sam stared at the door with the strange crystal-shaped keyhole.

Tom swallowed. "Moment of truth."

"Yeah," Sam agreed. He removed the crystal key and inserted it into the keyhole.

The crystal turned dark pink with the mellow glow of light filtering through its smoky center. For nearly two minutes nothing happened.

Then, the obsidian door swung open.

Chapter Twenty-Four

Sam and Tom walked through the massive obsidian door and in to the narrow passageway on the other side. The beam of Sam's flashlight washed over their new environment, reflecting off the glistening crystal walls. If he had to guess, none of the crystal was native to the region. Instead, it had all been brought in by the ancient Mayans.

Or the Master Builders?

He pictured the Mayans as the puppets and the Master Builders as the masters influencing their design and engineering feats for their own purpose. The question was, what exactly did the Master Builders want with South America?

Sam pondered, *if I could answer that I might know why the Black Muerte Cartel is so desperate to get inside.*

He hoped time would soon reveal all.

They continued down the passageway for approximately fifty feet before it opened up into a large chamber shaped like a horizontal rectangle, with a narrower vertical section made of sloping stone works in the middle and leading to an identical horizontal rectangle on the opposite side. Along each vertical section were two stone rings, tenoned into the wall at mid-court, not too dissimilar to those on a modern-day basketball court. Viewed from above, Sam imagined the entire vault must form a massive playing field in the shape of a capital letter "I," with serifs.

At the end of the second rectangular chamber, a small passageway appeared to head deeper into whatever strange temple it was they'd arrived in.

Tom's lips twisted into an incredulous smile; his amazement evident. "What the hell is this place?"

Sam met his smile. "Judging by Armando's theory that we've located the origins of Xibalba, Hell is probably an apt description."

Tom swept the entire playing field with the beam of his flashlight. High above, on each side of the sloping walls, were what appeared to be row upon row of stone benches, forming what must have once been a tremendous seating arrangement for spectators. At either end of the field, large rows of masonry stairs ascended to the heavens above. "It's an ancient sports field?"

"Yes," Sam confirmed, knowing full well what he was looking at. "The game is called *Pok-ta-pok*."

"You're kidding me!"

"No, I'm serious!" Sam replied. "The Mesoamericans have been playing the game for more than three thousand years. Of course, this is the first time I've ever seen a ballcourt constructed underground."

"Why do they play the game?"

Sam shrugged. "Why not? There are a number of theories but the most prominent one isn't too dissimilar to the 'why' of modern sports today."

"And that is?"

"Because we can and because we, as the human race, have a need for competition and without sports we'd probably end up releasing some of that pent-up desire on a battlefield."

"What do you know about the Mayans and their game… what did you call it *putt-putt*?"

"I believe that's miniature golf." Sam grinned at his own joke. "The Mayans played *Pok-ta-pok*, which is believed to mimic the sound their rubber ball made when it struck a player."

"All right," Tom said, "So how was this *Pok-ta-pok* played?"

Sam replied, "Ballcourts were public spaces used for a variety of elite cultural events and ritualistic activities like musical performances, festivals and, of course, the ballgame. Pictorial depictions often show musicians playing at ballgames, while votive deposits—a sacrifice, sacred in nature and made up of a variety of items and offered to gods—buried at the Main Ballcourt at Tenochtitlan contained miniature whistles, ocarinas and drums."

He walked farther across the main alleyway. "Although there is a tremendous variation in size, in general all ballcourts have the same shape – a long narrow playing alley flanked by walls with both horizontal and sloping surfaces. The walls were often plastered and brightly painted. The length-to-width ratio remained relatively consistent at 4:1 despite the tremendous variation in ballcourt size."

Tom asked, "How big are we talking here?"

"Well, the playing field of the Great Ballcourt at Chichen Itza is by far the largest, measuring just under 300 hundred feet long by 90 feet wide, while the Ceremonial Court at Tikal was only 45 feet by 15."

Tom glanced around the underground ballcourt. "This is somewhere in the middle of that, nothing spectacular by any means in comparison to what we know has already been built."

"With the exception of this being underground." Sam shined his flashlight straight up toward the domed ceiling. "Look at that. A masonry dome like this wasn't achieved by the Romans until 126 AD when the Roman emperor Hadrian built the Pantheon."

Tom nodded. "And this is a heck of a lot larger than the Pantheon."

"Agreed."

"So, what did they do? Kick the ball like some complex game of soccer?"

"Kind of…" Sam thought about it for a minute, recollecting the various tidbits of fact from his knowledge base on Mesoamerican history. "No one knows for certain how the game was played but most theories suggest its rules were similar to racquetball, where the aim was to keep the ball in play. The stone ballcourt goals, those rings up there along the alleyway, are a late addition to the game."

Sam took a breath and continued. "The players struck the ball with their hips, although some versions allowed the use of forearms, rackets, bats, or hand-stones. The ball was made of solid rubber and weighed as much as ten pounds.

"Games were played between two teams of players. The number of players per team could vary, between two to four. Some games were played on makeshift courts for simple recreation while others were formal spectacles on huge stone ballcourts and leading to human sacrifice."

Sam grinned. "Even without human sacrifice, the game could be brutal and there were often serious injuries inflicted by the solid, heavy ball.

"Points were lost by a player who let the ball bounce more than twice before returning it to the other team; those who let the ball go outside the boundaries of the court; or those who tried and failed to pass the ball through one of the stone rings placed on each wall along the center line. Points were gained if the ball hit the opposite end wall, while the decisive victory was reserved for the team that put the ball through a stone ring – a rare event given that the rings were barely larger than the ball and often as high as 15 feet off the ground!"

Tom studied the grand stadium. "It's quite something, especially for a game that kids might have played to stave off boredom."

"*Pok-ta-pok* was used for a lot more than entertaining kids," Sam warned. "Some historians believe it related to astronomy, with the bouncing ball thought to have represented the sun and the stone scoring rings speculated as signifying sunrise and sunset, or equinoxes. Then, there was the concept of war."

"War?" Tom asked.

"*Pok-ta-pok* was most likely a proxy for warfare. Two kings of opposing people may challenge their best players to the game, with the winner vanquishing their enemy. In many cases, that meant the losing king would be sacrificed at the end of the game."

Tom swallowed. "Brutal."

"You'd better believe it." Sam shrugged, as though the Mayans were no worse than the Romans or any other early civilizations. "There are also some theories that the games were played to promote the fertility of a kingdom or to determine the outcome of cosmologic duality."

Tom made a wry and incredulous grin. "Cosmologic duality?"

Sam smiled. "The game was a struggle between day and night, a battle between life and death, as seen in the underworld. Ballcourts were considered portals to the underworld and were built in key locations within central ceremonial precincts. Playing ball engaged one in the maintenance of the cosmic order of the universe and the ritualistic regeneration of life."

Tom sighed heavily, "So if this really is Xibalba, what do you think this ballcourt means? Were people playing to decide whether they were going — at least from their society's notion of the afterlife — upward to Heaven or downward to Hell?"

Sam bit his lower lip. "Well, if you're to believe the Popul Vuh, basically the Mayan bible, this was the ballcourt where the twin heroes, Xbalanque and Hunahpu, challenged the gods of the underworld to a multi-match ball tournament."

"They challenged the gods of the underworld to a game of ball?" Tom suppressed a grin. "How did that go?"

Chapter Twenty-Five

Sam said, "Mayan cosmology, which shirks neither from darkness and violence nor beauty and heroism, features one of the most strange and transformative tales of the underworld. The story is found in the Popul Vuh, the most comprehensive, remaining work of Mayan mythical literature and which was recorded through the Quiché language by a Dominican friar in 1701 AD. The most important and cohesive part of the Popul Vuh recounts twin heroes, Xbalanque and Hunahpu, challenging the gods of the underworld to a multi-match ball tournament…"

Tom said, "Go on."

"The story begins when Hun Hunahpu, the father to the twins, challenged the greedy and corrupt gods of Xibalba to a ball game. In important tournaments the losers were sacrificed and their severed heads became permanent additions to the court. When Hun Hunahpu lost the ball game to the gods of the dark house, they ripped him apart and left his head impaled on a tree."

"You're really selling the ancient Mayan times to me here, Sam."

Sam nodded in agreement and continued with the story. "However, Xquic, a lovely blood goddess of the underworld fell in love with the head of the brave and handsome Hun Hunahpu and became impregnated by his spit. She raised her own twin sons, Hunahpu and Xbalanque, keeping them hidden away from the eyes of the gods below but, when the two grew to manhood they inevitably found their father's sporting equipment. Learning of his downfall, they set out to defeat the gods of Xibalba, whose malign influence was corrupting the world of life.

"After deliberately losing several ball matches in order to obtain a strategic advantage, the brothers were forced to take shelter in a dark house in Xibalba which was filled with killer bats and the horrifying bat gods known as the Camazotz. To escape the bats, the brothers took refuge inside their blowguns but Hunahpu, mistakenly believing that dawn had arrived, stuck his head out to look around. A Camazotz promptly snipped Hunahpu's head off with razor claws and carried the bleeding head to the ceremonial ball court for use during the next day's ball game.

"Grieving for his dead brother, Xbalanque summoned the animals of the jungle and asked them to bring their favorite food. Many animals brought leaves or grubs or worthless carrion, but the coati brought a calabash gourd, which Xbalanque then fashioned into a surrogate head for his brother. During the ballgame, he managed to exchange the fake head for the real one and the brothers ultimately went on to win the tournament!"

"What did the Xibalban gods do when the twins won?"

"Enraged by the loss, the Xibalbans constructed a great oven in which they immolated the meddlesome twins. The deities of hell then ground the twins' burned bones to dust and threw them in a river. However, Xbalanque and Hunahpu were again, one step ahead. They magically regenerated as a pair of catfish which gradually changed into boys. Amazed by this miracle and not recognizing the now-transformed twins, the Xibalbans hired the orphans as magical entertainers. The twins performed increasingly spectacular magical miracles for the Xibalbans, for example transforming into animals and burning buildings—only to restore them, perfectly unharmed."

Sam took a deep breath. "Finally, the two magicians were called to appear before One Death and Seven Death, the ranking rulers of Xibalba. The twins performed a spectacular magic show and culminated with Xbalanque sacrificing Hunahpu, only to have the latter emerge more powerful and vigorous than before. One Death and Seven Death applauded and demanded the twins put them through the same transformation. Naturally the twins sacrificed the rulers of Xibalba, but they did not restore them to life. They then revealed their true identities and began to slaughter their former tormentors. The forces of Xibalba surrendered utterly, begging for mercy.

"The story ends with the twins granting clemency to the surviving gods of Hell on the condition that the world of life no longer need worship them or present offerings to the underworld. The brothers then dug up their father's remains and pieced them together, but their magical skills could not bring him fully back to life. Maimed and broken, he was left on the ball court where they found him. Some say he became maize and gave life to the world. Others say he became the fragile hope which lingers for all things lost and dead.

"The brothers then left the underworld but, as they ascended to the world of the living, they found that it had now become somewhat diminished from their purview. Their mighty magical transformations had put the affairs of life behind them. The two kept climbing and transcended the world entirely. They are still visible as the sun and the moon. Their story is the Mayan story of creation and how life was redeemed – at least for a time – from the greedy deities of the underworld."

Tom said, "Great. So, what did the Master Builders have to do with any of this?"

"I have no idea," Sam said, fixing his flashlight on the upward staircase at the end of the ballcourt. "But I think it's time we go visit the *Heavens* and find out."

Chapter Twenty-Six

They followed the passageway at the end of the ballcourt into a small alcove that harbored more than a dozen weapons, shields and warrior masks. They were presumably the remnants of long-forgotten Mayan victories on the ballcourt.

At the end of the alcove, they climbed the steps that symbolically led upward toward Heaven. The passage ascended at a forty-degree angle, almost identical to those found in the Egyptian pyramids. After climbing roughly a hundred and eighty feet, the diagonal passage opened into a large, empty chamber. Sam shined his flashlight along the walls. There was nothing. A completely vacant room, which probably took the better part of a decade to carve out. He wondered what purpose it had once served.

They turned around and backtracked until they reached a second opening in the ceiling that ran in an opposite, diagonal direction. This passage maintained the same forty-degree angle as the original but, instead of heading north, slanted south. Sixty feet along, a second passage opened. This one ran horizontal.

Sam caught his breath before continuing.

At the end of the ascending passage the tunnel leveled out again and then opened into another large chamber. Presumably the king's chamber, but there was no sarcophagus. Instead, an ornamental pedestal stood at the center. He ran his eyes across the chamber. It was made almost entirely out of pink quartz crystal, known as rose quartz. He looked up. The ceiling was a large, rounded dome, the surface of which was covered with both writings and numbers.

Tom focused his flashlight on the ceiling. "The writings are a mixture of pictographs, hieroglyphs and symbols. The same sort of gibberish I've seen you refer to as being written by the ancient Master Builders."

Sam grinned. "Yes, this is their work. Now I'm certain of it."

Sam stared at the ceiling trying to make sense of what appeared mostly as ancient, undecipherable markings. Although the domed ceiling was full of writing, none of the words were grouped together. Instead, it appeared as though a child had scribbled all over it, at random. A likely alternative, the individual words could mean something all by themselves.

Tom asked, "What does it say?"

"I don't know," Sam said, already taking a digital recording of the images so that he could decipher it later. "It can take hours to decipher a single word in the ancient language."

He lowered his eyes and examined the rest of the room in silence. On top of the central pedestal sat a small piece of glass or transparent stone, glistening. It appeared ornamental and yet valuable, like an orb. It stuck out of the pedestal, with some sort of metallic bevel material, like brass only more golden, blocking the surrounding sides and directing the light, reminding him of a microscope lens.

Sam shined his flashlight at it.

The light scattered throughout the small chamber, as if through a prism.

At the top of the brass-like sidings, where the clear orb stood proudly, were a series of markings dividing the circle into four equal portions.

Sam had seen a very similar device inside a flooded pyramid beneath the Mediterranean Sea. That one made sense out of some of the quatrains that Nostradamus had purportedly foretold the future by showing a vision of places far away.

Sam tried to rotate the pedestal. The device didn't move. He tried harder, but it may as well have been bolted to the stone flooring. Studying the markings in the brass, he tried to move the brass itself with no success. He then moved along to the lower section of the pedestal where a series of pictographs surrounded a single, beveled dial of brass, shaped like a spear.

Tom was the first to recognize the image. "That's a looking glass!"

"Another looking glass!" Sam was incredulous. "I thought we'd found them all by now."

"Apparently not."

The looking glasses were a network of communication devices built by the ancient Master Builders and spanned the globe. They projected light only, no sound, but allowed the users to see where the refractive tube opened, often viewing distant lands and at times, thousands of miles away.

The question to be considered—what was a looking glass doing inside the Mayan underworld?

Sam stepped closer to the pedestal and looked directly at the flawless orb. It was currently opaque, but he hoped to change that. Tom had found the first of the looking glasses in a pyramid nearly 500 feet below the Gulf of Mexico. The stone orb was made from a material harder than diamond and nearly two hundred times more translucent, meaning light and sound could travel through it much farther and faster than any other known material on earth.

It was designed for viewing other parts of the world during the ancient times.

A type of magic used long before the internet allowed such communication; videoconferencing, for example.

Sam rotated the dial shaped like a warrior's spear, waited, and then grinned like he'd just won a final hand of cards. He placed his eye up to the orb as though he was looking through the lens of a microscope. The opacity of the orb had dissipated, giving way to a very clear picture.

The image depicted an identical chamber to the one they were already standing within, only the next one was made of jade. He rotated the dial again and the image changed to another darkened and empty chamber. The walls were made of blocks of limestone. He made one more rotation, finding another made out of marble.

Tom said, "It looks like there are four temples linked together by this looking glass."

"That's right. Maybe they're all Mesoamerican? Maybe they span the globe? There's no real way of knowing from here."

"Any idea what these four temples relate to?"

"No. But I intend to find out."

It was nearly an hour before Sam and Tom finished digitally archiving the contents of the king's chamber in addition to images of the other three kings' chambers as they were viewed through the looking glass.

There was a connection there, somehow, but right now Sam sure as hell couldn't see it.

When there was no more to be learned at this particular location, they headed back down, toward the ballcourt.

They descended the ancient stairway, passed through the votive hall adorned with its ritual battleaxes, blades, shields and masks and out into the main *Pok-ta-pok*, the ballcourt of Xibalba.

And stopped…

Because blocking their path across the ballcourt's alley were two men in beastly masks. One wore a mask of a Mayan vampire and the other, a black cougar.

One of them looked like he had materialized straight out of one of the ancient Mesoamerican petroglyphs. He was six foot four with a muscular frame that challenged even Tom's massive physique.

Sam said, "Who the hell are you guys?"

One of the men was carrying a solid rubber ball. "My name is Xbalanque and this is Hunahpu. If you want to leave Xibalba alive, you'll need to beat us at a game of *Pok-ta-pok*."

Chapter Twenty-Seven

Sam's lips parted. "You've got to be kidding me."

The first man passed the ball to his teammate. To Sam, he said, "Are you ready to play?"

Now Sam grinned. He exchanged a glance with Tom and turned his gaze toward the one carrying the ball. "You want us to play a stupid, ancient ball game?"

"No. I'd like you to die and become a permanent member of the underworld. But I'm willing to give you a chance to survive. That is, if you can beat us at the greatest game on Earth."

Tom splayed the palms of his hands upward. "Hey, I don't know where you guys are from and all, but these days, *Pok-ta-pok* is out and soccer is *in*."

"Soccer?" The man behind the vampire mask queried.

Tom said, "It's a game those on the surface in South America prefer to play these days. You kick the ball with your feet and have to score a goal. You probably wouldn't understand it. The game's more for the living than the dead!"

Vampire mask said, "You think this is funny? Play ball or prepare to enter Xibalba forever!"

Sam's head swiveled on his neck toward Tom with an expression of confusion. It couldn't be, could it?

Both masked men were wearing a simple loincloth, only, and without a hiding place available to either man, each appeared weaponless.

"Sorry guys, we've got places to be," Sam said, pushing past the man wearing the black cougar mask.

He almost made it to the obsidian door before vampire mask heaved the *Pok-ta-pok* ball at him. The ball hit him low, below the hips, wiping his legs out from under him as successfully as a bowling ball.

For a second Sam wasn't sure he was going to be able to get back up, but one look at his opponents reassured him that quitting wasn't an option. He slowly pushed off the floor and forced himself to stand up. His joints protested in pain with each movement.

When Sam looked like he might not make it, Tom stepped in and lifted him up.

Sam felt a jolt of lightning running along the nerves in his right leg where the game ball struck, but he locked his knees in tight and refused to give his attackers the satisfaction of knowing that they'd inflicted injury.

Cougar mask picked up the ball and said, "That was just a warning. If you try and run again, we'll aim for your head – and I promise you no one gets to return to the surface after being hit in the head by a *Pok-ta-pok* ball."

Sam expelled his breath, slowly releasing the pain in his leg. "I bet."

As if to quell any further hope of escape, Cougar said, "Also, if you're thinking about taking the game ball and trying to escape while we're unarmed, you'll find the gamekeeper won't be as forgiving."

Sam and Tom glanced at the unguarded entrance to the ball court. Sam said, "Who?"

"The gamekeeper," Cougar said, gesturing toward the entrance, now guarded by a man carrying a double-sided battle axe.

Sam swallowed.

His eyes darted toward Tom, who nodded, crossed his arms and resignedly said, "It looks like we're staying to have a friendly match of *Pok-ta-pok*."

Chapter Twenty-Eight

Tom wasn't anywhere near as frightened as he should have been.

He'd played basketball, soccer, and gridiron and all had come natural to him. No reason *Pok-ta-pok* should be any different. Sam Reilly–was a different matter. Despite his athletic attributes and sharp mind, the guy had always been terrible at any game with a ball. Maybe he just hadn't found the *right* game yet. Tom sure hoped to hell that *Pok-ta-pok* was it.

Tom pictured the ballcourt as a sort of medieval soccer field, more akin to a gladiator's arena than a place to play ball. Then again, if you listened to what the history books said about Xibalba and the human sacrifice at the end of a game of *Pok-ta-pok,* he was starting to wish he was in a Roman arena instead.

The gamemaster stepped into the middle of the ballcourt.

Tom and Sam stood at the northern end of the I-shaped arena, with Vampire and Cougar at the southern.

An hourglass was turned over. Sand began to shift and sift and with the movement of each grain, Tom and Sam's time to prove their worth grew shorter.

The gamemaster shouted something in a language Tom didn't understand and then rolled the ball up the sloping wall of stone. The ball rolled all the way to the ceiling before falling down with the speed and force of a cannonball.

Tom tracked its movement, stepping in close to knock it, but stepped back at the last instant for fear a collision with the ball and his body at speed could prove lethal. Their two masked opponents made no attempt to touch the ball, confirming to him that doing so would have been dangerous, if not deadly.

The ball rolled all the way to the bottom of the court, across the narrow section and halfway up the opposite side of the sloping stone until losing its momentum and falling back to the ground.

This time Cougar moved in quick and caught the ball on his torso and sent it north, down the vertical lane of the field.

Sam dived to block it, but the ball was moving faster than he was.

Tom ran for it, blocked it with his legs, preventing them from scoring a goal. He knocked the ball to Sam, who kicked it hard at Cougar.

The man jumped to avoid the ball taking him out, and instead the ball struck Vampire at his hip – knocking him to the ground before ricocheting back to him.

Sam knocked the ball to Tom, who gave it a hard kick, sending the ball all the way down to the southern goal.

The gamemaster yelled something, presumably awarding them a goal.

Tom glanced at Sam and grinned. "See, nothing to it!"

Sam laughed. "I never doubted it."

Their opponents regrouped and started sending the ball north along the playing court, adeptly passing it back and forward, keeping momentum.

Cougar passed it to Vampire before Vampire headbutted it, propelling the ball up a sloping section of stone.

The ball rolled back down, its velocity similar to when the gamemaster had commenced the game. Tom shifted easily out of its way and slammed into Sam in the process. They both fell and got back up in an instant, but in doing so, had no preparation for the ball's second downward bounce.

The ball struck Tom in the back, knocking him over.

The gamemaster shouted again, apparently awarding double points to Cougar and Vampire.

Tom grinned. He wasn't injured but he'd forgotten he was playing an ancient ball game, designed to circumvent actual war, and as a consequence the game was meant to be played violently. Points were scored for sending the ball into goals, but more points were awarded for injuring one's opponents, with the near impossible and ultimate goal of making a winning score through the stone ring.

Tom rolled the ball toward Sam and said, "We're playing the wrong way."

Sam bit his lower lip and arched an eyebrow. "There's a right way to play?"

"Yeah. We need to be inflicting pain on our opponents!"

Sam winced, remembering the shooting pain down his leg from the hit he took earlier. "All right, I can do that."

With that, Tom turned the game around, successfully sending the heavy rubber ball hurtling in a constant barrage at their two opponents.

Vampire and Cougar, despite arguing that they were the best *Pok-ta-pok* players in history, appeared to have the reflexes of amateurs.

The gamemaster awarded point after point to Sam and Tom, until Tom was certain they were about to be pronounced the winners of this stupid game.

By his count, they were nearly ten points up.

The gamemaster held up the hourglass so that everyone could see that the end of the game was approaching fast.

Maybe it meant last five minutes?

Or even the last minute…

There was no way to know for sure.

The ball rolled forward, followed closely by Vampire and Cougar racing to send it through the vertical axis of the ballcourt.

Tom stepped out of the way.

So did Sam, following Tom's intuition for the game.

Time was on their side. The best thing they could do was let it run out, while their opponents made an easy goal score.

Instead, Vampire threw the ball toward Cougar who in turn kicked it hard against the vertical wall.

Tom watched in disbelief as the ball hit the side, ricocheted, and bounced back toward the opposite end of the narrow court – landing on the sloping side. It rolled downward and through the stone ring.

The last of the sand ran through the hourglass.

The game of *Pok-ta-pok* was over.

The gamemaster stepped onto the ballcourt and announced, "Xbalanque and Hunahpu win!"

Vampire and Cougar cheered.

The gamemaster pronounced loudly, "It is time to grant Xibalba its human sacrifice."

Chapter Twenty-Nine

Sam and Tom could only stare in amazement at each other.

The gamemaster didn't designate who, exactly, was about to be sacrificed but either way, it wasn't on his plans for the day.

Tom made an imperceptible nod and both players ran back toward the votive hall. Behind them, the gamemaster gripped his double-sided battle axe and followed them like the grim reaper.

Inside the votive hall, the small arsenal of ancient weapons still adorned its walls.

Sam gripped a spear and headed up the stone steps while Tom grabbed a massive, spiked club and hid behind the door.

The gamemaster entered slowly, then spotting Sam climbing the stairs, took off at a sprint. Tom didn't hesitate and swung the spiked club into the back of the gamemaster's head as he attempted to run by.

Sam heard a sickening crunch and knew instantly that the gamemaster was no longer a threat as he slumped forward onto the ground, his body perfectly still.

There was no noticeable rise or fall of the man's chest.

Tom waited behind the doorway again, holding the spiked club, ready to make a second assault if needed on the other masked men.

Sam watched and waited, but no one came.

After about ten minutes Sam slowly made his way down the stairs and checked on the gamemaster. The man was dead. There was nothing they or anyone else could do for him.

They then headed back out to the ballcourt.

The rubber ball slammed dangerously close to Sam's head before bouncing down the court. Distracted by the ball, Sam searched for the two ball players, but found no one.

Tom asked, "Where did they go?"

Sam frowned, his eyes searching quickly. "I don't know."

A split-second later, he heard a sort of war cry. Above him, both men jumped down, attempting to land on him.

Sam moved quickly. One of the attackers missed him completely, while the second caught his shoulder with his hand, pulling Sam down onto the ground.

Sam regained control fast.

He rolled over and tried to punch his attacker in his Cougar face mask.

Cougar blocked the first attempt.

Behind him, Sam heard Tom fighting with Vampire. Despite Vampire's muscular physique, Tom inflicted devastating damage using his spiked club.

Sam rolled on top of Cougar and tried to lock the man's throat with his elbow, squeezing until the man nearly passed out. Sam asked, "Who are you?"

When Cougar looked like he was about to lose complete consciousness, he suddenly rolled to the side and began running south along the ballcourt.

Tom ran in pursuit. He shouted, "Sam! Our dive gear! Don't let him reach it or we'll be trapped."

Sam picked up his spear and threw it.

The spear flew across the ballcourt true and straight, like an Olympian's javelin.

It struck Cougar in the back, right between the shoulder blades – penetrating all the way through his chest.

Cougar fell forward, impaled by the spear, dead.

Sam turned to Tom, "What about Vampire face?"

Tom lifted his bloodied, spiked club. "He's dead."

They went and removed the two masks from the dead men.

Vampire had a tattoo. It was a very different warrior mark. It was a series of small teardrops tattooed on the man's face. This particular brand of tattoo was well-known amongst members of Mexican Cartels and identified the number of people that a person had murdered.

Tom suppressed a grin. "They don't look like ancient warriors."

Sam bit his lower lip and shook his head. "No. If I had to guess, they work for the Black Muerte Cartel."

"So why play the ballgame at all?"

"That I don't know..." Sam expelled a deep breath. "Maybe they weren't sent here to kill us, after all. I mean, if they wanted us dead, why bother challenging us to a game of *Pok-ta-pok?*"

"Exactly. Why not just bring a gun and shoot us dead?"

"So, if they didn't come here to kill us, what did they come for?"

"And why make up such an elaborate ruse like a game of *Pok-ta-pok* to achieve their goal?"

Sam's eyes widened. "Unless they weren't trying to kill us at all? Maybe they just wanted to scare us? Maybe keeping people out of Xibalba was their real purpose."

Tom nodded. "But the question remains, why?"

"That I don't know." Sam turned toward the southern entrance. "Come on, let's get out of here while we still can."

"Agreed."

Sam and Tom raced back to the obsidian door.

In the dry chamber next to the submerged passageway was their dive gear, still intact and undisturbed.

Tom looked around and asked, "Where are our masked men's dive gear?"

Sam frowned. "It's not here."

"Which means… what? They entered Xibalba from another direction?"

"Yeah, maybe."

Tom said, "There were no other passageways. We explored them all. It's like Armando said — there's one way in and one way out."

"I don't know definatively, but I'm not in the mood to find out." Sam donned his closed-circuit rebreather, placed his facemask on and said, "Let's leave Xibalba, Underworld of the Dead, to the dead."

Tom nodded. "Agreed."

They raced through the flooded, labyrinthian passageways all the way back to the cenote through which they had entered.

Outside, Armando and his men still stood guard with AK-47s.

Sam asked, "How did they get past your men?"

Armando made a wry smile. "Who? We haven't seen anyone since you entered the water."

Sam frowned. "No one's been through here since us?"

"No. Why? What did you see?" Armando asked, his voice containing a hint of concern.

Sam lifted his hands. "I don't know. There were two masked men who challenged us to a game of *Pok-ta-pok* on an ancient ballcourt of Xibalba."

"Really?" Armando met Sam's eye through raised eyebrows.

"Yeah, really."

"What happened to them?"

Sam shrugged. "We sent them back to where they came from."

Armando shook his head. "And where was that?"

Sam said, "To Xibalba… that place of fear and underworld of the dead."

Chapter Thirty

Over the next forty-eight hours Sam and Tom returned the crystal key to the Mayan World Museum of Mérida and brought Armando up to speed on all they'd discovered inside Xibalba — keeping the truth about the looking glass a secret.

After exchanging digital data from their trip, it was agreed that they would examine the footage for additional clues before making a second expedition, unclear if there was even a purpose to doing so.

They parted ways with Armando and caught a commercial flight to LAX.

Tom asked, "Where will you go?"

"I'm taking a week off and spending it with Catarina."

"Heading anywhere in particular?"

"No. I think we'll go to my home in Lake Oswego in Portland, Oregon, and have a quiet vacation. You?"

"I'm going to Alaska with Genevieve."

Sam suppressed a grin. "What's in Alaska?"

Tom's eyes beamed with joy. "Wild animals, vast open spaces, mountains… anything you want."

Sam said, "Enjoy. We all deserve a break."

Chapter Thirty-One

Ethan never really wanted to go to Syria.

He had done SEAL training for an entire year of his life, and he'd expected more; maybe a para jump deep into North Korea to gather intel or even a covert mission into Iran, but where was he now? The middle of nowhere training Syrian soldiers to use their decades-old Kalashnikovs against the M14-equipped Islamic State.

Right now, his squad roamed the endless desert in their IFV – Infantry Fighting Vehicles – with walls of sandstone farther off to the left and nothing but sand dunes to their right. Was this what he'd suffered and sacrificed for? Was this it? He could neutralize five armed terrorists with a knife, hold his breath for three minutes at a depth of twenty feet, and even carry a full-grown man with both their packs of equipment for half a mile –through the desert. Ethan could survive anything, but he felt like he was in the regular, any-man's Army; not one of the elite, best-of-the-best, warrior few.

He stared out the bullet-resistant glass window and into a low sunset, dust billowing up as the unit's tires bit into nothing but dry, arid landscape and thus obscuring his view like water off a speedboat. An age-old paradox bounced around in Ethan's head – if his presence was enough to stop violence from happening in his area, he'd exceeded expectations. He often woke up to the sound of muffled shots, live-fire action just outside their base's perimeter and, right or wrong, found himself longing to be out there in the thick of it. He hadn't busted his ass for a commendation and a handshake; *this* soldier was born with fight in his veins.

And then, off in the distance, an all too familiar pop-pop rang through the air. Ethan swung around. Was he imagining it?

Soldiers could go insane from the paranoia and anxiety.

Ethan looked at his team's faces as they sat packed like mackerel, side by side opposite him, swaying together with every small dune the IFV ran over. They had clearly noticed the shots too. Min gripped his M16 a little tighter, the whites showing on the tops of his knuckles. Ethan carefully stood up and leaned over the driver's seat. He tapped on Bryan's shoulder through the uniform.

Bryan took off one side of his aviation headset. "What's up, boss?"

"I think we've got live-fire close by. Can you slow down?" Even as Ethan spoke, the pops sounded much more distinct than before, and with great frequency. He looked back at the other three SEALS and barked, "We're going to get out and check what's up. Stick together! I'll take lead, okay?"

With resounding unison, the men shouted, "Understood, sir!"

Ethan took a good look at each of the soldiers. Though he could barely make any distinctions beneath the layers of uniform and fully outfitted helmets, he still felt their connection. In a few months he'd gone from a fresh SEAL to leading his own squad of elite soldiers.

There was a pride in that.

But pride could get you killed.

The men jerked up from their seats as the vehicle gradually slowed down. Ethan shouldered his way through and opened the door in the back with the pull of a red lever. Heat flooded into the back and he had to squint against the blinding glare of the sun. With the rear now open, the sound was deafening. *Just the way I like it,* thought Ethan. Ethan shot a hard look backward at his men and flicked his fingers forward with a crisp, pointed snap. *Stay sharp, heads' up, boys.* Some hand signs were universal throughout the military and this one in particular tended to change lives. *Hammer time*, he thought.

As soon as they jumped out of the vehicle, Ethan knew in an instant he'd made a mistake. Bullets rained down at them from every angle, coming in heavy from their right, making small puffs of sand where they landed — scarily close to the squad. They had stopped where four dunes intersected from all sides, trapping them like caged mice waiting to get shot up with all kinds of experimental drugs. Stupid, Ethan-stupid! So proud of that training. Where the fuck is it now?

Instinct kicked in: Ethan pulled Bryan behind the vehicle for cover by the cuff of his neck and everyone else followed immediately. But the damage was done – the targets, now them not the enemy, had been spotted. Now the bullets were homing in, shots consistently bouncing off the IFV with loud pinging noises. He knew that if they simply remained in position, not only would they get overrun, the insurgents would bring to bear their RPG and blow the vehicle to smithereens. Though it could withstand less-powerful mines and rocket shot from close range, the vehicle's armor became relative when it came to a direct hit from an RPG.

Time was running out.

Ethan scooted in the sand to the edge of the vehicle. With a quickness of reflex he learned in training, he stuck his head out from the side and took the scene in. Five, six, seven men spread around the dunes held assault rifles in their hands, firing indiscriminately. Thankfully, none of them had any grenade launchers.

None that he could see, anyway.

He couldn't recognize them despite their lack of helmets or protective gear. If any of them lived to tell the tale, those terrorists were in for a lifetime of imprisonment in America. The enemy was slow to recognize Ethan's head, giving him time to pop it back in without injury. Now wasn't the time to take chances. His squad fired from the sides of the vehicle with far greater accuracy than the insurgents. Every time their M16s fired a volley, the return shots slowed as the insurgents were forced to take cover behind the dunes. *Eventually they'll grow some balls and cut through my squad like a hot knife through butter,* Ethan thought. Desperation and fanaticism made men bold.

He craned his head, looking behind him. The familiar hole-riddled caves with their red-colored walls of stone stood reliably. Too far though. He looked up. The machine gun nest sat stoic and peaceful in the midst of the intense firefight. Was it possible for someone to get to the other side, climb up, jump in the nest and mow them down?

Min was closest to the driver's seat. Ethan knew it was him because of his size. "Min!" he screamed. "Can you get in and turn this bad boy around? We need the MG!"

"I'll try, sir!" The little man fired a few more bullets then clambered inside. He hit the start button and the engine roared to life. Ethan could barely hear it rev up under the constant stream of bullets. The wheels began turning — but there was no movement.

Was the sand too slippery for traction?

Min switched the motor off and jumped out while ducking. "The tires on the right are completely blown out. Guess those motherfuckers were smart enough to do that."

"Smart enough to not let us escape, but dumb enough to attack us in the first place," he muttered. In his military voice, he barked, "Team! Retreat! Head for the caves!"

"What about the IBV?"

"Leave it! We'll come back for it later!"

His squad reluctantly detached from the safety of the armor in front of them and backed up through the squeaking sand, still facing forward. The insurgents seemed to notice. They climbed out from behind the dunes, stalking forward and shooting from the hip, Rambo-style. Ethan would dole out some hard, physical discipline if any of his men ever decided to shoot like that.

All of a sudden, Brian stopped firing and turned tail, combat boots kicking up sand as he struggled to get to the caves as fast as possible. They were only a hundred and fifty meters away. If they maintained their line...

Too late. One by one, his men submitted to their "flight" adrenaline reactions. Ethan was hardwired to avoid it at all costs; he could survive anything. But for novices, no matter how well they were trained as SEALs, human nature was always the first weakness. *Shit*, he thought as he followed suit. If they were going to do something, they would do it together.

He covered their retreat and bullets spiked up fountains of sand on both sides.

Fifty meters, forty, thirty... The sand gobbled his entire leg up with every step. The eighty pounds of weight felt like a neutron star. Ethan swore he would sink like he was crossing quicksand if he stopped running. But he kept going; they were too far to give up now. He wasn't going to die out here. Not like this. And not today.

In front of them was an unassuming cave, some of the interior lit up by the deeply angled sunlight. If it was just one large interior chamber with nowhere to hide, he and his squad were mincemeat. He did remember, however, from a lecture he'd heard somewhere, sometime, that the Syrian caves were long, complicated interconnected systems. If the insurgents started losing their supposed "Holy War," they would definitely retreat and hide in the caves. But now, it was his squad who had to hide.

They tumbled in, rolling through the sand. It was noticeably cooler without the sunshine beating down on the sand grains and making a miniature greenhouse effect underground.

"Lights." Five unusually bright beams lit up the dark walls in quick succession. In here, the bullets sounded much less imminent, but they couldn't drop their guard now.

"Spread out. In!"

The team fanned out as the rounds sounded nearer. Ethan found a tunnel leading to the back of the cave. It looked like an unassuming bump of sand in the farthest corner. To the untrained eye it would have been nothing. But it was *something* to the crew. Suddenly, the ground opened up under him. The horrifying sensation of falling swept over Ethan like a dread he'd never before experienced.

To his surprise and momentary relief, the fall was amazingly short. He landed on a hardscrabble mix of dead leaves, some wood and the usual, sand. Ethan scrambled to his feet and, with shaking hands, aimed his gun at the hole now above him. But no fight came.

Shouts and bullets could be heard from above, but no bullets landed on him.

Ethan didn't know what to do- those were his men up there! And he'd fucking ended up down here? He turned on his flashlight, at a loss for what else to do. He needed to find a way out of here. He cast around to get a look at his prison. And stared.

As the sound of fire died off from above, Ethan wondered if his men were alive or dead but couldn't focus as his brain tried to process the scene before him. On the wall next to him, an image of a maze stood out; almost as if in relief. And in the middle? An intricate stone key appeared to be embedded in… the wall?

Reaching out with a tentative, shaking hand, he touched the key.

A shout from above grabbed his attention. He spun around.

Chapter Thirty-Two

Sam Reilly's House, Lake Oswego, Portland, Oregon

The birds chirped outside. It was a calm day on the lake and summer scents of barbecue and sunscreen slicked the breeze.

Hot as hell inside, though.

Sam gripped the wrench harder, wedged it around the stubborn bolt and turned as hard as he could. His tendons stretched and his teeth ground together, but deep in the core of the thing he felt some imperceptible shift and knew he was going to win.

Sam coaxed the bolt loose and finished it off with his fingers. It took a few times to get some purchase what with the oil, but Sam didn't mind getting his hands dirty. Eventually the bolt turned free and Sam sat back with a satisfied sigh and regarded the Thunderbird. He wondered again how things got so tight when she hadn't been used since he first discovered Excalibur more than six months ago.

Sam's moment of triumph was interrupted by the distant ring of his cell phone.

It took him a moment to understand what he was hearing, still lost in the hum and puzzle of his vintage car. He shook his head and came back to himself. He eased himself out from under the belly, groping for a nearby rag. He wiped his hands as he got to his feet, wringing hard at the oil that coated his fingers.

He dropped the towel on his workbench.

Despite washing them as quickly as possible, Sam still felt the grease on his fingers as he strode into the house from his attached outside workshop.

The cell phone kept ringing.

Whoever they were, they were persistent.

Catarina, still wet from her swim in the lake, stepped down the hallway and handed him his cell. Sam mouthed the words thank you, his eyes glancing at her with a mixture of lascivious desire and affection, wondering why he'd felt the need to work on the T-Bird when he could have been swimming with her.

He smiled, smitten and content to have her in his life.

Catarina gestured toward the phone. "Are you going to answer that?"

Sam nodded. He wedged the cell phone under his chin, reaching for a kitchen towel off the stove and wiping his hands as he answered. "Hello?"

The voice was curt. "Thank you for finally answering your phone, Mr. Reilly."

Sam's eyebrows rose. "Madame Secretary. Good afternoon." Sam wracked his brains for a possible reason behind the call. "To what do I owe the pleasure?"

"What do you know about Palmyra?" she asked without further preamble. It was something he liked about the secretary of defense. She didn't waste words.

"Syria?" His lips twisted into a puzzled grin. "I read the papers and I hear the news, but if I'm to be honest, not a great deal at all. Why? What should I know about its ancient capital, Palmyra?"

He could almost see her smile as she spoke. "A small deployment of Navy SEALs stationed there discovered something that I… well. I think you'll be interested in."

Sam pivoted and sought the window, phone against his ear. Outside, the breeze blew stiff ripples across the lake. "Really? I'm not that kind of soldier anymore… what happened?"

"A group of men stationed in Palmyra got engaged in a firefight with some insurgents two days ago. They got pinned down in some ruins outside of the city, hard pressed."

Sam frowned. "Enemy fire?"

"Yes… and heavy, too. They fought their way out but during their escape one of the men got separated from his companions and found himself under the ground."

"Go on."

"You need to know what he found."

"What makes you think that?" Sam frowned. "I mean, what does this specifically have to do with me?"

She smiled through the phone. "Everything, Mr. Reilly. Everything."

Through the windows, Sam saw the breeze pick up on the lake. Sam thought of his car and his project, half-finished in the garage. Maybe he wouldn't get to finish it this trip after all. More importantly, he wondered if there would still be time to spend with Catarina. "Why?"

"I could tell you, but it's easier if I simply show you. Are you near a computer?"

Sam tossed the towel on the counter, put the phone on speaker and moved toward the laptop on the low wooden coffee table where he'd been enjoying coffee and the news earlier in the day. He settled behind the screen and opened his email. "I am now. What did you want to show me?"

"Open your email."

Sam did so.

In an unsettlingly brief amount of time, an encrypted email arrived. It wasn't the first time he'd received a communique from the higher-ups at the Pentagon, but their efficiency never failed to impress and intimidate, no matter how he tried to hide it.

Sam clicked on it and almost immediately a photograph loaded.

It was a picture taken inside what appeared to be a stone tomb. For a moment he thought it was a low-res image taken from some kind of handheld surveillance recorder, and he was surprised at the rare shoddy quality. Then the photo fully loaded into stunning resolution and all he could do was stare.

Along the stone wall was a detailed drawing of indeterminate age, carved in stone and painted. Sam leaned closer to see its details. There, at the center of the wall drawing, was a depiction of a labyrinth, with a strange key at its center.

"Mr. Reilly? Did you receive the file?" The sharp voice cut through his amazement.

"Yes." Sam struggled to process what he was seeing. "I got it."

She said, "I believe you know what this means?"

Sam Reilly swallowed hard and nodded to himself. "It means that my history has finally caught up with me."

The Secretary said, "The question is, Mr. Reilly... what are you going to do about it?"

Sam Reilly took a deep breath.

He knew the answer to that question, as much as he disliked it.

"It's time for me to return to where this all began... where I first heard about the Master Builders – and as much I don't want to, it's time for me dig something up that I had hoped would remain buried for all eternity."

The secretary of defense said, "I'm sorry it's come to this Sam. I had hoped that it wouldn't."

He'd hoped so, too. But more times than not, your past has a way of catching up with you. "I understand, Madam Secretary. I'll be ready for the flight within the hour."

He ended the call.

Catarina looked at him. Noticing the change in his demeanor, her brow furrowed with worry and her piercing gray eyes locked onto his. Her lips thinned. "Is everything all right?"

Sam took her hands affectionately into his, kissed them, and then kissed her on the lips. He closed his eyes and enjoyed the moment. He could happily spend the rest of his life with this woman, forget about his obligations...

He would do it, too.

If only his obligations would forget *him* and leave him alone.

She pulled back from him. Her trim eyebrows arched, and her lips parted questioningly. "Tell me, Sam… what's happened?"

He took a deep breath. "I'm sorry. I need to go pack. There's something I need to do. I'm really sorry." He kissed her on the lips once more, a long, slow, and passionate kiss. "I'll try my best to be as quick as I can."

"Sam, you're scaring me. What the hell is going on?"

He had already returned to his equipment room and begun packing two large duffel bags with what appeared more like military equipment than something a maritime salvage expert or archeologist might need.

Catarina grabbed his hand and stopped him. "Sam!"

"I'm sorry. I'll try and make this as fast as I can."

Her eyes narrowed, confusion and concern evident across the planes of her beautiful face. "Where are you going?"

"Palmyra, Syria, Washington DC, Nevada… among other places."

"Why?"

Sam ignored her question, continuing to pack.

She persisted. "When will you be finished?"

"Soon. No more than a few weeks. That is, if I survive."

"Sam!"

He stopped what he was doing and looked at her. "Yes?"

"I'm scared. Why won't you tell me what's going on? What is this all about?"

Sam closed his eyes and bit his lower lip. He swallowed hard. He knew she had a right to know. All the same, he wanted to protect her as much as he could. But he loved her and for that reason alone, he owed her the truth.

He opened his eyes and said, "Because it's time I go back to Hell—and retrieve the Labyrinth Key."

Chapter Thirty-Three

Portland International Airport

Sam sat on the couch as evening fell, still facing his computer. The only difference was that now, there was a glass beside him. The sun had set, and the light was like he was underwater without his realizing, lost in his own memories.

The last time he'd seen an image similar in nature to the cave drawing had been inside an ancient fortress in Afghanistan, somewhere near the Khyber Pass.

That had been fifteen years ago.

But the memories were as fresh and raw as they'd ever been – along with his memories of the deadly events that'd followed.

He remembered the smell of the dust and the oil. The gun smoke in the heat outside and the acrid scent of his own three-day old sweat.

He remembered leaving in the middle of the night to board a plane without being seen, heading to Washington to personally debrief the president.

It had been April, just as it was now. It was one of the last times he would see the President alive…

Khyber Pass. He'd been running from a band of armed militants that had surprised their party in the ruins of an old town – only God knew *how* old – which had been bombed to hell, outside the city. They'd gotten separated; Sam had run, foolishly, to try to head off fire.

He'd tripped on a branch and rolled down a gully… the ground had given way and before he knew it, he'd hit bottom under a shower of dirt, stone and dead leaves. As he brushed himself off, tense and anticipating an attack from above, he thought he'd fallen through some loose ground, common to the area. But as he waited, the attack didn't come and he slowly, painfully, climbed to his feet taking stock of any injuries and his overall situation.

He raised his face to take in his surroundings and stared.

Sitting in the airport, Sam could still remember the gut-punch of surprise, incomprehension. It was not a sinkhole into nowhere that he'd fallen. He'd actually found himself in a man-made corridor, a kind of tunnel. He thought for a wild minute that he was in someone's basement from the nearby town, but it was no basement.

He was confronted by a wall with a strange symbol; a spiral branching off with four toothed arms. Sam had stepped forward and touched the dusty wall with awe. It wasn't an image imbedded into the wall like he'd first thought.

Instead, it was a solid artifact.

A strange stone key, bearing the image of a labyrinth.

Sam reached for his glass and downed the rest of its contents, shaking his head. It was amazing to think his entire world could be changed in a mere instant. Always in just an instant and never in the way you'd expect.

If he hadn't found that tunnel, found that drawing, he never would have met those men. And if he'd never met those men… the president would have had a very different story.

He'd buried that afternoon, that image, and all it had represented. He had tried to forget it had even existed, hoping that its secrets might remain such until long after he was dead.

He should have known better. With one phone call from the secretary of defense, that hope was now being shattered.

The discovery of a second symbol only proved what he hoped had been a mistake back then. Now there was no other solution than to complete the mission he had started all those years ago.

All the way through to its grizzly end.

Chapter Thirty-Four

The Louvre, Paris

The city lights of Paris sprawled through the organized streets, the classy boulevards. The massive crowds of tourists flooded the courtyard of the Louvre around the famous pyramid, snapping selfies and chattering in languages from all over the world. African vendors, blue-black in the sun, sold knockoff fashion brands on the side from tables made of cardboard topped with sheets, easy to collapse and run with at the first whistle of the police. As night fell, they'd replace their fake Prada and Armani with cheap plastic glow sticks and toy helicopters that launched into the Parisian dusk like fairies.

The guard shuffled through the last of the visitors of the day and wiped his brow. He was always surprised at the number of people that waited three hours in line and then raced through the hallowed halls of art to the Mona Lisa, took a selfie among the masses, and then left, satisfied. He knew they'd go home and years later say with pride, "Oh, the Louvre? I've been there."

Anyway. Not his problem. He had one round to make and then he'd be off.

Inside the last stragglers trickled, weary-footed and hungry, through the massive and gleaming halls. Benches lined the walls near the windows. The guards called in and the people sitting on them stood and left, as requested.

Crisp heels clicked out and with a last glance around, the guard linked his arms behind his back and paced out.

The room went silent. The evening light trickled in; the curtains closed. Time lapse footage would show…

A movement. A hand slid down the leg of the bench. Its mate followed. Two feet, clad in soft material, similar to slippers, crept down and a slim form hit the ground silently.

Mia lay a moment and listened. So many people did stupid things when infiltrating museums, where there were sophisticated motion sensors, etc., but she was experienced; she only worked her magic utilizing pre-existing structures. There were no sensors on the benches because people had to sit on them during the day. And they never counted on her size.

She'd been working Michel for more than a month to gain his loyalty. She'd promised him cartel connections back in the mythical United States- which must sound like paradise to a small time Parisian thief trying to make his dreams come true in the big city. That she'd ghost him the minute this was over was of no consequence, and probably of no surprise to anyone who knew her.

Well. Anyone other than Michel, anyway. But just because you robbed a museum together didn't mean you really knew a person. No, not at all.

Mia slid to her feet, wearing circus shoes. No sound greeted her entrance into the hall, and she shifted her shoulders in the unfamiliar guard's uniform. The woman was a little bigger through the shoulders than Mia herself, but it couldn't be helped. She'd needed something that fit passably well on short notice, and she didn't want to be hampered by a man's tent of a costume. She'd spotted the girl on her breakfast scouting mission in the cafeteria over a cafe au lait and introduced herself. Amazing what a little kindness could render.

That her work uniform was in the bag that was stolen from her that afternoon would be the least of the girl's worries. It was the loss of her money that would have more serious consequences. Mia had shoved the cash in her bra and tossed the rest in the trash.

She smoothed her cap of hair and surveyed the scene. She had chosen her location well, in the midst of the antiquities. If anyone entered now, she'd pass easily as a guard as long as they didn't stay too long.

She just hoped Michel had gotten the security system out of commission. That was the least he could do.

One way to find out.

She squared her shoulders and poked her finger toward a painting, toward some woman's naked and fleshy thigh. She didn't touch the canvas though- wouldn't do to leave fingerprints.

The alarm sounded immediately. Fuck.

Mia snatched her hand back and glanced around, pushing down her adrenaline spike with long practice.

And sure enough, a very French-looking guard rounded the corner, gun drawn. He stalled when he saw Mia.

"What's- what's going on here?" His smile was charming, perplexed yet a bit flirtatious, his accent clear.

Mia smiled and shrugged. "Oh, me and my clumsiness," she laughed, her French passable. That was the good thing about big cities. You could disappear.

He folded his arms, skeptical, eyes trailing up and down her body. The guard's uniform didn't reveal much, it's only downside. Not, she reflected, that there was much to reveal. She gave him another smile. Bastard was making her late.

"I haven't seen you before." He holstered his weapon and she fought to keep her gaze from latching onto it. Beautiful piece. Maybe before she left, she could... "I would remember."

"First day." She twitched her lips in a Gallic expression of 'What can you do?'. "I'm afraid I don't know my way around the alarms just yet. Slipped."

"I can show you, if you want."

"No, I don't want to interrupt your round. I'm sure you-"

"I just finished."

Fuck. This wasn't supposed to be this way. She'd researched. She'd done specs. They didn't finish until nine. She had another full hour... She-

"Oh," she temporized, buying time. "Oh, that would-"

His radio blared. "Where the fuck are you? You think I'm doing this shit job alone?" An angry voice screamed at him in French.

The guard blushed. Mia laughed and waved him on. "Go. I'll be fine. You can blame me for being late." She winked. "Maybe after I get off you can show me around."

The guard pocketed his radio. "It's a date. Meet me at the pyramid."

Mia barely avoided rolling her eyes. How unoriginal. "I'll be there."

"Nine o'clock. That's the shift end."

Mia shook her head. Men were so predictable. "Nine fifteen." She plucked at her uniform. "Let me change clothes, at least. No way I want to go outside wearing this."

He laughed and ducked out of the room with a parting glance back at her.

His footsteps had barely cleared the door jamb before Mia dismissed him, her ears still tuned to any sounds of approach.

She checked her watch. 19:46. She shoved it back in her pocket. Michel was supposed to have deactivated this wing at 19:30. If he didn't have it done by now, he wouldn't have it done. Mia considered testing it out again, same painting, but she was fooling herself and didn't have time to waste. The ruse would only work once.

Mia moved to the cabinet silently in her rubber soled shoes. She pulled the drawer open, with its glass covered lid.

That was the great thing about France, she thought. France had quality. France had glass. Plexiglas didn't break, at least not as fast as she needed. She took a screwdriver from her pocket and smashed the butt into the corner of the glass with a quick jerk.

It broke with a clean crack, quickly muted. No alarms.

Mia barely spared her surroundings a glance. The job was now whole, complete… and hers. This is what she was born for. She pulled on her gloves, limbered her fingers, dipped into the broken corner of the door and grabbed the key.

She didn't look at it, didn't marvel at its antiquity or ponder what doors it might have opened once. That wasn't why she was here. She was here for the cash. She was here because this piece of metal and stone, apart from all the others, was special.

It didn't feel special, she reflected as she dropped it in the roomy pocket of the guard's uniform. Then, she reflected further as she closed the door silently and kicked the glass toward the base of the cabinet. No, in her experience, special things never did.

Quick measured steps saw her out of the regal hall. The slanted stone eyes of the Middle Eastern statues watched her go.

Mia found a bathroom on the first floor near the exit and slid in with a hasty apologetic smile to the woman cleaning it. She pulled the stall open, already unbuttoning her uniform, and closed the door.

The cleaning lady laughed, a big African belly laugh. "Hot date?" she said through the thin metal.

Mia laughed as she shimmied into a slinky shirt top and jeans. She shoved her uniform into the guard's stolen bag, glancing at the small metal trashcan on the wall. She lifted the lid. No tampons inside. Fresh bag. Perfect. She pulled out the slim cell phone she'd prepaid for this job. There was a text waiting from Michel, as promised. He was waiting outside. With a heart emoji. How boring.

Mia rolled her eyes and dumped the phone inside. She pulled off several handfuls of toilet paper and shoved those in too. Then she closed the lid.

The cleaning lady wished her a good date as she hurried out.

Mia couldn't help congratulating herself a little bit as she navigated her way out of the museum and into the Parisian night. She dropped the stolen bag unobtrusively near the exit door. She wiped her hands on her pants and was just starting off into the crowds before a voice behind her made her turn.

"Is that it? Think you're so clever. You thought you could just sneak out?"

Mia stalled, heart hammering. "What?"

She turned to find the guard from before leaning against the door with a smug smile. "We had a date."

Balls. She must have gotten turned around in the museum.

"Oh." Mia smiled and flirted, tweaking his collar. Now that she thought of it, she could use the cover, actually. Always helped to have a getaway partner, even if they didn't know that that was their job.

They wandered through the periwinkle night as the buskers sang Leonard Cohen covers and the streetlights winked on, the epitome of romance. When he pulled her into an alley, after a street-side glass of mediocre wine that tasted like victory, she let him. When he pushed her up against the wall covered in peeling posters and felt her up under her shirt, she let him do that too. The key, after all, was safe in her pants.

And when he bent his head to kiss her neck, she hit him on the soft spot at the base of his skull hard enough to black him out. She giggled as he collapsed against her with a moan for the benefit of the other passers' by. "Baby, you'll have to wait…"

Mia braced his weight against her with a grunt. When she was sure he was out, she let him slump to the ground amid the chip's wrappers and cigarette butts and slime.

She strolled to the end of the alley, looked right, then left. A police car loitered at the curb, lights flashing, cops smoking. She had no idea if they were here for her- frankly, she'd be surprised if they were. She'd planned this one to the hilt and execution was her specialty.

Still, no use taking chances.

Mia pulled off her shirt and tied it around her waist. Underneath she was wearing a chic sports bra. She did some quick toe bounces to limber up and to let off some of the giddiness, then started forward in a jog. She flashed the cops a smile as she passed. The breeze felt good on her bare skin.

She took off running down the Champs Elysee through the glowing Parisian dusk, flashing past the fancy designer shops and expensive cars, running full out, adrenaline surging in her veins, down toward the Arc de Triomphe.

Chapter Thirty-Five

Washington, D.C.

Josh straightened his sleeves as he took the two cups from the sidewalk vendor. Just another of DC's lawyers due for a morning jolt. He shoved a crumpled dollar in the sliced off paper cup that served as a tip jar on the steel truck window with a wink. "Morning, doll."

The coffee girl grinned at him. "You've got some…" She brushed at her nose and Josh realized with a shock he'd been sloppy this morning.

He wiped it off with an ashamed laugh. "Oops. Vitamins. I never learned to swallow pills, have to take them powdered."

She laughed with the practiced good will of a service girl. "Oh, I know what you mean, sir. Keep up the health."

"Always the health for Alfred and Stark." He took the cups and raised them in a toast.

"Ooh." She smiled. "Alfred and Stark."

"You've heard of us?"

She smiled. "Wanted to temp for you a long time, now. Once I finish school."

He leaned on the counter, ignoring the line forming behind him. "Oh? Is that so?"

Her glance flicked behind him. "Why'd you want to be a lawyer, anyway?"

Josh thought of Ethan and his damn nobility. He took the cups. "Friend of mine turned me on to it, actually. His dad was a real bastard, and I realized I could help people. Got me a scholarship to… oh, to somewhere with not too many letters… and the rest is history."

"You got the job before you came to the city, or after?" She blushed. "Sorry- it was your accent. Good southern boy. My aunt's down in Georgia."

He grinned at her. "Good ear, girl. You've got a future in a courtroom, yet." He picked the cups up from the narrow ledge by the tip jar and smiled at her as he sauntered off. "Oh- and I got the job after. Came here for a girl, like all poor schmucks." He winked. "My sister."

The morning was the kind of morning he loved, right down to the chemical smell used by the street cleaners and lightly mixed with sweat reek of the homeless.

The world was his.

The morning light entered through the plastic blinds as Josh trailed his fingers along the desk. They stopped at a pile of papers and rippled the edges, wondering what tale they might contain. Footsteps echoed in the hall, dull on the carpet, and he stopped his rippling. Maybe someday he'd find out, but not today.

The handle turned.

The senator entered, still looking at his phone or papers. He clearly wasn't expecting an audience: Josh waited, leaning against the desk, wondering how long before he'd take notice and found he'd even had time to cross his arms before the man even looked up.

Finally, look up he did, over the gold rim of his glasses. He stalled. Then he closed the door behind him with a small click.

"Mr. Rowe. Good morning."

"Senator." Josh nodded once, with the hint of a smile. It was a smile he'd perfected over years, designed to inspire a faint sense of unease.

It seemed to be working. The senator pocketed his phone. "How did you get in here?"

Josh shrugged. "Your girl at the desk likes her coffee too sweet and too light." He raised a brow. "Like she likes her bosses, apparently."

The man ignored the jab in a moment of self-preservation. "Is there something I can help you with?"

"I came to discuss what we'd spoken about earlier."

The senator shook his head with a flash of his campaign smile, all of his pearly whites front and center. "I told you. We can't. I'm sorry, Josh. I would if I could. But it's just not possible."

Josh took the decanter and tipped a healthy splash of whisky into his coffee. He held out one of the crystal glasses. "Want some?"

The senator shook his head. "Too early for me, thank you. But please." He gestured at the cup Josh was already sipping. "Feel free…"

"Aw, come on. No one's going to know. Or do you have a bunch of little cameras installed in here?" He grinned, glancing toward the walls but keeping an eye on the man's face. "Don't want anyone to see?"

The senator rubbed his neck, laughing. "No, no cameras in here… Well." He laughed. "We did have one but the cleaning people busted the wiring last week… It's still being repaired."

"Ah." Josh put his glass down and pushed up his sleeves. "That's good."

His punch caught the senator forcefully and without warning, in the nose. He was supposed to hit the man on the cheek but he'd turned his head like a girl and now, Josh had made a mess. God *damn it!*

The senator staggered back, clutching his face. Real fear sparked in his eyes. "What the hell —"

Josh shook his fist out, taking notice of the blood on his skin. He looked for a place to wipe it off but saw nothing within convenient reach.

The senator glared as he staggered forward, stumbling a step or two before a fortuitous grab at his desk allowed him to remain upright rather than prone pondering his reflection in the shine of his attacker's wingtips.

Lightning fast, Josh snatched the letter opener off the desk and grabbed the Senator's wrist. He trapped the man's palm on the desk and positioned the letter opener above the senator's hand and paused, the tip mere millimeters away.

The senator whimpered in abject terror. Josh could see his own tiny image in the man's glasses; make that two tiny images. Studying his mini-me's, he read nothing at all in his own eyes.

"I'll do it," he promised as the senator gaped with fear. "You know I will."

"But I—"

Josh smiled pleasantly. "What can I say. They want what they want. And you know what?" He pressed the tip of the shiny steel blade into the senator's flesh, causing a slight indentation. "You're going to give it to them."

The man broke. Josh had seen many people break. He knew the signs. "But… my campaign was built on…the fact that I-"

Josh laughed. "Ah, yes. Your campaign." Josh lifted the letter opener, running it in a meandering fashion along the senator's prominent veins. Age spots were just starting to show. The senator was getting fat and complacent in his prime. "You worked hard to build that campaign; I know. The people trust you. You *want* their trust. You worked hard to build your reputation on it." Their eyes met. "You know how fast I can unbuild that trust, that reputation?" He smiled in the man's face as the senator's glasses winked in the light. "Please don't misunderstand. I'm in no way threatening to end your career, okay? I'm promising, senator. And I always keep my promises."

The senator's lips opened. They weren't chapped. He took care of himself. But his mouth was dry. He touched his hand to his nose as the blood trickled- just a touch. His throat worked; his eyes hardened-

The door opened.

Josh palmed the letter opener like a switchblade. The senator jumped. His young aide peered in after his perfunctory knock, carrying a stack of papers. "Sir," he said, double checking his schedule, and Josh thought, *no wonder the senator was getting soft*. If your help didn't do their prep before they opened the door, you deserved just what kind of help they could give you. "Your meeting with SOMEONE important…"

He glanced up at the silence and saw the senator by the desk. Josh slowly released the letter opener, nudging it unnoticeably back to its place. The aide stared, not one blond hair on her head out of place. "Sir! Are you okay? Shall I call security?"

Josh and the senator locked eyes. Though the two men had both graduated from Ivy League schools, you didn't need to be smart to read the warning in the depths of Josh's.

The senator turned and smiled. "No, it's just nerves." He spread his hands disarmingly, at a loss for his own human failings. He touched the blood that trickled from his nose reassuringly. "I get nosebleeds when I get nervous. Always have." He laughed and glanced to where the cameras were supposed to be. Where no cameras were. He flicked lint off his pants. "It's hell on my dry cleaning. Should have picked a different profession. Not so many speeches."

The aide smiled, reassured. He offered the senator a tissue. "Well, we're ready for you when you are, sir." He took his bloody tissue back despite his protest and Josh frowned. "I'll tell them you're finishing up a call, sir."

Josh realized his hand was also bloody and tucked it under the clean one as the senator said, "I'll be right there. Let me just… clean up a bit."

The door closed behind the aide.

The two men sat in silence until Josh stood up by the desk and began to dust his hands on his pants. Then he thought better of it and held them in front of him. He smiled, poured some of the whisky onto his shirt tail, and mopped off the blood. "I'm glad we had this meeting, senator." He drank straight from the crystal decanter and swore it tasted better than if it had been from a plain glass. "I'm also happy to report you and I will never meet again. In fact, you'll never meet me or any of the boys again." The senator's shoulders relaxed imperceptibly, but his eyes narrowed, waiting for the other shoe to drop. Josh put the decanter back on the table. "Next time, it will be your family who suffer for his mistakes. You still enjoy that place on Abbey Court?" He shook his head regretfully but never dropped his eyes. "I hear the neighborhood is really going downhill."

The man blanched. "I understand." His lips tightened. "Sir."

Josh grinned and tucked the damp tail of his shirt back into his pants leisurely. "Have a good morning."

As Josh strolled out of the room, his phone vibrated in his pocket. Good timing. He smiled winningly at Jonas at her desk as he pulled out the phone to answer it.

"Hey, sis. Isn't it early in Paris?"

He noticed his hand was still bloody. He switched the phone to his other ear so the senator's aide couldn't see and continued down the hall amid the bustle of a D.C. morning.

He grinned. "Well. I guess that's worth staying up to celebrate." He jumped out of the way of a harried temp hurrying along and grinned. "Nice work. The boss will be very pleased with you."

Chapter Thirty-Six

US Military Base – Palmyra, Syria

The heat rose off the dry, dusty land, unstoppable, unavoidable. Sam wiped his brow. He'd spent the better part of ten hours in a dusty, tiny truck, hurtling over broken roads through the desert since dawn. Now the sun was high in the sky and Sam sighed, having never thought he'd be here again.

Ten young men and women cleaned up the area outside the ruins while they waited for the supply truck to come. Now, as Sam dismounted from the jeep, grateful for the chance to stretch his legs, he took a look at his welcoming committee. He'd attracted notice – he expected to, a civilian in this place – but they took it in stride. One in particular caught his attention – a striking man in his mid-twenties who wore his combat gear like designer clothes. *There's something about the eyes*, Sam thought, which seemed to convey a certain arrogance coupled with an intelligence beyond their years. A look that was hard to forget.

The man had spotted him too and was waiting to see what he'd do.

Shrugging off his uneasiness, Sam started unloading his truck. He had packed light due to short notice, amazed to note how much the desert had worn down his strength. When he heaved his bag to his shoulder and glanced again to the tent entrance, the startling man had gone.

Wordlessly, a couple of soldiers helped him and motioned at Sam to follow.

As he trudged through the base, Sam couldn't help but notice a certain air of boredom- almost a sense of longing for something, anything, to happen. *Everyone's seen pictures of marine super-bases in the desert*, he thought, *but no one talked about the tent-based camps that made up the majority of US bases.* Here were the absolute basics. As he passed through, he saw dusty books, well-worn, tossed on bedrolls with newspaper under them, spread out like a map. Sam had forgotten about that himself. You could hear scorpions coming on newspaper- their little claws scuttled very particularly. He still remembered the sound. And the newspapers made good reading if you managed to get a recent issue. Out here, you'd take whatever entertainment you could get.

Lost in thought, Sam almost bumped into the marine in front of him before realizing that they had stopped. He hefted his bag higher and peered into what had brought them to a halt; it appeared to be a small tent, big enough for two people, no more. All but one marine had left.

"Thank you, soldier."

"Pleasure, sir." He gestured to the dusty bedroll, the plastic stool that served as both table and chair. His face hid well-concealed skepticism that a man like Sam could get used to a life like this.

Sam set down his bag. "I was told that I could speak to—"

The marine looked like he never smiled, but Sam thought it was just a front. This kind of life made people alternately suspicious or amazingly open. Always a tossup. "Just get yourself situated, we'll send him over."

"Thank you." Once the marine had retreated Sam shifted the entrance curtains wider and stepped inside. To his surprise, there was a box fan linked into a mess of extension cords running to some main power unit. Sam loosened his collar in the breeze, grateful. Amazing what a little cool air could do. The tent almost felt secure.

Sam dumped his bag on the ground, making sure his cell and wallet were secure on his person. He wiped his dirty hands on his pants, then his hands over his sweaty face, feeling grit. Was there a bathroom he could use to wash up before meeting Ethan? It had been fifteen years and they'd parted ways under ambiguous circumstances. Now, after so much time, the least he could do was look presentable.

But where was the bathroom? Walking outside, Sam decided to just walk back the way he'd come. Hopefully he would find a bathroom. Or even better- a water pump.

He found some soldiers carrying heavy plastic water jugs that had seen better days on their shoulders, shirtless in the sun, laughing. Sam envied them their cleanliness but kept his mouth shut. He followed the way they'd come, aware in passing of the general day-to-day familiarity of soldiers all about, bored and awaiting orders. He felt a pang deep in his chest. For all the horror and toughness, the marines had given him a brotherhood of camaraderie he'd never found anywhere else. The crew of the Tahila were close, but it wasn't quite the same.

He finally found the pump on his own and crouched to rinse his hands and face, insanely grateful for the feeling of clean water sluicing away all the grime from his long journey. The water was hot enough to make him wince, heated to shower temperatures just by the sun. He rinsed his mouth quickly and spat it out in the dirt.

Damp with the oppressive humidity, thick as a blanket, he rolled his sleeves up past his elbows and found his way back to his tent with minimal wrong turns.

He checked his watch. He was early, too. That would give him time to collect his thoughts in preparation for seeing the man who had saved his life all those years ago. Saved his life, and…

Sam cut that thought off and pulled aside his tent flap.

He reached for his bag to pull out his notebook and gripped the bag in surprise. The man he had seen earlier was just sitting on his bed.

Sam released the bag and tried to look like he wasn't totally caught off guard. He straightened slowly, feeling water and sweat trickle down his neck. "Ethan."

Ethan nodded, but said nothing. *He hasn't changed*, Sam thought. He still had the wary arrogance that had played a big role when he'd saved Sam's life, but now older, he could see his bearing had been greatly enhanced by the military; hard to miss the muscles and tight buzz cut, all framed and showcased by the standard military-issued tank, fatigues and boots.

"Been a while. How have you been?"

"I've been all right." Sam watched the little boy who'd suffered his drunken father peer out from those hard eyes. A little kid longing for approval and acceptance. "How about you?" He smiled. "Good to see you."

And it was. Hard to fake that actually. Despite the man's arrogance, Sam liked him now just as he'd liked him then.

Ethan must have heard the ring of truth beneath his words. He shrugged but softened a bit. "All right. Didn't think you'd actually come. Long way to go just to look at a stupid wall." The suspicion lurked again. "Must be important."

Sam dumped his bag to the ground. "I think so. Well. I hope so. Get me off the hook."

"You and me both."

They sat in silence again in the dusty, stifling heat. Sam prickled with sweat and tried to tamp down his annoyance.

"Listen, kid. Quite frankly I don't want to be here anymore than you do. I wish like hell you hadn't found that tunnel, but now that you have, we may as well get to the bottom of it. I've found some things stateside that make me think that – well." He risked a glance at Ethan, who was now cleaning his nails with his pocketknife. "We can talk about all that later."

"Sorry." He didn't sound sorry, at least not much. But he didn't sound resentful either. He eyed Sam, judging how much to give away. Finally, he shrugged. "It's just that, it wasn't my choice to get involved in this, you know? All I did was do what I was supposed to do and report." He tossed his hands in the air and flipped his knife. "I thought it was going to be a cool tomb or something. I didn't think it would have anything to do with… whatever. It's been fifteen damn years, you know? I have enough on my mind without going back *there*. I've got things to do *here*. I can't afford to..."

Sam knew he was remembering the man who had held a gun to his head and a knife to his throat. A shady figure with ambiguous morals. Ethan looked like he'd done well for himself. Sam sensed the military had fostered a sense of honor and duty in his presence and the soldier's responsibilities seemed to have toughened him. Sam could see he took this life seriously and in him recognized something of himself. Ethan had found a family here; one he'd never dared to hope of finding and he'd die before doing anything that would risk his position among them.

Sam raised his hands and risked a smile. "You and me both, boy. I haven't forgotten, either."

He entered farther into the tent and sat on the floor, maintaining a low position and allowing Ethan, the position of power. He pulled out a bottle of water and offered it to Ethan, who shook his head. Sam pulled it back and drained half in a single gulp. "Man, that was a long ride. Don't know how you deal with this out here."

Ethan cracked a grin. "It's all right."

Sam stretched. "So, what did you find out there?" He gestured to the staggering heat. "I didn't come all this way in a damn truck to beat around the bush."

Finally, Ethan cracked a smile. "No?"

"Why don't you take it from the top."

Ethan considered him, then relented. He pulled his feet under him and fiddled with his knife, end to end. It seemed to help him think, having something to do with his hands. "We were on a scouting mission. Pretty routine. We'd been in the area a while- hell, we'd been there before- so no one expected any trouble." Ethan went to work on a splinter with the blade. "Before I knew it, we've got the pop-pops hitting us good and people are shouting and boom, we're in a firefight." He rolled his eyes. "Not routine, but still nothing to be scared of."

Sam kept his face neutral. "Seen a lot of action out here?"

"Some."

A troop passed by, laughing. Ethan tracked their shadows through the wall.

"As my team hid out in a small underground cave, we found that it almost looked like an abandoned city," he resumed after they'd passed. "Since we couldn't go back out, we decided to go deeper."

"Regulation, right?"

Ethan's grin slanted. "Not exactly. But what else were we gonna do?"

"Hey, I'm not judging you. I'd have done the same." Sam laughed. "What happened?"

Ethan glowered. "I fell down. Damned floor caved in. But it was a pain in the ass at the time. I wasn't injured. I got out a flashlight to see if I could find our way out and that's where the interesting part happened. On the wall beside me, there was a picture."

"A picture?"

"Now, all these caves, they sometimes have primitive drawings," Ethan said, as if he hadn't heard Sam. "But there was something different. It seemed like some kind of map. And it seemed... accurate."

Sam leaned forward. "A map? To what?" He was thinking back to the Yucatan, to his own find in the hills. "Was there anything else on it? Was there-"

Ethan threw up his hands. "Good God, man! Can you let me finish? Maybe you came all this way just to hear yourself talk?"

Sam had the grace to look abashed. He needed what this kid knew. And he owed him more than that. "Sorry."

"Gee, thanks." Ethan raked a hand through his short crop of hair, as if remembering the confusion he'd felt that day. "Everyone else had gone on but I told them I had to... tie my boot." He looked up with a slight, sheepish smile, the first Sam had seen. "I hung back." He shrugged in defiance. "Curiosity, I guess."

Sam grinned but pushed down a twinge of misgiving. "Killed the cat."

Ethan raised a sardonic brow. "So I've heard."

Sam gestured for him to continue. "Well? What did your curiosity get you?"

Ethan glanced up and to the side, trying to remember, as if reliving the moment. Sam knew because he'd felt the same thing. That image wouldn't ever leave his mind's eye. Ethan gestured and Sam watched him snap into report mode. "At the center of the map, there was a little platform. With a... a kind of key on top of it."

Sam's mind was racing a mile a minute now. Was finding another key really this easy? "A drawing of a platform? A drawing of a key? Or was it an actual..."

Ethan shot him a glance. "A drawing." Sam's eyes narrowed but, he felt the boy was telling him the truth. Not the whole truth perhaps, but truth, nonetheless. There'd be time for the rest of it later. "I knew it was something special. I didn't have time to think about it right then, though, you know? We were still getting shot at- or would be once we got above ground. You know, better position, up above I mean, versus huddled below down some damned hole in the ground, just waiting to be grenaded like dumb bunnies."

"Well, you're probably right about that."

Silence reigned again. Ethan glanced at him and reopened his knife, lounging on Sam's bedroll. Sam noticed he kept his boots carefully off the blanket. "We got out okay and no one else seemed to think there was anything weird about it. Hell. I don't know if they noticed anything at all. But I kept thinking about it. Christ. Don't know what possessed me to put it in the report. If I hadn't, this all would have…"

They looked at each other.

Ethan hunched his shoulders and stuck out his chin, "That's all I know. Promise."

Sam picked up a stone and played with it. "You did the right thing, putting it in there. Neither of us are who we were fifteen years ago. And if there's a chance we can close this once and for all, we should take it."

Ethan seemed surprised by the steel in his voice. Sam wasn't. He'd been thinking of these men and what they'd done to his life for the past decade. He tossed his stone away and picked up his water bottle. "Thanks, Ethan. I can take it from here. But you seem like a good man to have in a fight." He grinned.

He couldn't help but notice the spark of pride in Ethan's eyes. The young man appeared to reach some sort of decision and said, in a rush of trust, "You know… I never told anyone about… what happened."

Sam unscrewed the water bottle cap, feeling the ridges in his thumbs like fingerprints. "I know."

"You believe me?" Ethan's eyes narrowed. "How do you know that I didn't tell anyone?"

Sam grinned around the certainty in the pit of his stomach and drained his water. It felt like the same temperature as his blood. "Because if you had, you and I would already be dead."

Chapter Thirty-Seven

The sun was still high in the sky but sinking toward slumber. Ethan walked, making his way along the tree-lined avenue, barely noticing the smooth sandstone beneath his feet. Broken and misaligned sections here and there required his attention; bumps in the road were inevitable or, as his Dad used to say 'shit happens', and damn. Shit was happening.

The sounds and scents of summer swarmed around him. Nighthawks coasted on the thermals high above. Ethan had walked these streets countless summer evenings, just like this.

But, this time? This time was not the same. This time, Ethan walked the streets in a daze; the kind exclusive and born of first-hand experience and almost impossible to believe even happened in the first place — first time you've been in a fight, a particularly bad bike accident, a car accident — personalized discoveries that never needed to happen. During and after those moments? They jolt us closer yet further from ourselves and they keep the world at a distance while we move through it with a thousand-yard-stare. Like ghosts.

He shuffled along, scuffing through the grass. It was cool on his feet and brought him back to himself as the cars swooshed by on the old streets.

He saw it again and again in his mind: the knife on the back of the man's throat; the shimmer of heat rising from the pavement.

Ethan jolted awake with a shout.

He lay there rigid, panting, in the sweaty dark.

He'd never forgotten that afternoon. Never forgotten it, but he hadn't dreamt about it in years. It was seeing Sam that brought it back, he thought.

Ethan stared at the ceiling as the quiet sounds of bugs and camp stirring told him it was between three and four in the morning. Too late to sleep again, and too hot. Ethan put his arms behind his head and lay back. Instead of the ceiling, he saw memories. He remembered, as vividly as he had dozens of times previously, that fateful day that he'd met Sam Reilly.

He'd reached his house, the one with the peeling white paint exposing the cheap siding underneath. The trash reeked. He had to remember to take it out. He stood there with his key in his hand, hearing the television already on, blaring The Price Is Right reruns through the torn screen windows already attracting bugs. The creak of the ancient fridge, the clunk of the handle—home.

In this hot, trembling night where anything seemed possible, Ethan wildly considered the possibility of running away. Away from all of this and the men in black and the clunking empty fridge and the sweaty, hard hands.

His father heaved himself out of the nubby couch, hacking and coughing. "Aww, you dumb shit. Could have told you not to bet it all…"

Ethan's thin shoulders shook in a moment of cowardice… or courage. He never could figure out which.

He reached for the handle and pushed the dirty button on the screen door. It screeched open as it always did and slammed closed with a whine.

His shoes stuck to the dirty linoleum in the heat when he came through the kitchen. His father had shouted from the living room, made a villain by the flashing light of the television.

The burly arms under the fat, the beer bottle, the clench of fear in the pit of his stomach…

He remembered the shout, as it had been shouted many times before. "ETHAN!"

Ethan squared his skinny shoulders and prepared himself. He stepped forward into the living room. He kept his chin down. Better not to make eye contact. He'd learned that, at least.

Unfortunately, this line of sight brought what his father held into his vision. Ethan gulped. The gun rested in his father's palm like it was made to fit between those callouses.

He remembered how his father had held the pistol out. His voice had been quiet, the way it was before the particularly bad wailings and Ethan knew he was in for it. Split decision- lie or not?

Deep down, though, he knew it was no decision at all. His father always knew when he lied. And it was always, always worse.

"Boy. What do you know about this?"

Ethan looked away. "I- I don't know anything about guns. Or your gun."

He flashed again on the dead cats, the scene in the desert... irrationally hot tears sprouted behind his eyes. He couldn't blink or he'd make them fall, and he didn't have the courage to wipe them away. The scene blurred.

His father hefted the pistol in his hand and Ethan remembered the weight in his own. He wondered if his father would shoot him. Wondered if it were loaded. Sweet Jesus, what had he done? He slanted a glance around the room, trying to see how many empty bottles littered the furniture and the floor.

His father turned the gun in his hand. "Well ain't that the truth. Don't even know how to clean it properly. Stupid boy." Ethan kept his eyes on the floor. His father hawked and spat. "Did you shoot it?"

Ethan shook his head.

"Don't you fucking lie to me boy." His father's voice shook with rage, with some emotion that made Ethan think there must be quite a lot of liquor in him already, which was weird, because he hadn't seen that many bottles. Maybe he'd had a lot at the bar...?

"Don't you fucking lie to me! And look at me! LOOK AT ME when I'm talking to you!"

Ethan raised his eyes with all the courage he had. His father's eyes were red and blood shot and his face splotchy in the heat. He brandished the gun with a glare. Ethan shook his head, trying not to sound desperate. Trying not to sound weak.

"No... no... Josh did. I just took it. And the bullets."

They stared at each other. He shook and his father shook. He knew he was going to die.

His father pointed the gun at him, and Ethan started to cry. Snotty tears, hot and helpless. He couldn't stop. His father stared at him, shaking, brandishing the gun steady on his son's gleaming face.

Then he turned the barrel toward his own face and stared at it. His finger tensed on the trigger, just the tiniest bit.

Ethan could only watch him and sob, the snot slick and sweet on his lips. The birds and sprinklers sang outside. He didn't know what he hoped for.

Then his father threw the gun away and held out his hands.

Ethan didn't know what he wanted. When his dad reached out for him, he flinched back. He couldn't help it.

He watched his father's face crumple in unbearable pain. He put his meaty palm over his drunkard's face with the veiny nose. His shoulders shook. Ethan thought he was crying.

Ethan shuffled.

This time when he reached out, his hands empty, his arms limp, Ethan edged forward, tentatively.

The big hand cupped his neck. Ethan tried to keep the tears in, tried to be a man, but he couldn't. Didn't want to. He slid his small arms around his father's thick, strong waist and together they sat there on that gray nubby couch, so worn the stuffing shone through the way it had when Ethan was little, while the TV blared some game show and the evening light slanted on toward night.

The next shock came the morning after, when Ethan had turned on the TV as his father sat surly and stubborn at the breakfast table, rummaging the kitchen counters like a bear in a cabin. "Coffee in here somewhere," he'd growled. "Got to be…"

Ethan flicked the TV to the morning cartoons, feeling hopeful. Maybe he could get a glimpse while his father was distracted. He didn't trust this fragile peace. Didn't trust this new world of hope.

But the morning cartoons weren't on. It was some talking head on the news. Ethan flicked the channel. The next one had been replaced, too.

By the fourth station that had been replaced by somber news anchors Ethan stopped switching and listened.

A man who looked vaguely familiar in a slick suit that looked hurriedly put on, with too greasy hair that had been rumpled by hands, was speaking. His eyes were red, and his voice shook. Ethan didn't recognize him.

"Dad," he said. His father grunted at him. Ethan twisted in his seat to see. "Dad. Who's-"

"The Vice President, Ethan. Shut up." The coffee pot gurgled. His father looked sick. His shoulders dropped. "Christ, I'm sorry boy. Just- I want to hear."

Ethan stared. He'd never seen his father give a damn about the news. Now here he was, no longer rummaging, and listening. Leaning on the counter, clutching his cup of steaming coffee.

The talking head stared into the camera, shuffling his notes in shock. Ethan remembered the open carton of milk on the table had smelled just the little bit off. Ethan filled his cup anyway and sniffed. Still drinkable. He drank, keeping his eyes on the tiny grainy television set wedged between the empty bread box and the microwave with the crust of spaghetti sauce on the handle.

"The President of the United States has been killed. His plane was hijacked by a man who as yet remains unknown. Security footage from Air Force One shows…"

A man in black.

"The president's face was gouged with this symbol…"

Ethan spilled his milk.

Now, as Ethan lay there in the dark surrounded by the sounds of the rising camp, remembering back to that fateful day in the desert all those years ago, it occurred to him, not for the first time, that perhaps Sam Reilly hadn't been entirely truthful with him.

Men shouted outside. It would be dawn soon. Dawn came early in the desert. He had a busy day ahead. He had decisions to make.

Sam had looked good. Healthy, happy, whole. He looked like a man pleased with his life. He didn't look like a killer.

But if there was one thing that Ethan had learned serving his tours in the military it was that killers didn't necessarily look like killers. The ones that didn't were always the most dangerous. The ones that didn't, were smart.

In any case, Ethan recognized the signs of a man who was questing for something, always searching. A man who couldn't stop until he found it. A man who could feel victory, but rarely satisfaction. Fanaticism had many faces. Ethan had seen a few of those while serving here, too. He wondered how Sam Reilly had spent the past fifteen years. If he'd flown any planes in that time.

Ethan took the key he'd taken from that tunnel from beneath his shirt. He'd kept it hidden at the last minute during his meeting with Sam, tucked away safe. Now he felt the contours in the dark, wondering what the hell he'd gotten himself into.

Chapter Thirty-Eight

The Ancient City of Palmyra – Syria

As Sam approached through the camp, he saw the team waiting at the end of a dusty path. He saw Ethan shake his head at the offer of a cigarette and take a healthy swig from the canteen on his hip instead. The boys all ribbed him for it, and he took their teasing in his stride, dishing back as good as he got.

Sam grinned. Had they not been in state-of-the-art military gear, Sam would've thought of them as any other group of friends. Their manner was so friendly and colloquial that he wouldn't have even thought they were the world's top-tier killing machines if they weren't holding their M16's. And even still, the looks they shared reminded Sam of the bond he had with Tom, unbreakable to the end.

However, there was a hardness to them that Sam couldn't quite put his finger on. Sam looked more closely. They stood in a way that made it perfectly clear that they trusted each other with their lives. He remembered that feeling.

For an unexpected moment, Sam had the rare advantage of seeing them before they saw him. He sized them up in that moment and decided to trust them.

Then they looked at him.

Their shoulders went back, their hands went to their weapons and their stares bored into Sam. Sam suddenly felt very small.

Ethan walked up to Sam. "Mr. Reilly." His eyes were friendly but guarded. "Sam. Why are you back?" His lip quirked and his hands clasped in front of him as if in prayer. "Did you lose something?"

Sam shook Ethan's offered hand, silently sighing in relief. "I have a proposition for you."

"A proposition?" Ethan glanced at his companions. "What- what are you talking about?" His gaze suggested he knew why Sam might be here and he wasn't sure he wanted anything to do with it.

Sam shrugged, glancing around at the men, blatantly eavesdropping. "You gentlemen up for a mission?" He spread his hands. "You'd be helping out the secretary of defense quite a bit, actually."

Their brows rose and reassessed Sam's importance. "Ethan. Who the he- who is this?"

Sam looked straight at Ethan and made his case. "The key. We need to retrieve it."

"What's he talking about, Ethan?" asked one of the SEALs.

Sam clasped his hands behind his back and shifted his weight. He needed these men on his side. More importantly, he needed to get the key. But problems tend to be solved when you have trained military professionals at the ready to help. He nodded at them with a smile. "Ethan knows."

Ethan sighed and shrugged, as if humoring Sam, but his eyes showed some respect at Sam's name drop, though his face suggested he wasn't quite sure he believed it. "Remember that time we took fire back near Palmyra? In the dunes? When we had to break and head for the caves in the back?"

The men nodded. Ethan spread his hands. "You remember how I fell through the floor?"

Laughter, true affection. "Yeah, I remember how we had to haul your ass out after we done all the work."

Ethan grinned, letting them have their fun. "Yeah, you're a bad ass, man. Bring it here, I'll give it a kiss." More laughter and Ethan turned serious. "Well, there was some passageway down there, some tunnel-like thing under the cave floor. Should probably make a note of where that was in case it ends up being a hideout, if it's not already." He shook off the thought. "When I was down there, I saw a drawing on the wall." He gestured toward Sam. "This man came yesterday with a message from the U.S. Department of Defense. It turns out it might have been important. There might have been something I missed. An important artifact we need to retrieve from those caves. Something like a key, right?" He glanced over at Sam.

Not bad, thought Sam. "Yeah. That's right. It's a key."

"But what I don't get," continued Ethan, "is the timing. You do know this is-"

"Wait, what the hell? He wants us to go back?" A big man with a small goatee folded his arms, laughing.

"Didn't we just say we got our asses handed to us that day?"

"Maybe he likes it rough…"

Sam knew it couldn't have been that easy, but he was surprised by the tone of excitement that simmered amongst the men. Then, he reflected, maybe there wasn't all that much action out here. Good to whet their appetites. "Yeah, I do, unfortunately. Want to go back, I mean. Not that I like it-" He felt himself reddening. Been a while since he'd been around a military sense of humor. He spread his hands. "Hell, it's orders. I can't mention much, except that it's for national security reasons."

One of Ethan's mates stepped forward and crossed his arms. "Hey, listen man. You can't tell us what's good for the country."

A gleaming black man adjusted his cap. "We've done more than you'll ever know about for the - good of the country." The SEAL made air quotes with his fingers.

Ethan stepped forward but Sam spoke before he could.

"Listen. I know that I'm a foreigner to you guys- an outsider. But I served my time in the Marines. In the 47th. I saw action in Afghanistan and I've served on soil back home, since. I know I look like I've gone soft around the middle- hell. I have gone soft around the middle." Not too soft, though, Sam knew, or he wouldn't have said it. And the way the SEALs eyed his civilian middle made him think they'd noticed, too. "But you have to trust me. The fact that I'm even here means I know that this is important." Sam spoke with sincerity. He knew that he couldn't find the key without a team. He also knew that this was his only chance for a competent one. "It's already approved by the Pentagon. Black-label mission, everything off-book, yet still approved."

Sam saw the SEALs looking at each other. Their faces were expressionless. Sam knew that meant that thoughts whirred behind their eyes.

"You can trust him." Ethan raised his eyebrows and Sam started in surprise at the support. "And he's telling the truth. He does have connections to D.C."

They glanced at each other, a silent conference amongst themselves. Slowly, arms went behind backs in acceptance, military chins raised. Ethan's smoking friend ground his cigarette into the dust beneath his boot. "We'll do it. But just in-and-out, within a day."

Sam sighed in relief. He wouldn't have to go by himself after all. As competent as he felt in this area, he didn't know this exact terrain and he didn't know the threats. He was glad to have backup if backup was needed. He nodded at Ethan. "Thanks."

Ethan nodded back. "I'll get the gear." He checked his watch. "None of us are on duty until eighteen hundred. So, we've got some time. Should be enough." He quirked a brow at Sam. "Wonder if we told the Sergeant if we were on defense business he'd let us skip mess duty."

Sam shook his head. "You can't tell anyone. It's cleared with the Pentagon, but the fewer people here who know about it, the better. For now, let's just say you're showing me the sights."

Ethan looked at him a long time, weighing him. But finally, he nodded and cast a glance at his water canteen.

Right away, the team broke up and started loading weapons and other supplies that they would need for the expedition. Sam was astonished at the speed and efficiency with which the SEALs moved.

He was too used to low-skill locals packing for him, but the SEALs were certainly a different breed. They barely spoke to each other, yet the proper equipment was getting loaded on the truck. Communication was merely a series of finger gestures and one-word commands. Like a well-oiled machine, people went to and fro, each component, knowing their role. A sense of pride welled up in him. These men had sacrificed years of their life, and possibly even life itself, to serve the country that had given them so much.

A tap on his shoulder startled Sam out of his thoughts of admiration. "You do know we're in a war zone, right?" Ethan's level eyes gave nothing away.

Sam's gaze delivered the same, right back, letting the boy read the truth.

Boy. Who was he kidding? If he was right, this man hadn't been a boy for a long time, not even when he *was* a boy. He shook his head. "This is more important than you can even imagine."

One of Ethan's mates burst out laughing. "What kind of damn key is so important? Is it going to take over the world or something? Because in that case, can we hurry it up? Always wanted to rule the world."

Sam shook his head. "Guys, listen to me." They turned suddenly serious at his tone, for the first time recognizing one of their own as Sam assumed the mantle of command. Boots shuffled; hands stilled. Faces turned to his. "This key doesn't have anything to do with ISIS. But it's big." He turned his gaze to Ethan and Ethan looked back. "Bigger than we thought."

Silence as the men looked at each other, wondering just exactly what they were risking their necks for and curious to know if it was worth it.

Sam spread his hands. "Look- at the end of the day, I don't need you to come with me. I know you've got duties here. I just need someone to show me the way. Then I'll…"

A snort emerged from the ranks; Sam couldn't see from where. "You'll what? Go on your own?"

Laughter rippled. "That an AK in there, Marine, or you're just happy to see us?"

A short Marine in a QUEEN t-shirt slapped him on the shoulder. "Don't worry, old man. We'll give you a hand." He assumed a prim expression. "Just make sure you get us back by dinner."

Sam grinned even as he winced. Old man?

Ethan approached him as the men readied themselves to move out. Sam met him with open palms. Ethan quirked an eyebrow. "This is borderline insanity, Sam. You know that, right? I mean-" He gestured to the grit and the dust and the oven-like heat, fumes of gasoline and the sound of guns. "Do you even want to be here?"

Sam took a breath. Complicated question. Did he want action? Action that meant something. That made a difference. Action that obliterated all sense of self and time, and let you be simple, wholly animal?

For Ethan's sake, he just grinned. "Oh man. No, I don't. Frankly, I want to be SCUBA diving off a beach in the Bahamas, boy." He gave a dramatic sigh as Ethan graced him with one of his rare full grins. "But our country wants you and me to locate an ancient key holding incredible military value. It just so happens, that key is in a war zone."

Chapter Thirty-Nine

Ethan said, "Hey. Wake up."

Sam awoke to a tap on his shoulders; someone's hand shaking him. For a moment he didn't know where he was-why was he moving? What was happening? And then it came back to him. He realized that Ethan was speaking to him. "What?"

He had never slept on a helicopter before. He'd tried not to sleep on this one, too, but it had only been a week ago that he'd been underwater in Mexico and a mere day since he'd arrived in the Middle East. And, despite what he wanted the Marines he was currently in command of to believe, he wasn't as young as he'd once been. He'd closed his eyes to think, feeling his head knock and rock against the hard, plastic back of the helicopter seat... then blackness.

When he slept, his mind was blank.

Ethan released his hand on his shoulder. "We're landing in two. We need you alert." His tone was surprisingly gentle, Sam thought. Far from his ordinary gruff self. Maybe he realized that sometimes, shouting wasn't always the best form of communication in a high-tension situation like this. As if reading his mind, Ethan handed him a bottle of water with a wry grin.

Sam took it and twisted the top in thanks.

As he drank, Sam looked outside the window of the helicopter that he and the rest of the team were crammed in, plus all their gear. Beyond the tiny oval window he couldn't see anything but mountains for miles. Their snow-capped peaks formed a ridge of rocky tops going in a pair of lines, running side by side as far as the eye could see. Clouds surrounded the caps, like a thick layer of luminous fog. *The entire scene is just like a movie*, Sam thought. *Surreal.* There were no gunshots to be heard from up here and the mountains were picture-postcard perfect; as if it'd been untouched since God had proclaimed '*Let it be.*'

He looked at Ethan. "You sure this is a warzone?"

"Oh, they're down there, all right. You just can't see them," replied one of the SEALs, smirking.

Sam squinted and tried to make out what was under the high-altitude clouds. He thought he could barely make out a couple of land formations – a valley here, maybe a forest, there. On one hand he knew it would be suicide to explore the area in a combat zone solo. However, his natural curiosity was yearning to camp out and discover every secret that the mountains kept hidden. It would be so easy to disappear out here…

As he shook off his thoughts, the pilot's voice suddenly pierced through Sam's headset.

"Prepare for a hot drop at the LZ."

Sam felt a drop in his stomach as the helicopter quickly decelerated, losing altitude and speed. Soon they were hovering barely five feet above a grassy clearing. The helicopter blades beat the air so hard that the trees around the clearing bent beneath their force.

One of the SEALs leaned over Sam in his seat and slid the only door on the left, open. The deafening roar spilled into the cockpit, breaching the noise canceling function in his headphones. Sam unstrapped his safety belt and looped his headphones over the seat.

"Go, go, go." Ethan commanded with a shout, bellowing in his ordinary, military-style crispness. Sam held onto his sudden nerves, knowing how foolish it looked when you rushed- and how easily things might go wrong when you were in too much of a hurry. He made his movements quick and precise and hopped off the helicopter with the rest of the team.

As he hit the ground, the SEALs formed a defensive circle around Sam, their assault rifles equipped with optic scopes bristling. Sam hoped it was second nature and not because they'd spotted trouble already.

He hitched his bag higher, wishing for that gun instead of a radio. He checked its position just to make himself feel better but, frankly, what good would it be in a firefight? "What the hell are you doing?"

Ethan raised his left hand to pause his squadron. "Didn't I say this was a warzone? We can't be caught off guard here, especially when you've dragged us this far for, what was it? A key?" He used the same hand and pointed forwards. "Convoy formation, move out." Ethan gave his squad a glare and ushered them forward. "Make it quick. Don't none of us want to be here longer than we have to."

The soldiers fell out and pushed forward, in formation.

Sam followed them, jogging lightly as they made their way through the scrub and rocks. The high altitude in the mountains was something Sam wasn't used to. He was far more comfortable holding his breath at sea level, but the thin air gave him the sensation of being able to breathe, but just not enough. SEALs take huge steps. Sam found himself gasping for air as he attempted to catch up with their large strides.

For at least ten minutes the group navigated back and forth around trees and bushes, which gave way to scrubby sand dunes, until suddenly Ethan stalled, holding up his hands. The team froze, weapons out, scanning the trees. Sam froze too, going for his radio and on high alert, trying not to pant.

Ethan peered forward, then advanced cautiously, beckoning. It took Sam a moment to realize he meant him and even longer to see what he was beckoning toward; a small cave opening. He never would've spotted it unless he was looking specifically for it. It was hidden behind a small bush and he was amazed that the SEAL team even managed to notice it in the first place. Before he had a chance to comment, he was ushered forward by Ethan.

He gripped his radio and ducked inside.

Blinded by the sun glinting off the sand and rock, Sam couldn't see anything in the pitch-black cave. One by one the SEALs turned on their flashlights, expertly aiming their sights around the cavern, as if clearing a room. Sam heard a scoff behind him.

"You didn't bring a flashlight?" asked Ethan. "You wanted to explore a cave in the middle of a desert and you didn't bring a damned flashlight?"

"Uh, no." replied Sam, flustered. "Didn't have one." He shrugged, giving in. "Look, I wasn't expecting this to be a…"

"I know the speech. I've heard it hundreds of times from soldiers, citizens and people like you. And I don't give a damn if you're pissing your pants out of fear. Now set yourself straight before you get us killed." Ethan growled, tossing Sam a small penlight. "Don't turn it on. It's for emergencies."

"Thanks." Sam's cheeks flushed red-hot from embarrassment in the cool dark. He hoped with their flashlights they couldn't see it.

They might not see anyway – the team had already moved down the cave system. Sam shifted to catch up and realized the floor was wet. Why the hell- Of course. It's a cave. There's going to be water. Urgently yet carefully and with knowledge honed from years of cave exploration, Sam made his way over to the team, gingerly avoiding unassuming rock outcroppings that could trip them up. The SEALs somehow did this while looking forward and with guns out.

As he followed, Sam looked around the cave. The walls were rough, and the ceilings had more stalactites than Sam could count. It didn't look like the ruins of an ancient city. "Hey, Ethan, you sure this is the place?" he called.

Ethan glanced back from his exploration along a far wall. He kicked some leaves. "Yeah, I know it doesn't look like it. Just be patient." He grinned. "You'll find it soon enough."

"All right." Sam shrugged. "You're the boss."

Sam followed Ethan toward the wall, stepping around the uncertain terrain. At least in situations like these he knew that his body and training would prevail over his brain. Even if he did forget his flashlight.

He joined Ethan at the wall. "What are we looking for? How did you find it before?"

Sam took one step too many and barely saved himself from falling into the hole in the ground in front of him, which he hadn't seen in the darkness. He turned, fighting his pounding heart, to see Ethan grinning.

"Like that."

Asshole. Sam glared at him. "It's not funny. That could have been-"

"Save it, pops. I've got your back."

Oddly, Sam believed him. Reluctantly, he grinned back.

Ethan moved forward, shining his flashlight down into a hole in the ground. Below, about fifteen feet down, Sam could see a room. Now he understood. While the cave had been a natural formation until now... In the dim illumination of Ethan's light, Sam felt how Lord Carnarvon must have felt seeing King Tut's tomb for the first time – shadowy glimpses of a grand past. Pieces of a whole. The familiar high stairs, unfriendly ornamentation and impeccable stone works called back: It was exactly like Xibalba. Triumph sang in his veins.

But there was one crucial difference.

He turned to Ethan. He could hardly contain his excitement, his heart pumping at a fever pitch, but first things first. "How are we going to get down?"

Scoffing, a SEAL tossed him a rope. Sam silently cursed himself, then managed a smile. The SEAL was clearly expecting him to throw the rope back to set up, but Sam knelt and fixed it to an outcropping of rock perfectly positioned for the purpose.

Ethan folded his arms. "Might want to let one of us do that, Sam. Want you to get to the bottom all in one piece, you know?"

Sam finished the knot and gave it an experimental tug. It would do. He dusted his hands and looked up at Ethan. "She'll work. I've been climbing since before you were born."

Before they could scoff or mutter among themselves, Sam gripped the line and hoisted himself over the edge and into the abyss.

He wished he'd thought to bring gloves, he'd thought as his feet touched down. The rope was hell on hands. Water under the bridge and all, now. It also appeared to be the least of his problems.

Shaking his hand out, the first things he saw were the skeletons. Sam instantly knew these were old explorers, apparently several who'd come before him. They had probably arrived in this place, perhaps run out of air or food and been unable to climb- or navigate- their way out. They had chosen to perish with the key. Their bones lay in perfect, undisturbed silence around the entire clearing below the entrance. Some of them held their arms closely to their ribs. Did any of them have the key? Sam's skin crawled at the thought of breaking apart the dead to find what he was after, but he had to admit, had roles been reversed there'd only be one place they'd locate the key. Clutched in his cold, dead hands. They were probably clutching the keys as if their life depended on it before they died; apparently it hadn't made a bit of difference. Speaking of which, Sam wondered, how *did* they die?

Looking both left and right, Sam stepped delicately over femurs and skulls and unlike Xibalba, there were no spears or crushed bones — anywhere. It was as if the explorers' lives were sucked right out of their bodies and without a trace as to how or why. A shiver ran down his spine.

Would he end the same way? Sam glanced at the SEAL team shimmying down the rope. They were here because of him. Would all of them die, too?

He chided himself, feeling stupid for conjuring up trouble when historically, trouble found *him*. Following Ethan's earlier advice, this 'pop' needed to stay focused and deal with one thing at a time.

Ethan had already lowered himself to the room's floor and was busy inspecting the unsettling remains. As he advanced into the dark, one of the SEALS – Min, maybe his name — began kicking one of the skulls around like a morbid game of soccer. It rattled, teeth falling out with each push and roll.

"Hey," Sam said. Min stopped and stared confrontationally at Sam. "Mind if you stop? Doesn't seem like the best way to respect the dead, especially when we don't even know how they died and you're screwing up any evidence that might be visible in situ."

For a moment silence reigned. Except... a macabre ring of rhythmic sounds bounced off the room's walls, the notes plucked by Min's now abandoned 'soccer ball' grating against ancient floor's uneven rock, expending its last gasp of kinetic energy as it completed a series of ever-shrinking revolutions over and around a small indent it had found. In peace, it rolled to a full stop.

All of the SEALS burst out laughing. Sam felt his cheeks turning beet red. Not from embarrassment. From anger.

"You have no idea how much death we see. This is nothing," Ethan said between heaves of laughter that ricocheted painfully off the high walls.

"All right, all right. I get it. Still I'd appreciate it if you stop playing football in a temple."

Min suddenly looked uneasy. "Did you just say something about a temple, man?"

He glanced away from the skull resting at his feet and held up his hands, respectfully. "Sorry," he said, and gulped.

Sam took a deep breath, turned away and tried to just let it go. He took a step forward, trying to get his bearings.

He glanced at Ethan, watching him warily. Ethan's focus turned to the wall.

Sam followed. If he'd been nervous before...

In front of him on the wall was the giant map, engraved and at least thirty feet long. This must have been what Ethan was referring to. He'd seen this before, in Afghanistan. It had been a little bit different, but the clawing feelings of unease... same.

Ethan had said the key had been in the center. The key had been in the center of the one he'd found, too. He looked around. No skeletons nearby. Did that mean... Sam quickly took his borrowed penlight out and pointed its light toward the etching.

The light shimmered over an obstacle in front of the map that he hadn't noticed earlier in the dimness, assuming it was just another part of the shadows. It looked like a pedestal, but he couldn't see what was on top of it yet.

Sam walked backward as far as he could go, careful of his footing, never taking his eyes off the pedestal. The SEALs watched him with something akin to wary respect. Or they might think he was crazy and if spikes shot out of the floor, they were judging whether they had time to run or if the spikes would take them out with him.

He was crazy.

Sam jumped when his back hit the wall. He let out a little sob of a sigh and craned his gaze up. Still nothing. As far back as he could go, and he still couldn't see.

He made his way across the cavern until he was standing just under the pedestal. He reached up, but it was just as he'd thought- he was too short to reach. He wasn't entirely sure he had the strength to pull himself up. Better not risk it.

He glanced at Ethan. "Give me a boost?"

After a moment the younger man crouched and braced his hands. Sam steadied himself on the already steady palms and before he could say if he was ready or not, he was rising through the air. He clutched the top of the platform when he could, peering up over the obsidian column.

Damn.

"See anything?" Ethan called from below.

Sam struggled to pull his flashlight from his pocket and shone it over the surface just to make sure. Then he felt with his free hand. Carvings, yes. But...he went over it to make sure.

Nothing. No wonder he couldn't see what was on top. There was nothing on top.

"Come on!"

Ethan lowered him back down and Sam dusted his hands on his pants as, deep down, his heart sank. He hadn't ever expected it to be that easy to find the keys, but seeing the empty platform made it real. He took a deep breath. He couldn't let it get to him.

Ethan raised his brows. "Well? Did you get it?"

Sam looked at him. "You were down here alone. How did you get up there? WHY did you go up there?"

The two men looked at each other and Sam thought of his father, trying to catch him in a lie as a little boy. "Ethan," he said. "When you came down here the first time, you're sure the key was here?"

Ethan blinked, looking truly startled. "Yeah, right up on that platform. Did you get it?"

"No." Sam watched Ethan closely and wasn't surprised when the man laughed.

"Well, now I know why we came along." He pushed his sleeves up. "Min!" He called. "Give me a minute…"

"It's gone." Sam kept his tone low and steady, but not unpleasant. He furrowed his brows.

Ethan stalled, mid-call. "What? No way. It was right here a couple of weeks ago." Ethan bounded over to the platform, and, easy as breathing, crouched, then surged up in an impressive leap that took him to the top of the platform effortlessly. He hung there with his Marine-toughened arms and legs dangling, searching. Sam had a twinge of hope that Ethan would find something, crushed as Ethan lowered himself back down with a look of disappointment.

And yet, Sam's years of experience sensed something was off; instincts and intuition could be misinterpreted, but never wrong. But before Sam had any time to flesh his thoughts out, Ethan reacted with a glare, then looked around.

"It was right here, I promise. I don't-"

"It's fine." Sam scowled, running a hand through his hair. Though Ethan wasn't the reason the key was gone, he felt disappointed in the SEAL but showed restraint in showing it. "Sorry I wasted your time."

There it was again, that 'off' look. It was gone so fast Sam wondered if he'd imagined it in the dark.

Sam shrugged as the SEALs muffled their grumbles, remaining professional and climbed their way back topside. Ethan watched them go. "What's next?"

Sam sighed, watching their ascent. "Now, I have to go back to Washington." He turned his full-on gaze toward Ethan, and they stood, regarding each other with pure military-born stoicism. "And tell the secretary of defense that someone beat us to it."

Chapter Forty

Pentagon, Virginia

Sam sat, hunched over his laptop on his desk for the first time in what felt like years. Maybe it had been years, considering all his recent memories were of life-threatening journeys and explorations around the globe. Now it was like he was just another nine-to-five office worker, same as everyone else.

It was weird.

Sam rubbed his temples gingerly. The headache of the situation at Palmyra was wearing him down. He could feel his own exhaustion in his bones, starting with the dull ache at the small of his back and crescendoing to waves of pain spiking his neck and skull. He didn't know if it was the jet lag, the helicopter, the tension of imminent death, or the potential release of massively classified secrets, but he was in a bad way.

For a moment he stared at the screen, trying to get a grip on himself as the screen wavered before eyes that were on the verge of tears from exhaustion.

Maybe I should stop. *I've looked at nearly everything*, he thought, but he knew that he couldn't quit. He'd pulled some strings both stateside and in the Middle East and one of his military contacts had gotten Ethan's helmet footage from the day of the attack. It was likely grasping for straws, but Sam had a hunch and he couldn't leave any stones unturned. Sure, Ethan hadn't explicitly given Sam permission to look through the footage; in fact, judging from the depths of which his contact had pulled the reel, the SEAL looked like he was trying to hide it.

Sam tapped some more keys with a little more vigor. No worries. If Ethan thought that his contacts with the military were better than Sam's, he had another thing coming. Sam could summon the authority and clearance to snatch one of those chaotic helicopter rides, hopping from airport to airport in the Middle East, in his sleep.

Sleep.

Sam rubbed his temples and pushed away the thought, glancing around the sterile space. It was business as usual in the Pentagon: Printers hummed constantly and employees murmured and laughed, except the printed papers were likely top-secret and those workers probably needed a high security clearance to even talk about anything here. He still couldn't wrap his head around how casual it was.

Better not to think about it. Putting it out of his mind, Sam connected the hard drive into his laptop. The screen with the Pentagon logo faded out into a green background asking for user credentials. He entered the decryption key, then waited as the machine whirred to life. He opened the file and began to watch.

The video started as the team was in the middle of a desert. The camera was faced at two helmet-wearing SEALs in some kind of vehicle, but it was too shaky to identify exactly whom. Sam assumed they were the same ones that escorted him into the caves. Then the camera lurched and there was a confusion of light and dark, followed by an abrupt shift as all of them suddenly piled out of the truck and ran outside.

Bright light, chaos of sand, greenery and sky. Figures almost indiscernible in the distance, concealed behind shrubbery and stones. Ethan threw a smoke grenade into the desert in the insurgents' direction, presumably. Running under the bullets whizzing over his head, Ethan sprinted into the valley that Sam had been in only a few days before. As expected, the leader ushered his team inside the cave, then ducked in himself, making sure to cover the entrance with the bush. Even in a firefight, Ethan kept his wits about him. Impressive.

Sam kept his eyes trained on the screen as he leaned over and reached into his backpack to pull out a pair of earbuds; he never knew if any sort of clue might come up in audio form.

He fit them in his ears and had to admit it was going as expected. So far, Ethan's story checked out.

The screen now showed Ethan carefully making sure no one in the team had any severe injuries. The SEALs discussed what to do, eventually settling on going deeper inside the cave.

Yes, it was a military operation and insurgents could arrive at any moment, but Sam was starting to get impatient. He grabbed a bobble head of the President off the desk and started twisting it as he skipped forward in the video. Whose desk was this, even? All he had done was make a couple calls and he had been escorted here. Hopefully they hadn't kicked some intern off his workplace so Sam could stress out about some dumb keys.

Guiltily, Sam found the controls and continued to fast forwarded until he came to the part where Ethan fell down the hole. Then Sam slowed the video down to regular speed. Nothing at all. He leaned back in the office chair.

The video looked around the room as Ethan's head pivoted, then showed the SEAL walking toward the map on the wall.

Sam twisted the bobble head vengefully. The spring started to stretch.

Ethan surveyed the map then strode around the massive podium made of obsidian. Ethan said something to his mates that Sam couldn't make out, limbered up. Something about nervous energy, he thought.

Ethan made the same impressive leap. The first time, he missed.

Sam watched with increasing admiration as Ethan struggled up the pillar. *No wonder the key had remained safe all these years*, he thought. *There'd never been a goddamn Navy SEAL going after it before.*

Ethan hauled himself all the way up, muscles bulging. Clearly, he was stronger than Sam. He stood on the top of the stone pillar and surveyed the chamber. Then he bent and swiped at the top of it.

From the camera angle it was hard to see, but Sam thought he picked something up…?

A shout from the team and Ethan stood in a rush, as if embarrassed at being caught horsing around.

Ethan dropped back to the ground, but he didn't seem victorious. Sam shook his head in disappointment.

The cam's footage turned around as Ethan started to walk back toward the team, but Sam caught something on the screen. Wait, what was that? Sam rewound the footage and skipped back to where Ethan had hit the ground. As Ethan crouched, just before he got to his feet, Sam paused the video.

Sam couldn't believe it. Didn't *want* to believe it.

Ethan's hand was clearly inside his jacket pocket.

And just before that…

Sam went back five seconds and then inched forward frame by frame by pressing the right arrow button. It wasn't easy to see, but there was definitely something gripped in Ethan's hand.

Sam replayed back the entire minute of footage where Ethan had clambered to the top of the pillar, on the pillar, then his entire journey back down.

By the time Ethan hit the ground again there was no doubt in Sam's mind.

He rocked back in his chair, dumbfounded.

Ethan had the key.

Sam could feel his pulse quickening. Why would Ethan let it play out this way?

Even before he could ask, he knew the answer, no matter how much he wanted to ignore it.

Sam shook his head. No. There was no way Ethan was working for... them. Before he had called the soldier up for any information the man had about the entire case, he had done a small background check. Everything appeared normal.

Normal at first, his mind supplied. *Remember, the SEAL had refused a more extensive background check for supposed 'government reasons.'*

Sam grabbed the desk phone. He dialed quickly, his fingers trembling over the keypad.

He put the phone to his ear. The screen read: Forensics.

"Yeah, hello? I need a team. Yes. No, no, I'm a guest here, so I should —" He broke off and listened. His brows went up. "An appointment? I need an appointment? Sir, I'm the guest of the sec —" Sam grit his teeth. "Seven days? Sir, perhaps you don't understand. I'm —" Sam slapped the desk with his free hand so hard it hurt. "I'm sorry, sir. You either schedule me for this meeting immediately or I get off this phone and the next call I make will be directly to the secretary of defense herself, and you don't want to know who she'll dial next." He waited, breathing hard, locked on the frozen image of Ethan on the screen. "Yes. I'll hold."

He slammed the phone down and shook his head. Bureaucracy never changes. He shouldn't let himself get angry. Emotions clouded judgment and that was the last thing he could afford.

The green light beeped. Sam picked up the phone and pressed the button. "Yes." Stammering on the other end. "Conference room D? Ten minutes. Yes, I'll be there. Thank you very much for your help."

He hung up. Then he made another call. It was over quickly.

Picking up his laptop, he walked with haste to the conference room. He was pleased when he was greeted by the sight of a full forensics team, prepped and ready by the time he'd opened the door. People called the government inefficient, but it was highly efficient when it was needed to be.

"Hello, gentlemen. And lady." Sam announced, motioning at the lone woman. "I need consultation on some helmet footage. The file is closed to all, but analysis would still be possible without context. The file is being downloaded to all of your computers now."

As if on cue, the analysts' computers started pinging with the notification of a download. Sam had timed the download before his entrance and had done so to add a bit of dramatic flair. They seemed unimpressed. He continued.

"The footage is from a SEAL operative. He's with his team, under fire in an undisclosed location which the taker of this footage declined to describe further. They hide in a cave, fall, and then he retrieves something from the top of an obsidian pillar inside the structure. I believe it is a stone key and if it's true, that key is of utmost importance. I need you all to find any details that I may have missed, and more importantly, find any clues that could lead us to the key's recovery." They looked skeptical, exchanging facial expressions confirming such. Finally, an angry man unstiffened.

"Madame Secretary gave us clearance, sir. We'll get you what we can."

He didn't smile. Sam thought he'd probably never smiled in his life. Sam didn't smile back.

"Thank you. I'll be back in one hour." Sam left the room.

His heart had settled but it didn't stop the anger that was now tinging the already frayed edges of his emotions. Why would Ethan lie to me? The man was young, but he wasn't stupid. Then again, the inexperienced ones always tended to get into the worst situations. No one heard of senior citizens trying to join terrorist organizations or getting indoctrinated by a cult. Idealism made more than a few take crazy risks.

Sam wondered if that meant he was getting old.

After pacing back and forth in front of the door of the conference room for five minutes and receiving confused stares from the team working inside, Sam referenced a Pentagon map conveniently placed near one of the elevators to find the nearest cafe. Half of the buildings had no labels, most likely because they were confidential facilities. He sighed and took the elevator down with a woman in a blue uniform and a federal designator tag with her name proudly displayed as "MARY". The woman stepped off on the second floor and Sam waited an additional floor before he got off and headed for Starbucks. Sam had always found it ironic that among the largest fast-food franchises stationed in the top-security government facility, Taco Bell stood stoically in the middle. He approached the counter and got a coffee and sandwich to calm his nerves. His hand instinctively reached into his back pocket for his phone. Dammit. He'd left it with his backpack upstairs.

Sam had finished his coffee and sandwich by the time he made it back upstairs and was feeling slightly more human. He balled up the plastic wrapper and stuffed it into his coffee cup, then pitched both in a waste bin before wiping his mouth, checking his shirt and rounding the corner leading back into the conference room. "Report, please."

A different man stood up, portly and with the squinty eyes Sam called 'chronic computer screen stare'. "Sir. We found some interesting things that you would probably like to know about. Would you like a full report?"

"No." Sam checked his watch. "Give me a summary now and prepare the footage and data for me to review later."

"Three items of interest, sir. First, the key is certainly on the man. The helmet cams now have a lot of features that not even the soldiers themselves know about. One of them being, the camera is constantly on. The man is shown putting the key in his personal backpack back at base. He goes stateside after, so unless he jettisoned the key on civilian time, it makes sense that it would still be on him."

Sam bristled. More evidence against Ethan.

"Second, he was being watched. The camera has infrared and when they dropped into the cave, it saw a camera watching them in this frame." The man brought up a red and blue picture from the footage. The cave was shown in blue, and then a spot of red. Zoomed in, it was clearly in the shape of a camera."

Sam cut the man off before he had a chance to continue. "Show me, first." After furious typing and mouse clicking, he turned his laptop around and showed Sam the infrared image. It was as accurate as the man's word.

"Of course, only SEALs and other special forces I cannot disclose to you get technology like this. Typically, we only look through these cams during hit operations of high-value targets, or in the event one of our servicemen is killed in combat."

Before Sam had any chance to process the information, the man rambled on.

"This one is the most troubling, sir. The cam is programmed to detect any signal waves near or on the soldier that it's attached to. And it detected a bit stream output to a satellite."

Sam felt dizzy. "What does that mean?"

"The people have a tracker on said Soldier, most likely biological. We have no idea how, when or where it was joined with the soldier, but data doesn't lie."

Sam's heart felt like it was going to burst out of its chest. "Send me the full report, encrypted, with the data. Thank you all for your time."

He didn't hear the polite formalities returned by the analysts, having quickly exited the room. He had to show this to the secretary of defense as soon as possible. He called the Secretary's assistant. "This is Sam Reilly," he said without preamble. "Is she up?"

By now the woman knew his voice. Sam wracked his brain. Angela. Her secretary's name was Angela. "She's in a meeting, Mr. Reilly."

"With who? This is important, Angela."

"Classified, but I can say that it's diplomatic in nature, sir. As you know, Madame Secretary is… very busy. If you would like to leave a voice message or arrange a phone appointment for later—"

"Pull her out." Sam's shoes clipped on the tiles as he moved toward the elevator. Then he changed tack and headed for the stairs. Not today. Angela stammered on the other line.

"Excuse me? Mr. Reilly, I promise I will give her your message as soon as—"

"Just pull her now. I'll be at her office in about as long as it takes me to run down these stairs. I don't have time to wait. A man's life is at stake."

Sam disconnected before he could say anything else.

Sam clattered down the steps, the noise echoed loudly, competing with his chaotic thoughts. He had no idea what he should do. Ethan had seemed like a decent fellow, even going to the trouble of reentering the warzone to supposedly help retrieve the key. Why risk all their lives for something he knew would be a wasted trip; unless he had something major to cover up?

Was he in the glue?

Did they have something on him?

Were his actions of his own volition?

Was he under threat and ultimately innocent?

What was Sam going to do?

He reached ground level without reaching any conclusions.

Sam rounded the corner quickly, headed to the secretary of defense's office and barged in.

The Secretary was sitting at her desk, and with a scowl. Angela, at the desk nearby, looked like she was going to cry. Shit.

"Why the hell did you call me out from a meeting with North Korea?" The secretary was a formidable woman and Sam had huge respect for her. What he didn't have, was time.

"Well, I didn't know you were in a meeting with a damn nuclear superpower." Sam struggled. "I'm sorry, Madame Secretary, but I..."

"That will be all, Angela. You may go."

Sam asked, "You're firing her?"

The Secretary folded her arms. "I need a team who can protect me and the interests of this country, not letting just anyone through the damn door."

Sam shook his head. "Stop Angela, you're fine. This is more important." He took a deep breath to steady himself. He faced the Secretary full-on. "I found the key, ma'am."

"So retrieve it. What's the problem?"

Sam handed her the summarized report of the forensic analysts. He watched as the Secretary's eyes widened. He allowed himself a small smile of satisfaction: Never in his years working with her had he ever seen the secretary of defense frozen with surprise. I guess you learn, or rather see, something new every day.

The Secretary looked up. "If this is true, then others are coming for him." Her brow furrowed. "He's a SEAL; he'll be hard to silence."

"Which means that his life is in danger." Sam ran his hands through his hair. "For the most part he's on a military base, isn't he? At least on base it won't be so easy to get to him."

The Secretary shook her head. "I don't think he is." She glanced at Angela, who hovered, uncertain what to do. "Leave us, Angela. We'll talk later. For now, make sure no one comes through that door – and I do mean nobody – not even Rocket Man himself." She turned back to Sam as Angela ducked out, closing the door behind her. "Let me bring up his personnel file."

Sam impatiently waited for the database to load. The largest government backed by the most funding, undisputed, had a technical infrastructure requiring a minimum of 30 seconds to load. *If it took this long to spit out a few kilobytes of data, I'd hate to need intel in the heat of battle,* thought Sam.

The Secretary sighed. "He's stateside. He's had three tours of duty and is finally taking some much-needed and well-earned R and R."

Sam stood up. Time was absolutely critical. "Where?"

"I mean, his home, right?"

Sam could not believe his ears. Why would the secretary be joking around at a time such as this? He leaned forward and slapped both hands on the desk. "Where!"

Her easy tone evaporated. "Small condo. A mile from the Navy SEAL base, at Little Creek, Virginia."

Sam was already walking towards the door.

"A thank you would be nice!" the Secretary called after him.

Sam turned around. "The only thank you that's needed is from you to me after I rescue this rogue soldier of yours." Their eyes met, level. It was a little far, but he'd had a bad day. "I think we both know what happens if I don't."

Sam kept his front to her until he was out the door – barely – then turned and strode swiftly down the hall.

A wide-eyed Angela watched him go.

Chapter Forty-One

Little Creek, Virginia

Ethan trudged up the street toward the condo he'd called home for the past two years. He still had to count driveways to find which house was his. The rest of the houses looked eerily the same. The grass was brown from lack of water and too much sun. It rustled in waves with every small gust of wind, creating ripples along the road verge, where it slowly disappeared, like Ethan's thoughts, which floated and fell away.

He flexed the fingers of both hands around the heavy bag of groceries that kept him balanced and resettled his big hikers' backpack on his shoulders. He could have taken a cab to the grocery store three miles away, but he needed the action. He could think better when he walked. Who was he kidding? He hadn't walked six miles, round trip, in a summer heat which felt balmy compared to Syria, merely because he wanted to think. In all honesty, he'd walked to the store and back, even though he wasn't in any mood to cook, because he wanted to *not* think.

It had been two weeks since his last engagement as a SEAL. He'd made it back stateside without incident and had mostly adjusted to the green and the moisture and the unsettling sights of wood siding and asphalt with yellow lines and small-town signage in English. He'd suffered through the well-meaning salutations and proffered speculation about his tour from the small-town gossips and men who'd known him since he was a boy. He had made peace again with small-town-Ethan and he'd gotten used to showers without waiting in line, but he couldn't shrug off the feeling of edgy alertness.

It was like a constant feeling that eyes were watching him. That had always been the case here in Little Creek, par for the course in any small town. But now it felt like he had a weapon trained on his back.

Was this the dreaded post-traumatic stress disorder that was whispered about among all the soldiers, but never high-ranking officers? Sure, they had given the SEALs a lesson on mental health and talked about PTSD, but it was only one class. The lecturers just told them to reference the Health Division and their problems would be solved. But he knew friends who'd fallen away to the supposed "disease". One of them went on a rampage with his family before he was pulled out by the cops and thrown into prison. Others drank themselves into shadows of their former life. Others simply... went crazy. Was it happening to Ethan now?

He shook his head, even though there was no one there, and gripped the bag harder. He had to make sure for himself. No. He knew there were resources out there to help him adjust, but no one had told him explicitly what those resources might be. He was too proud to see a therapist, but he knew deep down that he would have to face his issues someday. He couldn't run forever.

Ethan wiped his brow in the heat. He paused in the middle of the sidewalk, glancing behind himself. It was 3 o'clock on a Wednesday afternoon and the quasi-gated community – with the glorified name of Fox Run – was completely deserted. It was a mile to town, on the edge of the city limits, and it was one of the reasons Ethan had chosen this condo. He didn't want to be bothered and after three tours he didn't want people to ask questions about his military ways.

The town had changed since he was a teenager and his father had moved them to the area. Back then, he'd raced around without a care, safe in the streets, safe in the security of a small town's collective care. Now he saw the hollow, empty eyes of junkies on his way home from the bar and, the kids didn't play on the streets anymore. At least when their parents had anything to say about it. The layoffs had hit hard.

Go off to fight for glory, he thought. *For duty. Come back home to shit. Nothing lasts.*

Three houses. First double driveway. He double checked the number on the mailbox just to be sure. Yes, he was home.

He turned into the drive, bag in hand. If he was lucky, he'd have two hours before he'd have to listen to the arrival of his neighbors.

At least his house was the same. Despite its vibe of constantly being on the verge of collapse, it was surprisingly sturdy, albeit a little sun-bleached. The white paint had faded to more of a yellow, Ethan noticed critically. He'd have to call the condo management and tell them they'd been slacking.

His small patio greeted him with its sad looking hostas and boxwood. He barely bothered anymore. *I should*, he thought. Their yellow leaves were depressing.

Ethan unlocked the door with the key he kept stereotypically under the flowerpot full of dying geraniums that he'd bought on impulse his first night back. His mother had always kept geraniums. As he put the key in the lock, he laughed at himself, wondering how a SEAL could be so inconsiderate of his own safety. But the town was small and everyone respected him. He had never had any problems. These people had known him since he was a boy and if they had tolerated Ethan's father, they would tolerate him, no matter how far down the rabbit hole he fell.

The door shut behind him with a whining snap and he jumped. He scolded himself even as he moved about, instinctively inspecting the room, surveying for any potential blind spots.

The plastic bag filled with vegetables and fruit cut into his fingers and he heaved them up to put them on the counter out of habit, even though the floor here was probably cleaner than any counter he'd come across back East. Ethan rubbed his fingers against the butt of the pistol he kept on his right hip.

Everything quiet. Everything… normal.

He snorted. *Normal. What was normal, anymore?*

Ethan stepped down the empty hall and peeked into the bathroom. Cold and dark as ever. His foot kicked the bedroom door wide open. It squealed in protest and bounced off the far wall with an unsatisfying thud. Dead as a doorknob. The blood rushed up to his cheeks when he saw himself in the mirror, shoulders tensed up and feet spread apart – a fighting stance.

He had to stop doing that. He cracked his neck and loosened up his shoulders. It didn't help.

Ethan entered the room and just stood there. It was the same. And it was different. He shrugged. It was always the same and always different. He blew a thin layer of dust that had collected in the time he'd been gone, off the top of the dresser, noticing that his reflection in the mirror was slightly blurred by dust, too. He looked like a ghost.

Ethan stared himself in the eyes, but wasn't sure what he saw. Then he sighed long and hard, and paused.

He had free time. What could he do? Back at base, there was always another thing to do, another thing to prepare, whether it be an insurgency ambush, another IED sweep, or even routine housekeeping. But back home, he felt purposeless. The problem? Ethan hated that feeling. Instead of relaxing, he would always end up spiraling into self-doubt and hatred over his lost feeling of purpose. The SEALs and Navy were all about *finding your purpose*. Ethan had been built up and trained to be a protector of America and its democracy. But, now what? Sleep at twelve, wake at six, go to the gym, make a healthy meal and repeat? *I need something to do.*

The rage built. *Do something*, his brain repeated. Like it was stuck in neutral, but his pent-up emotions demanded a shift in gears; start in first, jam the pedal and eat up some open road. *This isn't good,* Ethan thought, *I just got home. It's too early to wanna put my goddamn fist through a goddamn door already.*

But what could he do?

His drill instructor's voice flashed into his consciousness. He had found Ethan, green and naive and proud of himself, flipping through a handbook at base. When scolded, he confirmed he'd finished his chores.

The instructor's face had gone red. "Do you know what happened to the last guy that told me he'd finished his work and I found him sitting around, waiting for orders?"

Ethan was regretting his admission. He'd clasped his hands behind his back in an effort at salvation. "Sir, no sir!"

"I killed him!" the drill instructor roared, literally inches away from Ethan's face. It had taken every effort to not grimace as spit flew onto his nose and eyelids.

"Get busy! With anything!"

Good advice now too. Ethan turned his back on his room, shut the door and made his way to the garage.

She was right where he'd left her. Cars had always been an interest of his, one of the only things he and his old man had genuinely bonded over. And this one... this was a beauty.

He felt the tension ease up – a bit. Couldn't help but, in the presence of this, his old NSU RO 80. One of the last European rotary engine cars ever built.

The car had developed an early reputation for unreliability. The RO 80 engine suffered from construction faults, not its only problem, and some of its earlier cars had required a fully rebuilt engine even before it'd spent its first twelve months on the road. Originally, the rotor tip seals had been made in three pieces, out of identical materials. The motor's design caused the center section to wear more quickly at cold starts compared to the other pieces; the worn center pieces allowed the two other parts of the seal to move which in turn, allowed combustion by-product to escape the uneven trio. The tip-seal, center piece, ultimately had to be redesigned using ferritic material and the problem was entirely resolved.

The fact that the rotary engine design had inherently poor fuel economy combined with a poor understanding of the Wankel engine by dealers and service mechanics further deterred the success of this vehicle. By the 1970-model year, most of the reliability issues had been resolved but a necessarily generous warranty policy and damage to the car's reputation had undermined NSU's financial situation irreparably. NSU was acquired by Volkswagen in 1969 and merged with Auto Union to create the modern-day, Audi company.

They had pretty much been phased out of the automobile industry, save for Mazda and a few other sports cars. While the ordinary piston-driven engines had multiple pistons and each one performed all the roles of intake, compression, combustion, and exhaust, a rotary had only one moving part, with four chambers for each of the stages.

What drew Ethan to these antiquated, yet somehow barely relevant engines? He thought maybe it could be the fact that it was so unique – and worked completely different – from everything else. It could be merely because they were COOL: power wrapped up in a sleek package. A combination of impracticality and efficiency you rarely saw in a military base. Or maybe it was because Ethan himself sometimes felt like a car with a rotary engine: on the surface, all cars look ordinary, just like Ethan when he was in his civilian clothing. But pop the hood and take a look and it was a whole different beast. Ethan's muscles twitched with a different energy, and his brain brewed akin to storm clouds, building close by, but not quite close enough to feel the thunder's intensity.

It was still a curiosity, how he got the car. Wasn't even that long ago, he mused as he ran his fingers over the rusty housing. He tucked in his shirt, hitched up his shorts, and slid under the body.

He had walked into the sleepy and quiet auto store for no particular reason at all and before his decision to join the SEALs and realizing he wouldn't be needing a car. Then, he'd been fresh out of the Navy, seeking the American Dream: a wife, a house, and a car. Maybe some buds to have a beer with now and then, shoot some shit, some pool. But there wasn't much money left after his down payment on the condo at the edge of town; it was a bit far to walk to work, but it was also a distance from Ethan's childhood home and after his father's death, there was no way he was going back there.

Ethan recalled having smoothed his almost empty pockets and wandering into the showroom, just for fun.

It was a new place, put in after he'd left for base. Of course, the place had its pride and joy of sports cars lined up in the front. Folly, he had thought as he went straight to the sole person working there. Ethan looked around. Other than the conspicuous zoomers, their other selection looked solid: normal cars for a normal price. Just like he wanted. Ethan sized up the attendant as he approached and was glad he'd worn his uniform. The man looked the type to appreciate it. Maybe he wouldn't walk out of here empty handed, after all.

"How may I help you?" The man was clearly eager for some amusement from a slow day, no doubt.

"Just looking around." Ethan smiled. "Say, you have any cheaper cars than these?" He spread his hands. "Fresh outta base and looking to start. Gives you muscles, but it don't give you cash."

The man laughed. "You sound like my son, son." He beckoned. "We got all kinds of course, just follow me." They navigated the maze of autos to the back side of the store. The employee opened a door to a garage and turned on the light. Inside, were rows of dejected-looking cars that had clearly not seen the light of day in months, maybe years. Ethan's heart sank. These looked like something even his dad would pass up and cars were the only challenge the old man had never passed up.

Then, off to the side, he glimpsed something promising. Maybe. A beat-up, old, wine-colored sedan. Ethan pointed at it.

"Which one is that?"

"Heh, never have had anyone ask about that one. It's an NSU RO 80. Discontinued in 1977."

For some reason, it called to Ethan. He had no wife. He barely had a house. He wasn't entirely sure he had a legal, unexpired driving license. But without a second thought, he had bought it then and there.

The manufacturer had gone out of business a long time ago, swallowed up by Volkswagen, along with Audi. The parent company attempted to rebrand the car as an Audi 200; the campaign largely failed and it fell to obscurity. Ethan sometimes liked to think of himself as one of the only owners of this car left.

In a remarkable twist of coincidence, the car seller claimed the antique originated from a warlord's collection in Syria. The man had fallen instantly in love and pulled whatever strings he could back then to have it shipped stateside. He didn't expect for it to work, but somehow, here it was, in Ethan's garage.

No matter the history, it was one of Ethan's few possessions and he loved it. He intended to get full use out of every last part of the car.

Ethan opened the hood and inspected it. It was like a routine between he and the automobile now. Every time he returned, a quick check-up of the car was necessary. No wonder he hadn't felt grounded. He'd been remiss in his duties.

The engine modifications he was adding to improve the old beater's longevity and mileage looked just as he'd left it. They were nearly complete, but he did want to clean up the insides a bit. Messy work, but oddly satisfying. He picked up his toolbox and started working. He first removed the housing and, with the steam cleaner, methodically went in every nook and cranny. Almost no dust had accumulated, but it was procedure. Soft rock played in the background, and soon, Ethan was immersed. His hands moved as if they a sentience of their own, and the sense of purpose that Ethan longed for finally settled in.

Until Ethan noticed something. His family had argued against it, but he had insisted on setting up security cameras around the grounds. Of course, he didn't need it, but it gave him a sense of comfort that he knew exactly what was happening on his own piece of soil. The monitors live-streamed 24/7 every room of the house, including the garage. They barely ever kicked into action, only catching raccoons and the occasional deer rummaging around the trash outside of the house at night, but it was much better to be safe than sorry.

It was the garage monitor that Ethan had seen out of the corner of his eye. On one of the feeds there was a blurry yet completely unmistakable shape of a man. He was creeping through the bushes, scanning around, until he looked directly at the camera.

"What the hell?" This man was clearly looking for something. Ethan gripped the wrench.

Some townie come to rob him? Some drifter? If it was a townie, it was a good bet he knew exactly who he was coming to rob, and that made him stupid. If it was a drifter, some junkie looking for a score off the highway as it turned into the named road, then he'd gotten caught casing the joint. And he had the bad luck to stake out a SEAL. That made him double stupid.

If it was someone else…

The shadow stopped, completely still. Its left arm went to its neck, bringing up the collar to his mouth. Talking into a radio.

Shit.

Not a beat job, then. Ethan flicked his fingers on the floor. This was something else, a coordinated operation. Who were these people? He knew there had to be more than one; who talks into a radio, alone? Had they known this house was his? How had they found it to begin with?

Ethan swung to look at the other cameras, but his gaze was distracted by the initial scene: In grainy black and white footage, the man reached in his backpack and brought up the distinct image of a gun. He trained it at the camera watching him.

Ethan never heard the shot, but the camera went to static.

Silencers.

Double shit.

Ethan wiped his hands with the rag. Couldn't risk slipping on his weapon. He also wiped the wrench. He stayed calm and didn't panic.

He fell back fast into training, fighting the surreal collapse of space and time as Syria became Little Creek and he no longer considered who, or where, he was. As he'd learned in training, his heart rate didn't budge one bit. Just as Ethan had been dragged into a bunker alone, not knowing where his men were or if they were still alive. Even when he'd been tortured, held at knife point, gunpoint, or watched the concrete around his bare feet, stripped of boots, jump into the air as his captor shot for his toes, his heart rate maintained. With satisfaction, Ethan had remained collected enough to use the distraction of a rescue team hammering the door to take control of the situation, breaking the man's nose with his hand. Then killed him with his own gun.

Life or death situations didn't really faze him. Surely, these men couldn't be worse than that.

Ethan didn't know why people would be after him; all he knew was that apparently, they were. Without thinking, he had already put the rag on the ground. He slipped back through the garage door, closing it silently behind him and made his way over to the drawer in the kitchen.

He opened the drawer. Some people kept junk drawers in their kitchen. Ethan kept his own version of the practice: an M4A1 with a close-range receiver, a handgun, a tactical belt and vest, and more bullets than Ethan could count. Ethan quickly put on the belt and vest, loaded his magazines into all his pockets. He should be good. He didn't know what kind of firepower these men had, but he hadn't met something the M4 couldn't handle.

With the weapon gripped in Ethan's reactionary hand, he sidled around the half island and made his way down the short hallway to the stairs and to the second floor, blessing the carpeting, though it would make any approach also harder to hear. From the second floor he would have a better vantage point, but the stairs creaked and groaned if he went too fast. Ethan stepped up each one slowly and over the ugly carpet he'd never bothered to change and always hell to vacuum. He eased up slowly, with his gun squarely trained downward into the living room. The layout of the condo was the one downside; too many places to take cover with its "modern" alcoves and stairs that jutted into the hall and led to the bath and bedrooms, downstairs. The stairs twisted awkwardly at a short landing, obliterating his view. He had to risk it. He glanced out the window at the landing but, of course, could see nothing.

These men weren't stupid.

They weren't stupid, and they weren't yet knocking down his doors. Why? They had to know he was aware of their presence; taking out a security camera would do that.

As he crept into the half-second floor which he kept for guests and looked like no one lived there at all, another thought popped into his head. Ethan had built a ladder from the upstairs bathroom to the roof: It was his preferred smoking haunt, as he hated having to scrabble climb the awkward chimney to the tar. He mentally patted himself on the back.

He hoped they – like the condo managers – didn't know about his access to the roof.

The skies were now bleak, the sun obscured by blankets of clouds. He attached his ACOG scope to his M4 and peered through the sight, seeing that the red dot was activated. Perfect. He reached into his pocket and brought out his phone. The wireless security feed flickered to life on the tiny screen and Ethan started scrolling through the perimeter cameras.

Side door. Gone. Patio. Gone. Garage. Gone. Front door. Gone. Yard. Gone.

Shit, shit, shit. He was operating blind. Who were these people?

Things didn't look too good. Whoever they were, they were well armed and professional. The man on the screen had been dressed in a black and white suit, giving him the insane look of a lawyer who chose to spend his lunch break peeping in other people's windows- with a military grade rifle slung across his front.

Stupid? No. Ethan shivered. Wearing a suit in a combat situation served no purpose, except to look stylish. He was damn sure there was body armor under those cufflinks and tails.

They looked like Secret Service agents, out of place against the rural landscape of the country town. He wondered how the hell they'd found him, and what the hell they could possibly want.

Been home two weeks, boy, he thought to himself. Your own damn fault for thinking it was too quiet. What did you say? Find something to do. Couldn't you just stay satisfied with the car and the easy life?

Ethan shook his head. He was grinning. Action. He thought of his groceries, still on the counter.

If he lived through this, he'd have to put those away.

Ethan slid out the window and onto the roof, the gritty tiles cracking under his boots.

As he peered over the edge, he saw the figure of another man slip out of sight and under the eaves. He was sure there were more and sure they had the condo completely surrounded. Damn. Was there legitimately no way out of this other than fighting?

He prayed his neighbors wouldn't come home from work early.

Ethan used his scope to assess in a full 360-degree rotation for any possible escape. There was even a man stationed in front of the sewer exit, 2 miles away. The only possible chance he had was to climb across the roof and shimmy down on the other side, but that would be suicide. It wasn't terrain he knew.

No. There was no escape.

Cocking his gun, Ethan peered into the forest line. A man in black stood, assault rifle shouldered, staring at the house but not at the roof. A mistake he would regret for the rest of the short life ahead of him.

Breathe in. Breathe out.

Finger on trigger.

Squeeze. Gently.

The suppressed ping of the M4 was a familiar sound to Ethan's ears. Neck shot. No body armor on the neck.

Instantly, the suit-coated assassin collapsed, red staining his flawless shirt.

Ethan didn't have time to contemplate his kill. He didn't even have time to admire his perfect shot. Instantly, bullets rained down on his house. The ledge that Ethan was using as support shattered as a barrage of distant sniper fire seemed to hail from every compass point. Ethan threw himself on the rough tiles, wincing as his magazines jammed into his stomach.

He hauled himself back through the window and bolted for the stairs, heading back down. He'd be a sitting duck up here if they got in the house.

On the ground floor he sprinted to and ducked against the wall behind the open drapes. Glad they were open. Sorry and glad.

He peered out.

Men emerged from the cypress line that bordered the field behind his property in black suits, quick and quiet. Silencers on all the guns. Where the hell were the neighbors?

Ethan readied his phone to radio for help - RADIO- it's called 911, civ boy- but startled by a shot, he dropped the phone.

Shit.

He'd kept the windows open, just the screens letting in the air. Ethan kicked it hard. It popped out with a twang and into the grass below. Ethan leaned for a quick peek.

Bullets rained in.

Ethan winced, then took aim and started firing. Years of SEAL training took over, and his crosshair jumped from center mass to center mass as bullets flew. His phone stayed forgotten on the floor.

He methodically switched to the other side and fired off a round. Then he dropped to his belly and elbowed across the rug into the bedroom and fired off a round from there. As return enemy fire grew thinner, Ethan felt what little stress he had fade away.

By now he was in his office, with a view of his patio and the dying flowers. Ethan peered out from behind his fake fig tree and aimed.

The man went down with no sound at all.

Ethan stood in the silence, breathing hard. Heart rate a healthy 100, if he was any judge. Breathing hard.

Hands steady, breathing hard.

Ethan peered out again and cautiously inspected his view. It seemed clear, but he knew that all it took was just one assassin, hiding behind a bush somewhere. Even his dead foliage provided some cover. And that cypress line was suicide. They could fire from behind the screen of dense bushes until he died.

Silence. Police sirens? Neighbors? Nothing.

Christ. He should have picked a house closer to town and to hell with the questions.

Time to get out of here.

Ethan slung the rifle over his back and took his pistol out. It was a better weapon for close quarters. He made his way cautiously out of the office and back down the hall into what passed for his kitchen. He glanced at the garage door. If he could manage to get the car out, he could hit the highway and figure out what the hell had just happened from a safe spot.

In the distance, car engines grew closer. Ethan didn't know whether they carried more assassins, help, police, or some unlucky (or was it lucky?) neighbors. But he didn't intend on staying long enough to find out. Ethan wasn't taking his chances betting it was the police. Not in this town. They wouldn't be much help with their outdated firepower anyway. And when it came down to it, he'd shot first. Could he claim self-defense?

Military hero, white, male, lower thirties. In this political climate? Of course he could. No doubt whatsoever.

Ethan stepped out of the blind spot of the hall and into the...

Blinding pain; he staggered back, feeling warm blood stream down his temple like an unstoppable cry. A pistol whip. Ethan stumbled onto the floor, already getting his pistol up to fire. He shot blindly, aiming ahead until his vision cleared, but a black boot kicked the gun away and Ethan screamed at himself for his stupidity. The screens he'd kicked out. Of course they'd come in the house. And he hadn't heard a thing.

Ethan looked up. The edges of his vision were red, but he could make out the man towering over him. Black suit and cold eyes stared down at Ethan as he cocked his pistol.

"Wait." Ethan struggled to sound calm. It was the best thing when talking to terrorists. "Who are you? Where are you from? And what do you want from me?" He coughed and tasted hot iron. "I haven't done any-"

"You don't need to know." The man smiled, slick. It enhanced the legal appearance. "You won't live long enough to care anyway." With that, he aimed his gun at Ethan.

Ethan prepared to kick. He had to time it just right, though- if he misjudged, this man would shoot him dead here and now and none of it would matter at-

His execution was interrupted by a yell.

Ethan opened his eyes to see the man and Sam Reilly, grappling, smash into his mother's cherry dresser and dining table, breaking a chair leg as they slammed together to the floor.

What the-

Ethan sprang into action and threw himself into the fray, trying to haul the man off Sam. There was no way he could get a shot off in the chaos, even if he could reach the gun-

The three men wrestled, racing desperately for the gun. Ethan wrenched an arm out of the thrashing mass of bodies and with all his strength nailed the assassin in the face with his elbow, bloodying his nose.

It was enough. Sam lunged forward, grabbed the pistol and in one move swung it around and struck the hitman hard across the ear.

The assassin went limp. Ethan checked for a pulse. It was there, and strong. He was just knocked out cold.

The two men panted in the dusty scent of carpet and fabric softener and gun smoke and blood and sweat. The milk Ethan had bought had gotten knocked off the counter during some part of the scrabble and now sat in a puddle on the fake wood floor of the kitchen.

Ethan stared at it, trying to process all that had just happened, but the brain recovers at its own pace, likely busy shunting the last vestige of adrenaline back to where it belonged.

He turned and held his hand out to Sam, the last person he'd expected to see here, spitting blood out of his mouth. "Thank you."

Sam grinned. His face was bloodied and scratched, and he had grass stuck to his dirty shirt. He took Ethan's hand and shrugged. "Don't thank me," he said, trying to catch his breath. "I was only repaying the favor."

In the distance, the sound of cars got louder. And was that a helicopter Ethan heard? Sam glanced toward the window, pushing himself up. "We can talk about who owes who later. Right now, we have more company to deal with."

Chapter Forty-Two

Sam checked his pistol, doubting he'd many shots left. "I'll drive. You can do the shooting. You're the SEAL anyway."

Ethan nodded in agreement. Sam still had a plethora of questions for Ethan, but he would have to save those for later. "Where's your car?"

"In the garage." replied Ethan. "It's a rotary."

Sam threw up his hands. "What do I care what car you drive? You could tell me it's a Schwinn bicycle, do we have a choice?"

Ethan shot him a look. Sam shut his mouth.

Sam and Ethan crept towards the garage door, careful to check around the corners for any more possible assailants. Ethan shook his head. "We'll have to full steam it out. Garage is vulnerable."

Sam raked his hands through his hair. They came away bloody.

Ethan didn't know it, but Sam had been staking out Ethan's house since before the assassins came. He'd come armed, but not with much. It was only by pure chance that Sam had managed to save Ethan's life. As Ethan eased open the in-house door to the garage, gun at the ready in case they'd already breached, Sam hesitated.

Ethan looked back. "What? Now's not the time for-"

Sam shook his head. He'd wanted to mention the key, but the talk would have to wait. There wasn't time. Sam had to trust that Ethan fighting those men he'd interrupted was a good sign- if they'd thought the key was hidden in the house, they'd have shot him on the spot and taken their sweet time looking. As it was, they'd seemed keen to keep him alive. And the only reason they'd need him alive would be to tell them where the key was.

Ethan tightened his lips and cautiously opened the garage door, aiming inside. The garage seemed to be clear. Twitching his head to notify Sam, Ethan eased inside. Sam gripped his pistol and followed.

Ethan slowly walked the perimeter with the M4 carefully aimed up.

Sam waited. When he was younger, he might have been impatient at such a check. But he had had too many brushes with death and solely due to his own carelessness. He was wiser now.

Ethan finished his round, and then beckoned Sam forward. The car chimed as Ethan unlocked it. Sam, already heading to the driver's side, barely caught the car key when Ethan tossed it to him. That would've been embarrassing, he thought. He wrenched open the door.

Sam slid into the leather interior and twisted the key in the ignition. He expected the loud yet smooth roar of a muscle car, but he was greeted with a rough, almost distinct chop, chop, chop as the car started. Christ. What had they gotten themselves into?

"Is there something wrong with the car?" Sam tested the gas as Ethan fumbled for the garage door opener and Sam braced himself for attack.

"No." Ethan's look was a cross between embarrassed and pissed off and pressed the button without warning. "I told you. It's a rotary!"

Right. He'd said that. Sam gripped the steering wheel and craned to look behind him. Rotary, eh? Well. That was good and that was bad: He knew from experience that rotary engines could output a huge amount of power from very little fuel- he'd done his share of drag racing along the shore in Georgia on college breaks- and so he also knew that they tended to be very unreliable.

"Can she handle what we have coming up?" The door opened methodically behind them with an even, measured pace. Sam grit his teeth. Over the whine of the motor he couldn't hear if anyone was coming. Better to keep the windows down?

Sam reached for the button and found a crank. He cranked furiously as Ethan did the same on the opposite side and as if his life depended on it.

Which it did.

Ethan loaded the gun, knocking in another round of ammo. "I fixed her up myself."

There wasn't time to ask his credentials. Sam tapped the gas tentatively, smelling gas and oil and the mustiness of Ethan's garage, the plastic scent of the garbage bag of a man who had just gotten home. He hoped like hell Ethan was a good mechanic.

The garage door had barely cleared the top of the car before Sam hit the gas and the car pushed backward. Ethan braced himself on the passenger seat and craned out the back window. He had hoped to see an empty field- and for the moment, it was. But it wasn't going to be empty for long- even in the distance, Ethan saw a convoy of black hummers screaming down the street. One of them cut through the field behind Ethan's condo. Through the thin screen of trees Sam saw a building. In the heightened sense of a man fighting for his life, he realized that the building was a funeral home.

"Go! Go! Go!" shouted Ethan.

Sam stepped on the gas and felt like he'd been punched in the gut as he slammed backward as the car roared to life. The pair were pushed back into their seats as if it were a roller coaster as Sam peeled around the short driveway and spun the wheel to straighten her out, thump, thump, thump. He stared down the convoy approaching the drive. If he hit it now, he could make it.

He tested the throttle. Sam had never felt this much power in a car. He knew it was no time to admire the mechanics of the rotary engine beneath their ride's hood, but Ethan did have a sweet ride.

As if on cue, the convoy started firing at the NSU. They were just sparks in the distance, but Sam knew that sparks in the distance meant deafening gunfire very soon.

He punched the gas pedal again. The driveway wasn't long. "ARE THERE ANY OTHER ROADS OUT OF HERE?" shouted Sam over the racket of bullets peppering the ground next to the car.

"TAKE A RIGHT AT THAT DRIVE!" bellowed Ethan. Sam tightened his lip. Screaming wouldn't help.

He took a right just as the cars got close enough and he could see drivers but not make out any faces.

"Tell me!" he shouted over the sound of the wind- the windows were down.

"You got it! Left when you- RIGHT. Go RIGHT when you hit Wooster!"

"You sure?!" The caravan was gaining on them.

"It heads for the bay! Out of city limits – we can go 120 and no one'll give a damn."

Sam shrugged. "Worth a shot."

They were on a dirt track now, with the tires scraping for traction against the mud. Sam silently thanked himself for learning how to rally-drive a long time ago. There was no way they would have gotten safely out otherwise. Behind the car, the convoy continued to gain on them. The gunfire was starting to get annoying, with some bullets starting to ping the car.

"Hey, bud, can you use that gun of yours?" asked Sam.

Ethan probably nodded, but Sam was too focused on the road. He heard Ethan recheck the ammo in his gun. All he heard was, "Can you keep clearance on the right side? I'm not trying to get crushed."

Sam shifted the car a bit to the left, gritting his teeth. It was work enough to keep the car on the road, much less worry about the person hanging out the window.

The shot Ethan fired off took him by surprise. It was precise and measured. Sam had expected the hopeful spray of a desperate man but was pleasantly surprised when Ethan aimed and shot cautiously. *Smart*, he thought.

Ditches full of wildflowers whizzed by. Fields and woods. Now and then, a driveway. Up the road, Sam spotted a split coming up. "Which way?" he shouted. Coolness went out the window. Ethan shouted an indiscernible response over the wind, still focused on the firing. Screw it, thought Sam. He twisted the steering wheel hard to the left, almost launching Ethan out of the car.

Ethan slammed back inside, swearing like a sailor. "I told you to turn right! What the hell are you doing?"

"I couldn't hear you!" responded Sam. The road had turned to asphalt, so it was a lot easier for Sam to drive smoothly. Now that he didn't have to focus on keeping the car on the road, Sam realized they'd emerged on a road traveling along the bay. From what he could tell they were still heading away from civilization, but for how long, he couldn't say.

"Christ- we're headed back to town!" Ethan growled. "You should have gone RIGHT!"

Damn.

Sam cast a glance in the rear-view mirror, then one out front again. Far in the distance he saw a bridge spanning an inlet off the bay and gripped the wheel as the car quivered under him. He jerked his chin at the bridge. "Where does that go?"

The men behind them were driving hummers. Hummers couldn't corner worth a damn. *This baby handled like a dream,* Sam thought. So far, anyway.

"Kittridge- this little town on the other side- it's like the last place before we really come back into-"

"Great." Sam hit the gas. Ethan's eyes went round as he realized what Sam was up to.

"Are you serious? You know if we lose it that bridge is-"

A shot took out Sam's side mirror. He flinched, then glared at Ethan. "Got a better plan?" He couldn't take his hands off the wheel, but wished he could. He'd love to punch the boy in the face. This was all his damn fault. If he'd just told Sam he'd taken the key in the first place-

Ethan delivered a sharp glare toward Sam then whipped around like a petulant child. He fired furiously out the window. A few seconds later, he screamed.

Sam bore down and kept all his focus on the upcoming bridge. He couldn't afford distractions. Could. Not.

Ragweed. They'd just passed ragweed; he'd bet his life on it.

Bet his life. He might have to, he thought as his eyes started tear up and itch.

Damn his allergies. He couldn't afford distractions right now. He sniffed back a massive sneeze and blinked hard, his streaming eyes squinting through tears. The bridge was closer. Thirty yards. He just had to make it onto the bridge. There was no way they'd be able to follow.

If they could…

Well. If they could, he'd have time to sneeze when he was dead.

Twenty yards.

Ethan fired more shots. It didn't seem to slow them down, but Sam heard the screech of tires. He flicked a glance in the mirror. Still there.

Ten yards.

Five.

The sneeze descended with a vengeance.

Sam gulped it back, fighting hard. His eyes teared, blurring the road.

He started to slow.

Ethan swung to him. "Sam!"

Sam blinked, choking, and wrenched the wheel.

The car shrieked and roared up the narrow, picturesque ramp. It was a blur of blues and grays as they shot across the causeway.

"Are they coming?!" he shouted, not daring to look.

"Coming!" Ethan barked in full military mode. He was almost all the way out the car window, M4 trained on the hummer. "They're-"

A sickening crunch and crash as the guard rail broke.

Sam lurched forward and took his foot off the gas.

The world outside, spun.

Chapter Forty-Three

Sam rolled to a stop at the other end of the bridge. He sat in the car and willed his hands to unclench from the steering wheel, but they weren't obeying him.

The hummer had gone over, just as he'd planned. Shakily he opened the car door as Ethan did the same on the right and pushed himself out into the world.

He went to the edge and peered over. The wreckage of the car was already sinking with great sucking, hissing noises of scalding steel. Gasoline made rainbows on the surface; flaming wreckage flickered, then went out. Sam tried to catch his breath.

"We'll go down. See if anyone survived. We…"

"You think anyone survived that?" Ethan turned to him, skepticism, awe, and grudging admiration warring in his voice. Sam ran a hand through his hair.

"I hope so," he said, fighting his sneeze. He pressed his hand to his nose. "We can ask them…"

Two heads bobbed to the surface. Thrashing. Sputtering. Too far away to get a close look but close enough to see them open their mouths to scream—

An unexpected pop made him jump. Red spread from the first head into the rainbow swirls and smoke.

The second pop shot the second head into the flaming body and Sam lost sight through his watering eyes.

He wiped them, grainy, itchy… Ethan looked at him, stunned.

"You're crying?"

Sam shook his head. "Allergies." It sounded stupid, even to him. He gestured to the men in the water, already sunk, just the blood remaining. "They were our only link. Was that really nec—"

He stifled his sneeze, gasping. "Necess—"

He sneezed so hard his head felt rattled. He wiped his nose on his sleeve; wiped his streaming eyes. "Necessary?"

Sam wiped his face again. When he emerged from beneath his shirt, he found Ethan's eyes fixed on his, and with the piercing defiance of a trained killer.

"Hey," he said. "They're the ones who came to me looking for a fight." Ethan surveyed the wreck one last time, shouldered his weapon and made for the car.

"All I did was finish it."

The gravel rumbled under the wheels and Queen Anne's lace and goldenrod thumped the sides of the car. Sam pulled over, off the shoulder, and tilted down into the road that led under one of the small bridges that dotted the creeks and inlets of Kittridge. They'd driven into the tiny town to get away from the wreck. Ethan assured him there weren't any security cameras on this particular bridge. When Sam demanded how he knew, Ethan surprisingly blushed and snapped, "Just do."

Kittridge felt like a movie set after the horrors of Ethan's house and the mad chase along the bay. Sam drove through the quaint streets like he was in a dream.

He pulled left when Ethan said 'left', following his lead. He saw the bridge up ahead. "Another one?"

"And if they have drones watching?" Ethan snapped, gesturing at the structure. "Get under it!"

It was a good idea. Sam could feel Ethan's steel gaze watching him as he navigated the rough terrain, but kept his eyes on the windshield.

Finally, he slowed, and the car rumbled to a stop, shaded beneath the rusty bridge. Sam craned his neck out the open window, squinting up.

"Should be okay," he said. "If there's anyone tracking us via satellite, they'll be—"

Ethan laughed. "Yeah, I know. I have a question for you."

Sam steeled himself and faced Ethan's glare as the other man folded his arms. He was still carrying the gun. "You want to tell me what this is all about?"

Chapter Forty-Four

Sam gripped the steering wheel and met his eyes squarely. "No," he said evenly. "And, I have a question for you."

"Go on."

Sam asked, "What do you know about the Labyrinth Key?"

Ethan hid his surprise fast, but not fast enough. Sam had enough experience with men in dire situations to know that the ability to lie, well, was among one of the last skills to return after fighting for your life. If Ethan was going to slip up, it was going to be now.

He didn't slip much, though.

"What labyrinth key? Oh, you mean that key? The one you wanted from Palmyra?"

Sam shook his head. "No. I mean the one you stole." He glanced at the gun and the way Ethan's hands clenched it and grinned. "The one you took—as a souvenir—from Palmyra."

Ethan wasn't expecting the smile. He weighed Sam under his gaze, remembering what he'd just done, what he'd just seen.

Hopefully, Sam thought, *he's remembering that without me and this Sam Reilly's impeccable sense of timing and duty, he'd be worm food by now – or worse.*

Sam repeated the question. "What do you know about the Labyrinth Key?"

Ethan shrugged a shoulder as if he couldn't give a damn. "That it doesn't look like it's worth all this trouble. THAT's what all this is about?"

Sam shook his head. "Afraid so. Where did you hide it?"

Ethan didn't quite meet his eyes. "What makes you think after all this it's not just stashed back at the house somewhere? Maybe in my sock drawer."

Sam allowed himself a wry grin. "Because you aren't an idiot. Besides, those guys were still chasing us. They've been watching you, and if they thought it was in your house, they would still be back there, searching for it after we… left. If they had already known where it was, they wouldn't give two shits about you."

"But they know *I know*. And they know it's not there." Ethan turned to him, a challenge in his eyes. "How the hell would THEY *know* that, Sam? Someone giving them intel?" He threw up his hands. "And frankly, how did you even know where I lived?!"

Sam held up his hands and faced Ethan fully. "Listen. Ethan. You've saved my life; I've saved yours. This isn't going to work if we keep not trusting each other. Despite what just happened, our lives are both still in danger because they don't know where the key is, and the key is the most important thing to them. If you don't want to end up like those men in the bay back there—" His voice rose and he couldn't quite stop it. "Tell me now, and sooner is way better than later, where it is, so we can end this!"

His shout echoed with anger inside the small car as he sat breathing hard in the driver's seat. Outside, the Queen Anne's lace waved in the breeze and he glanced in the rear view mirrors and the side mirrors. Still nothing. He wiped his running nose.

"All right." Sam turned in surprise at Ethan's voice. It was soft, determined. "I've left it secured in a safety deposit box." The voice hardened a bit. "I'm not telling you the location. Not yet."

It was the last thing Sam was expecting. Especially from a SEAL who probably didn't have many valuables to begin with. He'd opened the box specifically for the key. "A safety deposit box? Really?" He scratched his forehead. "Why?"

Ethan rolled his eyes. "Because I'm not an idiot! The image," he relented, fiddling with the strap on the gun. "It was the same one I'd seen on the USB stick you and I buried all those years ago."

"You remembered that? After all these years?"

Ethan bristled. "Have YOU forgotten it?"

It was a fair point. "No. Sorry." Sam sighed. "Listen. I don't mean to —"

"Ahh." Ethan jerked his head and squished a gum wrapper in his fingers. "I figured there might be a connection, is all. Maybe it was nothing. But after you came all the way to Palmyra looking for it…" He shrugged. "Either way, I wanted to keep it safe." Ethan held his gaze for another moment. "Good thing I did, I guess."

"Very good." Sam flexed his grip on the wheel. "Why did you take me all the way out there, anyway? When you knew you had it all along?"

Ethan looked at him like he was the stupid one. "I didn't know you. I didn't trust you. You want to learn about a man, take him to a war zone."

There was some logic to that, and Sam's estimation of Ethan rose a notch. "And what? You trust me now?"

"That depends." Ethan folded his arms. "You going to tell me what this is all about?"

Sam sighed. "I suppose you have a right to know, seeing on how you have the key, right?"

Ethan didn't move, but Sam felt his eagerness. "Know what, exactly?"

Sam glanced at him. "Well…" he said, and Ethan's lip tucked in. Sam grinned, himself. Against all odds, he liked the boy. "Have you ever heard of the Black Pyramid?"

Chapter Forty-Five

The dusty road gleamed under the dying summer sun's waning rays. More Queen Anne's lace waved from each side in the gentle breeze, but Sam didn't notice. He was seeing another field, at another time. This one was far away from here, even more remote than this. It had smelled of dust and gun smoke too, though, with the same distant cry of birds…

Ethan sat beside him in the passenger seat, leaning against the window. He still held the gun in his lap and Sam thought it a mercy they hadn't been pulled over. He didn't know the conceal-carry laws of Virginia.

He almost snorted. Like those were the only laws they'd broken today.

Ethan's hands were steady as he cleaned the assault rifle methodically, wiping it down without seeing it and stripping it with long, familiar practice.

Sam watched his competence, remembering the men in the bay. He rubbed his lip with a sigh. "I suppose you want some answers?"

Ethan's focus shifted from the gun, slightly. "Be nice. Yeah. Just killed three men for you — betting that's gotta be worth something."

"They were coming after you, son. Not me." Sam fought to keep his voice calm, telling himself sarcasm wasn't going to help right now. His stress level wasn't Ethan's fault. His brain disagreed — Ethan stole the key and didn't tell me; Ethan's a liar — and Sam couldn't keep the coldness completely at bay, despite his best effort. "Wasn't *my* house they ambushed."

The competent hands resumed their cleaning and Sam cautioned himself to tread carefully here. He didn't know this man's loyalties and he'd seen what those hands could do.

Ethan glanced at him, completely expressionless. "Yeah, be nice to know why that was, too." He snapped the pieces together with a click.

Sam scratched his temple and stared into the flat field beyond the window. The nature scene was soothing, deceptively so. Nothing about the world of men had touched it yet. Shaking himself mentally, Sam wondered where the hell to begin.

The beginning, he supposed. It was usually the best place. He turned to Ethan. "What do you know about the Hawara Pyramid?"

Ethan's eyes narrowed and he lifted the gun, then leaned back far behind him into the back seat and grabbed his kit bag. He hauled it up front, plopping it in his lap. "Nothing. I'm guessing it's in Egypt?"

Sam smiled, but it was thin-lipped. Most people thought of the Egyptians when they heard the word 'pyramid', not knowing that the pyramids were one of the oldest-type structures known to man. It was more stable than a straight tower and its elegance of shape suggested a yearning toward heaven for many cultures. For now, he let it go – not everyone was a historian and the American school system sucked. Whatever. As it happened, the man was right. "Yeah," he said. "Near the ancient city of Crocodilopolis, sixty miles southeast of Cairo."

"Crocodilopolis. You're shitting me."

Sam raised his hands, though he remembered having a similar reaction himself. "Hey, I don't make up the names. Apparently, they have a lot of…"

"Hippos, yeah. Sounds like it."

Sam bit back a chuckle. Ethan just stared in a non-committal way. "Okay. Crocodilopolis. And?"

Sam went on drumming the steering wheel. He wondered if this was the best place for this conversation. Wondered if pursuit was coming. If they could see for miles along the flat open fields, others could too. It wasn't likely that there'd be more – Ethan had taken out the last of the visible ones. But that's what Sam had thought before, that day that they'd…

Ethan said, "Hey. Hippos?"

Sam jerked back to the present to find Ethan eyeing their surroundings, the same as him. They'd be okay. And this was important. This was … everything.

"Amenemhat III was a pharaoh of the Twelfth Dynasty of ancient Egypt," he continued. "He ruled from c. 1860 BC to c. 1814 BC and was notable for building the Black Pyramid, the Hawara Pyramid, and …" He glanced at Ethan. "The Labyrinth."

The last word grabbed Ethan's interest. His gaze flicked from his recon of the fields to Sam, sharpening. "Go on."

Sam increased the air conditioning a little bit and leaned back in his seat. Sweat ran down his neck.

"The Black Pyramid was originally about two hundred and twenty-five feet tall. It had a base of three hundred and fifteen feet long, an incline of fifty-seven degrees." He knew Ethan's mind would supply the visuals that matched the numbers, a skill used often in laying out prospective target hits. "It was a typical size for pyramids of the Middle Kingdom. Not massive but, not tiny either. But something was different – the Black Pyramid wasn't made of stone."

Ethan snorted. "What's it made of? Crocodile bones?"

Sam grinned. "Nothing so glamorous. Just clay and mud brick, I'm afraid. But it is—was—covered in thin sheets of limestone."

"Yeah? So, we're looking at a tank; back in its day."

Sam blinked. He hadn't thought of it that way. "I guess you could say that. Though it probably has more to do with weight than armor – there weren't any internal walls, either. Considering how close the pyramid is to the Nile ..." He shrugged. "There's a pyramid nearby, at Dahshur. The Bent Pyramid of Sneferu. The land is clay and not stable, so close to the river. The Bent Pyramid had already begun to sink centuries before. The two pyramids are only about two miles apart."

Ethan flipped out his pocketknife and started to clean the blood from under his nails. Sam risked a glance at himself in the rear-view mirror and wished he hadn't.

"So how big is this thing anyway? Were they worried about it falling through the earth?"

Sam put his appearance out of his mind, but realized they'd have to find a place to clean up before they made their public debut. He rubbed at some dirt on his cheek, trying to look casual. "The ground-level structure consisted of an entrance opening into the courtyard and mortuary temple, surrounded by walls. There are two sets of walls. Between them there are ten shaft tombs, which are a type of burial structure formed by graves built into natural rock. The pyramidion," He glanced at Ethan as the other man opened his mouth to make some remark, "which is the capstone of a pyramid, was covered with inscriptions and religious symbols. Some of these were scratched off, leading researchers to conclude the pyramidion was never used or it was defaced during Akhenaten's rule in the years to come."

"Researchers?" Ethan's brows rose. "Someone actually found this place?"

"Several 'someones', actually. It was a team effort."

Ethan rubbed at a hole in his worn jeans and Sam could tell his interest was piqued. "You said 'ground level structure.' That means there's more?"

Sam laughed. "Much more." He drew a finger down the wheel like he was traveling into the earth. "Below ground level, subterranean, is a network of complicated passages. There were burial chambers for two of his queens – one of them was named Aat and the other had no name."

"Nice guy."

"That's history. From what I've read, the king's section remained mostly intact- they found a sarcophagus, canopic jars, the whole enchilada. But no king."

"Grave robbers?"

Sam nodded. "That's what they think, anyway. The section for the queens had definitely been broken into and looted. The pyramid was abandoned after it began to crush the underground chambers- remember how I told you it was too heavy for the land it was built on?" Sam shrugged, marveling again at how much the ancients had accomplished with minimal technology. "The builders installed supporting beams and mud brick walls to stop the sinking, but it was too little, too late, and the pyramid was abandoned." He glanced at Ethan. "You already know what happens to abandoned buildings in the desert."

Ethan grinned. "Yeah. They fall down or they get used."

"Exactly. This one got used. By the 13th dynasty, the lack of security meant that locals had usurped the Valley Temple nearby to be used as a granary, so they think the first breach of the pyramid happened at about that time. There is evidence of restoration work around one hundred years later though so, someone gave a damn. Or they just didn't want to bother building another tomb: King Auibre Hor and his princess Nubheteptikhered were buried in two of the ten shaft tombs on the northern side of the outer enclosure."

Ethan laughed. "Cozy."

Sam laughed with him. "After they abandoned the Black Pyramid, the pharaoh changed tack and went on to build the Hawara Pyramid." Sam stared out the windshield, remembering the first time he'd seen the massive structure, back when he'd just finished his first tour of duty and stopped in Egypt on his way back to the States... "To this day, it has the honor of being the third highest ancient Egyptian pyramid in existence."

"Third highest." Ethan waved his hands. "Oooh."

Apparently, Ethan chatted after he killed. Sam wondered what the real problem was. Nerves? Sam himself had been shaking like a leaf earlier. Still was. He clasped his hands tight on the steering wheel to hide the small tremors. "It has its distinguishing qualities."

If it was nerves, Ethan displayed no other signs. "Yeah? And what are those?"

Sam looked at Ethan as the cool air blasted from the vents. He loosened his collar a bit. "It's said that beneath the Hawara Pyramid exists an ancient Labyrinth that housed a Forbidden Library with the greatest body of human knowledge in all of ancient times."

Ethan's eyes narrowed. Then he slapped his pockets and opened the glove compartment, rummaging inside. "A labyrinth. I don't suppose this labyrinth would require a key?"

Sam grinned. "More than one. But wait. We're getting to that. What is the labyrinth? It's purported to be a vast underground complex of caverns and chambers...a maze, if you will. They say it held the secret to the origin of mankind. They say it holds secret, ancient texts from Atlantis." He glanced at Ethan. "Heard of Atlantis?"

"Yeah, I've heard of it. City under the sea, right? Fairy tales." He shrugged, dismissive. "Really bad Disney movie."

Sam laughed. "Maybe. Maybe not. Something must have existed for so many to have written about it. Same with the labyrinth. No one knows if it existed, really. But Strabo wrote of it in his ancient treatises and even Herodotus apparently had the chance to visit and record its wonders — before it disappeared into history."

"Record its wonders. Don't suppose he recorded what they actually were, did he?"

Sam's lips quirked. "Afraid not."

Ethan rolled his eyes but Sam could tell; he was intrigued by the story. The young man was smart and perceptive. And, he wanted answers. Sam thought he might have made a great historian if he hadn't gone into the military. But then, he supposed war was a way of seeking answers, too. "So, what does this have to do with me? With those men I killed?"

Sam spread his hands. "The labyrinth was said to hold an untold wealth of knowledge: the histories of unknown civilizations, great empires, and powerful rulers that lived centuries before history as we know it, even began. There are lots of people who would risk a lot to access the potential power of that magnitude."

Ethan shook his head. "I've never understood that. How does knowing about ancient civilizations bring men power? What about life? What about NOW, what we're building NOW. We have the most advanced technology the world has ever seen. Why spend so much time looking BACK?"

Sam shrugged. It was a fair point. "Wise humans learn from the past and the surprising lessons it sometimes holds. If for no other reason, I suppose men want to find the labyrinth because it is, or at least it was, very was beautiful. They say that once one entered the sacred enclosure, there was a temple surrounded by columns, forty to each side, and this building had a roof made of a single massive slab of alabaster and carved with panels richly, further adorned by excellent paintings. You ever seen alabaster?"

Ethan's voice softened, caught up in the tale. "Glows in the sun," he said. "My...mom had this tiny box, when I was little. She kept her jewelry in it." He looked out of the window. "That roof must have been beautiful."

Sam wondered, not for the first time, what kind of home Ethan had come from. He sensed it may not have been carefree and all-day laughter. "I think so too." He, also, looked out the window, imagining the glories of another time.

"But – just a legend."

"No, actually." Sam shook himself at Ethan's dismissive tone. "It's located less than a hundred miles from Cairo at Hawara. A team of researchers from Belgium – and Egypt – excavated in 2008. The expedition was able to at least confirm the presence of the underground temple, not far from the Pyramid of Amenemhat III."

Ethan turned to him in surprise. "It's real? This labyrinth, these keys? This..."

"Everyone thinks of Greek history and mythology when they hear about labyrinths. Theseus and the Minotaur and all that. Just like they think of Egypt when they think of pyramids." He slanted a glance with a grin at Ethan. "Even though there are pyramids all around the world. The world holds many secrets. Most of them are still hidden."

"Well, I can't argue with that." Ethan fiddled with his bag, then dropped it and faced Sam directly. "Does all this have something to do with the day we met?"

Sam squinted into the lowering sun. He should get the windshield washed. Rain had dried dusty and the evening light made the dust look like tears... "This has *everything* to do with what happened that day we met."

Chapter Forty-Six

The sun slanted through the car windows in the parking lot outside the dive bar, early patrons laughing and loitering outside. Sam killed the motor and the car hummed to a stop. He flexed his hands on the wheel. "I could use a drink. You?"

Ethan glanced at the bar, then at Sam. "How do you know all this?"

Sam scratched his ear and watched a biker gang rumble into the lot. "It's a long story, actually."

Ethan watched the bikers shudder to a stop and slap each other on the back. The streetlights clicked on. Music swung out into the night as the men entered the bar; Ethan turned to look at Sam. "Tell me about what really happened on the day that we met, before those two Federal Agents tried to kill you."

Sam spread his hands. "How about that drink?"

Ethan's lips were set hard. "Something happened that morning, before I met you, that ties in with everything that's happening now, doesn't it?"

Sam shrugged. "It does."

Ethan put his hands on his knees, the hands that had just killed four men not more than two hours before. "How?"

Sam shook his head. "I can't say."

Ethan reached for the handle and snapped his door open. "We're done here."

Sam held out his hand. "Listen, Ethan…"

Ethan swung his head back around. "You can't say? Or *won't* say?"

They stared at each other in the confines of the small car. Finally, Sam shrugged one shoulder. "I guess, won't say."

Ethan glared. "Because you still don't trust me? After I killed in your defense?"

Sam stared down the challenge in his voice. "No. Because the less you know about the truth behind that day, the safer we'll both be."

Ethan folded his arms and raised a brow. "Bullshit. I'm not buying it."

Well, he wasn't an idiot, Sam knew that. "Well, you don't have to buy it." He spread his hands. "But you do need to trust me. Please, Ethan. It'll need to wait."

Ethan leaned forward. "Men are after both of us. Wait until when, exactly? In the grave?"

Sam shook his head. "Until we finish the mission. Then I can tell you the truth." The door opened again, letting out the music and revelry. They both turned to watch. When the music died back down, Sam turned again to Ethan. "Listen… if we make it, I promise we'll both go back and dig up the security box from that day. Back in Rhyolite. In Nevada." He reached out for his own door's handle. "Come on. Let's get a drink. Best we get the lay of the land."

After a long moment, Ethan nodded. "Promise?"

"On my honor — and as a marine."

It seemed satisfactory. "And what's in that box… it will reveal the answers to everything? Everything I want to know about your past? That you won't TELL me, now, anyway?" He all but spat the words.

Sam nodded, thinking of who else had told Ethan that he couldn't have what he wanted. He wondered what had happened to *those* men. "I promise. Everything's there." He held out his hand to shake. "When this is over, we'll go together and set its secrets free." He raised his brows when Ethan still didn't move. "Deal?"

Ethan looked at him a long time, then reached out. The two men shook, strong. "Deal. And yeah." He scratched his ear, glancing toward the bar. Sam noticed his hand shook, just a bit. "I'll take that drink. And you can tell me what you know about this Labyrinth, right?"

Chapter Forty-Seven

The bar was a dive, full of colored Christmas lights strung in front of band stickers and glass bottles. The clientele turned at their entrance, sized them up, and then turned back to their drinks and pool games as the live entertainment tuned up on a small stage to the side.

Sam gestured to a small booth near the back. Ethan moved through the crowd like it was a war zone and walked with the certainty of a military man. Sam flagged down a server as they sat. "Lager," he said, then looked at Ethan. Ethan shrugged as he slid in. "Same. And a water. No ice."

Sam laughed. "Really? No ice, in this weather?"

Ethan shrugged. "Got out of the habit in the desert. Too cold, now. Like drinking glass."

The men faced each other across the scarred wooden table. Sam rubbed at some graffiti, wondering if there was a way to get out of this.

The server brought their drinks, frothy and frigid. He smiled his thanks as he took the first sip, keeping his eyes down; same as one does around wild animals. Maybe he'd be spared.

But it didn't look like it. Ethan drank, wiped his mouth, then set his beer aside deliberately and leaned on the wood and hit him with that intense stare. "So?" He spread his hands. "We have our drinks; we've got mood music. We're all set. Tell me what you know."

Sam tapped the table, wondering where to start. "Okay," he said. "There was a temple attached to the Hawara pyramid. It was a temple for the dead."

"A mortuary temple."

Sam toasted him. "A mortuary temple. It was referred to as the Labyrinth by the ancient Greek philosophers, Herodotus, Diodorus Siculus, and Strabo, who praised it as a wonder of the world."

Ethan snorted. "More ancient praise, more ancient names. Ooh."

Sam held up his hands. "Yes, yes. Just, hear me out. You said you wanted to know." Ethan gestured for him to continue. Sam did. "But of the three of them, Strabo—"

"Sounds like some kind of protein powder. Or like, a camping equipment company."

Sam laughed. "Strabo was a Greek geographer, philosopher, and historian who lived in Asia Minor when it was transitioning from the Roman Republic to the Roman Empire." He quirked his brow. "In fact, he was instrumental in drawing up the original treaty. Not common knowledge, but true."

"So, you're an authority on Greek-Roman peacekeepers with an interest in politics?"

Sam again quirked a brow, ignoring Ethan's sarcasm. "He had an interest in many things; one of which was the labyrinth. He documented its purpose and how Amenemhat III had kept the place secret for nearly four thousand years." Sam grinned. "Strabo describes that Amenemhat left a key to his secret labyrinth, and a forbidden library to each of his children."

"Nice man. My dad didn't leave me a library."

"Well. You were an only child, maybe. In any event, in order to access the labyrinth and all its secrets, you needed all four keys. His children were Sobekneferu, Amenemhat IV, Neferuptah, Hathorhotep. And their family was... fractured, shall we say. He hoped that giving his children group-dependent access to the library would force them into closeness."

Ethan grinned. "I take it that it didn't go as planned?"

"Of course not. Each of the children became focused on securing the hidden labyrinth for themselves. After their deaths, each child sent their own key to the four corners of their world to keep the others from ever finding it."

"That sounds more like it." Ethan drank, finally sounding interested. "So where are these keys now?"

Sam drank deep and licked his lips of foam. "One went to South America, where it was buried with the Mayan King in Xibalba – and presumably stolen by someone…"

Ethan quirked a brow at him. "You're quite tan, Sam. You spend some time in Mexico recently, perchance?"

Sam grinned and toasted him. "Good eyes. Another key went to Afghanistan. That's the one I found. Another, to Syria…"

"Which I found. What about the last one?"

"The last one went to France. It stayed there awhile, until its owner took it to North America as part of an expeditionary quest—for the other three keys—during the French colonization of the Bay of Fundy and Nova Scotia, in 1608."

Sam shook his head. "And then, history happened the way history does. The things that can't possibly happen, the impossible, happens. Somewhere, somehow, during the process of the American Revolution in which the French sided with the American colonies against Britain, the last French owner of the fourth Labyrinth Key, on his deathbed, gifted the key to – George Washington."

Ethan laughed outright. "Shut up."

Sam held up his hands. "I'm not joking. It's true. Took me a damn long time to find that out, but it's true." He grinned. "You don't believe me? Come on, Ethan. You're a military man. You know how little civilians, and thus the history books, ever really know about what goes on behind the scenes of any country. It wouldn't be the first secret to be passed down from American president to American president, and I'm sure it won't be the last."

Ethan cocked a grin into his beer. "I guess I can't argue with that. What else was passed along?"

"Just a story." Sam shrugged, but looked at him shrewdly. "A story that claimed how the four Labyrinth Keys were required to enter Amenemhat III's Labyrinth and Forbidden Library."

Ethan grinned, the light finally dawning in his eyes. Sam was impressed. It had only taken him one beer. "And that was fine and good and just a story, wasn't it? Until President Harris discovered another key had been found."

Sam spread his hands, half wishing he'd never found it. "Yes. Everything was fine and good until I went and found a labyrinth key and was summoned by the president of the United States in the middle of the night to brief him." Sam's gaze darkened and he drained his beer. "A meeting that never took place…"

Ethan summoned the server. "Another round, please." He looked at Sam as the man retreated. "What happened?"

Sam shook his head. "Like I said, I can't say… not yet… but, hopefully soon."

Ethan settled back. "'Hopefully soon'. Is that before or after more men come to gun me down?" Sam just looked at him. Finally, Ethan shrugged. "What about the others?"

Sam took his new drink as the band started to play old-time country and the crowd cheered. "What others?"

"If George Washington was looking for the keys, there must have been others?" Ethan hunched his shoulders. "Other men who knew about it? Who were looking for it too?"

"Oh." Sam shrugged. "Yes, of course there were others. In fact, there's a whole Brotherhood of the Keys that's been around since the Middle Ages. They believe Amenemhat III knew that the knowledge contained in his library would cause tremendous harm, capable of destroying the world, and thus decided to prevent any of his children from ever harnessing its powers."

Ethan shook his head. "Medieval fanatics, medieval mass destruction and magic." He took a napkin from the metal holder and mopped up the condensation caused by his glass, precisely. Then he folded the napkin into tiny squares.

"They did like their magic."

Ethan flicked the napkin to the middle of the table. "But these are real keys to unlock a real door, right?"

Sam laughed. "That's right. They're real keys to unlock a real door. A large obsidian door, said to be somewhere beneath the Pyramid of Hawara."

Ethan looked up at him from beneath furrowed brows. "The one that requires four keys to unlock. Two of which, we have no idea where they are?"

"Yep. That's the one."

Ethan rolled his eyes. "So why don't you just use dynamite to open it?"

Sam grinned at such a practical solution. "It's a *really* big door, Ethan. Made from nearly twenty tons of stone."

Ethan shrugged. "So? Use a *really* big amount of dynamite. Or C4, if you're new-fangled."

Sam shook his head as the band lights swung between sets and their table was bathed in blue and red. "It's not that simple. The labyrinth and library system are built beneath the Nile. One false move and the entire chamber floods—washing away the knowledge of the ancients—forever."

Chapter Forty-Eight

Ethan folded his new damp napkin into tiny squares.

It gave him something to do with his hands and, he thought better when he did something with his hands. He was a man of action. The feel of the gun in his hands, the way the trigger felt as he pulled it when he'd killed those men… he could still feel it in his body. He felt every single one. He didn't know if it was the heightened sense of life or senses, when shooting, but he could feel every man he'd ever killed, recall details, clear as day. The way the air smelled, even the feel of his fatigues brushing across his leg hairs that stood up in fear.

Ethan folded the paper and took a covert glance at the man across from him.

Secret labyrinths, ancient brotherhoods… Ethan had never put much stock in conspiracy theories. He'd learned early that there was enough monstrosity in the world without inventing fake boogeymen.

And yet those men had come. Those men had been real. "So, in summary, there's a secret labyrinth and the keys open it and we need all of them to do it." He shrugged and flicked his napkin away again. It was too wet to fold. "What exactly are you expecting to find inside this Forbidden Library?"

Across from him Sam made a rueful smile. He knew how far-fetched it sounded. He was down to earth. Ethan liked that about him. "Answers."

Sam didn't seem like a nut, Ethan reflected. He wished he hadn't thrown his napkin away; he couldn't take another without looking stupid and he needed something to do with his hands. He slung an arm over the back of the booth and slouched instead. "Answers to what?"

Sam spread his hands. "Some of the greatest questions to plague the human race since the dawn of time."

Maybe he was a nut, after all. "Oh yeah? Like what?"

Sam settled in, but his eyes were serious. "Where did we come from… where are we going…"

Ethan threw up his hands. "Right. The meaning of life and shit. What makes you think some ancient Egyptian, who's been dead for nearly five-thousand years, could possibly tell you about any of that?"

Sam quirked a grin. After a moment he took a sip of his beer, then dug in his jeans' pocket. He reached across the table and handed Ethan a beat-up piece of paper. "Because of this."

Ethan took the paper, realizing it was a printed photo. Ethan scanned the image. It was a pictograph carved in stone and painted; and he could only assume he was looking at the vaulted chamber of Amenemhat III. Ethan remained unimpressed. The guy looked like every other picture of an ancient Egyptian pharaoh he'd seen — neat cylindrical beard, slanted eyes, full lips. Change the hat and take off the hair, take off the beard and it could be a woman.

Ethan flicked the photo. "Looks like every other photo of a pharaoh I've ever seen. What makes him different?"

Sam grinned. "Look closer."

Ethan did, skeptical. But he turned his attention to the task at hand. He might think it baloney, but those men were real.

Still… nothing.

"See anything different?" Sam smiled at him from across the table. "Maybe… somewhere around the eyes?"

Ethan's gaze went straight to the eyes. And he blinked in shock.

They weren't black, as most of them were. What he'd thought to be a simple act of time, fading the paint, turned out to be something different entirely.

This man's eyes weren't black at all.

And they weren't faded by time.
They were a dark purple.

Chapter Forty-Nine

Ethan raised his eyes to Sam in surprise.

Sam leaned back in the booth. "Weird, huh?"

Ethan flicked the photo to the table. "A bit, yeah. What's up with it?"

Sam pulled his drink close. "The eye color. It's a genetic mark of a Master Builder."

"So, this PHAROAH person was the one who built the pyramid?"

Sam shook his head. "No. Well, yes. I mean, he did. But a master builder is more than someone who... well. Builds things."

Ethan drained half his beer. "Go on."

Sam settled in. "The Master Builders were instrumental in the construction of the Egyptian pyramids. The Mayan ones, as well. They—"

"Get you gentlemen anything else?"

Sam glanced at Ethan. "How about it? Hungry? Use some substance to soak this up." Ethan shrugged. Sam turned to the server. "How about some potato skins. Bacon and chives."

When the server went off to fill their order, Sam leaned back and continued. "The Master Builders have purple eyes and are genetically predisposed to extraordinarily long lives."

Ethan laughed. "What—they're like, immortal or something? Next you're going to tell me something about the fountain of youth."

Sam shook his head. "No, it's actually true. Based in science. It has something to do with their DNA telomeres. They don't shorten with age, like us, for some reason. Consequently, they live for hundreds of years. There's a girl on our ship who—"

"A girl on your ship who what?"

Sam shook his head. "Nothing. She has purple eyes, is all. To be fair to her, sometimes they're teal, sometimes, they're topaz. So is her hair." He leaned back for the arrival of their potato skins, the fragrant steam rumbling his stomach. Sam took two for himself and gestured to Ethan to partake. The younger man did so, taking a bite as if he hadn't eaten in days. Sam wiped the grease from his chin.

"Jesus, these are delicious." He opened his eyes wide. "Anyway. With the wonder of years came intelligence far beyond that of ordinary people with ordinary lifespans. The Master Builders spread out across the globe, offering their services to various leaders in order to build great monuments."

Ethan snagged a napkin and wiped his mouth. "Fancy."

"Constructive." Sam wondered if they weren't a little drunk. He pointed a finger at Ethan. "The ancient Egyptian pyramids are believed by many to have been built by the Master Builders."

Ethan leaned back in his booth. "Yes. The Mayan pyramids too, or so I hear."

Sam laughed. "You ever heard of Atlantis?"

Ethan raised a brow. "You asked me that already."

"How about the Temple of Zeus? The Gardens of Babylon? Just to name a couple of the world's greatest wonders," Sam said, laughing at Ethan's face dancing with multi-colored Christmas lights. "You name it, they were built by Master Builders."

Chapter Fifty

The bar's parking lot smelled of hot asphalt and cold summer rain, diesel, stale cigarettes, cheap beer, and even cheaper, perfume. They'd stayed around for last call, a move that was questionably safe, but they'd kept their backs to the wall and Ethan was reasonably sure they hadn't been followed. When Sam had asked him, what made him so sure, he shrugged. "Been coming here since before I was legal. Cramer always let me in."

"You were a drinker?" Sam asked.

Ethan gave him a level stare. "I liked the music." He gestured at the stage where the band was packing up, slurping water and lager from thin plastic cups with gratitude and smiles as Cramer, presumably, congratulated them on a set well-played. "Howard's always had the best."

Now the canned sound of hard rock slid out and into the night as Sam stretched his back and checked his watch. It was close to midnight and neither of them had thought of a place to sleep for the night. Sleep would be necessary very soon.

Sam surveyed their ride, wishing Ethan had bought something a little less conspicuous. He shoved his hands in his pockets.

Ethan turned to him. "Now what?"

Sam offered up a wry grin. "Want some ice cream?"

Ethan blinked. "What?"

Sam laughed at his face. "That's what my dad used to do when he had to give me some bad news. We'd go get a soft serve from Tasty Freeze and sit on the fountain steps…" He trailed off at the look in Ethan's eyes. It was obvious Ethan's dad hadn't done many things like that with him, and from the way Ethan's shoulders loosened but the tightness stayed in his jaw, he would have killed to have those kinds of memories.

Sam shrugged elaborately to cover his mistake, feeling a little more warmly toward the kid. "Way I see it we've got two of the four labyrinth keys, thanks to you."

"Talking about keys…" Ethan said, "I'll drive."

Sam tossed him the keys to the car. "All yours."

Ethan snagged the keys out of midair and closed his fist around them, tight. "And the ice cream bit?"

Sam scratched his ear. "The ice cream bit is that our enemy is likely in possession of the other two."

Ethan snorted. "Likely possession. Come out and say it – they've got them. I'm a worst-case scenario man; SEALs are born prepared. I was trained 24/7, dead-dog exhausted, until I was prepared. Wouldn't make it out alive, otherwise. SEALs don't drop into war zones and fall through cave floors all 'cause of huntin' unicorns."

"Fair enough. So, worst-case scenario says it's safe to assume then the enemy has both the remaining labyrinth keys."

"Who are *they* exactly?"

Sam wavered. "Honestly, the less you know the better. I don't want you compromised in the future. What I can tell you is that someone is hunting the keys. I don't know if they've got their eye on other ancient relics too or if it's just these, but I can assure you, these are definitely in the plan." He held up one finger. "First, someone beat us to Xibalba and took the Mayan key. Then, a week later, George Washington's key was stolen from the Louvre in France."

"Sounds like they're organized. An expert team and most likely heavily backed by the financial support of a collector."

Sam's gaze sharpened in surprise, then Ethan grinned. Sam was strongly reminded of the boy he'd met that first day, all those years ago back in Rhyolite. Ethan appeared to be confident, more than a touch arrogant, and certainly convinced of his own superiority. "That's right, keep going."

Ethan's eyes narrowed. "So we're looking for a collector with a bunch of thugs who has access to some really nice suits. Is that about right?"

Sam blinked at the summary and assessed it. "Yeah," he said after a moment. "Sounds about right."

"And they've taken two of these keys out from under your nose."

Sam bristled. "Yeah. That sounds about right too."

Ethan grinned. "Then why don't we just take them back?"

Sam held up his hands. "Hey, son, I'm all for the idea. Don't know why I didn't think of that. I'll get right on that as soon as I know who to take them back *from*."

Ethan opened the car door, gesturing Sam to do the same. "Well then, you're in luck."

Sam paused on his way to the door's handle in surprise. "Why? Do you know who the collector is?"

"Nope," Ethan admitted and slammed the door, leaving Sam out in the hot night. Ethan rolled down his window and stuck his head out. "But I think I know someone who does."

Chapter Fifty-One

They waited until morning to attend the meeting.

After checking into a dingy motel off the beaten path, Ethan slept like a soldier – dead to the world and alert in an instant. Sam had knocked into the bathroom door on his way in because he hadn't wanted to turn on the light. Within a split second he found himself shoved against the door with an arm around his throat.

Ethan stilled then released Sam. "Sorry."

Sam rubbed his neck. "It's just me."

Now they were drinking coffee in awkward silence in the buffet room that looked like it doubled as a bingo hall at night. Ethan drank his coffee black with lots of sugar. Sam waited for the fresh pot.

He wiped his cup's rim and took a sip. "You still haven't told me where we're going."

Ethan nodded. Like this answered everything. He pulled his keys out. "Why waste the silence? It's going to be a long drive."

The morning had dawned clear, but the air was already becoming hazy with summer heat. They'd hit the highway with the windows down, Ethan driving the NSU RO 80 fast but careful among the morning commuters. They passed strip malls just waking up, empty fitness centers and secondhand computer stores, chic coffee shops on the edge of areas culled through gentrification. Ethan drove without taking his eyes off the road, but every now and then he'd flick a glance to the other lane, to passersby on the sidewalks. Sam knew without asking that he was on high alert.

Ethan said, "You want me to swing by and pick it up?"

Sam turned his attention from a car wash to Ethan. "Pick what up?"

"A hooker for the ride." sniped Ethan, rolling his eyes. "The labyrinth key I stole from Syria, Sam. What else?"

Sam shook his head, ignoring the quip. "Probably best to leave it wherever it is for now. Safer. Don't need to invite more trouble than we've already got. It's safe, where you have it hidden, right?"

"It's safe," Ethan confirmed.

"Good."

Ethan continued to drive in silence for a few minutes.

"So that'd be a *no* on the girl?" Ethan flashed a quick grin, and Sam had to laugh.

It was clear Ethan knew these roads and that he'd made this drive many times. When Sam started to recognize the signage, he kept his mouth shut, but was surprised. When they crossed the Potomac and into Washington D.C., Sam asked "Capital man?"

Ethan glanced at him. "How do you know it's a man?"

Sam considered. "Fair point."

They drove in silence a while, emerging from the suburbs and heading toward the center of town via a maze of streets that made Sam glad he wasn't driving for a change. He'd had enough of taking the wheel after yesterday.

"It is, though." Ethan spoke as if revealing some kind of truth, the tone of someone who's made up his mind to trust. He'd been quiet the entire ride and Sam wondered if that was what he'd been wrestling with. He wondered what Ethan had come from that made him wake up with karate moves in the middle of the night and that taking enemy fire came easier than having faith in his fellow man.

He'd lost Sam, though. "It is, what?"

"A man." Ethan kept his eyes on the road and made a careful turn across traffic. He shot Sam a glance from the corner of his eye as they stalled at a light. "You've actually almost met him." He tapped the wheel and cruised forward as the light changed. "Josh Rowe. He was there that morning back in Rhyolite…"

Sam swallowed and shifted his body weight, somehow uncomfortable in the seat. "Any chance he might recognize me?"

"Not a chance in hell."

Sam's eyes narrowed. "You're sure?"

"Certain. He left as soon as the shooting started."

"Smart man."

Ethan laughed. "Yeah. I'm the idiot that stayed."

Sam said, "And how exactly do you know that your friend is connected to the collector?"

"Josh knows everyone." Ethan shrugged, checking street signs and the rearview mirror. "He's a lawyer," Ethan said, as though that explained everything.

He caught Sam's face as they swung into a wide boulevard and Sam began to recognize the corporate, slick side of town. "He's a good man," Ethan hastily added. "Don't worry. He's just got a colorful past."

Sam nodded dubiously. *Didn't they all?* "In what way?"

Ethan sighed, relenting, but didn't take his eyes from the road as he said, "Josh got involved with a drug lord from the Black Muerte Cartel."

Sam raised his eyebrows but said nothing.

Ethan's brow furrowed in loyalty. "Don't," he said. "I know what you're thinking, but it's not like that. He got involved with the cartel because his little sister developed a drug habit. They hooked her in because she was pretty and lonely and, well, people can do some really stupid things sometimes."

"It happens," Sam acknowledged, his voice level, noncommittal and not judging.

Ethan took one hand off the wheel to run it through his buzz cut and fix his collar. "In this case, it turned into a habit she couldn't afford." His voice turned bitter, and Sam wasn't entirely sure who the rancor was for. "It always does, doesn't it? In the end, she ended up having to work for them to pay her bills. And once that happened, they owned her." He shifted his shoulders, but his meaning was clear.

Sam faced him head on. "Is she still hooked?"

Ethan sounded surprised. "On heroin? No. She got clean." *There was more pride in his voice than his friend's kid sister warranted*, Sam thought. "But just because she stopped using doesn't mean she can leave when she wants. They've got her, now. She knows too much. And she's useful to them. She's had to be, to survive."

He glanced at Sam as if begging him to understand. "That's how Josh got involved with working for them. He can keep tabs on his sister, maybe help her out. He's a lawyer – always good to have in your back pocket if you're on the wrong side of the law, and he's good at his job; makes himself useful, works the angles to get them to owe him favors, make himself indispensable. He's hoping he'll be able to get her out one of these days. Pull enough strings, and maybe you get somewhere, right?"

"Yeah, he sounds like a decent guy."

Ethan rounded on him in fury. "Yeah, and since when were you a saint? Mr. Harvard or wherever the hell you went to school on daddy's dime. You think that people just step into life without mud on their shoes?"

Sam raised his brows. "I'm going to pretend I didn't hear that."

Ethan's fury morphed to sullenness. "You do what you want. I'm not going to pretend I didn't say it."

Sam held up his hands. "Hey! I'm not trying to judge. I've known my share of men in dire straits." Hell. He'd been in dire straits. "Family is family. And friends are friends. And I did mean it, you know—it sounds like a more noble cause than just winning cases to get rich and buy new cars."

"He's good at that, too." Ethan grinned, despite himself. "And if you can say one thing about the cartel, they do pay well."

Sam grinned too and the mood lightened. "Maybe you and I should apply. We've got the dispatch arm taken care of already."

Ethan sounded surprised to laugh with him. When he spoke again it was a little easier. Sam felt he'd taken the chance to be vulnerable and it had paid off. He hoped the other man would trust him a little more easily in the future. Trust streamlined things, so he'd take it. They were going to need all the help they could get.

"Nah, I don't think it's a good idea. But I'm thinking there might be a vacancy soon." At Sam's raised brow, he shrugged. "See, that's why I figured there was some connection to your collector or whatever. He called me a few days ago to say hey, grab a beer someday, we should celebrate! So I asked him why. He said his sister had just finished a big job in Paris and they'd been really pleased. Said she'd mentioned it'd been the second part of her operation, or something like that, but that she only had 'two more' to go and that if successful, they might talk about her release."

"That is great!" Sam kept his voice light though; in his experience the cartel didn't just 'release' assets, nor that easily when it was someone who'd been privy to their inner workings. He expected that when, or if, she did get out, she'd have to set up quite a different life than she'd had to date—if she wanted to keep on living for any length of time.

Ethan grinned a broad, genuine smile, though worry lurked in his eyes. Sam thought he knew what a risky move it'd be. "Actually, she wants to be a circus performer. But not just in any circus; she wants to be part of something really special. As in Cirque Du Soleil kind of special."

"She any good?"

Ethan's smile flared a hundred watts. "She's amazing. You'd never think someone that small could pack that much power. She moves through the air like she's moving through water. Immune to gravity. Just… weightless. Free."

Something clicked. "Ethan," Sam said. "Your friend's sister wasn't SCUBA diving in the Yucatan, recently, was she?"

"What?" Ethan blinked at the non-sequitur. "I don't know – Josh didn't mention anything like that. It wouldn't surprise me, though. I know she's one hell of a diver. Did all kinds of training here in D.C., then went down to Mexico to take some on-site courses specific to cave diving."

Sam shook his head. "There can't be that many cartel-working cave divers with the body of a dancer. It's more than likely the same person who stole the key hidden in Xibalba." He glanced at Ethan. "If they're trusting her with this mission, she must be in pretty deep."

Ethan's chin came up, a hardness in the set of his jaw. He kept his eyes on the road, but his voice was steady and sure. "She's a good person. She deserves to be free."

Sam looked at him with curiosity. "You sound like you have a soft spot for her."

Ethan shrugged. "She's my best friend's sister. I've known her since I was a kid and, yes, I've loved her a long time."

"Childhood sweethearts, hey?"

Ethan shook his head. "No. She hated my guts when we were kids."

Sam smiled. "Is that so? Why?"

"To be honest, because I wasn't the nicest of kids. My father beat me and I took that out on just about anyone around me, including my friend's little kid sister."

"So, what changed?"

"I got the shit kicked out of me by a bigger kid, and a stranger saved my life. After some reflection, I decided I wanted to be that stranger instead of the bully. That's why I joined the Navy SEALS. I wanted to help protect those who couldn't protect themselves."

"And the girl?"

Ethan grinned. "She grew up and as time went on, she and I seemed to have more in common than she and her brother."

Sam watched him levelly. "That sounds… complicated."

Ethan shrugged. "Not really."

"Man. You're dating your best friend's sister. Tell me how that's not complicated even if she wasn't working for the cartel?"

Finally, Ethan laughed. "Yeah, okay. It's not ideal. And he doesn't know. We're going to tell him, but first we need to get her out of there. If he knew, and they knew he knew…" His eyes dimmed. "I've seen what people do for leverage. No one knows. And no one can know if she's going to stay safe." He turned to Sam, gaze sharp and piercing, suddenly furious. "The boss would execute her if she escapes. He'd track her down and… she's told me stories of what he'd do to her."

"Terrible?"

"No." Ethan's face went flat. "She didn't make it sound that bad. That's how I know."

They drove in silence for a while.

Ethan turned to him and burst out. "Sam. I don't know what the hell you're doing here, or why I met you that day in Nevada, but Mia's in there, she's stuck with these people trying to kill us, and she doesn't deserve to be. Josh and I we're doing our best, but we're just not that well connected. But you know something about these men we don't know. Otherwise they wouldn't have been after you. You scare them. That's good. Maybe with your help, we can end this, once and for all."

Sam watched the gleaming buildings spin by. "Let me ask you something. The cartel boss. What does he look like? Do you know?"

Ethan shook his head. "Nothing really. Mia just said he goes by the name of…"

"Carlos Gonzalez."

Ethan turned to him surprised. "Yeah, actually. How did you know?"

Sam's mouth tightened in the memory of vengeance as something clicked into place that had been missing for fifteen years. "Because Carlos Gonzalez ordered President Harris killed after he discovered that I had found one of the Labyrinth Keys."

Chapter Fifty-Two

Sam watched as they passed through the city center and headed toward a bustling, chic neighborhood full of activists in crocs and secretaries in suits. Everyone glued to their phones. The summer air fanned his hair through the crack in the window.

Now Sam raised his brows as Ethan slowed down and cruised for a parking spot. "We've been trolling these streets for twenty minutes, Ethan." He glanced at the clock, the sun that was now noticeably higher in the sky. "You sure this is where Josh wanted to meet us?" The sidewalk was packed with morning commuters and tourists eager to experience the nation's capital and they weren't budging an inch.

"Yep," Ethan replied as he peered out the window, then slowed to a stop as a sedan in front of them flashed its taillights, preparing to pull away from the curb. "There's no way anyone is going to pay attention to a few more people here. The worst that could happen is that someone's going to think we're meeting with a man on his morning coffee break."

Sam had to admit that there was a good chance they wouldn't be noticed in the crowd. His stomach growled and he wondered if they'd get some breakfast.

Ethan raised a hand out the window to signal to a dump truck waiting behind him and slid into the parking spot with his bad-ass car like a pro. He slapped his pockets as the engine died, checked the console, then glanced at Sam. "You got money for the meter?"

Sam hopped out of the car and shut the door gently. He dug in his pockets and pulled out some change. He slid the quarters into the meter and the little ticker swung to half an hour. Sam shook his head. Two dollars of quarters for thirty minutes. He hoped this meeting was going to be quick. "Next one's on you, man," he said, putting his remaining change back in his pocket. "You ready to go?"

Ethan was already on the street. "Come on."

Sam started after him but turned and looked ruefully at the car. He knew that he would probably be back, but he did love that car.

Ethan noticed Sam's glance from the curb. He grinned. "Nice, isn't it?"

"Yeah." Sam started out of his trance. "Someday you'll have to tell me how you wound up with it. So. Anyway. What about this friend of yours? Where is he?"

Ethan pointed across the street toward a busy Cuban cafe. Quaint iron tables outside the café were packed with tourists and Sam couldn't see anyone who looked familiar. Sam squinted, but still saw no one. Ethan raised an arm in a wave and finally Sam saw one of the men sitting alone raise a hand in acknowledgment. He put a finger in the book he was reading and sipped his coffee with a grin.

Sam started walking, then stalled when he felt Ethan's grip on his elbow. He turned. "Keep your eyes open," Ethan said, glancing around. "We have no way of knowing what we're getting into."

That was for damn sure. Sam nodded and straightened his shoulders and let Ethan take the lead as they crossed the street.

Ethan grinned as they reached the table. "Starting early?"

Josh laughed and toasted him with his coffee cup. "Busy morning, my man. Cracked ten skulls already and it's not even noon."

Sam watched unnoticed as the two men caught up. Ethan's friend Josh wasn't that tall of a man, even seated, but he carried himself with the assurance of someone used to getting out of sticky situations, one way or another. It was a good quality in a lawyer, even if it did make him feel a bit slippery. Then again, Sam reflected, slippery was probably a good quality to have when you were trying to double-cross the most powerful cartel in North America to rescue your sister.

He extended his hand with a polite smile.

"Hey, you must be Josh. I'm Sam…"

"I know who you are." Josh interrupted his introduction with another grin and shook his hand firmly. "Ethan told me." He gestured at the table and snagged a chair from nearby. "Mind if we use this?" The chair shrieked as he pulled it close. Knew I was coming, but couldn't get the chair before now?

Sam ignored his annoyance and took the offered seat. "So, you know why we're here?"

Josh turned his gaze to Sam. It was the sharp, assertive gaze of a politician or a playground bully. Sam was generally unbothered by anyone else, but he couldn't help but feel dirty as Josh inspected him. It put him on guard, and he wondered what the hell Ethan had gotten them into. But if this man had information about the keys and how to get them, then it was a necessary evil.

Lots of things were necessary evils.

Just as Sam was about to say something, Josh steepled his hands and leaned back in his seat. "Yeah, I know why you're here."

Sam wondered why Ethan had suddenly gone so quiet. "And?"

"It's impossible."

Sam fought to keep himself under control. He wanted to punch this slick man in the face.

"It's impossible? You like to waste people's time, don't you?" He shook his head. "You're a lawyer, you're paid by the hour. Of course you like to waste people's time." He slapped the table and prepared to stand. "We're done here. If that's the best you can offer."

"I've been told that you're in the business of doing the impossible." Josh regarded him calmly over the Styrofoam cup. Stuck halfway to his feet, Sam looked over at Ethan. Ethan nodded. Sam realized that Josh was just messing with him, gauging him.

"That is my business, yes." Sam sat back down, tugging at his pants.

"I needed an idea of how committed you are." Josh eased off. "You have to forgive me. I don't know anything about you. But Ethan says he trusts you and he doesn't trust many men."

Sam glanced at Ethan but Ethan wasn't looking at him. Josh noticed the look. He nodded. "Because he trusts you, he'll probably have told you I have a personal investment in how this all plays out."

"Your sister?"

"Yes."

They sat in silence in the busy street. Finally, Josh shrugged. "There might be a way. I have some favors I can call in; from people who know some people."

"What kind of people?"

"People who owe me. They're good to have."

Sam narrowed his eyes. "I think that…"

"Sam. If he says they're good to have, then they're good to have. He knows how to get what he wants."

Sam shrugged. "If you say so."

Josh leaned forward. "You want the Labyrinth Keys, right? We need to get in and get out."

Sam laughed in disbelief. "Hang on just a second. Ethan says you know where these keys are, but how the hell do I know you really do? Where do you get this information?"

Josh glanced at Ethan. "I don't know if Ethan told you, but I'm a lawyer. I know a lot of people. Some of them are…" He waved his hand back and forth. "On the other side of the tracks, shall we say." For the first time he looked Sam in the face without trying to hide anything. "Ethan told you about her. I know he did. And I found out from her what she was up to. She tells me, keeps me in the loop because she knows the more information I have, the safer I am." He shook his head. "I wish she wouldn't because it's dangerous as hell for her. The only thing that keeps her safe is that everyone in the crew knows I'm true to my word. Or, that I have been so far." He fiddled with his coffee cup in a sudden show of vulnerability. "Because she's still in there. She told me there's a man who wants these keys. He didn't tell her why, but that's what they're after." He looked at them levelly. "She's still in there. She's my kid sister and I'll do anything to get her out. Seems like a fair trade – some stupid ancient stone keys for a life."

Sam didn't reply. That seemed a little dramatic. But, he reflected, it was very likely true.

Josh glanced at him. "Like I said, there is a way. I have a guy ready to receive a call, but I need you to know something."

"Which is?"

"We get one shot at this. It's not like you can just walk out and try again. If we go in for this, it's going to take everything you've got and there's a good chance that everything you've got might not be enough. Though it will be enough," he added, as Sam opened his mouth, "if you're as good as he says you are- but there isn't much wiggle room for slipping up." He grinned, but his eyes were serious. "Like, no room, actually."

Sam leaned forward on the table. "I'm in." Out of the corner of his eye, he saw Ethan shake his head.

Josh glanced between them, then reached for his pocket. Sam tensed, but he just pulled out a pack of cigarettes and tapped one out like a pro. "Listen, bud." Josh slid the cigarette in between his lips and lit it. "This isn't about if you die or not. If they get a glimpse of your face, never mind a picture or a corpse, everyone you've ever interacted with is dead. Family, friends, all of them."

Sam glanced between them. "That's ridiculous. There's no way they would spend that many resources on what amounts to a nobody."

Ethan grabbed Sam's arm. His eyes bore into Sam's. "He's serious, Sam." said Ethan. "These men are connected." He didn't look away. "You know they are."

Sam fixed Josh with a steady stare. "I've seen what they can do. I need these keys. If they get the second two, they'll be unstoppable." Sam took a deep breath. "I'm ready. It's you who has to decide. She's your sister."

"Don't."

Josh looked around as if people were watching. Ethan looked around too. There was nothing but tourists and now the influx of the early brunch crowd, which could hide anyone. Sam fought to keep his hands on the table, to not scratch his neck.

Finally, Josh drained his coffee and pushed to his feet. He hadn't even asked if they wanted anything to drink, Sam thought. "I'll be right back."

Sam raised his brows. "Where are you going?"

Josh grinned, but his eyes were haunted. "I'm going to make a call. Make a man an offer he can't refuse."

Sam watched him walk off into the crowd and loiter near the parking meters. Sam checked his watch; they had ten minutes left before they had to go feed their meter. Josh spoke into the phone while watching Ethan's car.

Ethan turned from watching him to Sam as Sam watched Josh. He saw a similar expression on the other man's face – a resolute determination. "You ever done this before?"

"Just part of the job," replied Ethan, with a hard look in his eyes.

Ethan's hands remained steady on the table and not for the first time Sam wondered what exactly had happened in this boy's past. Before Sam had a chance to ask him about it, Josh reappeared, pocketing his phone with the ease of a man who spent most of his life staring at a screen. That was really quick, Sam thought.

Josh sat down; his shoulders hunched. His face was closed, and he was deep in thought. He opened his mouth as if to speak, then closed it again and fiddled with a ring on his right hand – a flat black stone set in silver. It's a nice piece, Sam thought. He wondered at its significance.

Sam briefly considered speaking first, then closed his mouth again and decided to wait.

"They're in a drug lab," Josh said. "Along a remote jungle section of the Yucatan, in Mexico."

"So we can just fly over there, steal the Labyrinth Keys and rescue your sister — does that sound about right?"

"Sure, that is, if the people with all the guns paid to make sure the cartel's millions of dollars' worth of drugs don't disappear and don't kill you in the process."

"That doesn't sound so dangerous," Sam said. "I know people in the DOJ. I'm sure you know people in the DOJ. I can put in a call." He had been about to say the secretary of defense, then thought better of it. No use putting all his cards on the table just yet. He still didn't know how much Ethan had shared. "We'll get the feds to back us. We can bust down a drug lab, easy. They want to bring down the cartel just as much as us."

"No! Not the feds." Josh's eyes were wild and then he got himself under icy control. "If the cartel gets one whiff that this is an outside job, it's going to be worse. So much worse you don't even want to think about it."

Ethan broke in with a steady stare. "He's right, Sam. If they think the government is involved, it becomes an issue of national security."

Sam slapped the table. "It already *is* an issue of national security!" He threw up his hands. "We've got the firepower of the biggest army on the planet on our side and you don't want to use them?"

"Not with her life on the line!"

"What firepower?"

The two men spoke together and glares sliced around the table in tense silence. What Josh hadn't said – would never say, because he was a macho man who wanted Sam to think he'd made his peace with it, was that if the feds got involved, they'd kill his sister for sure.

He was probably right.

Standoff.

Finally, Josh raised his hands, almost in apology, and looked Sam straight in the face. "It's in the Lacandon Jungle," he said, and Sam realized why he was reluctant now. His heart sank. The remote location meant two things. The cartel had enough money and enough motivation to put the drug lab in the middle of nowhere. That meant that they had some serious resources lying around. Second, if they pursued them, it wasn't like they could lure them to some public location where they might easily get the jump on them. No. Here, Sam's team would be walking in blindly, entering the cartel's home territory without any real chance of recon. No. This wasn't going to be easy.

Sam glanced again at Josh and was struck by the cautious hope in his eyes beneath the bravado, beneath the fear. He glanced at Ethan, confirming his suspicions. Josh didn't give a shit about the American population or protecting the president. The only reason Josh was helping them was to rescue his own sister.

Sam stood up. His chair shrieked. "Let's do it."

Josh stood, startled, and Ethan did the same. Sam reached out his hand to the lawyer, who took it after a moment, his eyes full of gratitude. Sam grinned at him, trying to be reassuring. When he looked at Ethan, the thanks in his eyes, the faith, made him stronger. Maybe it would be okay. They'd be walking into a death trap, but maybe, just maybe, they'd pull off the impossible.

Chapter Fifty-Three

On board the *USS George Washington*, Gulf of Mexico
The Bell Boeing V-22 Osprey sat in the middle of the liftoff pad in all its magnificent beauty.

It was shaped like an airplane yet was the size of a helicopter. It had two huge propellers on the ends of its wings. The true novelty of the vehicle, however, was that the propellers rotated up and down. This allowed for vertical take offs, which basically meant the Osprey was both a helicopter and a plane, and at the same time.

Needless to say, it was Sam's favorite thing. He was very excited that he was getting to run an actual mission with it. It made the almost certain death risk worth it. Well, almost.

The roar from the propellers deafened him as he, Ethan, and Josh jogged across the tarmac and clattered up the shaky steps and into the Osprey. As they entered, waiting soldiers in non-descript uniforms handed them the headsets that they would wear during the flight. Sam settled them over his painful ears with gratitude.

As Sam slipped his on Ethan tapped him on the shoulder and gestured to two seats at the center of the craft. Sam made his way down the narrow aisle and strapped himself in.

The Osprey was even better inside. He'd never seen such engineering. The seatbelts were designed so that they would never break during a crash yet could be released instantly with the click of a button. He wondered what Tom would have had to say about her.

Tom. He wished Tom were here to save his ass in this.

"Beautiful, isn't she?" Josh had to shout to be heard over the headset.

"How'd you notice?" Sam could feel himself bellowing but it sounded like a whisper. He realized that Ethan and Josh were both looking at him. He suddenly felt self-conscious.

"Everyone is surprised their first time." Ethan said with a grin, speaking with the ease of a man so used to life and death situations that he was able to roll with just about anything; content with taking the good as it came. "Consider it a treat. I had to pull a bunch of strings to get this for us." He strapped himself in next to Sam while Josh made his seat across the aisle. "Definitely worth it."

The rumble of the engines couldn't be described yet reminded Sam of a lion's roar he'd heard in Africa a while back. Sam gripped the arm rests and ran through the plan.

"Loaded. Lifting off." Sam heard the pilot's voice over his headset. He checked his gun one more time. He would usually be fine with a pistol, just in case, but Josh had insisted that everyone be armed to the teeth. As a result, Sam had a Kevlar vest and throat guard, fireproof pants, two belts of ammo strapped across his chest, with the entire ensemble topped off with two pistols, couple of knives, and a handful of grenades. All in total, Sam probably had hundreds of thousands of dollars' worth of equipment on him. He'd never worn this much firepower in his life. It felt heavy.

He turned to Ethan.

"How long was it again?" asked Sam. But Josh answered.

"Ride's going to be four hours, but we'll be notified when we hit air space over the Yucatan Jungle." He braced his elbows on his knees and leaned toward the two men who were putting their lives on the line with him. "When we get that far, the pilot's going to shut off the engines and glide in until we hit X-Factor." He glanced at Ethan. "What about landing?"

"If the pilot has to, he'll turn the engines back on. But this guy's good. I've seen him coast to a stop on a dime in the desert. We all took bets." He flipped his lighter. "Hopefully that'll catch them unaware."

Sam nodded. It was smart to make sure that no one could hear them when they flew in. He looked out the window. Finally, the base had faded into the trees and all he could see was green below.

It was a tense four hours and they each spent it all inside their own thoughts. Ethan triple checked his weapons. Josh spent time on his phone. For his part, Sam stared out the window, lost in the past, lost in the future and what he hoped was coming.

When he looked out of the window, all he saw was clouds. For a moment he was taken aback, and then realized that the pilot was forcing the Osprey to go as high as possible so they'd get the most distance out of the glide.

"You think we're all going to make it?" asked Ethan unexpectedly.

"What can we do, besides believe it?" Josh shot back. Sam agreed with a wry grin. They couldn't do anything besides trust themselves.

He nodded at Josh. "She's his sister, trapped in a life of terror and lies." He glanced at Ethan. "She's your friend." Ethan glanced away. "And I'm trying to stop criminals from unlocking ancient secrets that will let them take over the world." He spread his hands. "If those aren't good reasons, I don't know what are. We're all the best at what we do." Sam sent Ethan a reassuring smile. "We'll make it out, trust me."

Ethan nodded, but Sam could see that he was still nervous. Sam remembered what he had learned from his marine training – being brave, especially in a military setting, didn't mean you didn't feel fear. It meant that even in the face of fear, you could operate perfectly and Sam was confident Ethan would perform.

"Starting gliding sequence." The pilot's voice shook Sam out of his trance. They glanced at him.

Sam held up his hands. "Let's run through the plan. We glide in. Team A covers the doorways, team B comes in toward the inside."

Josh nodded. "Mia says there's a room they've set up to store their hoard. Gonzales likes to go in there and preen. She says that's where the keys will be."

"Guarded?"

"Mia said there's two men at all times, but sometimes they're in a good mood." He threw up his hands. "Whatever that means. Now. Mia is going to be in there; she set up a meeting with Carlos—"

Ethan turned on him, stunned. "You ASSHOLE. You put her in there? Straight in the line of fire?"

Josh threw up his hands as if he wished it weren't so. "You think I had a say? *You've* met her!" Ethan glowered, but apparently this rang true. "Listen." Josh ran his hand through his hair. "It's the best I can do! She'll be safe with him. He trusts her. He won't expect it to be a lead-on. He's a bragger. He'll want to gloat about their success, talk about the next phase of the mission. She said she'll keep him there until we get past the guards."

"How the hell is she going to do that?"

Josh grinned. "She's a smooth talker. Trust me. That's the least of our worries."

"How are we going to get in?"

"My man on the inside is going to poison the morning brew. Nothing serious, but enough to knock out as many as he can. He's got others lined up who'll create a diversion. It's not going to get them totally out of the way but should give us a chance to find and get in through the cracks. Get to the treasure room, get the keys…" He shrugged. "Take as many of them out as we can. Get Mia. Get out."

"What happens to Carlos?"

"We'll have to deal with him."

Silence for a moment. Then the static interrupted, announcing their descent.

They looked at each other.

"And the entrance?"

Ethan cocked his weapon. "We've all got silencers, don't we? Let's use them."

Chapter Fifty-Four

The jungle was hot and humid and, not for the first time, Sam thought he was going to die. That he'd come all this way to extract two keys to save the world seemed utterly ridiculous. But he knew it was for more than that. There was an innocent girl in there, and this was to end a battle that he'd gotten involved in fifteen years ago that he'd never wanted to fight in the first place.

Sam checked his weapons as the pilot guided them closer to the trees, silent as death. It was time to end this.

Beside him he saw Ethan doing the same and grinned.

The Osprey set down in the jungle, almost vertically. Almost like a hovercraft straight out of science fiction. She was without a doubt, hands-down the coolest ride he'd ever encountered. He turned to Ethan as they unbuckled. "This ride alone almost makes it fucking worth it." He rarely swore. *It's the nerves*, he thought, and got a grip on himself. Nerves made you nervous; they couldn't afford to be nervous.

He pulled himself deep into his mind and set the controls. They'd already made it out. It was already finished, Carlos dead, the cartel beaten, Mia rescued, the keys regained. It was a visualization technique he'd developed back in the army – almost like a copy and paste of reality. He never really knew if it worked, but it helped ground him and it made him feel centered, focused.

In his mind, Sam released the keys as the plane touched down.

Ethan gave him the thumbs up and they swarmed off the plane and down the shaky steps. It was completely silent – just jungle sounds and the soft metallic creak of their feet on the stairs. A sharp contrast to when they'd boarded back on board the *USS George Washington*.

The dense jungle pressed in close and Sam and Ethan both turned to Josh, who had the GPS map on his phone. He gestured forward and they fell in line behind. Josh took point as discussed; in the off chance they were spotted he could say he was coming to speak with the boss. He'd make something up, he'd said.

But the plan wasn't to be spotted. They stuck to the shadows as they crept along. Sam didn't see any cameras, but it didn't mean they weren't any. They were banking on the fact that so few people knew of this location and the general remoteness of it to put the cartel at an advantage: They didn't expect attack. People who didn't expect to be attacked got lazy. Sam hoped to God they got lazy.

Regardless, he knew going in that they couldn't leave anyone alive.

They also couldn't be seen. Couldn't be recognized. He scratched at the mask covering his face, sweating in the heat. It was a pain in the ass and dangerous but couldn't be avoided. If it was true- and he knew it was true- that the cartel could track them down and make their lives miserably long or miserably short- then they couldn't take the chance of being recognized.

"How far?" He whispered at Ethan's back, ahead of him.

"Two hundred yards." Ethan was deep within himself, on high alert, like a jungle cat stalking prey. Sam remembered that feeling of power himself.

They continued on.

The plan was for Josh to introduce them at the gate- they were collectors who had information about the last two keys. Once they were through, the team behind would take out the guards and Josh's man on the inside would take care of the security cameras. Sam, Josh, and Ethan would head for the treasure room and take out the boss, where Mia was supposed to be detaining him.

That was the plan, anyway.

The bunker came into view: a squat, ominous building of cinderblock and concrete and barbed wire fences. Cameras on the posts. It looked like a scene straight out of any military man's nightmare. An outpost in the middle of nowhere, packed with a hundred border patrol hostiles just itching for action.

They stopped to collect themselves. Josh looked at Ethan and Sam. They took a collective breath and stashed their weapons.

"Ready?"

Ethan didn't grin. "As we'll ever be. Let's go."

There wasn't much to add to that. Sam followed as the two men stepped out of the shadows and into plain sight.

They were stopped immediately by the guard at the gate. "Who the hell are you?"

Josh offered up his lawyer smile. "Brought by some clients for the boss. This place is hell to find on a map, you know that, right? When he said it was easy to find, *Jesus*. Never heard such bullshit."

The guard glared. "Clients for what? He expecting you?"

Josh didn't back down. "The boss's business is the boss's business." He shrugged. "Sorry, man. I just follow orders. He said bring them here, don't tell anyone. I haven't told anyone."

The guard cocked his gun. "Consider me no one?"

Josh held up his hands. "Listen, I don't want to get my asshole stitched or opened, okay? I just want to get these men to the boss so he's happy, making everybody happy. I set it up with Mia. She's been working a beat getting keys for Carlos. Don't ask me what they're for; I honestly don't know." He gestured to Sam and Ethan. "But they've been having a shit time finding the rest of them. Finally, she tracked down a source – these two know where the others are – but they won't talk to anyone but Carlos."

The guard gestured the gun toward Ethan and Sam. "Why they in masks?"

Ethan didn't waver. "Self-preservation. Faces get you killed; this is deeper than you know."

The guard wavered. "Gotta check." He went for a radio. They waited, tense. This was Josh's man's time to shine. If he didn't come through…

"Castro. Men here for the boss. You know about it?"

"Cleared." A massive click and the gate opened. "Send them through."

The guard didn't seem convinced. He put down the radio but continued to glare suspiciously. "How do I know –"

There was a brief "pft" and then he slumped forward, just a bit, and the one next to him jerked as if to go for his gun, and then he, too, slumped. Ethan caught the second while Josh caught the first, and Sam's hand came out of his pocket where he'd kept the pistol with the silencer out of sight.

Josh propped the guard against the wall with a nail gun. "Man, this heat," he said. "Gotta be careful."

He slipped the nail gun to Ethan who slammed the long spikes into the other guard's dead palm and into the concrete wall. It wasn't too convincing, but they didn't need much time. At least he hoped they didn't. They just had to get inside.

They left the gate open behind them. Sam, Ethan and Josh slipped inside.

The bunker was armed to the teeth. It looked like a demented version of Sam's high school with small rooms, all branching off a main corridor. He smelled coffee and disinfectant and wondered if Josh's contact had succeeded in poisoning the brew. If not, they were going to need every piece of ammo they'd brought with them.

Now that they were in, they had no idea where to go. Mia had promised to get in and keep Carlos in the treasure room, but she hadn't given them the map like she'd promised. They didn't know if this meant the whole plan had gone to shit already or she didn't want to blow her cover.

They were also supposed to get a guide but that, apparently, hadn't worked out either.

Sam checked his watch. They were five minutes late. He didn't know how long Mia would be able to detain the boss. They didn't have time to figure it out.

Ethan took point. "Fan out. Shoot if you have to — meaning, if you think they're going to run."

They nodded. Sam gripped his pistol, touching the ammo on his vest.

Ethan turned and without warning kicked open the nearest door, gun in hand, hot and ready.

Beyond his shoulder Sam saw what looked like a break room. He swung around wildly and spied a camera. Take it out?

Ethan sliced his hand through the air.

Sam took out the camera.

The men in the break room looked like mules, just there shooting the shit over coffee in the morning and doing their best to wake up from a night of hard partying the day before. Sam thought they were either mules or chefs. None of them looked too important and they certainly looked terrified at the sight of the gun. Their paycheck wasn't worth their lives to them, it seemed.

If that was true, they were in the wrong line of work. Nothing was certain in this goddamn world.

Ethan snapped his fingers, swinging the gun around at them.

"Boss!" he barked, low and urgent without shouting. "Tell me where the boss is, and no one gets hurt. Get back to your coffee and churros. Got a meeting with the boss and the motherfucker didn't tell me where the hell he'd be waiting."

A stammering mule babbled something in Spanish. Sam could barely make out the words 'middle' and 'room' and 'floor'. They were looking for a middle room on one of the floors? That narrowed it down.

The mule coughed then slumped forward. For a moment Sam thought he'd been shot, but no one looked as if they'd fired. He smelled no gun smoke. Just coffee and cleaning solution and stale sweat.

The mule nearby slumped forward.

It looked like Josh's contact had come through; at least in one regard: Innocent casualties were getting knocked out of commission. Sam fervently hoped it'd be enough to help them out.

Sam and Josh and Ethan looked at each other with desperation.

"Split up? Cover more ground?"

Sam shook his head. "We stay together. We need to cover each other's backs."

They backed out of the door and headed down the halls, kicking in the unopened doors and peering in; clearing each room as they went. No luck. They hurriedly secured any men they came across.

Eventually, they came to the third floor. Sam was starting to despair they'd never find it. Josh bled onto the linoleum, his white shirt ripped into strips and tied around his bicep, tightening each with his teeth. Ethan took over point, gun raised. They paused, waited in silence, hearing voices inside.

A man's voice and a woman's voice. In Spanish. Too hard to hear what they were saying. Sam, Ethan and Josh exchanged glances.

"Whoever the man is, shoot to kill as soon as we get through that door." Josh's eyes were hard and certain. "I'm not taking any chances with her safety. We need to get her out; time to end this."

Ethan nodded. Sam stepped forward and turned the handle.

The door opened without a problem. They swung inside.

A man who could only be Carlos, the drug lord, reclined on a plush couch that looked lifted from some French chateau, covered in dust. His expensive shirt was open to his navel, showcasing a thick mat of dark hair on his chest. He had mean, intelligent eyes and a stupid, self-assured smile.

The woman straddling him was thin and small, her crop of dark hair styled in curls.

Sam recognized her instantly, even with her hair now dry.

Something was unfamiliar, though – she was entwined around Carlos, his hand down her shirt, cupping her breast.

Ethan stalled at seeing this scene and for one crucial second, his gun faltered.

Carlos gripped Mia's arm in surprise, consternation on his face at having his dalliance interrupted. Then he saw the guns and his hand went to his pants – open at the top, Sam saw – and pulled Mia in front of him as he realized his gun was on a table just out of reach.

Mia was dragged into the line of fire. She winced in pain as his meaty hands locked around her thin throat.

"You shoot me I'll break her goddamn neck," he growled. Mia's wide eyes were steady and calm as the men stood there trying to get a clear shot at the boss. Sam had no doubt he'd let her take any bullets meant for him. "Who the fuck are you?"

"We want the girl," Sam said, hoping his mask disguised his voice and that Carlos wouldn't remember what it'd sounded like fifteen years earlier. "And we want the keys. Give us those and no one gets hurt."

The boss laughed and a light of recognition sparked in his eyes. "If it isn't Captain America. Who are you? More capital stooges?"

Josh stepped forward, but Sam gripped his arm, holding him back. They needed Josh, of all people to remain unrecognized. He needed to keep working for them as they might need him in the future.

Ethan stepped forward; gun trained on the drug lord. He stepped to the side, clearly hoping to get a shot at Carlos's fleshy middle, but the boss's gaze followed him, tightening his grip.

"I swear to Christ and your whore spawn mother, I'll break her neck if you come one step closer!"

Mia turned to Carlos in panic, trying to twist her hand free.

"Carlos," she babbled, desperation in her voice. "Baby, don't let me die. They want me. They won't shoot me. I'll get your gun, just don't break my neck."

Ethan cocked his gun and trained it on her chest. "We want the keys. You're secondary."

Her eyes flashed fury for an instant as they stared at each other.

Please, girl, Sam pleaded silently, *don't do anything stupid…*

"Carlos," she said soothingly, "I'm going to reach for the gun, just let me get it."

Many things happened at once.

Carlos eased his grip on her neck, Mia leaned across his body for the gun on the table, and Ethan's finger tightened on the trigger.

Steel flashed in Mia's hand.

Carlos screamed.

Ethan fired.

Mia pushed off the couch, covered in blood. She wiped the tiny knife on her shorts as the drug lord gurgled from where she'd sliced his jugular.

She held onto the knife as the men stared at her.

"Come on!" she shouted. "You never seen a woman? Get out of here!"

Ethan snapped out of his reverie. "Keys."

She rummaged in a box. "Take your damned keys and let's get out of here."

Sam tucked the keys in his pants. Mia looked up at Josh and then she threw her arms around his neck. "I knew you'd make it, big brother."

He held her tightly, then released her. "Always do."

She turned to Ethan with a tentative grin. "You were gonna shoot me?"

"We'll talk later," he snapped. "Once we're out."

She touched his face. "He was going to leave," she said, as if they were the only two in the room. "I had to keep him here somehow."

Sam ushered them out of the room. "Romantically touching, yes, but can it wait until we're out?"

They hurried out the door and into the hall. "What about the knife?" Ethan asked as they clattered down the stairs. Their cover was blown anyway. Josh fired a shot at a man with a pistol coming up the stairs. Head shot. They kept moving, past his body, continuing down. Two floors to go.

"I always carry it," Mia said breathlessly. "You would too if you lived with them." She flashed a quick grin and Ethan blasted a horde of men coming at them from behind, shielding her with his body. "That's the good thing about having boobs. Keeps a lot of things hidden."

The men collapsed in a heap of death.

One more floor.

Ethan cocked his gun. "Surprised he didn't find it. Looked like he was on the hunt."

"Nah, he's a pussy. He only gropes the sides." She grinned.

Josh panted after her, gripping his arm in pain. "Mia," he gasped as they reached the ground floor and Sam hurled a grenade at a window, blasting through wall and wired-glass, alike. "You don't have boobs."

She turned on him, knife to his belly as they climbed through the window. "Say that again and *you* won't have any balls."

There was no sign of the Osprey.

They sprinted for the trees anyway as the men on the walls opened fire. "Now what?" Mia yelled.

"Get to the…"

Sam's instructions were drowned out by the arrival of the craft as it landed vertically. It was as if they'd planned this mission right down to the last second. The stairs descended, they ran up, and the door closed behind them, as enemy fire peppered the hull. By the time the men got close enough to make any kind of difference, the doors were closed, and they were pushing off again, straight up into the canopy, straight up into the sky.

Chapter Fifty-Five

Sam stared at the two Labyrinth Keys.

They were housed in a purpose-built metallic suitcase.

His eyes drifted out the large windshield and across the shimmering waters of the Gulf of Mexico, far below.

Ethan said, "I'll pick up the Syrian key from where I have it hidden, a quick stop in Rhyolite then off to Egypt – last stop, Strabo's labyrinth."

The corners of Sam's lips curled upward, offering up the slightest of grins. "Why? What do you think we'll find there?"

Ethan frowned. "Is that where you buried the last labyrinth key?"

Sam tilted his head to the side but remained silent.

"All those years ago," Ethan persisted… "You and I buried something. I glimpsed the sign of the labyrinth key. Isn't that what we buried there?"

Sam shook his head. "Goodness, no! I knew something like that was way too valuable to bury. My Labyrinth Key has been stored in a bank's private vault under a name that can't be traced back to me and as an item that in no way could ever have been connected to the labyrinth key."

"Then, what did we bury?" Ethan's forehead furrowed in puzzlement. He cursed. "I mean, what sort of secret have I kept all these years, if not the location of the last labyrinth key?"

Sam smiled. "Secrets which are going to come out soon, but not yet. If anything, they're even more dangerous now."

Ethan asked, "Will I ever learn the truth?"

Sam's eyes aimlessly drifted across the ocean, before landing hard on Ethan's firm gaze. "If we reach Strabo's Labyrinth and get out alive, I promise you, we'll go back to Rhyolite together and bring to life secrets that have been buried for far too long… or possibly, not long enough."

Ethan locked eyes with him, his jaw set firm. "Agreed. I'll go with you to Egypt and help you reach the ancient library beneath Strabo's labyrinth – and then I'm going to hold you to that."

Sam grinned. "Please, make sure that you do."

Chapter Fifty-Six

Nile River, Egypt

The motor-yacht formed a dark silhouette along the river. At a length of one hundred and eight feet, with a width of forty-five feet, it was shaped more like a bullet than a traditional yacht. She had a long black hull and narrow beam, tapering to a razor-sharp prow.

The trailing whitewash, a stark contrast against the near black river against the night sky, was the only demonstration of the vessel's unique combination of raw power. The twin Rolls Royce 28,000hp MTU diesel engines and twin ZF gearboxes which projected the force of the combined 56,000 hp into four, HT1000 HamiltonJet waterjets; and did so all but silently. This massive power was married to her unique hull, which used a series of hydraulic actuators to alter her shape in order to achieve the greatest speed and stability under any type of sea conditions. She was able to lift out of the water and into an aquaplane at speeds of 60 knots—making her the fastest motor yacht of her size in the world.

Now she sliced up the river that had seen the birth and death of a civilization thousands of years before like a silent angel of vengeance, like a river god herself. The Nile sliced through the desert like a snake, a dark thread scaled by the wind rippling its obsidian surface.

Sam felt, more than heard, the power humming under him and knew he was home. There was something about the unique thrum of the *Tahila* that comforted Sam in a way that nothing else did. He'd worked his whole life for this sense of release.

They'd met up with the ship as the last of the sun's rays drained from the sky and Genevieve had a veritable Egyptian feast waiting for them; a very welcome sight after the flight from the jungle to D.C. to Egypt. Sam hadn't set foot on dry ground in what felt like a week.

Now Sam and the crew sat around the table with empty plates and the carnage from dinner before them as the engine pumped in a pattern endlessly, droning on and on in Sam's ear until it became background noise, like the rhythmic drum of a clock's second-hand tick. The rumbling never left. It made the table at which Sam sat shake just enough that an empty plastic cup rattled loudly without cessation until he stood up and filled it with Coke—just to quiet it down. As he began to lower himself back into his seat, the entire boat lurched forward, pitching Sam's balance off-center. He steadied himself and reached for the cup again, taking a quick sip as he sat. No sense in risking a doused lap; a wardrobe emergency ranked pretty low on his priority list right now.

He groped for a napkin then broke off laughing as a big, fluffy golden retriever pushed his head adoringly into the hand holding the cup. "Caliburn," he scolded, fielding the cup and drinking again. "Caliburn, stop it!" The dog panted with a happy, adoring dog grin. "It's good to see you too. I've missed the hell out of you."

Tom laughed from down the table and snapped his fingers. "Here, Caliburn." The dog shifted his attention and wiggled up to Tom. Tom slipped him a slice of roasted lamb, which the dog snapped up greedily.

"Tom!" cried Genevieve from the door. "That's not allowed!"

Tom raised his hands in self-defense. "I'm just doing my job, taking care of the crew. Am I not allowed to take care of my crew?"

She grinned. "It's all right, Caliburn should know better than to take food from you."

Sam turned in his seat. "How long have we got, Matthew?" Matthew Sutherland was the best skipper Sam had worked with in his entire life. He could navigate everything from rivers to ocean waves, and always with smooth, professional finesse.

Matthew said, "We'll be there in less than two hours, if all goes according to plan."

Genevieve set a bottle of ouzo in front of them, along with a set of tiny glasses. "Two hours, yes," she said, as she poured. "But there may be some delays as we get closer to the temple. The Nile might start out in the North as a really big tributary system – so there aren't any issues up there with boat traffic." She shrugged. "But as we navigate farther south, it gets tighter and tighter. There's a few marine checkpoints along the way, too, and you never know how long it might take to get through those."

"How far are we from the first checkpoint?" Sam asked, wondering if Matt had factored bribe money into the monthly accounts before they'd made their way to Egypt.

Genevieve whipped out her phone, unlocked it, and stared at the screen for a few moments. "About thirty minutes, give or take." She glanced at Tom. "You've got about thirty minutes, Tom, if you do want to take a rest. I've made up the cabins for both of you. Regular berths. It wouldn't be a long nap but might be worth it."

Tom watched her go with a drowsy smile. Then he turned to Sam. "You know, this reminds me of the old days."

Sam laughed. "Oh yeah? Like when?"

"You know, back when we started this. Back when it was simple. We would go find the treasure and bring it back."

Sam sighed. Such an optimistic retelling. "You're forgetting about the percentage we had to pay to the governments of the territories we dodged in and out of; then having to avoid publicity so we didn't get robbed, and…"

"Yeah, blah blah blah. But my point still stands – we were living simply off untouched valuables and, after it was all done, we would relax, just like this, dreaming of our next haul." When Tom reminisced and spoke of their past like that, it surely did feel sentimental. "Now we're getting shot at – and shooting back, mind you – over four goddamn stone keys. They're not even worth anything on their own but somehow, the United States government is involved? What madness is this?"

Tom threw up his hands as the yacht bumped through another patch of rough water.

Tom and Sam exchanged a glance – their way of talking things through, although via vibe versus verbal and a method they'd perfected over years of missions, milestones and occasional mishaps together – that said it all.

Sam said, "I would say it is pretty important madness. You know the stakes."

Tom shook his head. "I don't know about that."

"We're not new to it, anyways," Sam said. "Now you find it the right time to complain?"

Ethan opened the door and sat down next to Sam. "So this is what the two of you get up to? Drinking and eating and traveling by luxury yacht?"

Sam snagged a glass and poured Ethan some ouzo. Ethan toasted him and drained the bitter drink. "Hey. You might have the best air transportation the military can provide, but you have to admit we travel in style." He suddenly felt a prickle at the back of his neck and turned around to see Josh standing in the door, too. When Sam made eye contact with Josh, he looked away timidly and innocently, but Ethan met Sam's gaze evenly. As expected from a SEAL, Sam thought. They certainly were taught to show no weakness. Gaze still unbroken, Ethan's raspy voice sounded.

"Yeah, you can talk all you want about the boat, but it's just alright." He gestured outside beyond the porthole. "You guys should go topside. The Nile is a real beauty, especially this part. It's where the tributary becomes the singular river. It's like watching raindrops come together on God's windshield."

Tom stood up and unfurled the yacht blinds. Ethan was right, it really was beautiful. The algae that bloomed over the surface of the water was a deep shade of green, making the Nile look like a green snake in the desert sand surrounding it. The snake slithered over a third of Africa's length, giving life and sustenance to all the lands around it.

Josh asked, "You been this way before?"

Ethan shrugged and handed Josh a glass of ouzo, declining Sam's offer of a refill. "I've been up and down this river a couple times during one of my Middle East tours. Even a few years back, the algae wasn't this bad. The pollution makes the nitrogen and the algae population spike." He shook his head. "It's going to murder the economy and all the people living here and they don't do a damned thing to stop it." Beside him, Josh drained his glass and pulled out his phone to check a text ping.

Ethan turned his gaze back to the window. "But it is beautiful."

Sam tilted his glass. "Speaking of beauty… what are your plans with Mia after all this?"

Ethan glanced at him. "That depends on what happens to the Cartel. She'll probably stay with some friends of mine who are currently stateside on R and R leave until we can be sure that the Cartel is no longer looking for her."

Sam made a wry grin. "You're going to leave her with some of your SEAL buddies?"

Ethan shrugged. "Only way to be certain the cartel won't get a chance to attack her."

Sam was about to ask what their plans were, for the long term, when they were interrupted.

Matthew stuck his head in the room. "First checkpoint, mates. Look alive." He grinned. "We're here."

Chapter Fifty-Seven

Crocodilopolis, Egypt (Modern Day City of Faiyum)

Egyptian cities were some of the most beautiful, vibrant places Sam had ever been. The markets bustled with tradesmen trying to catch unwary tourists with the allure of gifts. Sam, Tom and Ethan sat at a street side cafe and drank some rose spritzers and tried to stay out of the sun.

Sam loosened his collar, feeling the sweat track down his neck. "This heat makes Georgia feel like Norway," he said as he finished the last of his soda and realizing it didn't help.

Ethan waved away a grimy child forcefully selling roses for exorbitant prices. "Don't worry. The sun's setting right now, it'll get cold soon."

Sam glanced over into the street. Above, on the window panes of the buildings, Sam could see a red light slowly creeping down the glass and stone. He was sure that the Egyptian sunset would be very beautiful from a good view. It was the kind of light that artists dreamed of, the kind of light that had a physical weight, like you were swimming in it.

"Speaking of that." Tom turned his attention to Sam. "Sam, do you even know where we're going? I swear I've seen this street before. I think we circled a couple times now."

They were looking for a hotel. Sam had decided it was better not to stay on the ship in case they were being tailed. There was no reason to bring his crew into this.

Sam flicked his glass. "A little rusty on my Arabic, Tom. Ethan? This would be a good time to…"

Ethan laughed. "A little rusty on my Egyptian. Sam." He reached over to summon the waiter. "We'll get back on the streets and find it."

The waiter leaned down with the check and Ethan handed it to Sam. "Sorry. You'll have to get the tab."

Sam dug in his pocket. Of course he would.

Tom pushed to his feet and cracked his back. With his height, he shaded his eye against the sun and pointed across the street.

"Wait, isn't that it?"

Sam looked up. Tom was pointing to an obscure sign that was clustered among the endless red and green storefronts. The sign read, "Armenzia, quality hotel," in somewhat sketchy letters.

Sam and Ethan glanced at each other. "There's no way," Ethan said incredulously.

Sam agreed, but how many hotels in Egypt were called Armenzia?

He grinned in sympathy. "He's a big lout, but we keep him around for a reason. Let's just go check it out."

The trio pushed their way out into the street, fighting through flower vendors and beggars and workers on their way home. Tom was the one who reached the storefront first and pushed. The door opened with an old ding, and Sam peeked inside.

"Hello?" he called. Inside, there was an old Egyptian man sitting behind a counter. He didn't even look up when Sam called.

"I'm Sam…" Before Sam could finish, the man nodded, and fished out a key from behind the counter. The tag read, 34. The man pointed upstairs. Sam looked back at the group, and only saw uneasy faces looking back.

"I guess this is it." With that, Sam walked down the hallway, lugging his bags behind him, until he finally came to room number thirty-four.

Sam put the key to the door and turned. The hinge squeaked, but the door didn't move.

"Is there a problem?" Ethan asked from behind Sam. Sam grit his teeth and pushed his annoyance. They were all tired, and they were all on edge.

Sam heaved again. With a final budge from Sam's tired shoulder, the door squeaked open and the men made their way inside. Surprisingly, for a motel on the edge of an empty street, the room wasn't bad. The sheets looked clean and the lighting, when Tom flicked the switch, was bright, yet atmospheric. Moths immediately flocked to the glow in the evening light.

Ethan went straight to the bed and stretched out. "Wake me up when it's time, guys."

Tom and Sam looked at each other. They waited until Ethan's eyes were closed and then Tom walked forward and shook Ethan on the shoulder. "Hey. Ethan. It's time to get up."

Ethan's eyes snapped open. "What the hell?"

Tom shrugged and glanced at Sam. Sam knew that Tom was already thinking what he was thinking, but he wasn't sure about Ethan.

Before Sam had a chance to explain, Tom stepped in. "We'll explore the pyramid after nightfall but we want to get in place." He wiggled his fingers. "I'm sure you don't want to do it when the Ra's glaring down on you."

Ethan frowned. "Ra?"

"It's the Egyptian god of the sun."

"What?"

"Never mind." Sam shook his head and checked his pockets, double checking that he had his phone and the maps it included. The keys were stashed tight around his neck. "We need to go. Grab what you need and lock your bags."

After a long moment Ethan slapped the bed and pushed himself to his feet. They all spent a few minutes securing their bags. They couldn't do much about someone stealing their entire bag, but the least they could do was make it difficult.

Back outside, Sam pulled his jacket closer around him. He hated to admit it, but Ethan was right about the temperature. It was getting cold surprisingly quickly. Yet, the city seemed more alive during the night. Guess it's not so different anywhere else, Sam thought as he zipped his jacket, glad he hadn't been too proud to bring it with him.

They threaded their way through market stalls and ships and revelers toward the outskirts of the city where the pyramid waited at the edge of the desert. As they left the older center behind, the streets became more and more deserted, more and more dark, and Sam fought off the feeling that they were walking into some kind of trap. Even from inside the streets, every now and then they glimpsed the pyramid in the distance, looming over them all. It looked far away, but Sam assumed it would be like all things in the desert, not exactly what it appeared.

Their boots crunched over the ancient cobblestones and the citizens they passed gave them suspicious looks. Sam didn't make eye contact with them, but he kept a wary eye. Beside him, he saw Ethan doing the same.

"Guys." Tom's voice interrupted Sam's thoughts, and he was surprised to hear a grin of delight in his friend's tone. "You do realize, don't you, that we're in Crocodilopolis? Literally the city of the crocodile?"

Sam and Ethan exchanged a wry grin. "No," Ethan responded, deadpan. "You're shitting me. That's why it's called this?"

"Well..." Sam thought that Tom had been checking their location on a map, but now he realized that Tom was flipping through a guide book, squinting at the words in the dim light. "The city of Crocodilopolis was located on the western bank of the Nile, southwest of Memphis in Egypt. Known to the ancient Egyptians by the somewhat less redundant name of Shedet, this city was the center of worship for the Egyptian god Sobek, the- you guessed it!" He adopted a game show style voice with a grin. "Crocodile god! Ever the subtle geniuses when it came to naming foreign places, the ancient Greeks dubbed it "Crocodile City", or "Crocodilopolis", as it is now remembered."

Sam shook his head, stifling a grin as Tom continued.

"The inhabitants of Crocodilopolis worshiped a manifestation of Sobek through a sacred crocodile kept at... kept at the city... city named 'Petsuchos' – a name that means "son of Sobek"" He frowned. "How the hell do you get Sobek out of Petsuchos?"

"Suchok? Sobek?" Sam shrugged.

Tom shook his head. "And I thought English was bad." He went back to reading as they rounded a corner, pausing under the dim glow from an upper level apartment window. "It says here that- Hey! They actually HAD a crocodile! That's where it gets it's- The crocodile was adorned with gold and jewels, and was kept in a temple with its own pond, sand, and special priests to serve his food. After the residing Petsuchos died, the body would be mummified and given a special burial –and then promptly replaced with another 'son of Sobek'". Tom flipped the page, enthralled. "The new son would then-"

"Yeah, yeah, we get the idea," Ethan said.

Tom glanced up and his face fell as he realized the game was up. He tucked the book in his pocket. "Sorry," he muttered. "I thought it was cool."

"It is cool." Sam sent him a grin. "We'll get into it later."

Tom ducked his head and brought up the rear.

For the rest of the walk, the group stayed silent. Everyone was tired, but Sam knew that he couldn't slip up again. The obsidian door was the last piece of the puzzle, and if someone beat him to it, everything would have been for nothing.

He broke off as they rounded a corner and stalled immediately.

The pyramid loomed before them with sudden, unexpected glory, rising from the night like a ghost of the past in the gloom.

Despite themselves, all three stood and stared.

It was a good three minutes before they collected themselves enough. Sam and Ethan looked at each other.

Ethan looked at Tom. "Your guide book have anything useful to say?"

Tom shook his head and Sam was surprised to see a knife suddenly flash in his hand. Tom pushed between them, headed for the tomb.

"Yeah," he said as he passed. "There are ghosts inside."

Ethan and Sam looked at each other.

Then they followed Tom's lead.

Chapter Fifty-Eight

Sam and Tom and Ethan stalled, staring at the structure. "Looks like some pretty active ghosts," Ethan said. A line of people stretched to the entrance. "Want to find out exactly what's going on? When I came for military tour here, our squad only had free time at night, and the attractions were all closed."

A stream of tourists milled around outside in newly-bought shirts proudly displaying EGYPT and pictures of the pyramids in various angles. "Clearly not here." An admissions and ticket booth stood proudly in front of the Hawara Pyramid. A man at the counter marked entries on a tablet, glowing ghostly computer blue in his face. Clearly, nothing was left unmonetized in a country where tourism was a huge part of the national gross domestic product.

Sam shrugged, not taking his eyes off the scene. "Maybe that's just because you were in a warzone."

Ethan looked skeptical. "Maybe."

Sam started forward. "I'll check it out."

Tom shook his head. "We'll go with you."

They all headed forward. When Sam reached the back of the line he gestured to the crowd in a friendly manner. "Didn't know we could get night tours!"

The man glowered. "You pay for it?"

The three of them glanced at each other. "Uh-"

"It's a special tour." A breathless woman who might have been his wife smiled at them. "WE had to sign up four months in advance to get a place in line." She held her husband's hand. "We're so excited. It's our two year anniversary."

Sam kept his smile in place, barely. "Congratulations!" he said. "You'll have to tell us how it was."

They moved away as the line started to move.

Ethan snorted. "Now what? We sneak in at the back of the line?"

Tom shook his head, quickly scanning and counting the mob. "Only about twenty of them. Not enough to disappear, and too many to just buy our way in."

While Sam and Ethan were discussing, Sam caught Tom from the corner of his eye, jotting down notes furiously on the beat-up steno notebook his friend had held on to for years. He could never tell how Tom managed to never run out of pages. Regardless, Sam knew that if Tom was writing in it, he was thinking up a storm over the situation. Eventually his curiosity overwhelmed him.

"Relax, Mister Anxiety. I'm sure everything will work out according to plan. Once we're inside. We've already discussed this on the yacht."

Tom looked up from the paper judgmentally. "Yes, once we're INSIDE. None of us expected there to be tourists!" He hissed the last word so loudly that a gaggle of Americans in Hawaiian shirts glanced backwards. Ignoring this, he continued. "More pedestrians forces us to change our entire plan. There are simply too many people around for us to get off the beaten path and slip past unnoticed. Plus, since their business hours are apparently 24/7 like a goddamn McDonald's, there will be more guards."

"If we need help dismembering some of the security personnel, I've got it." Ethan shrugged nonchalantly.

"Pipe down. I'm not done," Tom raked his hands through his hair and glared. Tom hated when his plans went awry. "Anyways, we now have two options: either find another way in like a secret passage, or attempt to blend in with the pack and find a way to split off."

Sam knew the first option was impossible. "We're already looking for a hidden door inside the pyramid. There's no way we're finding one on the outside of it along with that."

Ethan shoved his hands in his pockets. "I guess that leaves the second option. Question: how the hell are we going to get in if this thing has been booked for months?" He looked the crowd over.

Surprisingly, Ethan grinned. "Give me five minutes."

He strode off into the line and returned dragging a skinny Iraqi kid by the arm. The kid was grinning ear to ear. Ethan introduced him as Ali. "Ali's willing to give up his place in line; he and a friend run a business on the side."

Sam shook his head in admiration. "Scalpers? Man you are good."

Ethan shrugged modestly. "Spot scammers a mile away. All part of the job." He turned to the skinny kid. "Okay, Ali. Name your price."

The kid sized up their American features, their carefully hidden desperation. "390 pounds," he said and Tom sputtered.

"That's three times the price! 260 and you've got a deal."

Ali's teeth flashed white. "That was 130 pounds each, man."

They gaped at him as the line started to move. Soon they'd be out of luck. Ethan turned to the skinny kid and revealed the M16 at his side. It was a beast of a weapon and meant business. "How about now?" he said.

Ali shrugged. "130 each."

Sam shook his head. "Pay him," he said. "We don't have time." He dug in his wallet and counted out bills. He counted again. "I've got three hundred, three... forty," he said, squinting to count in the dim light. "All I got. Tom, spot me fifty quid. I'll pay you back."

Tom slapped his pockets and came up with nothing but the guidebook. His face fell. "Motherfuckers," he breathed. "Gone."

Sam pushed down his rage, turning to Ethan. "Etha...."

He turned to Ali with a charming smile. "Get you three forty, Mr. Jobs. Best we got."

But Ali shook his head. "Sorry. Couple of tourist waiting up there, ready to pay full price. Give you two."

Sam shook his head. "We need three, one for each of us." He cracked his knuckles, fighting the urge to pound Ali in the knees.

Beside him Ethan was digging in his pants pockets and Sam thought he was checking for smokes when Ethan said, "Here! I found some!"

Sam turned. Sure enough, the SEAL held a wad of Egyptian bills in his hand. "I found them in one of my cargo pants. Maybe it was a nice little surprise for my future self."

Sam laughed. "Or you just didn't want to pay for the room."

Ethan grinned, took the bills from Sam, and handed them to Ali, saying something in Arabic that made the boy grin. Ali flicked him three tickets and raced off into the night. The bills had already disappeared.

Tom surveyed the group, mind working. "Okay, entry accomplished. Second question: are we inconspicuous enough to enter without attracting attention?"

Sam surveyed the group and felt his heart sink. Tom wore a tank top and camo tactical pants, which would have been relatively ordinary if his backpack wasn't a full military-style pack. Meanwhile, Ethan sported an unusually large hip of his jeans, under his black shirt that read "US NAVY" in conspicuous yellow lettering.

"We're going to need a wardrobe change," Tom noted. Sam inspected the admissions kiosk with his eyes for anything of help. To the right sat a dejected, sand-dusted plastic box filled to its brim with clothes.

"Bingo," Sam said. In no time all three looked like ordinary citizens, save for Tom's huge stature. His T-shirt was at least a size too small for him and made Tom look like a bodybuilder, but at least he wouldn't get noticed as anything out of the ordinary. For now, at least. Sam grinned and took a photo with his phone.

Tom batted away the flash, "The hell you doing, Reilly?"

Sam pocketed his phone. "Evidence for Genevieve of just how handsome you can be."

Ethan laughed and Sam wondered if he was thinking of Mia.

They pushed themselves to the middle of the line to blend in among the crowd. Tom turned to Sam and Ethan with instructions. "Okay. From what I remember, the tour guide will probably give us maps, so we can explore the places that aren't listed in it. They wouldn't put details about the private areas in it."

Ethan shook his head. "How the hell do you know all this?"

Tom glared at him. "I do my research. Just because we were coming at night doesn't mean you shouldn't be prepared for all contingencies."

As he said this, a stout dark-skinned man with fair hair waddled up to the tour group and began to speak.

"Everyone. Please listen. I will be tour guide for you this evening. Follow me." He then yawned and walked off for the tour group to be left trying to collect themselves and follow the guide.

The three men looked at each other.

"Let's just... get us some space." Ethan pushed through the crowd and they soon found themselves at the front of the horde, eyes set straight on getting as close to the tour guide as possible. For now.

Sam, Ethan, and Tom followed the tour for half an hour, inspecting every rocky cavern they entered and the fake sarcophagi lined up along the walls under thin glass displays lit by hot flood lights. As the guide droned on and on, often overrun by the continuous clicking sound of cameras, Sam leaned into Tom. "Now that we're inside, you think we could get a hand? Think we could get a map?"

Ethan shook his head. "What good is a map? We're looking for something that's not ON a map, aren't we?"

Without replying, Tom strode up to the guide and tapped him on the shoulder. "What do you want?" the man said in broken English.

"Do you have a map?"

They clearly did. The man sighed, rummaged around his paunch and dug up a crumpled sheet of paper from his fanny pack. He threw it at Tom. "Here."

Tom brought the map back and spread it flat, and Ethan and Sam came to his shoulders to see it. The only marked path was the one being toured.

"There has to be more than this." Ethan grit his teeth in frustration.

Tom threw up his hands. "This map tells me nothing."

Sam shook his head. "What exactly did you expect? We have to find it ourselves."

"Wait. Guys, take a look at this." Tom pointed directly to the left of them. Instead of the same boring wall, there was another passageway cordoned off by yellow tape with Egyptian writing that Sam could only assume said something along the lines of "WARNING" or "CAUTION".

Sam knew that if anything, this was the chance to break off the tour group unnoticed. The Americans and Chinese were presently ogling over a mask supposedly worn by a pharaoh thousands of years ago. Somehow, seeing as it was out in the open and rusting at the edges, Sam doubted the legitimacy of that.

Sam looked left and right, then nodded sharply. "Break away. Now!" With that, Tom vaulted over the tape, and Ethan scuttled under it. None of the tour group appeared to notice. Sam checked one last time, and moved the post holding the tape up and walked past.

The tunnel beyond the tape was surprisingly spacious and wasn't claustrophobia-inducing, as Sam had feared. It was wide enough for the three to walk side by side comfortably. Even more so, this made him nervous. The Obsidian Door was here for a fact, but what if it was hidden away so well that none of them could find it? Their efforts would be wasted. He supposed they could talk their way out, claim they'd gotten lost from the group, but what if they really did get lost from the group? There was no map of the places they wanted to go. And there was no end in sight of the tunnel.

As they walked, the ground began to angle downwards. They all felt it, but the scenery never changed. Normally, Sam would be staggered by the designs on the walls, the paintings and inscriptions that glowed in the light of his phone when he deemed them safe enough away from the group to risk the illumination. But now, so close and with no real knowledge of what lay before or behind, he gritted his teeth and continued.

Suddenly Ethan tensed. Sam, walking next to him, stopped too. "What is it?" he whispered, ready for anything.

Ethan shook his head. "I don't know. It just feels-"

Suddenly the ground under them gave way. Sam had no time to open his mouth and shout as rubble rained down, the floor dropped out, and he felt himself falling. Dirt and rocks struck his skin and he defended his face as best he could. He thought of the keys around his neck and was glad he'd double chained them with tungsten cord.

Then he wasn't glad of anything as he hit rock bottom hard and fast. He gasped at the pain in his back and prayed he hadn't broken anything.

Miraculously he still clutched his phone. Its flashlight still illuminated the scene before him, faint and eerie.

"Is everyone fine?" Sam shouted as quietly as he could. He didn't want to risk being overheard and didn't know how far sound echoed in these tunnels. From nearby, he received grunts of affirmation. He shone his phone around, but all he could see was male bodies hunched in pain and recovering. It was all they could see of him, he assumed.

Sam gripped his phone and pushed himself aching to his feet. As he brushed off the debris from the fall, he inspected the path. The only difference appeared to be the light, which was coming from somewhere. Sam had assumed it was some trick of his lighting, but now realized that was not the case. Rather than a harsh fluorescent, it was warm and welcoming light like a campfire. He clicked the light on his phone off and the light in the distance remained.

Sam tipped his head back in wonder.

The ceiling was inscribed with ornate hieroglyphics, none of which Sam could translate. They bore the stamp of weather and time, of soot and dust. Sam shivered with the sudden feeling that the past was here and it was real. Other men had stood in these halls. Other men with lives like his. Kings and robbers had breathed this same air.

"Wow."

With the echo Sam couldn't quite be sure who had made the sound, but he thought it was Tom.

As Tom and Ethan collected themselves and dusted their clothes off, Sam swung his light down to inspect the walls. Unlike last time in the caves in China, there were no secret passageways hidden into the walls. Sam wrestled with himself. Which way to go? There was no way to know and all he did know was that this was a maze. Which didn't help at all. He steadied his shoulders and glanced at the others.

"Rock paper scissors?" he said.

They put their fists in the circle and hit. Ethan won and jerked his head down the passage Sam himself would have chosen. "This way," he said. There was no hope but to keep trekking.

The tunnel continued on a downward slope, and the three checked the ground for any more trapdoors thanks to the unusual ambient light.

"We've got to be getting close to something." Ethan wiped his sweaty brow, and Sam didn't correct him, even as he felt the uncertainty in his stomach. He squinted forward, but it did seem that Ethan was right: there seemed to be a solid wall some distance away from them, where the ambient light stopped.

Tom pushed past and Ethan and Sam followed him, grinning at each other, their pace renewed, and their strength restored.

Tom walked fast to the wall, his footsteps getting quieter as he fell away from sight.

"You guys might want to check this out," he called.

There was nothing at the wall except for another inscription.

"Are these hieroglyphics?" Ethan asked. "I still can't tell the difference."

Tom squinted at it and ran his fingers over the engravings. "No," he answered. "It's just a diagram, and it's depicting something important."

"What?"

"Looks like a picture of them burying something… in some kind of tunnel." He turned to Sam. "Didn't you say this place had been a mine at some point?"

"They built one nearby, yeah. Why?"

Tom leaned forward. "It looks like this is…"

In Sam's head, everything clicked suddenly. He looked at Tom, whose face was lit up with inspiration as well. "Oh my God. It's genius."

Ethan folded his arms. "What's genius?"

Sam turned to him, tracing the drawing. "This place used to be a mine, just some utilitarian space that no one thinks twice about, right? And what are mines vulnerable to? What are we next to?"

Ethan's mind worked. "Water... a river..." He frowned. "You're saying he buried the entrance in the river? But how?"

Sam tapped the stone, feeling thousand-year-old grit beneath his sweaty fingers. "He used the mine shaft to hide the excavation of the library labyrinth. No one would ask questions, they just assumed people would be doing the pharaoh's orders."

"How would he ensure they wouldn't talk." Ethan shook his head. "Never mind."

Sam spread his hands. "So they build the labyrinth disguised as the mine, but he knew there had to be a way to hide it permanently. So... man, this guy was smart, so he designed it, positioned it originally just before the second cataracts in the Nile."

"The second what?"

"Cataracts – they're like small waterfalls...navigable waterfalls..." Sam shook his head impatiently. "We passed through them last night. Once he had the library dug out, and they'd excavated what they needed from the mine, he just dumped tons of granite into the water, causing a backflow."

Tom's appreciative smile spread across his face. "Wow. Wow, wow. They'd all just think their ruler was bettering the city, being smart. You make a backflow like that you widen the river, making the cataracts more navigable by large boats, increasing trade ability for the whatever they'd just mined..." He shook his head in utter admiration. "And In the process, it flooded the entrance to the library passageway, burying it forever..."

Sam said, "All right, let's go find the obsidian door."

Chapter Fifty-Nine

Aswan, River City – Egypt

The *Tahila* floated along the Nile River. Although the waters weren't smooth, the boat's automatic stabilization system made the ride feel stable, as if they were riding over land. Sometimes, Sam thought, depending on the land, it was even smoother.

Sam looked down at the Nile.

It barely wound to and fro, sometimes linear enough boats could continue moving straight without turning. He breathed in the air of the Nile. It smelled full and slightly musty with the tinge of the algae brimming on the surface.

His eyes squinted. About a mile down, he could make out the cataracts. Though he had never been there, he knew the cataracts frothed and churned the blue river into a muddy foam. The white bubbles were already visible from the yacht, and Sam could only imagine what their chaos looked like up close. They would soon drive head-first through the mess of liquid, once again unsure of the outcome.

"Hey, Matthew." Sam turned and sought the skipper, finding him at the wheel. Sam made his way over. "We're going to have to go past the cataracts," he called against the wind of their passing, watching his footing around lines and cleats. "Are you sure *Tahila* can handle it?"

Matthew, standing amidships, hands clasping the glossy padded wheel, shook his head.

"Look," he said, "The *Tahila* might be able to survive it, but she will take a beating and for no reason. No, better to take the FC580."

A puzzled grin came across Sam's face. "The FC580?"

"We picked it up during the last maintenance overhaul," Matthew said, retreating back into the cockpit and Sam followed, stepping over the small metal steps entirely. They passed the steering and went all the way to the back of the yacht, ignoring Sam's friend's inquiries about their intentions. Matthew stopped randomly at the floor of the stern.

"Right here. You're going to be using this to get through as fast as possible." As he spoke, Matthew crouched to an unassuming hook in the floorboards. He pulled it, and an entire trap door opened, revealing a hole filled to the brim with rubber.

Sam was still confused. "It's just rubber."

"Not just any rubber. Watch this." The captain pressed a button on the rubber. Almost instantly, it expanded, popping out of its home under the boat. Little by little, the form revealed itself. A rubber boat.

Ethan's cold voice startled the two. "I know that boat. We used it all the time during marine amphibious training." He walked up with calculated steps. "Really fast, somewhat impossible to get outside of the military, much less in Egypt. How the hell did you get your hands on this?"

Matthew winked. "I have my connections."

Sam grinned. This was excellent. He clapped the skipper on the shoulder. "Matthew, you always come through."

Now that the FC580 dragged behind the bulletlike *Tahila*, the Zodiac looked like an unwilling prisoner forced to parade with a king. Even with this rather ill omen, Sam knew that he would feel infinitely safer in the nimble zodiac.

"We're approaching the cataracts," Matthew called out. "Get your men ready for diving."

Sam decided to get his suit on first- that way he could pilot the zodiac while the other two got theirs on to save time. He jumped on the zodiac, shifting his weight to counteract the swells and falls of the water. The zodiac wasn't stabilized like the *Tahila* and he could feel it.

Sam struggled to get the diving suit on. He forgot how difficult it was to get a quality suit on sometimes. Having no success, he flung the suit onto the deck of the *Tahila* and hauled himself up after it. Putting the suit on here was a little bit easier, but it still took Sam a solid five minutes to finish securing the connections.

Satisfied with his setup, Sam opened the door that led below decks.

"Ethan!" he called. "Tom! Hurry up! We're here!"

There was no response.

"Ethan!" he shouted again.

Failing to get even a call back, Sam went below decks. In the cramped space below, he found Ethan and Tom fast asleep. Tom was lying on the chair, jacket huddled up as a makeshift pillow against the wall, and Ethan was just collapsed on the floor. Sam smiled. They'd all had a long night.

"Hey, wake up." he said gently. Ethan jerked awake and Tom rolled over, grumbling. He flung an arm over his face.

"We here?" he mumbled.

"We're here." said Sam, more loudly. "We need to dive. Now." Ethan stood up, the discipline of the watch deep in his DNA, used to the Navy SEAL call times. Tom was a little bit less disciplined, but wasn't a complete slob. In moments, Sam succeeded in getting both of them to deck, where they stood blinking and looking more excited.

"Ah," said Matthew when he saw the trio. "Ready to go? I'll keep the *Tahila* waiting for you here. You take the zodiac and dive."

"Thanks, Matthew." Sam turned to Ethan and Tom, who were already pulling on their dry suits and had them loose around their waists. "Hop on. I'll drive us while you two get dressed."

Ethan and Tom clambered over the rail and onto the zodiac first. Sam unknotted the bowline in the rope keeping the boats together, tossed the end to Matthew, and quickly jumped on before the zodiac could float away. Sam revved the outboard and the military spec'd engine purred as smoothly as a new car. The zodiac jerked, then surged forward, cutting through the choppy water.

In minutes they'd reached the cataracts. Sam cut the motor and let it idle as he glanced at Ethan and Tom, who were just finishing putting on their suits. The Zodiac drifted toward the eastern bank of the river, settling next to a large boulder, where Sam quickly tied off.

"So now that we're out here, how do we find the passageway?" Ethan adjusted his dive bag.

Sam grinned. "I thought that would have been obvious."

Chapter Sixty

They squinted at the blue sky.

"It's dive time," Tom said as adjusted his suit and his mask. The gear muffled the last few words, but he knew that Sam would pick them up.

From beside him, Sam heard a snort. He turned to see Ethan fully suited up in the SCUBA gear save his mask which he now raised.

"You trying to get out of some work, here at the end of the line, Bower?"

Tom grinned. "You wish. Worried about looking like a girl in swimming lessons?"

Ethan rolled his eyes. "You want to say that again? Say it again. First in my class, second in my squadron, an…."

Sam cut him off. "Gentlemen, as much as I'd love to hear your pissing contest, we don't have time for that." He grinned at Ethan. "Look, Tom's already swimming into the passageway." Ethan swiveled his head and saw the tall figure of a man in a SCUBA suit paddling away into the darkness. Without a word, he sent a glance to Sam behind the mask, placed the regulator back in his mouth and flipped over the side of the boat. Sam pulled his own mask down and went in after him.

They followed Tom's lead. It was Tom who, with Elise's help, had painstakingly researched online sources for any information about the layout of the mines from the inside.

According to their findings, the tunnel was about fifty feet long. Now that they were inside, Sam discovered it was wide enough for all three of them. He turned on his flashlight and shined it ahead of him. The tunnels' carved walls still showed signs of chisel marks from the mining excavation and before them it wound ever deeper into the ground.

Ethan turned to Sam in concern. "We're not going to have enough oxygen," he said through the radio of his full facemask.

Sam shook his head. "We'll see how far we get. Treat it as a recon mission." Ethan nodded. "If we can't find any dry passageways, we'll turn around and come back up."

Sam turned back around, barely keeping up with Tom, who was eagerly swimming down the passageway. The passageway itself had flattened out, and now they were gliding along a flat floor.

Their voices echoed eerily from the regulators as they continued down the passageways. "What do you even think we'll find?" Ethan kept pace easily next to Sam as they both followed Tom down the corridor.

"Honestly…" Sam called out to Tom ahead of him. "What do you think, Tom?"

Tom had stopped up ahead in the passageway and was now staring at something into the distant dark. Sam and Ethan quickly caught up and joined his friend. "What did you find?"

Tom gestured to the passageway. "See there how the dark looks a little different and it goes up and up?" Tom swam forward and pointed up. "I think there's a dry hallway up ahead. Let's go check it out."

The trio quickly swam up until the water became too shallow to swim well. The light of the flashlight distorted, indicating a surface just up ahead. Sam paddled, then broke the surface. He shined the light around. They had emerged into a small circular chamber full of water, which fed into a hallway. Sam was sure now that the passageway had been intentionally designed this way.

He pulled himself to his feet and took off his flippers and mask. The water reached his ankles. Beside him, Ethan and Tom did the same.

Ethan shook out his wet hair. "You know more than I do, boys. What's coming up?"

Tom gestured to the hallway before them. "According to the plans I was looking at, there should just be another chamber right up ahead." He grinned. "Should we go see if the tales are true?"

They sloshed their way down through the passageway. The walls were covered by mysterious Egyptian markings that Sam had only seen in books before. Sam saw images depicting all kinds of scenes: some depicting a parade next to a line of temples, marching through a city's street. Others were more surprising, showing a shining disk above a pyramid.

"Do these mean anything?" Sam touched the wall. Though he tried to keep it out of his voice, awe filled his words, the weight of history hanging over his head.

"Of course they do." Ethan spoke surely, much to Sam's surprise. He'd never thought Ethan to be much of a scholar. "But it would take a full research team years to decode them all. I thought we were only interested in one thing."

Sam nodded. Excitement sang in his veins as the full weight of what he was seeing fully sank in. This was the gateway of the ancient library of the pharaohs that had been lost to the centuries. What else would he find within these walls?

Sam shook his head. As much as he wanted to take their time and study everything on these walls, the ancient history and artistry they depicted, everything else would have to wait.

They were confronted with a short horizontal passage. They tipped their heads back and stared.

Ethan pointed. "There," he said, his flashlight sweeping the damp stone and the symbols. "That."

Faintly visible in the roof was an opening, with barely enough room for a man.

Ethan grinned in triumph. "That's it!" He scrambled up a pile of rubble and hauled himself through. Sam shouted up.

"What do you see?"

Ethan's legs dangled and his voice echoed as he reported back.

"Empty passage at a right angle to the one you're in now," he said. "It's got wooden doors, another passage parallel to… and it's filled with mud and stone! It's not just random, it's deliberate!" His voice rose in excitement. "I think this is it! Why else would they go through all this trouble to…"

But Sam shook his head.

"It's a decoy. If you look around, you'll find another one. A second one in this roof. The whole pyramid is circled by these passages."

But now Ethan shook his head again. "They're open. The doors up here. They're open. Didn't Tom say the burial chambers were up here? Somewhere?"

Tom called up. "They say the real entrance to the burial chamber is even more carefully concealed- between the decoy shafts and… is there an alcove? The right thing is opposite the alcove."

Ethan kicked as he looked around. "Alcove, check!" he shouted down. He twisted around and back to the men below. "What are you waiting for? Aren't you coming up?"

Sam and Tom looked up and climbed up after Ethan. They pulled their way through.

The chamber was not tall enough to stand upright, but as he crouched, panting from the climb, he saw Ethan was right. The doors that led away were open. He exchanged an excited glance with Tom.

"Let's go."

Ethan stepped out of the way and let Sam go through before him.

He emerged into a massive chamber, big enough to stand. Sam stood in awe.

The burial chamber he was standing in glowed with a lambent gleam of quartz and well-polished limestone that gleamed even with the dust.

The ceiling was made of three quartz slabs that made Sam suddenly very aware how much stone they were standing under and that the pyramid above them was crumbling.

This could only be the burial chamber, Sam thought. Above he could barely make out two relieving chambers propped to form a pointed roof. An enormous arch of brick a full meter thick built over the pointed roof to support the core of the pyramid.

Sam and Tom and Ethan stared. They slowly paced the chamber. To Sam's surprise, the room didn't have any other entrances or exits. This was it.

The walls were decorated with elaborate pictographs, depicting the Black Pyramid in fading paint and carvings.

He stared in awe, yet he still didn't understand. Wasn't the labyrinth supposed to be below Hawara? This was not a maze. Not… anything. Just a chamber. Sam turned to Ethan and Tom. He felt like an idiot, but it had to be said.

"I thought there was a labyrinth. Where is the labyrinth?" He shook his head. "I thought it was buried under the Hawara Pyramid."

He was surprised to find Tom shaking his head. "Let me run this theory past you. Just…hear me out." He raised his hands in the dimness. "When Strabo referred to the expedition below Amenemhat III's pyramid, he wasn't referring to the Hawara Pyramid. We all thought that's what he meant since it's the more famous one, the stronger one." He shook his head. "But I don't think he was talking about the Hawara Pyramid. I think he was talking about the Black Pyramid."

"Oh, no. You have got to be kidding me. Wait. Just wait." Ethan held up his hands, then used them to scrub his dirty face and hair. "I thought the Black Pyramid was reduced to a bunch of mud?"

Tom nodded, his face a study in wry sympathy.

Sam's shoulders slumped against the unavoidable weight of the words. It made sense, when he thought about it. He desperately wished it didn't, but it did make a strange kind of sense. "So you're saying the ancient maze that the entire world has been searching for- searching for centuries, no less- the one that holds invaluable treasures and the secrets of the ancients that could unlock the secrets to more secrets, is not given a fitting burial under a triumphant monument of stone." He looked between them in despair, begging them to convince him otherwise. "It's actually hidden under a crumbling mess of a pyramid? Under nothing but ruins?"

Tom nodded again.

Ethan shook his head in disbelief. "It doesn't make sense." He turned to Sam. "You told me this… what was his name? The historian guy."

"Strabo," Sam said.

"Strabo," Ethan agreed. "Smartest man in history or something like that, first rate source, actually saw this labyrinth with his own eyes." He glared at them with a touch of desperation in his eyes that Sam chalked up to the late hour and exhaustion. He couldn't blame the SEAL, really. He felt pretty much the same. "How could Strabo, a world-renowned geographer, make such a mistake?"

Tom smiled, but it was wry. "Easy," he said, tapping the floor. "He didn't make a mistake.."

Sam finally understood. He put his head in his hands with a long moan. "Right. Damn. You're saying he was being intentionally obtuse."

Tom wiped his hands on his wetsuit. "I'm certain of it. It's the only thing that makes sense." He shook his head and slapped Sam on the back. "I think the whole damned thing was a ruse. Amenemhat knew that the Black Pyramid wouldn't support the weight he was putting on it. I think he built the labyrinth in stealth first inside the mine shafts, and then, to deceive his own children, he secured it with the crumbling, failed wreck of his first pyramid. He even showed it to Strabo, who wrote about it, as being beneath Hawara to throw them off his track."

"But… why?" Sam watched Ethan rummage around in the debris, then stop near a wall and pull out the old map they'd taken from the tour guide. He pressed the map and began to rub.

"I don't know." Tom threw up his hands. "Test their intelligence, maybe?"

"It doesn't make any damn sense. I can't believe we came all the way here for nothing. Now what? We go tomorrow night to the Black Pyramid? What's left of it? Ethan!" he called over. "What are you doing?"

Ethan didn't answer. Sam turned back to Tom, glaring. "This is bullshit."

Tom spread his hands in sympathy. "I know. The only chance we have is to backtrack, go tomorrow to the Black Pyramid and start from the beginning again."

A piece of paper fluttered between them. Tom broke off, staring at it. "What's this?"

Sam leaned over Tom's shoulder as he snatched the paper off of the damp ground. "What the hell is this?"

Ethan put his thumbs in his pants. "Looks like some kind of map." He gestured behind him. "Found it on the wall over there, looked familiar, so I scribbled it down while you old guys were bickering like two little ladies." He smirked. "Sorry about the paper choice. Didn't have any ancient papyrus on me at the time. Hopefully that will do." His voice changed, a little more serious. "I mean it. Hopefully you can make it out on top of the new map. It's the only paper I had. Do any of you have something better…"

Sam waved him down with a frown. "Hush. I can't look if you're yammering like that. Shut up and let me see."

He studied the paper in the dim light. If he squinted past the modern depictions of the pyramid's interior, it did look like a map. At the very least it looked like more than they had before.

A hell of a lot more, actually.

"Well, I'll be damned," he said, turning to Ethan, to find the boy watching him anxiously and trying to hide his nerves. "Aren't you just a first-class thief?"

Chapter Sixty-One

Sam turned his attention to the map again, drawn to its secrets.

Despite the dangers of handling it, he couldn't bring himself to stop. He couldn't wait to get it back to the *Tahila* where they could analyze it properly. He'd look at it then with Elise's skills, too, he consoled himself. But now... at least he deserved a peek.

Sam held the map closer to the flashlight and studied it. It was intricate, but complex, and frustratingly familiar. But still... Sam shook his head.

"I feel like this whole thing was a waste of time. I feel like it should make sense... but..." He threw up his hands, trying to keep his voice low across the open water. "I can't really tell what this is leading to."

His confidence was starting to fall. All the work they'd done to get inside the pyramid, the unexpected surprises that they'd suffered and overcome... Was it really worth diving after this map - merely just a bunch of symbols on brown paper – or had this trip all been in vain?

"Maybe we need to decipher it. Like a code," Ethan took the map back and studied it in the light of the flashlight.

Sam said, "Pass it over. To be honest, I feel like an expert in that. After looking through all these hieroglyphics in these pyramids, I think I have a rough idea of what this means."

Ethan snorted. "Sure."

Tom made a face at Ethan and took the map from Sam.

He bent his big body over the tiny parchment. "Come on! Isn't it obvious? This thing here, means..." Finally, he gave up and shook his head. "You know what? Never mind. This isn't some sort of code. This looks like an awfully drawn map. You can't even tell what that is," Tom said, pointing to a cluster of circles at the center of the map.

Giving up, Tom made his way back to the walls of the cave, reading through the thousands of symbols that decorated the stony confinements.

Sam and Ethan kept staring, looking at it from the top, the bottom, upside down, and even tried shining the flashlight on it from different angles.

Nothing happened. The map's secrets stayed hidden.

Suddenly, the sound of an engine began to grow louder. It was definitely from outside the cave.

Making eye contact with Tom, Sam knew exactly what was happening.

"Looks like we've got company." Tom's eyes showed fear but also determination as he quickly opened his backpack, withdrew a gun, and enclosed the rest of his belongings back in the bag. "Let's give them a welcome."

"No." Sam slapped the gun away. "None of us are prepared for a proper welcome party. Let's get out of here." He looked at Ethan. "Now!"

With Tom leading the group through moss and rock, the sounds of the engine grew louder and louder.

It only meant one thing...

They were in trouble.

Chapter Sixty-Two

Even as they scrambled to pack up their belongings into the bags on their backs, Sam couldn't help but appreciate the raw power behind the engines fast approaching them.

"You hear that?" Sam asked as Ethan attempted to stuff a small generator back into his camo backpack.

Tom looked up with a look of infinite exasperation. "I think we both hear it, Sam. That's why I'm packing up. Why I'm packing up, at least. It would be great if you could help me out with this." He threw Sam a flashlight, which bounced off his chest and rolled into a dip in the mossy rocks.

Sam shook himself out of a trance, brought on by that approaching roar that crashed through the pyramid tunnels like the rush of fate. He knew he should move, but he found himself gripped by the power of the night and all he could think about was the power behind the consistent drone of the engine spinning the propellers, creating the thrust, and pushing the enemy to them faster and faster... A small part of him inside screamed for Sam to wake up, but this too was overtaken by the speedboat.

"That's a lot of power behind it. I wonder if it's faster than our zodiac."

Tom grabbed Sam by the SCUBA respirator hanging off his neck. "That won't matter if you don't get off your ass very soon and start hauling it out of here," he muttered through gritted teeth. As he spoke, the familiar pop drip sound of bullets hitting the water around them filled the air. The engine of the speedboat also got louder, and all of a sudden, Sam snapped out of his trance.

He wondered if the air was drugged with some kind of poison. There were stories of pharaohs defending their tombs in such ways and just because it hadn't been written about didn't mean it wasn't true.

There wasn't time to think about that. They needed to get out as soon as possible. That's all there was to it.

He shot to his feet, shouldered his backpack, and began following Tom and Ethan in a full sprint. The rocks suddenly became very quiet as their attackers cut the power and got off. Sam forced himself to focus. That silence could only mean one thing.

They were on land too.

Running forward as fast as he could, Sam struggled with the pocket on his SCUBA suit and procured his trusty pistol. The worn-in rubber grip and perfect weight fit familiarly in his hand and he felt steadier. At splashes and shouts and the whisk of shoes on rock, Sam took a breath and looked behind him.

Five men clambered out of their larger speedboat, guns in hand. Even from here, he could easily make out the models of the guns and wondered what the hell they'd gotten themselves into. Trapped themselves in here like...

Mice in a maze.

Two of them held Heckler & Koch UMP 45's, and another a Beretta. While three of them were in SCUBA gear as if they were ready to dive at a moment's notice, two were in street clothes. Sam made out a pale face dressed in an impeccable black suit, while the taller man sported khaki shorts and a T-shirt and Sam thought irrationally that he must be freezing in the desert night, and then thought, why the hell do I care?

He didn't give a damn what they wore, as long as they died wearing it.

But he did care. Some part of his brain must: the black suit looked familiar. So did the glasses the other man wore. But before Sam had a chance to look further, bullets whizzed past his ears, making him duck before firing random shots in the enemy's general direction.

Ethan seemed to notice the unusual familiarity too and frowned at Sam as they fled. "I've seen those two people somewhere," he shouted as he aimed his own AK at the five men running after them.

Sam panted as they fell naturally into step. "Same as me."

"Look, there!" Tom pointed directly in front of them. They'd reached the entrance, and the silhouette of the Tahila loomed in the distance, with the FC580 closer, just off the rocks.

But the men were gaining on them. While the trio were bogged down by the water still in the SCUBA suits, their pursuers were nimble and easily jumped over the large rocks in their way.

Sam's breath rasped like fire in his throat as he leaned over his thighs, gasping. "We're not going to make it."

Tom slowed to a stop, panting. "You're right." He then brandished his gun, which glinted in the morning Egyptian sun. "But we can fight."

He, Ethan, and Sam exchanged grins.

They ran for cover behind three rocks large enough for them to lean their backs on. It was a gamble: they could try to catch the bad guys by surprise when they went past the rocks, looking for their suddenly vanished quarry, or they could confront them in a firefight now.

Sam looked at Tom, asking the question with his eyes: Which would it be?

Sam didn't have to answer his own question. A voice rang out against the hard, wet stone and Sam clenched his fist.

"There's no point in playing games, Mr. Reilly. We know you are there and we know where we want you. I have guns trained on you from all angles." The voice sent a chill down his spine.

Ethan's eyes swung straight to Sam's with a cold, calculating look. Tom dropped his gun, which clattered onto the stones. "Bastard," he swore, almost without sound. "Goddamn bastard."

The voice went on, all cultured calm and so smug Sam wanted to slap it out of the air. "So I would suggest coming from behind those rocks, hands raised, before I take you all to hell." It was Armando.

Sam gripped his gun, preparing to charge out and blast these men into oblivion. To hell with caution, to hell with tact. Rage boiled up in him at men who would like to get what they want. Men who thought there was no other way.

He was just about to stand and face them, expose himself to bullets and rage, when Ethan surprisingly rose first. Sam hadn't expected the Navy SEAL to give himself up so easily.

Maybe if there was no way out Ethan thought it was better to cooperate? Sam looked up at the soldier's face. He was gritting his teeth, pain and fury warring in his eyes. Ethan's hands suddenly clenched on the gun. "Josh! What the hell are you doing?"

Now Sam recognized where he'd seen that suit before. He peered out from around the edge of the rock, trying not to get his head blown off.

Josh stood with Armando and the three other men in black suits and rough homespun, the only thing linking them as a united force the ruthlessness in their eyes and the deadliness of their weapons.

In his hand he held printouts. Sam could only imagine they'd been taken from the *Tahila*, a ship where the man had been welcomed as family.

Sam's heart leapt. His crew? Were they safe? What had this bastard done to them?

Josh spread his hands. "I'm sorry, Ethan. But that was the deal. They would never have let Mia go if I hadn't cooperated with them." His grin crooked. "You do want what's best for her, don't you?" He gestured at Sam and Tom. "Come on. They promised to let you come back with us, start a life with them, just give us the keys."

"Just like you promised?" Ethan stood his ground. "What about them?" His gritted teeth made the words a low growl. "What about Mia? Was she in on this too?"

At that, Josh had the grace to look contrite. "No. She didn't know anything about this." A glimmer of fury sparked. "When were you going to tell me you were fucking my sister?"

Ethan's knuckles tightened on the gun. "None of your business." It was a voice Sam had never heard the SEAL use, no matter how angry or commanding he got in other situations. "You fucking crook! I thought we were friends!"

Josh stood there in the tuxedo and dress pants, fidgeting and wiping his sweat beaded forehead with a handkerchief. Somehow the water splashing back and forth into the speedboat had completely ignored the lawyer's clothes.

Josh gave a crooked smile, holding hard to the arrogance and the cruelty that had helped him survive and climb. "Family over friends," he said.

Armando grinned and took off his sunglasses to reveal eyes frozen over and cold as ice.

"Ethan, is it? Pleasure to meet you, Ethan." He gestured to Josh. "Please, don't hold it against him. Your friend has talent. I couldn't have done it without him, really. He was the best mole I've ever had work for me in the cartel. Relayed your every single move every moment." The new drug lord gave a wet slap to Josh's back. He stepped away from it. "And without him your Mia would still be in Carlos's... clutches." He grinned lecherously, out of place on his distinguished features. "I lost a rival and gained a cartel. You lost a friend but gained a lady love." He shrugged. "All of these seem fair trades, yes?"

Tom shucked his gun and the noise carried loudly over the predawn water. Sam saw him glance at their Zodiac out of the corner of his eye and shook his head. As close as it was, it would still be suicide. Tom glared and shouted around the rock.

"So, what are you going to do with the map?" Now Sam could see Tom's hand reaching for the gun he had carefully set onto the rock. Instantly, he knew what their plan would be: Tom would delay Armando and his goons long enough for Ethan and Sam to reach for their guns. Then they would all fire, making a mad kamikaze dash for the zodiac in the process. Was it risky as hell? Sure, but Sam thought it was a hell of a lot better than working as a slave to the Black Muerte.

"-and that's a lot of money I can use for goals. My goals, of course." Armando finished his winding speech, and grinned. "Josh here was kind enough to draw up the contract."

Ethan snorted. "Oh yeah?" he glared at his friend. "Better check it for holes. Bet it's as tight as damn Swiss cheese."

Armando laughed. "Oh, the American expressions. Always so amusing." He bowed, gallant. "It was a pleasure to see you again Mr. Reilly. It was a good day when we struck up our correspondence. I always knew you would be most helpful."

"Glad to be of service!" Tom shouted with a glare.

Ethan saw him tense to make his move and shook his head. Before Sam could stop him he poked his head beyond the rock outcropping, putting himself directly in the line of fire. He slowly raised his hands.

"Truce!" he called, echoing across the water. "Truce." He held Josh's eyes. "You can have them. Just let me come with you. I've got the map." He held up a piece of paper in the growing dawn.

Sam sputtered. "Ethan, what the hell are you doing?"

But Ethan wasn't looking at him. He just kept waving the piece of paper that Sam knew wasn't the map because HE was holding the map and he and Tom shared a glance and that's when he saw Ethan beckon at them behind his back – where he was holding his gun at his belt…

All he had to do was reach for it.

Sam lunged forward to stop him but Ethan brought his hands down and back and then the gun was in them and he was firing, firing into the men before them with abandon, with rage, bullets hitting flesh and stone and water with hisses and sizzles and pops.

"GO!" he shouted as the bullets rained back and red opened in his arm, black in the dawn, and Sam dove for his own gun, heedless of the firing squad, got it up and shot from his stomach into the fray as Ethan grunted with another hit and a gasp and then Tom was there, boots scrabbling on the wet stone, and Ethan had tears running down his face and Sam saw that clearly and then his mind went blank.

Then Tom dragged his arm as Ethan covered them and, firing in quick succession, Tom dragged Sam toward the boat. Under the increased fire Armando and his group ducked, but not before one of them got hit with a bullet square in the chest, falling over and dropping his UMP. Sam and Ethan brandished their own weapons and provided cover fire.

"Sam! Let's move!" Tom shouted, racing for the water. Sam followed suit, but Ethan wasn't moving.

"Ethan!" he shouted. But Ethan just shook his head, fury filling his face. "I'm not leaving before I strangle that son of a bitch with my own bare hands!" He pointed at Josh, who was curled in a ball on the moss.

"There's going to be plenty of time to do that, but only if we reach the zodiac!" Sam said as he grabbed Ethan by the scruff of his suit. Almost instantly they were met with return fire, but this time, they kept running. Sam shot over his stomach and under his shoulder with his pistol but did not dare to look back. For all he knew, they could be right behind him. The zodiac got bigger and bigger in his sight.

"Almost there!" He dared a look behind him. Armando and his team were gaining, already shouting and gesturing to their boat, giving a moment of reprieve as they gave chase.

Shit. If they kept running at this rate, they would never make it. Sam didn't know which was worse- a pitched sea battle or here on the rocks.

At that instant, Sam's foot lost traction with the slippery moss a few feet in front of the zodiac. He felt his body accelerating full force into the rocks. "Keep going," he called to Ethan and Tom when they stalled, seeing him on the ground. "Save yourselves first."

"No way," Tom panted as he struggled to drag Sam's sprained and limp body into the wildly-rocking zodiac as Ethan covered their retreat. Sam slid into the squeaky rubber and the motor revved and his leg pulsed and ached under him. He turned to Ethan with a glare. "Your goddamn good man is a goddamn-"

His voice died in his throat. Ethan's chest was riddled with holes. Blood streamed from cuts in his face. He drew breath with a staggering gurgle that didn't sound good at all.

"The *Tahila*!" Sam shouted. "Go! Now!"

But he remembered the power of the motor he'd heard in the caves. The enemy had more horsepower than them.

As if to prove it the cartel's motorboat roared past the rock outcropping and around the shallow falls.

Tom glanced at the gas while Sam gasped in pain as the harsh flight jostled his leg. "Got her full throttle, Sam, and can't do much more!"

Sam grit his teeth. "Do more."

Tom shook his head as bullets splashed the water and they all flinched.

Then, over the horizon, another noise. A silence, more than a noise. Some kind of presence. Sam couldn't have said what made him turn – maybe the feel of sea air all his life. But he faced the stern and his mouth dropped.

There in the distance was the *Tahila*.

He squinted. Too much to hope. But no. He could see it now. Definitely moving toward them.

"Tom!" he shouted.

Tom stopped firing and let the tiller go for an instant to look behind them. That's when Armando fired at their hull and the bullets finally pierced the toughened multi layered rubber with a bang.

Air whooshed out.

Ethan fumbled his fingers into the hole, plugging the gap. Injured as he was, it was the best he could do. He still cradled his gun in his lap, but it seemed beyond his strength to use it.

Armando and the cartel closed in fast as the Zodiac limped along toward the *Tahila*, sputtering spray.

The men got close enough to see their faces. Josh huddled in the boat with a gun in his hands, shooting. His next shot put another hole in their hull.

Then he splattered backward. Ethan's gun was out and level.

But now there were other guns – suddenly the men in the oncoming boat jerked and shuddered and fell as fast as puppets whose strings have been cut.

Sam spun as best he could in the slick rubber, with his ruined leg.

Genevieve stood at the rail of the *Tahila*, spray splashing in the rose gray dawn. Mia stood at her side, her mouth hard as she stared at her brother's corpse in the boat with their enemies, and then falling open as she saw Ethan's bullet riddled body in the boat with Sam and Tom.

Genevieve waved. In one hand, she held a minigun with the barrel glowing orange from the raw firepower.

"Morning!" she called, a little too cheerfully. "Fine day to be out on the water!"

None of them replied and sat there, catching their breath as the boat gurgled around them, the walls slowly deflating. Finally, Sam twisted towards her and managed to grab the rope she threw overboard, attached to a float. The boat sank faster as she dragged it through the water toward the ship, but it couldn't be helped.

Another rope slapped down and he heard Mia shout for a doctor, a medic, someone as Ethan grabbed hold weakly.

Sam could barely hold the rope and he felt Tom's steady support from below as he was lifted into the air for the deck.

There he found Genevieve, Mia, Elise, Matthew Sutherland… and the approaching sound of Egyptian police sirens, drawn to the sound of shooting. Matthew looked at the approaching white spray and tightened his lips. Sam wondered if he was thinking about bribes. Just another day on the job.

Sam realized he was still clutching the map. He unclenched his fingers but it wouldn't leave his grip. "Morning," he said weakly, before collapsing onto the deck and everything went black.

Chapter Sixty-Three

Dahshur Necropolis – Egypt

Staring off into the distance, Sam let the burning sunlight reflected off the sand fill him, trying to scorch out the events of yesterday. He'd slept the rest of the day and most of the night, Matthew tending to his leg which wasn't sprained as he'd feared but just very badly bruised. He'd be up again soon if he had anything to say about it.

Still, it had been five days since the shootout on the water and Sam and the crew of the *Tahila* had been lying low. Ethan's wounds took time to heal and they all thought it best to let the madness die down before they slipped back into the pyramid with the map.

There was no way Sam was leaving this godforsaken town without seeing what he'd come to see. He and Ethan deserved that much, at least.

The last he'd seen of Ethan the night before was a brief glimpse of him in the galley looking for a drink with Mia seated at the table and a low murmur of voices between them. Sam, going for water, had passed by and made do with the filtered water from his faucet instead. Whatever they talked about was their business, though he hoped it got resolved without bloodshed, this time.

Sam leaned back on his elbows and winced as it twinged his leg. His time at the Necropolis had been a long and wild experience, no doubt about that. Now he was taking a small moment of quiet before the rest of the storm. He hadn't told anyone where he was going or that he was going and he was sure he was going to catch hell for it from Tom, but he needed to be off the boat and he needed to clear his head to prepare for what was to come.

As he stared at the mounds of tombs and small pyramids, he could make out the Egyptian masterpieces that somehow endured for centuries. Located conveniently on the west bank of the Nile, it was the perfect location, he thought. The pharaoh had chosen well. Not too close to the river, but not too far. Just about right.

As the red sun gilded the tops of the dunes and distant pyramids, the rippled steel roofs of shack houses and stores, Sam reflected on how history is passed down. He wondered if the Egyptians had known when they had buried their dead and prepared them for a life in the afterlife full of all the bounty of this world that they would one day be a source of historic and artistic interest centuries later. He bet they wouldn't have, but anyone who believed that much in the afterlife had to have some interest in legacy, after all.

His eyes were particularly drawn to a lumpy mound of brown dirt, looking like a failed attempt at a sharp five-sided pyramid. To his knowledge, it was only towards late 2600 BC, after the Great Pyramid of Giza was built, when the Egyptians finally discovered the trick to building sturdy structures that had sharp edges. This only meant that this mound was built around 2613 BC and was one of their tests. Nonetheless, the mound was surrounded by a handful of tourists walking around on a mixture of sand and clay.

Sam remembered reading about this. He tried to remember as he stared at the structure, willing the name into his mind. What was it? Dahshur? No. They were in Dahshur. Certainly not the Black Pyramid. Was that the name?

Suddenly, the name of the mound hit him. The Bent Pyramid. Appropriate. Vaguely remembering the name from the map he had seen hours ago, he knew the name made sense. Sam could picture generations of ancient Egyptian architects pouring all of their knowledge in transition from step-sided pyramids to smooth-sided ones and this was the result. These were the fumbling attempts that had led to such masterworks as the Pyramids of Giza, wonders of the ancient world, a shining testament to humanity.

So this is what I was exploring, thought Sam. It looked much different in daylight.

Clearly, the Bent Pyramid was not a success with its collapsing walls and dirty look - yet tourists seemed to still admire the ancient aesthetic and architectural value. It was one of the best preserved in the area and something had to have worked: its outside limestone was still mainly intact, unlike many of the pyramids in the surrounding area.

Pyramids, right. Remembering that there were two pyramids drawn on the map, he found the motivation to start moving. After all, he couldn't spend his entire day just staring off into space.

Watching a tourist couple starting to walk north, Sam began to follow. Maybe they actually knew where they were going. Which meant where he was going. Or at least he could ask them for some information on where exactly he was.

Walking through the sandy ground, Sam's shoes began to slowly sink into the ground, making him more and more tired as he walked through. That was one of the miscalculations that had contributed to the collapse of the pyramid, he knew. Another was the weight of the blocks themselves – their weight was not distributed evenly and as the awkward weight proved to be too much for the unstable foundation the massive stones had settled wrong, giving the pyramid its hunched shape and its name.

What kind of idiot decides to build a structure on sand? Sam thought. But he knew who it was. If only he could remember. Anyway, he thought, the ancient Egyptians didn't have much choice- most of the terrain was sand. It was remarkable they'd done what they'd done. And it seemed they'd learned from their mistakes, as the pyramids of Giza were many times as large, with perfectly cut blocks weighing two tons, and they'd been standing for thousands of years without a hint of collapse.

Done with pulleys and ramps and mud and water and manpower. Sam shook his head and continued on. As his leg grew tired, Sam's mind offered up a fact like a bubble from the depths unbidden, unexpected, one he had heard from his tour guide days ago.

It started with an S... I know it.

He touched the side of the pyramid, hoping that there would be some sort of clue; his eyes fell onto the hieroglyphics carved on the side of the pyramid. It looked suspiciously like a snake.

His mind clicked. It was Sneferu! King Sneferu. The ambitious pharaoh who supported mathematical and architectural endeavors under his financing, and was actually in charge of the Bent Pyramid. There had to be another one nearby. Sam was sure of it. He was on the right track.

Regaining his motivation to walk, he continued his journey northward, enjoying the sound of the rustling bushes, the trickling water in the Nile, and the clicks of the tourists in the background. Boats skimmed the surface of the blue water.

Slowly, a red tip began to surface upward out of the ground in the distance. Getting excited, Sam picked up his pace. Was it the Red Pyramid?

Sure enough, the famous structure towering at three hundred and forty one feet and boasting a glorious red color stood majestically only a couple hundred feet away. Sneferu had learned from his mistakes with this smooth sided edifice. A fitting monument to a king.

Sam had seen enough pyramids in the past few days to get the full spectrum, and The Red Pyramid looked much more like what people expected to see when they heard the word "pyramid". The learning curve was steep, Sam thought as he gazed at the structure. It was only the second true pyramid which was ever built, but it had come damn close to achieving the ideal of the pyramid builders' art. Or maybe, he thought, they'd been too tired to improve on it, but he doubted this. As he circled it now, there seemed very little to improve on. He knew that it was still the third tallest pyramid ever built, behind the two largest at Giza and shook his head, impressed. It was really amazing that so little was known about it, despite the fact that it had been hidden in a restricted area, safe from the prying eyes of the public, ripe for study, until 1996. Sam suspected that the slightly greater distance of Dahshur from Cairo – about twenty five miles south of Giza and ten miles south of Saqqara - made it a bit more of a hassle for tourists and a bit less attractive for tour operators, especially since there weren't any tourist shops in the area for merchants to earn commissions!

Sam looked at it now and had to admit that this is what made it an especially attractive place to visit.

There was a plaque outside, though, an impressive amount of signage for the area. He brushed the dirt off so he could get a better look.

There seemed to be three rooms inside the pyramid, joined by a single corridor.   Sam knew that the ancient Egyptians hadn't come up with the idea of the arch as a load-bearing mechanism in stone buildings- he was fairly certain that distinction went to the Greeks and the Romans- so when they did construct rooms in stone structures they either used lots of stone pillars spaced close together to support the weight of the roof like a forest of stone – a common sight in temples and one familiar to tourists, synonymous with ancient Egypt; or they used large slabs of stone to make "corbelled" ceilings. He'd read the term before, but he hadn't seen it close up and he looked at it, interested. The one in the first chamber allowed the ceiling to reach twelve feet high – constructed by flat slabs of stone laid on top of each other moving slowly in towards the center, the huge mass of stone above the room keeping the ceiling from falling in on itself.

He rubbed his thumb over scratches in the plastic plaque cover. Some hopeful tourist had inscribed their initials, eager for their own brush with immortality.

There was a staircase which led up to a passageway to the final chamber and Sam studied closely, wondering how much of this information he could use in navigating their descent into the Black Pyramid when Ethan was finally well enough to go.

He didn't expect it to be easy. Thieves had been breaking into burial chambers even from the earliest days, so the passageways inside the pyramids had been deliberately made to be difficult to follow, with deep pits for unwary grave robbers to fall into and stone blocks called portcullises which could be lowered from the ceiling to block the path.

Still, Sam knew that almost all of them were eventually ransacked and looted, and his heart stopped as it had before, at the thought that they'd come all this way to find nothing when they finally reached the heart of the maze.

Sam squinted at the structure before him, marveling again at how time worked. The architect had been clever: some archaeologists believed that the Medium pyramid was the first attempt at building a smooth-sided pyramid, and that it may have collapsed when construction of the Bent Pyramid was already well under way. That would have clued the architect in to its potential for instability, Sam thought... prompting his decision to hide the labyrinth under something that was already crumbling as a way of keeping it safe from prying eyes. Hopefully.

He still wondered how he had expected his children to find it if they had to fight through a collapsed ruin to get there, but that was a question for another day.

He could only deal with so much.

The Necropolis was worth it, Sam thought. Who knew I could ever be standing face-to-face with this? "Wow" sounded anticlimactic, but it was the best his tired brain could do.

Now this, the Red Pyramid, was known to be the resting place of King Sneferu. It only made sense that it was. After all of his investments and dedication to the project, of course he would want to be buried there.

His son, Cheops, had learned from his father's mistakes. He had constructed the Great Pyramid at Giza based on this design, but that rose almost five hundred feet in the air, a testament to the ages.

Sam shook his head, impressed as he always was at the powers of mankind. He wasn't a philosophical man by any means, but he could give credit where credit was due, and there was definitely something humbling about standing next to such power. He thought about legacy. He thought about the man who had built the Black Pyramid and thought about what kind of man he had been. What kind of father.

So he should expect staircases, he thought, when they made their entrance into the Black Pyramid. He should expect portcullises and booby traps and passageways that went nowhere.

He brought out the map Ethan had copied from the hall onto the other map, but it didn't tell him much more in daylight than it had at night.

Someone must have found their way in to make the map, he thought.

Yes. Someone. Many someones. All dead.

He knew the pyramid before him had already been breached and defiled by Europeans - he was sure of it. What he didn't know was if it was worth going in. After all, rumors had it that there was already black graffiti on the insides of the walls, left behind by the finders of the pyramid, who wanted to leave their mark on the sacred structure.

Those fools, Sam thought, shaking his head. That they would disgrace such a magnificent structure was beyond him.

Sam sat down on the gravel, took out his journal, and flipped the book open to a free page. Rummaging in his pack, he held the book open with his thumb and carefully took out his sketching pencil and began measuring out the sides of the pyramid. Slowly, he became more appreciative of the Egyptians' intellect.

How did they make the rock line up so linearly? Sam wondered.

He had heard tales of how advanced the Egyptians were in terms of mathematics and astronomy, but in the presence of these majestic structures, Sam could only stand in awe of the pure power of the Egyptians. Soaking in the energy that the Red Pyramid seemed to seep out to him, Sam started to sketch.

Sam had no illusions about being an artist, but he did like to make records of his travels and drawing was always something that had shut off the logical part of his brain. He wasn't as technically skilled as he'd like, but he was improving and he'd found that drawing – with its reliance on measurement and perception- was as good a way as any to sharpen the skills of vision and sight.

But Sam's hand never stopped, as it seemed to have a mind of its own. He was drawing the Red Pyramid, standing with the Nile flowing beautifully in the background. Labeling the land as Necropolis, Sam stopped to admire the page.

Not bad, Sam thought, critically regarding the page. Good enough for now, anyway.

Pulling out his headset, Sam leaned back on his hands and began to listen to music as he let the wind rustle his hair. Tonight. They would go tonight, tomorrow at the latest. It might take Ethan quite a while to heal and they couldn't wait that long, not with the cartel on their ass. Not when he didn't know how much Josh had already said. Not when he didn't know how much Mia knew, or where her loyalties truly lie. He knew Ethan trusted her- or had trusted her- but he'd trusted Josh, too. Love made people blind.

He laughed as a song came into his ears. "All you need is love." Playing *The Beatles* always made him feel more hopeful about the world. Good art did that, that's why people loved it. It made you feel connected to something greater than yourself, and remember your own purpose in this mad play called the cosmos.

Sam lost himself in his thoughts once again. He imagined the Egyptians dancing to the music of British rock bands, the Egyptians drinking beer and trying fast-food. He pictured the Egyptians teaching the Americans how to write hieroglyphics and drawing murals on the subways to promote the importance of aesthetics.

His thoughts turned to what they would find later, when he and Tom entered the Black Pyramid and tried to follow the map, as he squinted at the structure. In the distance, date palms dotted the floodplain of the Nile and Sam thought that it was part of the reason the whole thing had collapsed, and part of the architect's genius. It was only ten feet above sea level, here. Well, if the man could use it, he could use it, too.

Sam packed up his book in the setting sun, fighting the sudden chill. Faintly in the distance he could see the *Tahila* riding the waves like a goddess.

Tonight. They'd go tonight.

Chapter Sixty-Four

Tom and Sam had snuck off the boat as quietly as possible. They hadn't told Ethan they were going and when they'd asked Genevieve where he was, she'd shrugged and said he was resting. He'd been resting and didn't want to be disturbed.

That was good enough for them.

But when they reached the Black Pyramid they found a man in the shadows already waiting. Sam tensed, hand reaching for his gun.

Then he recognized him and his hand didn't drop but his face did, into a scowl.

"What the hell are you doing here? You're supposed to be resting."

Ethan wore bandages under his shirt, but he looked hale and eager with a defiant glint in his eyes.

"There's no way I'm missing this after everything that's happened." His eyes blazed a challenge. "I have every right to enter this place, just as much as you. I found a key-"

Tom snorted. "You stole a key."

Ethan glared at him. "Men tried to kill me for it; I killed them. I helped you get the other two keys. Without me, you wouldn't even know where they were. I-"

"And almost got us killed with your help. Slimy turncoat."

Ethan swung on him. "And all your friends are perfect?" He swallowed. "We do what we have to in war."

Tom stepped forward. "How do we know you won't leave us in there? Take the-"

Ethan punched Tom in the stomach. The other man, caught by surprise, stumbled back, winded. Before Tom could retaliate and do serious damage to Ethan's already damaged physique, Sam stepped in the middle.

"Hey. He has a right to be here, just like you do. I'm not playing nursemaid. To either of you."

He turned a level gaze to Ethan. "I want you here, you're a good man to have in a fight and you do have a right. But I'm not going to drag you along. You keep up on your own steam or you don't keep up at all."

Ethan met his gaze with a level gaze of his own. "Understood." He grinned, surprisingly. "Boss."

Sam flicked a glance at Tom. "Can we all play nice?"

Tom looked mulish. "Sure, if he does."

Sam rolled his eyes. Ethan and Tom shared a look. Tom's lip quirked. Ethan's did too. Sam wondered just how the man had managed to get off the *Tahila* in the first place.

Depending on his future plans, he wondered if Ethan would be interested in being a part of the crew. He was useful and he was shrewd and he was persuasive. All good things to have at your back.

Sam grinned and faced the challenge ahead. One thing at a time.

This one happened to be the military fence around the encampment. Sam and Tom had been planning to duck under and sneak in, but Ethan dragged them toward the manned gate entrance.

"Got your back, boys," he said and saluted the guard in impeccable SEAL fashion. "Been working while you been taking your sweet time."

As they passed, Ethan tossed the man a whole carton of cigarettes.

Even Tom laughed. "What did you tell him?"

Ethan fought a grin. "That we wanted to perform satanic sacrifices on holy ground to protect us from the demons that surround us drawn by your ugly face."

Sam laughed. "Sounds about right."

The fence was a fair distance away from the structure itself and it took them some time to cross the open ground under the moonlight.

Sam fought the prickle of unease at the back of his neck, glad Ethan had come with them after all. Always good to have another man in the fight, even if he was recovering from injury.

The three men cautiously approached the entrance of the Black Pyramid as they took in the ancient monument that had withstood so much history. From afar, it was almost unrecognizable, blending in with the sandy, desert landscape that surrounded it for miles around. To the casual tourist, it seemed like an old pile of rubble that had been decaying for years unless you knew what to look for.

"No wonder it's called the Black Pyramid. It just looks sad." Tom observed as they crossed a narrow dirt path, approaching the massive structure. They called it "mid-sized" in the information, but it looked damn big close up. Sam whistled appreciatively, inhaled a lungful of dust, and doubled over, coughing.

"Don't die on us now, Sam." Tom said teasingly. Sam gave a small grin. They stopped in front of the entrance, which was a small hole covered in cobwebs. Limestone crumbled off the top of the entrance, and clay that once encased it was completely worn away.

"Well, here it is." Ethan eyed the structure warily. "We came all the way for this?"

Tom shrugged good naturedly. "Definitely not your dream pyramid, but she has curb appeal, I'd say."

Sam stepped in front of them, crouched down to pass the low lintel. "Well we definitely didn't come all this way just to talk by it." He glanced at them over his shoulder with a grin. "You coming?"

The musky, distinct scent of ancient ruins wafted in the air as the men waddled inelegantly into the structure one by one. None of them were small men and their entrance was ungainly, but they made it inside with nothing more untoward than heads full of cobwebs.

The sun from outside dimmed fast once they'd entered and Sam held up the glow of his flashlight to light their way. It was not as poetic as the torches of old, he thought, but it got the job done. The blue sterile illumination threw their shadows huge and bent onto the walls, and it was dim but it showed them enough: they'd found themselves in a narrow corridor barely tall enough to stand in, in which the walls seemed to be pushing increasingly inward. Isn't this just cozy, Sam thought? Sam glanced at the others, but they seemed too awed by their surroundings to move forward. Just as well, he thought, as he'd done most of the research. Much good it might do him.

Sam held up his flashlight and squinted, trying to make out any shapes or corridors – or booby traps – in the darkness in front of him. So far it seemed like a fairly straightforward aisle.

Tom tapped his shoulder and gestured him forward with his chin.

They went.

Here and there, the men spotted hieroglyphs that weren't scratched off during pyramid looting raids, but they were so faded that it was impossible for Sam to decipher. For the first fifteen minutes from the beginning of their entry into the pyramid, only one path seemed to exist that led deeper and deeper within the pyramid in one big spiral towards the center. Sam had heard tales of false passageways constructed to fool tomb robbers, but that didn't seem to be the case here. They didn't see any alternate passageways at all. He desperately put all B grade horror films from his head and the visions they brought of rocks sealing the passageways or someone flooding the entrance, trapping them underground like moles in a maze.

The passageways grew wider as they traveled deeper into the pyramid, which, Sam remembered, had caused many structural problems. He hoped these had been fixed somewhat in the myriad renovations over the years, but it was not a big hope. The group walked in complete silence, everyone fully submerged in their own thoughts.

Then Sam's flashlight began to flicker.

"What?" He thumped it in his hand, but the light wouldn't turn on. He shook his head. "Second one today."

"Here." Ethan reached out to him in the slowly dimming light as they stood in the ancient tombs in almost complete pitch black. "It's small, but it'll do for now." He gave Sam a rough grin. "Is it possible you were never a boy scout? Always come prepared."

Sam took the small flashlight and he took the lead.

The single corridor didn't last long.

Soon, branches spun off the main hallway and Sam and Ethan and Tom muttered about what to do. Yes, they had the map, but that didn't mean that it was easy to follow. Sam remembered reading about a queen's section and assumed they'd found it when they entered a lavish tomb full of crumbling pottery and skeletal, painted wood. The chamber held a magnificent sarcophagus, and the hallway was unusually wide. As they wandered down the hallway, it became clear that in the alcoves off the sides were actual houses.

"Priest's houses, maybe." Sam glanced at them, wondering at the power of such a civilization. Wondering what people two thousand years from now would think of theirs.

They'd taken turns and wrong turns and backtracked for more than two hours before frustration finally got the better of them. Sam shook his head, staring at the map. "I know we're going the right way," he said, not for the first time. "We're on the right track. We just need to…"

"Keep going?" Tom finished. "Heard it."

Sam rounded on him. "What do you suggest we do? We've been shot at, drowned, kidnapped, and betrayed to get these keys and you just want to make snide remarks-"

"Hey."

They turned at Ethan's voice to find his flashlight shining on a feature they'd missed during their squabble. It was big, but that wasn't what set it apart. It was a door, which made it different from anything they'd found so far. Before they'd found empty archways or partially moved stone slabs. But this was covered in a mural- Sam picked out figures and leaves and rows and rows of hieroglyphics.

Instead of being decorated with fading paint, however, this mural was deeply carved into the stone and filled with a type of red paint. It looked unnervingly like very old, very dried blood along the sandstone grooves.

While faded, it was clear that more effort had been spent on this door than on the walls around it. And that was saying something.

Sam felt a flicker of excitement. Had they found the king's chamber after all?

"Are you guys thinking the same thing I am?" Sam gestured to the door, standing closer to it and peering up at its height. "This might be it, boys."

"That door does not look like it's going to budge." Tom shook his head with an engineer's certainty. "It's got to be at least three hundred pounds and considering the age of this pyramid, it's probably stuck to the walls at this point."

Glancing around their surroundings, Sam noticed a medium-sized hole towards the right, on the top of the door.

"Hey, anyone got something long enough to fit through that hole and possibly open the door?" Sam asked, as he began to search his own backpack.

Pushing aside his water, food rations, gun, and some ammunition, he came across his belt that he had taken off a while ago.

This might work, thought Sam. "Ah," he said. "Never mind. Let's see what happens with this."

Moving aside his backpack, Sam had to go on his tiptoes to fit the belt through the crack, then slowly moved it around trying to make out the door from the inside.

"You got anything?" Tom asked, rather impatient. "I feel like that crack is a hint to how to get in… I just don't know how a belt is going to help us Sam."

"Yeah, you're right," Sam said, giving up. "You think we should just try shooting a hole through the stone?"

"Nah, don't upset anything. Let's go back out where we came from to see if there's a different pathway. Maybe the king's tomb is more towards the top of the pyramid."

Silently agreeing, Sam followed Tom as the group made their way back up, and took the stairs towards the top of the pyramid. On their way, they encountered different rooms, completely looted, but obviously still intact as a tomb.

We're not the only ones who've been in here, Tom thought. That means that King Sneferu's treasures might not even be here anymore.

Losing some faith but not yet giving up, the group slowly made their way all the way to the top… only to be faced with the dreaded dead end.

The group just stared. Undeniably crushed, there were no words to be said. After a long moment of silence, Sam opened his mouth for some kind of moral attempt. "Come on." He spread his hands with a winning smile, covering his own disappointment and frustration. "We're on the right track. I think we just need to keep going!"

"What does that even mean," Tom snapped. Obviously annoyed, he plopped down on the hard ground, twisting his flashlight in his hand.

"I mean maybe one of the things that we've seen already is a clue." Sam cuffed his head. "We've got the map, even if it is confusing. We've got our own eyes, dammit. What if… what would you say if one of those tombs that we saw had a sort of clue?"

"I'd say you're an idiot," Tom said. "We've been trying to search for any type of clue for hours under ground, and every single one we think could help ends up leading us to these dead ends."

"Oh," Sam nodded. "Right. I forgot that sitting and moping is preferable." He gestured magnanimously. "Please, by all means. It's sure to be a great help. Not sure why I didn't think of that."

Tom snorted, but when Sam turned away from him he heard Tom push to his feet with an oath and shot Ethan a very small grin. Ethan shook his head, fighting to keep his own optimism. Both of their discoveries had not prepared them for this. The finding of the keys seemed like fate, like a walk in the park to this. Even shooting out the cartel compound had basically dropped the precious pieces in their lap. This was something else again.

Even remembering how far they'd come to be here filled Sam with a little more confidence. They'd done it once; they could do it again. Sam picked up his pace towards the room that had been looted but still had a sarcophagus. It was massive, glorious, covered in carvings. He wondered if they were in the king's chambers, the man who had left keys to his children to bring them closer to wisdom and instead had ensured that that wisdom would go unfound for centuries.

The more he thought about it, the more certain he felt about a clue here. He ran his fingers over the dusty wall. There had to be.

Glancing back towards the group, he saw Tom sulkily scuff his feet. Sam slowed his pace and waited for Tom to catch up.

"Come on, Tom. We've survived worse than this. We all just got shot a week ago! We're not giving up just yet."

Tom's only response was a thin smile, and Sam just let him be.

Finally reaching the open room, Sam whistled for everyone to gather.

He gestured at the sarcophagus, which was lying open. "Look. The body is gone. What if…" He knew he was grasping at straws but he had to get them talking to share ideas. It was the only way this was going to work and Sam didn't mind looking the idiot for the good of the team. "There's no way this was meant for man." He looked around at all of them. "If it was, why would any thief want to steal the body? It just doesn't make sense."

"Because they're twisted grave robbers who'll take anything they can get?" Tom put a finger to his cheek. "Because in the nineteenth century there was a huge market for mummy dust? Improved the virility."

"Ugh." Ethan grimace. "You tell bad jokes."

"Not a joke. Just the facts. Maybe they burned the body for fuel. Just some dead guy, once you take off the jewelry, right? And eBay."

All good points. Sam held his ground. "But this is the king's chamber, I'm almost sure of it. It has to be."

Tom shrugged. "If you say so."

Ethan looked around. "You want to know what I think? Since I've seen these desert men and I know how they think? I think it's weird that the sarcophagus is so out in the open. It's almost as if they're telling us it's not important."

Sam shot him a relieved grin. "That's what I think. Otherwise keep it hidden. Or maybe there's something hidden in the ordinary. Wouldn't be the first time…"

Sam stepped forward and put his hands on the sarcophagus. He shoved, put his whole weight behind it, but Sam immediately knew he was in trouble. It was heavy.

Very heavy.

Nothing budged, not even an inspiring grate of stone on stone. "I'm definitely going to need some help here," Sam called back. "Come give me a hand!"

Tom and Ethan joined him around the tomb. Tom reached out and put his weight behind Sam's. This time there was the grate of stone.

Ethan joined them but Sam shook his head. "Sorry, man. Can't risk you opening that chest of yours." He grinned. "You can be the moral support."

Though the stone had budged a bit, still, the massive sarcophagus wouldn't budge more than an inch. It's like it's been locked or something.

"Take out anything metal that you have," he gasped, trying to collect his breath and gearing up for another go. He gestured weakly at the stone. "We're going to need to pry this thing to move it."

Tom laughed. "You must be joking."

Sam shook his head. "You got a better idea?"

Taking out his belt, Sam slipped the it under, and tugged.

Ethan was wandering around the tomb critically, casing it like he'd case a potential weapon. He asked, "What about the keys?"

Sam swung to him in surprise.

Ethan traced the designs on the sides of the huge box. "Here," he said. "There's a groove, a hole. It looks like a hole, anyway. But it's filled with nine hundred years of dust. It might be a key hole."

Sam stared. "I... am an idiot."

Tom was way ahead of him, already at the side. "There's one here too!" he shouted, the excitement crashing around the walls, deafening in its echo.

Ethan grinned. "Pick out the dirt." he said, digging in his pants for his army knife. "That, at least I can help with."

It took them longer than expected to pry out thousands of years of dirt. But pry they did.

Sam turned to Ethan, who was already pulling the keys out from under his shirt where he wore his dog tag. Sam pulled out his own. He looked at Tom.

Tom leaned down and kicked off his shoe and then handed two keys to Sam. He laughed.

"Your shoes?"

"You think of a safer place for them?" Tom huffed, shoving his foot back in his big boot and jerking tight the laces. "No one's going to pick my shoes."

"Right." Sam confronted the casket, holding the key. "Let's see what we've got."

The first one didn't work. The second one did. It turned.

He turned to the others with a huge smile. "Gentlemen," he declared, "I think we've got something."

They found the keys that fit the other holes, and it still didn't help with the weight of the lid, but when they all got their backs behind it they'd been buoyed up by their triumph and when the lid slid back a few inches they cheered and by the time they had it back the width of a narrow man they were breathless and cursing and triumphant.

"One more should do it…"

Tom shook his head. "Don't push it all the way. Don't let it hit the ground. Not sure this place could take the impact without coming down around our ears."

It was a fair point.

Red and gasping, they heaved.

It took some minutes to recover from the stars flashing in front of his eyes. When his vision cleared Sam gripped the edge of the tomb, hauled himself up, and peered over the edge. He couldn't believe his eyes. He glanced over to find Tom doing the same, his face thunderstruck.

They grinned at each other with excitement.

Dim and shadowy beneath where the tomb had previously lay was not a body. Before their eyes, was a staircase leading down toward the deep crevices of the earth.

"We've done it!" Sam said. "Let's see where it leads."

Sam lowered himself down to the stairs on the other side, carefully. Ethan's small flashlight lit the descent five steps and Sam stopped. He didn't want to think what would be waiting; it was all he wanted to think about.

He grinned up at them, a flutter in his chest. "Let's go."

Chapter Sixty-Five

Sam peered down the stairs.

Under the beam of his flashlight the passageway was lit in a way that made it seem almost staged. Sam could tell that no one had been here in centuries. The first couple of steps were well designed, almost inviting, yet quickly disappeared into the shroud of darkness.

"Hey Tom, can you hand me another flashlight. This one doesn't do a damned thing." He held his hand behind his shoulder without looking, knowing that someone in the group would hand it to him. He felt the cold metal touch his fingertips, and suddenly shuddered at the unexpected chill. What's wrong with me, he wondered? He shrugged the feeling off as nerves and pointed the flashlight into the depths.

The staircase descended for a solid three hundred feet, and appeared to turn at the end. Sam squinted, but he couldn't see more than that.

"What's down there?" Tom asked.

"Nothing much. I think it turns at the end though," replied Sam. His mouth twisted up, but he kept his tone light. "How much do you want to bet there's some Egyptian trap inside?"

"Only one way to find out." It was Ethan who hopped over next, surprising Sam, but he didn't know why he was surprised. It wasn't like Ethan had a history of caution and he had a personal stake in the matter of discovery, just like Sam.

The two men shared a grin and Sam stepped down a few steps cautiously to give Ethan room. He crept down the stairs quietly, signaling the others to do the same. If one of the steps triggered anything, he wanted to hear it.

"High alert," he whispered back, and felt Ethan nod behind him, grin forgotten, deadly serious. This was a warzone. This was war.

They had gone about five hundred feet, it felt like, without any incident and no change in scenery. Sam hung hard to his mode of caution, but it wasn't easy the further they got, tense and jumpy and wanting it to be done. He was just eager to get to wherever the obsidian door was. Then, he noticed something.

"Hey." He stalled in surprise and Ethan almost bumped into him from behind. "There aren't any hieroglyphs here."

Ethan stopped too. "Yeah," he said. "I was just about to say that, too."

"I think I know why," chimed in Tom. If Sam had space to turn around, he would have. It was rare that Tom inferred, rather than just quoting some history textbook.

"I think I read about this somewhere." Tom continued. "This must be more of a transitional tunnel, rather than an official hallway. Even in secret passages, they had hieroglyphs. The only reason why they wouldn't here is because this must have been built quickly and secretly, probably only by a couple of workers."

That made sense. The hallway must be at the bottom. Sam jumped down the last couple of steps, and beamed his flashlight forward. Indeed, it was a hallway, walls lined from bottom to top with ancient markings that Sam had never seen before. He squinted towards the end of the hallway.

He couldn't see the end. Tom and Ethan caught up to him.

"What do you see? Where's the end?" asked Ethan.

Sam shone his flashlight, but no more secrets revealed themselves. He shrugged. "I don't know."

Tom glanced at them. "What should we do?"

Sam glared back. "I mean, what can we do? We go for it."

As if on cue, there was a deep thud at the top of the staircase. Tom, the last of the line, turned to jump up the stairs, but it was too late. The entrance that they had come from had closed. There was nothing there but a wall of stone.

"Oh, shit."

There didn't seem to be anything else to say.

Ethan shrugged with a wry grin. "I guess you're right." said Ethan. "Forward we go."

"This really isn't the time for being a smartass." Sam glared at him, annoyed. "If we run out of air in here, we run out of light…"

"No, he's right." said Tom. As Sam looked at him, ready to retort, Tom held up his hand. "Look at the walls. There are some hieroglyphics on them now. They depicted ancient Egyptian people, either looking or running toward the end of the hall."

Sam stopped his tirade in surprise. He turned and inspected the wall and found that Tom was right. The last people who had seen these markings were probably the ones who created them- they had to be true somehow. And all of the tiny Egyptian people were running with a look of hypnosis towards whatever was waiting for them at the end of the hall.

Sam hoped like hell it wasn't the afterlife.

But they were right. Nothing to do but go forward.

"All right. The figures on the wall point the way. Let's go." Sam put one foot in front of the other back into the dark. The hallway was wide enough to now fit the three of them side by side. They walked forward, Tom occasionally turning and seeing if anything had changed behind them.

Nothing had.

About ten minutes later, the hallway showed no signs of stopping. Sam was contemplating running. They could all handle it- well, maybe not Ethan, but he could stay behind and guard the rear- and at this point, it would probably save more energy than dying of asphyxiation under an ancient pyramid.

Without thinking, he picked up his pace and began to walk faster. Fast enough that his breath caught in his throat and the others made sounds of surprise nearby. But they didn't comment, just matched their pace to his.

Sam locked his eyes on the darkness and soon he was jogging, the slow lope easier on his aching body than the pounding quick walk.

The others followed suit.

The hall was filled with their panting breaths and footfalls. Wordless agreement pushed them on.

He quickened his pace. The two next to him followed.

The corridor narrowed and Sam's breath caught. Were they close?

And then suddenly it was there. The hallway stopped. Sam stopped. Sam didn't even feel tired.

Before them at the end of the hall was a massive black door that gleamed faintly in the glow of the flashlight, like dark glass.

The others stopped beside them. Ethan's ragged breathing cut through the silence, hitching on his wounds. But Sam knew he wouldn't have traded this for the world. He was a soldier.

Sam reached out toward the door and realized that his hands were trembling. Normally, that would have surprised and annoyed him, but today, it did neither.

"Is that actually it?" Ethan's whisper broke his trance behind him.

"I think it is." Tom's voice was hushed with awe.

As he stood and looked at the fruits of their success, Sam felt the desire to laugh. He'd been so focused on getting the keys and finding the door, he had never imagined what he would do when he actually reached it. It didn't matter now.

Idiot, he chided himself as he reached into his pocket and took out all of the keys he'd put there after opening the tomb. Didn't seem any point in keeping them separate or safe since they were the only ones here. How many things can you do with a door?

He weighed the four heavy keys in his palm and handed one each to Tom and Ethan. The surface of the door was smooth and blank, not carved as he'd expected, not carved like the tomb. The keyholes sat in a diamond directly in the center, like a small flock of birds or an alien symbol. It was eerie and unsettling and Sam's blood hammered in his veins.

It was a tight fit for all three of them in front of the door but they managed. They each stood in front of the keyholes, and held the keys in front of them, Sam having one key in each hand.

"On three?" Tom's voice was hushed with anticipation.

"On three." Sam took a breath, held it for eight beats, and let it out to a count of eight. It was a trick one of his army buddies had taught him, a meditation secret from the east. A way to calm the mind, to link body and heart and bypass the brain.

He glanced into the obsidian. It was so reflective he could see his face in it like a ghost. It almost seemed to invite him in to whatever otherworldly realm waited beyond its barrier.

"Let's go. On three."

Their breathing quieted.

"Three..." They stepped closer, shuffling in the dim light.

"Two..." The keys entered the holes, soundlessly.

"One..." The weight heavy in their hands.

They turned the keys.

With a deep rumble, the obsidian door slowly moved to the side. Sam briefly wondered how the door moved without any gears or motors, then threw the thought aside.

They walked in.

Chapter Sixty-Six

Strabo's Labyrinth

The massive chamber spread before them.

It was larger than Sam had ever imagined. He had heard tales of a mysterious underground complex of caverns and chambers, but this put them all to shame.

Strabo had written that when one entered the sacred enclosure one found a temple surrounded by columns, forty on each side. He had written that the labyrinth had a roof made of a single stone that showcased carved panels and that was richly adorned with excellent paintings. He made note that it contained memorials of the homeland of each of the kings, as well as of the temples and sacrifices carried out in it, all skillfully worked in paintings of the greatest beauty.

Well, Sam thought. Someone had to put words to it. That words couldn't do it justice was hardly Strabo's fault. The man had tried.

"Christ!" Tom muttered nearby, then crossed himself and glanced around guiltily. Sam understood. The holy name spoken such sounded profane in this place. He stepped forward into the massive chamber, awed. The three men drifted off on their own, taking in the splendor.

Sam couldn't catch his breath, it seemed. Was it possible they were finally here? Had that turn of luck – accident, total accident – in Afghanistan all those years ago, finally led to this? Loss of life, lack of sleep, secrets covered, secrets revealed… it all fell away as he stared up and up and up.

Elaborate hieroglyphics covered the walls, scenes of ritual and royalty, court life and daily life. Boats sailed stone rivers, painted cows chewed painted grass contentedly with wise slanting eyes. Sam saw treasure chests and resurrections, men coming from the stars, creatures emerging from underground. River gods and women with birds' heads and birds with the heads and hands of men... there were islands and depictions of elaborate civilizations, carved palaces and scientists and delicate flowers. He saw statues that looked like Easter Island but even more ancient, ships voyaging on painted seas. He thought back to what the ancients had written- that the labyrinth contained the key to mankind's history. That inside its hallowed halls, secrets of ancient civilizations and great empires and the rulers who shaped history on the planet before history as we know it began.

It certainly seemed true.

Sam stood under the weight of the glorious alabaster ceiling amid the mysteries and the wonder. His heart twisted tight in his chest and something in him rose and tightened and spread its wings. Something that had been trapped inside since he was a boy, he felt. Since that day in Nevada. Since long before.

He wept.

They weren't sad tears. They were tears of wonder at the glory of it all, at the mysteries of man, at the unmappable human spirit. This was why he did what he did. This was why, so he could leave a legacy, uncover a little piece of the legacy that they'd already left for themselves.

Jesus, he thought, trying to collect himself, hoping the others hadn't seen. Sitting here sobbing like an old woman about ages past, pining for the days she'd never see. Get yourself together, Reilly. His eyes stung as he stared around him and he shook his head. According to Strabo there were three thousand rooms like this.

There were scrolls.

Sam didn't know how they'd been preserved in the damp and in the dark, some combination of low temperature and the right amount of humidity, maybe. He wasn't a historian or a restorer. And as pristine as they seemed now, he couldn't bring himself to touch them. He-

Ethan didn't have the same restraint.

He reached out and touched just the corner of one of the scrolls with a wondering caress.

The papyrus crumpled to dust before their eyes.

Ethan staggered back, horrified. Sam just stared.

Their eyes met in dismay. "I didn't-" Ethan stammered. "I didn't know it would-"

Sam shook his head. "Not much you can do about it now." He turned his gaze to the room, where hundreds, perhaps thousands of scrolls sat in cupboards with tiny cubby holes cut just for them. The secrets of the world, he thought sadly. Known and unknown- and all just out of reach. There was a chance, maybe, a slim one, that with the right research tools and archeological equipment experts could excavate these precious secrets, but somehow Sam doubted it. He felt in his gut that these stories were meant to stay hidden and remain so.

The men exchanged wry looks and drifted off again.

Sam didn't know how long he wandered, lost in the majesty of it all. Dimly he was aware of Tom making rubbings of the walls, of him touching the floor, making sketches in his small book to record these feats of engineering. For Genevieve, Sam thought, as much as for posterity's sake. He wondered what Mia and Ethan had talked about the night before.

He saw Ethan trailing his fingers over the walls, his expression as staggered as Sam himself felt. He was glad it had been true. He was glad Ethan, of all people, had been able to see this.

Sam approached him and Ethan jerked, startled. But it wasn't like it had been in the hotel room- a defensive reflex. This was merely surprise, the awareness that he was a human being with a body and he was not alone in this room. Sam nodded at the wall.

"Pretty incredible, no?"

Ethan shook his head. "I can't believe it's real." He gave a wry smile. "You were right."

Sam grinned. "Well. I can tell you it makes me wish I'd learned ancient Egyptian, that's for sure." He touched the dusty wall reverently.

"That's the sign for bread," Ethan said unexpectedly and Sam turned to him and stared.

He gestured at the walls covered in line after line of script. "You can read this?"

Ethan shook his head with a sheepish smile. His voice was wistful. "Just a few things. My… dad. Brought me a book from the library once, on one of his sober binges. He knew I liked old stuff, puzzles and things. He thought it would make a good secret code."

Sam smiled. Ethan rarely talked about his dad, leading Sam to believe that their time together hadn't been altogether pleasant. But he was glad the boy had happy memories too and that bitterness hadn't buried them completely.

"Hey Tom!" Sam called over to where Tom was still sketching in that little black book. He became aware that the other man hadn't moved from one specific spot for quite a while, now.

Tom was diligent. "What about you? Any unrevealed linguistic skills?"

"I don't even have any revealed linguistic skills. But I can tell you one of these things is not like the others." He ran his hands over the wall in front of him, a frown in his voice and between his big brows.

Sam and Ethan glanced at each other, then shrugged. Curious, Sam made his way through the tables and the artifacts, trying not to touch anything, to where his friend stood staring at the wall on the other side of the room.

"What do you mean?" He asked as he approached. He was still too far away to see properly.

"This." Tom frowned again. "Now, I'm not a linguist and I'm definitely not an artist, but these… they don't look like the rest of the hieroglyphics we've seen. Did they have different languages? I mean, different sets of symbols for different things?"

Sam shook his head as he got closer, trying to remember if that was the case or not. He'd never read anything about it. "I don't think so. Ethan?" he called, only to find the other man close by his shoulder. "What about you? Do you know?"

"I don't think so either." Then Ethan's grin quirked, wry. "But I'm not an expert, either."

"Well." Tom shrugged. "Then I don't know what this is. Maybe it's graffiti, but I don't know how anyone would have ever gotten past those doors…"

Now Sam was close enough to see but he didn't think he could possibly be seeing right. He stopped in front of the wall and peered closer, and then his mouth dropped open.

"This isn't Egyptian," he whispered, trailing his hands across the dusty wall. The writings were complicated, like a cross between hieroglyphics and ancient Sumerian and Sanskrit, something born from the crossroads of all civilization, handpicked to secure the secrets of the ages. The letters even felt powerful under his fingertips. "This is the language of the Master Builders."

Chapter Sixty-Seven

Ethan looked at him sharply. "They're the ones who built this place, right?"

Sam couldn't take his eyes off the text. "Right."

Tom looked back at him. "You're certain?"

Sam laughed. "Yep. After fifteen years, I've developed a pretty good understanding of the language. Not quite as good as Billie, but pretty good."

Tom said, "You want to bring Billie in on this?"

Dr. Billie Swan was the world's leading expert on the Master Builders, an extraordinary archeologist, and a complex friend who seemed to hinder as much as impress Sam Reilly during his various expeditions over the years. She had also nearly married Tom years earlier. They had parted ways amicably, but there was still tension.

Sam paused for a minute. "Yeah. I'm going to have to. Look at the amount of work here, it could take years to decipher it all, and I'm not sure we have the time to waste."

A moment later, Sam began reading a very specific piece of text.

We came before.

We will return.

We have never left.

Tom asked, "What the heck does that even mean?"

Sam shrugged. "Beats me."

His eyes scanned the rest of the ancient inscription.

"The race to locate the obsidian chamber will be triggered. There will be a fight to decipher the cipher in the stars. The whole world will want to possess its awesome power. Destroy the macroscope for the good of mankind, I pray no one ever deciphers its ancient mysteries."

Tom asked, "Great, so now we need to find the obsidian chamber?"

"It looks like it." Sam grinned. "And destroy a macroscope?"

Ethan asked, "What is a macroscope?"

Sam shook his head. "I have no idea. The only time I've even heard of the name was the classic 1970s science fiction book by Piers Anthony, but I can hardly imagine that the author of this ancient work intended to make any reference to the works of a sci-fi great."

Tom asked, "Any idea who wrote this?"

Sam shook his head. "I don't know. Wait... there's a name down here."

He fixed his flashlight on a small engraving toward the bottom of the stone wall.

It was a type of signature.

Sam read it.

Michel Nostradamus.

"Good God!" Sam said, "Nostradamus toured Strabo's Labyrinth long before us!"

Ethan expelled a breath of air. "How can you be certain?"

"He left his name."

Ethan wasn't convinced. "Maybe there's another Nostradamus? Anything else?"

"Yeah, look at this, Nostradamus chiseled the date into the solid stone. The date has been carved there for centuries."

Ethan fixed the beam of his flashlight on the date.

That's when he swore. "Holy shit! That's today's date!"

Chapter Sixty-Eight

Sam greeted Dr. Billie Swan at the now open obsidian door.

Despite having not slept for more than twenty-four hours, she looked every bit as beautiful and arrogantly stubborn as Sam remembered her. With a unique mixture of European and Asian descent, she had the sort of delicate, yet striking features of a porcelain model.

Of course, that's where any apparent weakness ended. Billie was up there with some of the toughest, most intelligent, and determined women Sam had ever known.

For the most part, he couldn't stand to be around her, but when it came to understanding the ancient Master Builders, he needed her insight more than he needed anything else in the world.

She was wearing olive cargo pants, and a white tank top. Her face displayed all the signs of a person who hadn't slept much. There were slight bags under her almond shaped, hazel eyes and her untidy dark hair had been tied back in a careless ponytail, a pair of Ray Bans propped on top. A flashlight in her right hand.

He shook her hand. "Thanks for coming."

She took it and grinned. "Thanks for inviting me."

"You've been on a flight all day. Do you want to rest?"

Her eyes were wide with wonder. "Are you kidding me? You found Strabo's Labyrinth… a place that people have been debating even existed for centuries. I can sleep tonight… or tomorrow… or possibly the next day, but first I want to see this."

"Good. Because I really need your help."

Her lips twisted into a wry smile. It wasn't very often that he needed her. "Why?"

Sam swallowed. "Because, we need to find the Obsidian Chamber."

She made a half-grin. "Come again. You need to find an Obsidian Chamber?"

Sam nodded, leading her toward the section of writing made by earlier Master Builders. He fixed his flashlight on the section regarding the Obsidian Chamber. "Look at this, Strabo wasn't the last person to enter the labyrinth. Nostradamus was."

Billie's eyes lit up in wonder, her mouth opened with awe. "Nostradamus was here!"

"Yes. Look at this, he says that on the day we entered this room, we unintentionally triggered a global quest to locate the Obsidian Chamber."

"Did he leave any proof that it was really him?" she asked.

Sam smiled. He knew exactly what she was referring to. In general, Nostradamus liked to leave clues in his secrets, that allowed the future intended recipients to know that it was really left by him. Sam said, "Nostradamus engraved the date that this deadly global quest to find the near mythical chamber…"

She frowned. Puzzled. "And?"

"The date was the very day that we opened that secret door and entered Strabo's Labyrinth – and it was carved centuries before we entered."

Billie didn't put up an argument. "Okay, that seems like a pretty impressive magic trick to me. It sounds like Nostradamus. Did he leave any clue about where such a chamber exists or how it can be found?"

"No, but he does leave a drawing of a ship over here." Sam fixed his flashlight onto a second wall, where a ship, frozen solid in ice, with a large mountain in the distance, appeared. "According to Nostradamus the last person to ever set eyes on the Obsidian Chamber was onboard this ship."

"Do you even know the name of the ship?"

Sam swallowed. "Yeah, the *RRS Discovery*."

Billie met his eye. Incredulity plastered across her face. "Ernest Shackleton's ill-fated ship?"

"Afraid that's the one."

"Ernest Shackleton was the last person on Earth to enter the Obsidian Chamber?"

Sam shrugged. "Apparently."

"Well that's great," Billie said, licking her lips. "People have been looking for his ships for over a century. Besides, it's meant to be buried in ice somewhere in the worst portion of the worst sea in the world."

Sam grinned. "That would be the one."

"You should leave as soon as possible."

"Where?"

"Antarctica of course. Where else? You need to find the *Discovery* before anyone else does."

"There won't be a lot of competitors, racing down there to locate it in Antarctica."

"Are you sure?" she asked. "Given what Nostradamus wrote, it appears that you should go with the full might of the *Tahila's* weapons system. Mark my words, you won't be the only one down there, scouring the frozen lands for Shackleton's damned shipwreck."

"It will take a few weeks to get the *Tahila* rigged and provisioned for the icy conditions."

"Then you'd better get going straight away."

Sam shook his head. "But why? Why do we care so much about finding the Obsidian Chamber?"

Billie arched an eyebrow. "Do you really need to ask that?"

"I'm serious. We're in Strabo's Labyrinth! One of the greatest catchments of ancient history ever found, a sacred storage place of knowledge, once thought to be nothing more than a legend… so why should I go on some wild goose chase to locate an Obsidian Chamber?"

She grinned. "Why?"

"Yes!" Sam said, his voice emphatic. "I'm asking you, why?"

Billie grinned. "Because this Obsidian Chamber that Nostradamus writes about doesn't refer to a place where the Master Builders visit, or once lived, it describes a place where the Master Builders derived their great powers." She took a breath. Grinned. "Don't you see, we're talking about the birth place of the most powerful race on Earth, a place that allegedly still exists, and potentially is still capable of providing those who visit it with unimaginable powers."

Sam swallowed. "Nostradamus said that by simply entering Strabo's Labyrinth, we've set in motion a terrible quest, a race that will entrap some of the major players on the world's globe, to hunt for the Obsidian Chamber…"

Billie nodded. "Of course it will! And why wouldn't it? Those who find the Obsidian Chamber might just have the chance to harness all the knowledge and power of the ancient Master Builders."

Sam cursed. "Which means we need to find it first… before such power falls into the wrong hands!"

Chapter Sixty-Nine

Rhyolite, Nevada – Two Weeks Later

A hawk's scream pierced the blinding blue sky.

The air was cloudless but hazy as the summer sun streamed through the dust kicked up by their rented jeep. The flat fields of Nevada stretched out in front of them, featureless and nondescript as Egypt and yet a world away.

The jeep puttered to a stop at the side of the road in a scrub of saw grass and dusty sage. After a moment Ethan killed the motor.

They'd entered the city limits of Rhyolite, Nevada, almost ten minutes ago and the tension had been building ever since.

Ethan glanced at him but didn't take his hands off the wheel. "Are you sure this is the place?"

Sam looked out at the caves and the rock outcroppings he hadn't seen in fifteen years. They looked exactly the same. "Sure as I'm sitting here," he said. Then he wiped his brow and wiped his hands on his jeans, twisting around to the back seat and hauling out an unwieldy package. "You want to do this or not?"

Ethan's jaw was set firm. "I'm certain."

"All right."

The sun beat down as they removed a shovel and Sam counted out the paces. The sage bush was right where he'd left it – only bigger.

Sam went first with the digging. The blade bit into the hard ground for a long time, the dirt as tough as old cement. When Sam tired, he passed Ethan the shovel with a grimace. "Here," he said, breathing hard. "You do it."

Ethan took the shovel with skepticism, but he took it. "I don't even know what I'm looking for. What if I miss it?"

Sam grinned. "You won't miss it."

Ethan shot him a look, and then brought the shovel down into the earth with a sharp shuck. He dug for almost five minutes, long enough for the sweat to trickle down his back and stick his shirt to his spine. When the shovel hit steel with a muted ring, he stopped in surprise.

His eyes darted to Sam, emerging from the digging rhythm he'd lost himself in order to avoid thinking about what might be waiting for them underground.

"Is that the old container?"

Sam dusted his hands and crouched down to brush away the loose clods of earth and sage root pieces like thick grubs. "Let's find out, shall we?"

The hole was as deep as his arms were long and Sam had to stretch out flat to reach the box, getting the red dry dust all up in his nose. He snorted, but it didn't improve the situation.

His groping fingertips hit metal and he felt himself slide.

Ethan grabbed his legs.

Sam grabbed the box.

"Okay," he said. "Got it."

Ethan hauled him back by the heels, the dirt scraping his skin where his shirt rode up in transit, until Sam could wrench himself up by his elbows. He did so, panting. He didn't remember it being in so deep. He hoped like hell this was it.

But when he brushed the top free of dirt, streaking slightly red from his sweat, he recognized the same symbol embossed in the top. Just a circle, slightly embossed, and a line.

It could mean a great many things.

Or it could mean just one.

He let out a breath he hadn't realized he'd been holding.

There was a lock on the front. Though rusted, it had held strong over the past decade and a half.

Sam rummaged in the bag he'd brought and pulled out a key.

It barely fit in the lock when he inserted it; it sure as hell didn't turn.

"Here."

He looked up barely in time to catch the can of oil Ethan threw at him.

He placed a few drops into the lock, inserted the key, and waited. It took a frustratingly long time, but eventually the key turned, starting and stopping as necessary, all the way.

The lock sprang open slowly. Anticlimactic, but true to life.

Not everything was fairy tale, he thought. Even if it felt like it sometimes.

He looked at Ethan. "Well?"

Sam lifted the lid, showering off bits of rust and roots.

Inside was another box, this one military grade and water proof. No lock, just a latch, which Sam lifted as he brought it out.

Inside nestled a Tyvek pouch. He pulled that out too with a strange jolt of déjà vu. He half expected them to come for them now, barreling down the road in those black Crown Vic Secret Service vehicles.

Sam fought a glance at the road. He'd hear anything coming before he saw it, out here.

He dumped the pouch into his hand. A pen drive slid out.

Sam rolled it over in his palm. Didn't look like much, he had to admit.

Ethan peered over his shoulder, wide eyed and fighting it. He shrugged. "So that's what this is all about, huh?"

Sam held the drive up to the light. Black plastic with a red slide, 32GB. At the time it had been outrageously high tech. Now you could buy these beauties at the corner shop for less than you could buy a cheap bottle of drinkable wine.

"Yup."

Ethan regarded it with interest. "What's on it? What does it say that they want so bad?"

"Say?" Sam turned to him in surprise. "It's not what it says. It's what it shows." At Ethan's raised eyebrow and skeptical gaze, Sam pushed himself to his feet with a strange sense of inevitability. The handle of the jeep burned his palm when he pulled open the door. The heat from inside the car hit him like he was opening the door to hell. Sam slid inside and pulled his laptop out of the glove compartment, the coolest place he could think of.

He wedged it behind the steering wheel and opened the screen. It booted up with a happy chime. Before he could think twice about it, he slid the drive into the slot. He clicked on the icon when the new hardware was recognized; he was glad it had been. He hadn't been sure about that. Fifteen years old was ancient in terms of technology. The video app opened and he turned the computer to face Ethan, who had slid into the passenger side and turned the air on full blast. "Here," he said, as his sweat chilled immediately in the breeze. "See for yourself."

With an apprehensive look at Sam, Ethan set his jaw and took the computer as the video began to play.

Chapter Seventy

Ethan's eyes narrowed in on the old surveillance footage.

The video was primitive and had the same look some home movies had, but hard. This was as hard as it comes.

It appeared to be filmed from a soldier's bodycam.

The unsteady video feed revealed the inside of what appeared to be a private Learjet. Probably the best maintained Learjet 23 at the time. What made it stand out even more was the unique emblem over leather seating along the fuselage.

It was the seal of the President of the United States of America.

"That's President Harris's Learjet 23!"

Sam nodded. "That's his bird."

It was no secret that President Harris, once a decorated fighter pilot during the Vietnam War, had never truly relinquished his love of flying. He kept a private jet at Andrews Air Force Base. And, if the secrets were to be believed, he took it out from time to time, with no one but his Secret Service Agents onboard. Once a pilot always a pilot. It was also said that the president liked to use the private space to host secret meetings that he didn't want publicly recorded.

It was also no secret what happened to President Harris on the flight that day.

The video continued.

A man in casual slacks and a white shirt sat straight and tense on one of the couches along the edge of the fuselage. Secret Service members in black manned the walls, arms clenched tight at the ready. A glass of clear liquid sat on the table before them, water, judging from the bottle beside it. Papers spread out between him and an aide with a rather stunned expression, scared and alert, like the thing he'd been warned about when taking this job but had never believed would ever happen had finally happened.

Ethan looked at Sam. "That is President Harris!"

Sam nodded. "Keep watching."

The President shook his head in the footage under the eyes of the servicemen. "Aimes!" he called and one of the servicemen stood at attention. "Bring the whiskey. I'm damned if I know what this is." He ran a hand through his hair, rumpling the professional appearance. Beyond the windows, the sky was dark. The time stamp read 1:53 in digital white letters. "Where did he go?"

"Head, sir." The aide tried and failed to not sound curious at the images spread on the table before them. The president grinned, wryly.

"Good man. Come at me with news like this and escapes into the toilet. Can't say I blame him."

"If I can ask, sir... what news is this...?"

The President looked at him. "Well, I'd love to tell you, Elliot, but then I'd have to kill you." He gestured to the cockpit. "Run on and see what's taking Aimes so damn long with that drink." He laughed. "And pound on the head if you pass it. Make sure he didn't get flushed out at thirty thousand feet."

Elliot smiled professionally. It's clear this President inspires loyalty and love. "Of course, sir."

"And bring back a glass for you, too!" the President called after him. He turned to the servicemen. "Anything in the constitution say I can't give liquor to my employees?"

"Only if they're underage, sir." A serviceman in black – short and stiff with a ramrod up his ass, thought Ethan – nodded like the social climber he probably was.

"It's legal even if they are, actually." The voice came from the man wearing the bodycam. Then, when the President looked surprised, the man said, "What? We're in airspace. It's above the law."

The president looked unsure about whether he was being had or not. "Really. Well, will you look at that. I had no idea." He gestured magnanimously at the soldier wearing the bodycam. "I think you should be President instead of me, my man. Spare me all this bullshit." He squinted. "What's your name, anyway… soldier?"

"Sam Reilly."

Ethan paused the video. "What the hell were you doing on that flight?"

Sam said, "I was supposed to be debriefing the President on the strange Labyrinth Key I'd found in Afghanistan."

"So why the hell were you on board the President's private jet?"

"Bad luck, I guess… I was flown to Andrews Air Force Base straight from Afghanistan. I hadn't slept. I was meant to debrief the President in the morning, only somewhere along the way, the President found out I was there, and a Secret Service Agent asked me to join him privately."

Ethan swore. "They wanted another body on that jet when it went down, someone of a similar height and build to that of the President. It would all look the same after the jet went down."

Sam nodded. "It would appear so. Press play, you can see how it all went down."

Ethan pressed play.

The next few events happened with lightning speed.

One of the Secret Service Agents pulled out his SIG Sauer P229 and leveled it at the President.

President Harris' forehead furrowed in puzzlement. "What the hell are you doing with that? We're not anywhere near the drop zone yet."

The Agent said, "I'm sorry Harris. Every man has a price… they had my children."

Sam Reilly dived forward, kicking him hard as the Agent squeezed the trigger. The bodycam footage went fuzzy and all over the shop as the soldier moved.

The shot went wide, killing the Agent behind the President.

Harris, once a decorated Air Force pilot, moved quickly grabbing the second Agent's SIG Sauer.

Sam gripped the Agents forearms, fighting to keep the barrel of the pistol away from the President. The Agent slammed his forearm against the mahogany doorframe in the fuselage, but Sam refused to relinquish his weapon arm.

The Agent used his spare hand to reach in and retrieve a second pistol.

He focused it toward Sam.

A shot fired.

But it wasn't from the Agent. Instead, President Harris had fired it, killing the Agent.

In the cockpit, the pilot was shot in the head, and the aircraft began to nose dive.

Sam raced upfront, ripped the man out of his chair, and fought to regain control of the aircraft. Next to him, President Harris, who knew the aircraft better than anyone else, worked to return them from the near freefall.

It was a challenging operation, but they came through it, leveling the aircraft steadily, and bringing it back to a cruising altitude.

Sam glanced around the cabin.

In total three Secret Service Agents were dead and so was the pilot.

The President, still at the controls, glanced back at Sam and asked, "Now what?"

Sam shrugged. "Now we go back to Andrews and get you help, sir."

"No. I'm afraid that won't do, son."

Sam looked puzzled. "Why not?"

"I'm being blackmailed by a Mexican Cartel."

The president pulled himself together with the force of personality that endeared him so much to his people. "My death was always the plan. It's just they…" He gestured to the servicemen. "They weren't supposed to actually do it."

Sam stalled. "Come again?"

The President crumpled for the first time that night. "The cartel has been blackmailing me for over a year. We've tried everything to get them to quit, but they're like animals. They've got information on me that will ruin my presidency and if I don't comply with their requests they'll…" He shuddered, his gaze frank. "Like you said. A man can pay for his own sins. Hell, sometimes I think it's right, even. But not my wife. Not my daughter…"

He gestured at the death. "That was the plan. They knew that. We were to stage my death and I would pass power onto Rowlands and go into hiding with my family. Once everyone knew I was dead they would be safe. We'd planned it for months. I knew, and they knew, that it was the only way I would be safe for good. That my family would be safe for good. We were supposed to crash the Learjet over Rhyolite, Nevada. Engine malfunction. There are parachutes on board, we were going to jettison and hit the desert. Cars were waiting. But…"

His voice broke and he looked around at the carnage. "Frye. Anders. I trusted them. With my life. My god, they've monitored Sofia." He looked at Sam, pleading. "Is there a chance it was still the plan? I know it would make you – but is there a chance they were just…" He trailed off, lost for words. "Doing their duty?"

Sam shook his head. "Those men shot to kill. How they missed you I'll never know. I'm just glad I was here. This story would have been very different otherwise. Your wife would have been a widow in fact."

The man sighed, shaking. "What do we do?"

Sam's gaze bore into him. "We go through with the plan."

"You're right, we can still pull this off."

"Do you trust the people on the ground?"

"Yes. I have two Secret Service Agents who I can trust with my life – I have to trust with my life. They are waiting for me. There's a car waiting for me. There are some parachutes in the back and a specially built exit point. It will be a rough ride. But we'll survive."

A few minutes later the President set the aircraft on an irreparable nose-dive.

And Sam and the President jumped out through the exit point.

The video showed them freefalling until their parachutes opened. The two men parted mildly in the air, and Sam landed first.

He met the President when he landed a few minutes later.

On the ground, a black SUV approached.

Ethan recognized that vehicle. It was the same one he'd seen fifteen years earlier, chasing Sam Reilly.

From the opposite direction, a young man riding a motorcycle approached.

The President landed with the ease and grace of a seasoned paratrooper.

The Chevrolet Suburban pulled up alongside the President. The camera moved toward the gathering as it appeared the younger Sam Reilly walked toward the group. The President was talking to two Agents. There was already a hot discussion going on, but it was impossible to tell what was being said from the bodycam footage.

Sam Reilly reached the President, who introduced him to the two Agents, and said that he owed the man his life.

A few seconds later, a young man on a motorcycle pulled up next to them. He couldn't have been more than twenty. The rider said, "Woah… are you guys all right? I just saw your parachutes! Did you just jump out of that plane before it crashed?"

The President gave a curt nod to the two agents, and then to the rider, said, "Yeah, that was us… we got really lucky."

One of the Agents got the message, drew his Sig Sauer and shot the rider dead.

On the bodycam, Sam Reilly's voice protested. "Good God! That man was just checking to make sure we were all right… you didn't have to kill him!"

The President turned his palms skyward in supplication. "Hey, I wasn't happy about it either, but a lot of lives are at stake here. If the story gets out that I survived a lot more people are going to pay with their lives."

"There must have been a better way…" Sam's voice was calm, cautionary.

One of the Agents whispered something into the President's ear.

The President turned to Sam Reilly. "Are you wearing a bodycam?"

The digital video ended.

Ethan asked, "What the hell did I just watch?"

"You know what it was."

"Yeah." Ethan looked out the window. "What happened in the end?"

Sam shrugged. "Frank Rowlands got to be president. Harris's widow and daughter died tragically in a car accident. As far as anyone knows they really died. Who knows? They might really be dead." He tapped the computer. "This is the only copy of this footage in the entire world. They'll be safe, as long as it stays hidden."

Ethan looked at him, his gaze unreadable. "Now I know about it."

Sam met his gaze the same way. "Now you know."

Ethan turned to him in earnest. "You didn't kill the President."

"Kill President Harris? Are you kidding me? Of course I didn't kill him."

"No, he died because you found that key… and the Cartel, having discovered that a second Labyrinth Key had been discovered went to kill Harris."

Sam grinned. "You think President Harris is dead?"

Ethan shrugged. "Even if he didn't die in that plane, he was never seen again. There was a state funeral and everything."

Sam shook his head. "No. President Harris survived, but he knew that so long as Carlos Gonzalez was still alive the cartel would use his family to blackmail him. But as you know, having served, no matter what happened, the President of the United States of America can never be placed in a position in which he needs to submit to the whims of another nation."

"So…" Ethan swore. "President Harris knew this. He needed to be dead."

"Exactly. A plan was made to fake his death. The only problem was, the Cartel got wind of it, and instead of letting it play out fictionally, he tried to make it real. Thus, they nearly succeeded in killing President Harris for real."

"Except you were there that day, to talk about the Labyrinth Key."

"Yes. I was there to talk about the Labyrinth Key. I realized what happened and I saved the President's life."

Ethan frowned. "There's one thing I don't understand."

Sam bit his lower lip, knowing where this was headed. "Go on."

"If President Harris is still alive, who were those Secret Service Agents sent to kill you?"

Sam expelled a deep breath. "President Harris was a good man, but he needed to complete the ruse. You see, if anyone found out the truth, his family would be murdered."

Realization dawned on Ethan. "Those were President Harris's trusted Secret Service Agents who tried to kill you."

Sam nodded, the palms of his hands turning upward. "I'm afraid so. I can't blame President Harris. After all, he needed to clean up loose ends." Sam steepled his fingers. "After I left Rhyolite, I sent him a message, explaining what I had done and that his secret would be safe with me until the day I died – upon which, a video depicting the truth would be revealed to the world. When that happened, it became paramount to Harris that I remain alive for a very long time."

Epilogue

Washington, D.C.

Inside Sam Reilly's father's D.C. apartment, Caliburn's ears perked behind his thick mane of golden hair, his brown doe-eyes passively taking interest in Sam and Catarina's somewhat heated discussion.

Sam sighed heavily. "I'm sorry, I don't know how long I'm going to be away. At least a month, probably many more."

Catarina nodded, taking his hand in hers and kissing his fingers. "I've seen that look before, Sam."

Sam pulled back, just a little, enough to see her face and look her in the eye. "What look?"

"You're going after the Obsidian Chamber, aren't you?"

Sam nodded. "I have to."

"You're going to give it everything you have."

Sam grinned. "You bet I will! I've been chasing this my whole adult life…"

Catarina asked, "What about Caliburn?"

Sam looked at the golden retriever, who raised a benevolent eyebrow to let him know he was listening. "My aunt can look after him while I'm away."

"What about the *Tahila*?"

Sam shrugged. "What about it?"

"I thought the benefit of living on board a ship was that your house goes with you wherever you go?"

Sam's eyes narrowed. "You think I should bring Caliburn?"

"Yes. Why not?"

"Caliburn's not going to like where we're going."

"Why?"

"Because Caliburn hates the cold."

She kissed him on his lips, then pushed him away. "Where are you going, Sam?"

"Antarctica."

Her lips curled upward into a wry smile. "Antarctica... whatever for?"

"To find a ship that went missing during the early 20th century."

She expelled a frustrated breath. "All right, I'll bite. What does a missing 20th century vessel have to do with the Obsidian Chamber?"

Well," Sam said, "Rumor has it, the leader of the expedition, a man named Ernest Shackleton, was the last one to physically see the Obsidian Chamber. Shackleton was on an expedition to reach the South Pole when his ship, the *RSS Discovery*, became trapped in ice and abandoned – never to be seen again."

"Good God! Sam, you're looking for a needle in a haystack."

"No. I'm looking for a frozen ship beneath a sea of ice."

Catarina could see she wasn't getting anywhere. "All right, so you're going to leave Caliburn with your aunt?"

"Sure. Why not? She loves that damned dog more than anyone!" Caliburn gave a curt bark in a not so subtle retort. Sam came and patted the golden retriever behind his ears. "It's all right, Caliburn, you know we all adore you."

Caliburn nuzzled into his arm, before settling onto his lap, as though that was penance enough. Sam turned to Catarina and said, "Besides, I wasn't lying when I said my aunt would love to look after Caliburn for a while."

Catarina sat down and gave Caliburn an affectionate pat. "Can you trust your aunt with him?"

"It's okay, this is the good aunt, remember?"

Catarina said, "Hey, I've met the rest of your family, Sam. Good, as a comparative term, isn't necessarily great."

Sam met her gaze. "In this case it is. This aunt is good. She's been a sort of role model to me. An erudite, compassionate, and gentle soul. A confidante, and someone I can turn to for counsel. She'll take good care of Caliburn while we're away. Besides, don't let Caliburn's growl confuse you. He loves spending time with her much more than he's letting on."

Catarina met Caliburn's raised eye. "Is that true? You want to go visit Sam's aunt?"

Caliburn licked his lips and set his tail wagging happily, betraying his real emotions. Sam shrugged. "My aunt tends to spoil him far more than our jobs allow for."

Someone inserted a key and let themselves into the house. Caliburn stood up and immediately started barking playfully. Sam turned his gaze to meet Catarina's eye. "See, I told you he was just waiting for her to arrive."

A fit, healthy looking woman in her mid-sixties walked in, followed by a gentleman of similar age. Caliburn ran right up to her at the speed of a much younger dog. She kneeled down and embraced him, working hard not to get knocked over in the process. "How are you, darling?" she asked, talking to Caliburn first.

Sam caught Catarina's eye. "See?"

They waited a good minute before Caliburn and Sam's aunt settled, unsure which one was more excited to see the other.

His aunt stood up and embraced him.

Sam said, "It's good to see you. I would like to introduce you to my girlfriend, Catarina."

She smiled. "It's a pleasure to meet you, Catarina. Sam's told me a lot about you."

Catarina embraced her. "You too…"

Sam's aunt smiled and put Catarina out of her misery. "Colleen."

"It's nice to meet you, Colleen."

Colleen turned to the gentleman with a kind smile behind her and said, "Meet my husband, Wayne Mundis."

The four of them talked over coffee. While Sam brought his aunt and uncle up to speed about his next project, Catarina talked about herself and what normal adults do for a living, and Colleen filled Sam in on her and Wayne's latest sailing trip in the Caribbean.

When they were finished, they headed out the front where their SUV was parked. Sam opened the rear tailgate for Caliburn to climb in, but Colleen wouldn't hear of it. Instead, she pressed the lower button and opened the front door, exchanging the trunk for the front seat.

She gave a curt nod to Caliburn, who provided a happy bark, and jumped up onto the front bucket seat, beside Wayne.

Her eyes leveled with Sam's suddenly serious. "I recognized that voice when you called. There's something terrible going on and you're going to try your best to stop it."

Sam said, "I have to. There's..."

She raised a single hand to stop him. "I know. You don't have to tell me it's important. I just want you to be careful and know that I'm thinking about you."

Anyone else and he would have protested, maintaining his lie. Instead, he just said, "I will."

"Good." Then, her voice more cheerful, Colleen said, "Now don't take too long or I promise you we're not giving Caliburn back."

Sam grinned. "I'll try my best."

He watched as they drove off. Wayne wound down the passenger window and Caliburn comfortably nudged his head out into the wind as the SUV pulled out of the driveway.

Sam wrapped his arms affectionately around Catarina's waist and watched them disappear down the road.

She turned her head to look at him, parted her lips, and kissed him.

When they stopped, everything was serious again. Catarina said, "Now what?"

Sam swallowed. "Now I have to beat the rest of the world to find it."

"Are you sure the rest of the world is looking?"

The lines in Sam's face suddenly darkened. "They're looking for it all right, the same as we are. It contains secrets that will change everything about the world, from political alliances, world economics, and even the future of the human race."

She nodded. "All right, then we'd better make sure we find it first."

"We?" Sam arched an eyebrow. "Do you mean it?"

"Yes." She kissed him again.

His lips straightened into a hardline. "You're sure?"

She grinned. "Sam, I'm coming with you to find the Obsidian Chamber."

"I'm glad," Sam said, and he squeezed her hand. "Because I believe we're close to finding it."

"Finding what?"

"Answers."

Her lips parted in a wry smile. "To?"

"Everything." Sam grinned. "We're on the verge of finally learning the truth about the origins of the Master Builders and why they're here."

The End

Printed in Great Britain
by Amazon

36109619R00253